TRESPASS

TRESPASS

Clare Clark

virago

VIRAGO

First published in Great Britain in 2022 by Virago Press

1 3 5 7 9 10 8 6 4 2

A CIP catalogue record for this book
is available from the British Library.

Hardback ISBN 978-0-349-01694-8
C format ISBN 978-0-349-01695-5

Typeset in Goudy by M Rules
Printed and bound in Great Britain by Clays Ltd, Elcograf S.p.A.

Papers used by Virago are from well-managed forests
and other responsible sources.

Virago Press
An imprint of
Little, Brown Book Group
Carmelite House
50 Victoria Embankment
London EC4Y 0DZ

An Hachette UK Company
www.hachette.co.uk

www.virago.co.uk

To my family, for being precisely and perfectly themselves

It's a hell of a responsibility to be yourself.
It's much easier to be somebody else or nobody at all.

Sylvia Plath, *The Unabridged Journals of Sylvia Plath*

Prologue

There are flowers in the memorial vase, bright splats of red and pink and orange like a kid's painting. Zinnias. He has always hated zinnias. The sun blazes against the dark granite of the headstone, making the gold letters gleam.

In Loving Memory of Harry Taylor
An Angel on Earth and an Angel in Heaven
Rest in Peace

He wipes his forehead with the palm of his hand. He can smell the booze sweating out of him, the stale morning-after reek of it. His mouth tastes sour. In the thick dazed heat of the afternoon he hears the distant roar of traffic on the A59. It sounds like the sea.

The last time he was here, the only other time, it was February. He remembers it exactly, the sharp burn of ice in the wind and his feet half frozen, white tulips in the vase. The first flicker of unease. The first hint that maybe this was more than just a game, a game with serious intent but a game all the same. A beautiful, intricate game where you were both player and piece, practised over and over until you never made a mistake, until the game was the safest thing you had.

He squats by the headstone. The flowers are fresh. Zinnias are like cockroaches, indestructible, but everything wilts in this heat. She has been here today. Perhaps she is still here. What will he do if she asks him what he is doing here, what will he say? His skin prickles. He wants to run. He straightens up and slowly, very slowly, he turns round.

No one is there.

He closes his eyes. Sweat greases his scalp. His head throbs, his hand too. It usually only bothers him when it's cold. He presses his thumb hard into the scarred skin, presses till the pain is in his shoulder, the base of his skull. He should never have come. It was stupid to think it would help, that it would make things clearer. Stupid and deluded.

Rest in Peace.

How long since any of them have been able to do that?

I

Tess made coffee properly for once, the French way, in the battered old aluminium espresso pot with the black handle. She even heated the milk, twirling the pan as she poured so that the foam made the shape of a heart, a heart with one side much fatter than the other, maybe, but a heart nonetheless. It was early, or early for a Saturday, but it was already hot. Upstairs Mia was still sleeping. In a month she would be a teenager and then presumably she would sleep all day and only come out at night, like a badger. Maybe, like a badger, she would even learn to make her own bed.

Tess took her cup outside. The garden chairs were grimy, silvered with snail trails. She had bought them as a set on eBay last summer, four of them with a matching table. The purchase was intended to mark the official end of six years of neglect, a declaration of commitment to a proper grown-up garden. A year later, it remained the full extent of her efforts. The tiny lawn was a jungle, the tangled grass studded with dandelions. Weeds pushed up between the flags of the patio. Dragging the least dirty chair into a triangle of sunlight Tess sat down. This summer, she thought idly, sipping her coffee, this summer I am going to get it into shape.

3

The sun was bright. Tipping the chair onto its back legs, Tess rested her head against the warm brick of the wall. She could be in Rome or Barcelona. She put her cup on the table and closed her eyes, pushing down the narrow straps of her top so that they looped around her arms. She was pretty sure women in Barcelona didn't have suntan marks from their pyjamas.

Something landed softly on her arm. Tess brushed it away. All along their street in Palmers Green the houses were being tarted up, lawns being replaced with Astroturf and wooden decking, front gardens concreted over for off-street parking. By letting the garden run wild, Tess thought, she was at least providing a valuable habitat for wildlife. She could feel the heat of the sun sinking into her skin like oil. Stretching luxuriously, her eyes still closed, she reached out for her coffee.

She felt it in her mouth before she swallowed. Something insubstantial but also solid, like a tangle of threads knotted together. Grimacing, she spat. A flying ant, its ant body capped with pale papery wings. She pressed her tongue against the roof of her mouth, trying to extinguish the memory – or had she just imagined it? – of the creature writhing against it. She could still taste its bitterness at the back of her throat.

Another ant landed on her thigh. She slapped at it. Glancing irritably down at her leg as she flicked it away, she recoiled. The ants were everywhere. The patio seethed with them. They swarmed over the flags, oozing up from between the weed-clotted gaps like the ground was sweating them out. They clustered on the legs of the table and over the shallow step to the kitchen and along the sill of the garden door, a rolling boil of black bodies and glistening wings. There was one on Tess's bare foot. She kicked out blindly, folding her knees tight into her chest.

Abruptly, too loud, she heard someone calling her name. Her phone, it was just her phone. Mia had personalised the ringtone.

Jeez, Tess, pick up already! Mia's laughter breaking through her terrible American accent. Tess ran into the house on her tiptoes, the soles of her feet shrivelling. Even after she closed the door she could feel the whisper of ants on her skin, in her hair. The number on her phone was international, +33. France.

'Hello?' she said. Her mouth was dry, the word stuck to it. The espresso pot was where she had left it on the hob. Its faceted side caught the light and she thought suddenly, wildly, of Aladdin's lamp and the genie inside who granted every wish.

'Hello, Tess. This is Delphine.'

Tess's fingers tightened around the phone. Tess's father and Delphine had been divorced for ten years. There was only one reason she would call Tess now. Don't say it, Tess pleaded silently. Please, Delphine, please, whatever it is you are about to say, don't let it be that.

'It's Sylvie,' Delphine said.

Sylvie, Delphine's mother and Tess's – Tess's what? If there was a word for it, in French or in English, Tess had never known it. Dark clumps of ants clotted on the sill outside the window. She stared at them as Delphine talked, her voice quiet and flat as though everything she said had been said too many times before. She told Tess that Sylvie had been feeling under the weather for months, not that she admitted it, of course. That two days ago she had woken in the night with pains in her chest and abdomen. She called an ambulance, she thought she was having a heart attack, but when they scanned her they found tumours in her liver, her lungs and her stomach. The one in her stomach was bleeding. They gave her a blood transfusion but the cancer was too far advanced, there was nothing else they could do. Delphine's English was as flawless as ever, almost without accent. Tess made herself look at the ants on the window, their wings glittering like splinters of glass. The consultant had told Delphine that they would need to keep Sylvie under observation in the ICU for at least the next few days. After that, if her condition was stable, there was a hospice in Brest. The staff were wonderful and it had a garden. They would do everything they could to make her comfortable.

'A hospice? But surely—'

'Please don't.' Delphine exhaled wearily. 'Sylvie – I cannot fight you too.'

In all the time she had known her, Tess had never heard Delphine call her mother by anything but her first name. She had never found it strange till now. She pressed her phone to her cheek and looked at the espresso pot, the flare of sunlight on its lid. A hospice. The place you went to die, when dying was all that was left.

'Look, the consultant is here, I have to go back,' Delphine said. 'I wanted to call, that is, the reason I am calling, I am not sure if this is appropriate, perhaps you will decide that it is not, it has been a long time, I understand that, but the doctors, they are not hopeful. If you wish to see her, if that is what you want, then you should come soon.'

Sylvie was dying. The words were sharp and clear, cut into Tess's brain, and yet there was no sense in them. It wasn't possible, not Sylvie, not yet. Sylvie was never ill. She was never even tired. The force of life ran through her like she was where it started. Tess tried to picture her in a hospital bed in a hospital gown, tubes running into the backs of her hands, but all she could see was Sylvie standing on the rocky promontory in her faded black swimsuit, her arms outstretched and her face turned up towards the rain, her hair streaming like seaweed down her back. The shout of laughter as she arced into the air and was gone.

In the garden the ants were taking flight, clouds of them swirling upwards like ash from a bonfire. When Tess closed her eyes, the ants went on rising in the darkness, only now the swirls were silver.

'Look Tess, I'm sorry, I need to go. I'll ring you back, OK?'

Tess put her phone down on the kitchen counter. She thought of the tumours growing silently in Sylvie's body, making new shapes from the meat of her, sucking and twisting her into themselves to make bodies of their own.

'Making art is like keeping a dragon in your cellar,' Sylvie told her once. 'Some days you feel utterly invincible. Some days you go up in flames.'

Sylvie couldn't be dying. She was Sylvie. And she was only sixty-four.

Suddenly Tess's head was too heavy for her neck. She leaned against the garden door, resting the weight of it against the glass. Above her, above the roofs of the houses that backed onto theirs, the sky was filled with birds. Seagulls, perhaps, though they didn't scream the way seagulls usually did. They wheeled and swooped in silence, feasting on the glutted air.

It was eight years since Tess had left Sylvie's house for the last time. There must have been cicadas that day, birdsong, the distant shush of the sea, but Tess remembered only the silence and Sylvie standing at the gate, her face like the face of the wooden saint who proffered his bread in Quimper cathedral, sombre and unshakeable. She was still standing there when Tess turned the corner out of sight.

A few months later she sent Tess a letter. It was March. Mia was five years old. There was snow in London and white blossoms like scraps of tissue on the spindly cherry trees along the street. Sylvie's handwriting was like Sylvie, too big for the page. Tell her, the letter said. There will never be a better time than now. Tell her and bring her home. There is something I need to tell you too. The letter reawakened all of Tess's anger and her fear. She knew that, if she did not answer, Sylvie would not write again. Sylvie never tried to change people's minds. She couldn't see the point. The people she loved, the people that mattered, those people made their way as she did, unerringly, their compasses turning them towards true North. As for the others, they hardly mattered at all.

Tess looked at the letter for a long time. With each sentence she felt Sylvie's hands on her shoulders, turning her against herself. When it was time to fetch Mia from school, she tore the letter into small pieces and put them in the bin. Later that night she took them out again and burned them in the kitchen sink. Mia couldn't read and she couldn't reach the bin but Tess couldn't shake the fear that she would find the torn-up words and put them together. That somehow the words would find her.

She never wrote back. Since then many years had passed. Tess noticed them pass, with a child you couldn't help but notice, but she did nothing. What could she do? What Sylvie asked of her was impossible. With every year it grew more impossible still.

Eight years of not speaking. And yet she had always believed that the silence would come to an end. The weight of their past required a future to balance it. One day, not yet but soon, they would shake things out between them like one of Sylvie's much-darned linen sheets, the ones they used to launder together and lay out over the rosemary bushes to dry in the sun. When they put them back on the beds, the scent of them was the scent of something just beginning.

When Tess looked up again the sky was empty. The birds were gone. Already the flying ants were thinning. By this afternoon only their wings would be left, scattered like torn-up ticket stubs across the patio. Then the birds would eat those too. Her unfinished coffee was still on the garden table. The coffee Sylvie had taught her how to make.

She closed her eyes, her arms tight around her ribs. Her heart howled. There was supposed to be so much time left.

Mia glared out of the window at the dry yellow grass, the rubbish strewn along the side of the motorway. She had pulled down the plastic visor above the windscreen but the sun was still too strong. It burned her bare arm through the glass. Her legs fizzed from sitting still too long and she was starting to feel carsick. Beside her, her mum leaned forward, her hands so tight on the steering wheel that her knuckles shone like teeth. She kept blinking and rubbing her eyes but she wouldn't stop, not even when Mia said she was hungry and needed the toilet. She said it wasn't very far now and there was chewing gum in the glove compartment and went on driving.

It was an hour earlier in London. Yaz would be getting ready. They all would, everyone except her. Mia bit her thumbnail savagely. She wanted to scream at her mum, to tell her she had ruined everything forever because, if it wasn't for her, she wouldn't be in this stupid car at all, she would be going to Lauren's, Lauren who had invited Yaz to her party and not Mia but who finally messaged her yesterday and said she could come if she wanted, Lauren who had never asked her before and now most likely never would again because Yaz said girls like Lauren only ever gave you one chance, and for what? For an old woman her mum hadn't seen since Mia was little, a woman she wasn't even related to, not since Grandpa Ivo and Delphine had got divorced, a woman who never visited them or asked them to visit or even sent her a birthday card, only none of that mattered when someone was dying; when someone was dying you weren't allowed to be angry, all you were allowed to be was sorry and sad, even when the person dying was a total stranger, and anyway that wasn't the worst part, the worst, most angry-making part was that it didn't matter how mean and unfair it was, there was nothing Mia could say because her mum didn't even know about Lauren's party, she thought it was just an ordinary sleepover with Yaz because, if she knew about the party and Lauren's parents being away, there was no way on earth she would ever have let Mia go.

They drove through a pine wood for a long time, then down a narrow lane with long grass like a mohawk in the middle that rustled against the belly of the car. Halfway down, where the lane turned sharply, her mum stopped the car.

'Look,' she said, pointing towards a clump of twisted pines.

'What at?'

'The sea, can you see it? We're almost there.'

'Then why are we stopping? I told you, I'm desperate for the toilet.'

Tess nodded absently, staring out towards the sea.

'I'm serious,' Mia said. 'For God's sake, Mum. I'm literally about to pee my pants.'

Tess blinked.

'Sorry,' she said and, jamming the car into gear, she bumped down the lane to the house.

The back door was open. Tess called but no one came. She told Mia to use the bathroom at the end of the passage. The toilet had a tank up near the ceiling and a chain to flush it. It looked like something out of a museum. When she came out, Tess was gone. Mia walked back along the passage and into the kitchen. Her mum was leaning on the counter, her back towards the door. Her head was bowed. A thin woman with shiny dark hair and gold buttons on the shoulders of her sweater stood beside her.

'Mia,' the thin woman said. She tried to smile but her face didn't want to. 'I'm Delphine.'

'Hi,' Mia said. She waited for her mum to turn around, to smile at her, but she didn't.

'They just called from the hospital,' Delphine said. 'Sylvie died.'

Mia looked at Delphine, then at Tess. 'Mum?'

Tess's shoulders jerked. She made a strange strangled noise in her throat. Mia stared at the floor. Then, darting across the kitchen, she hugged her mother tightly, her face pressed against her back.

'It's OK, Mum,' she said, and Tess turned round inside the circle of her arms and cried into her hair.

2

Tess walked across the garden towards the cliff. She wore a swimsuit and sunglasses, one of Sylvie's threadbare hammam towels tied sarong-style around her waist. It had rained in the night, the grass was still wet, but already the rinsed cool of the morning was giving way to something heavier. It was going to be hot. Blades of grass clung to her bare feet. She thought of the nights she and Sylvie had lain on their backs in the darkness looking for shooting stars, Sylvie toasting their wishes with Armagnac and exhaling a thin ribbon of smoke up to mix with the Milky Way. Through the black grid of the pines the sea was an inky blue. The people who settled here believed that this jut of land was where the world stopped, Sylvie told Tess the first time she came. Finistère, the end of the earth.

Tess was twelve. After a protracted and acrimonious divorce her parents had both remarried. Tess lived with her mother and stepfather in London for most of the year but when the summer holidays came round her mother packed her off to Ivo and Delphine in Paris. She told Tess that Ivo was still her father, that just because he had married a child – and a French child at that – didn't mean he didn't have responsibilities. Tess was glad. She imagined a summer sipping Orangina by the Eiffel Tower but when she arrived in Paris Ivo announced that he was taking her to Delphine's mother by the sea. No one with a crumb of sense, he said, remained in Paris in July. He drove her to Sylvie's in a sports car with the roof down. Delphine didn't come. She said she had to work. Tess pretended to be sorry. A whole summer, she thought, just her and Ivo, hugging the thought like a present. She didn't think about Sylvie at all.

Ivo stayed at Sylvie's for one night. The next morning he called Tess a jammy so-and-so, kissed Sylvie on the cheek, and drove back to Paris and Delphine.

The narrow path down to the beach was overgrown, the air heady with the coconut scent of gorse. Out beyond the bay a boat with white sails tilted towards the horizon. It was like a hologram, Tess thought, everything the same and none of it real. She could reach out her hand and the picture would resolve around it, the saturated colours moving over the screen of her skin. All the way here, on the deck of the ferry, driving from Caen along the old familiar roads, Tess had tried to order her thoughts, to find the set of words that would put things back together, but each time she tried to clear a space in her head for them the memories pushed their way in: the stormy crossing after her mother died when she was sixteen, the drive after Mia was born when she never stopped screaming, both times weary to the bone and weighted down with grief that was not just loss but anger and fear and confusion and the disorienting blankness of not belonging anywhere or to anyone. Tess never pretended that she could belong to Sylvie, Sylvie did not believe in owning or being owned, but she knew that if she could only make it to the house at the end of the earth then Sylvie would show her how to belong to herself. That was Sylvie's gift. When she loved you her power ran through you, you could feel it as she looked at you, the fierce magnet of her certainty drawing you closer, gathering the filings of you into something solid, something resembling a whole.

Sylvie was dead.

The lurch in her chest was like vertigo. Tess swayed, covering her face with her hands. Sylvie was dead and she was going swimming. But what else was she to do? She had no idea what came next. When Tess's mother died it was like a machine took over, the messiness and confusion shaped and sealed safely like sausages in their skins: funeral, burial, memorial, the same words repeated over and over until they were sounds with no meaning. A life catalogued and accounted for and filed away, case closed.

Sylvie had refused a funeral. According to Delphine, she thought that burial poisoned the earth and cremation released too much carbon into the atmosphere and that a corpse should anyway be put to good use, so instead she had bequeathed her body to the university in Brest for medical research. When Tess asked if she could see Sylvie before they took her away, Delphine said it was too late. Her body had already been collected by the faculty. It had to be stored in precisely the right conditions or it would be of no value to the students. No one could say when they would be finished with her. Sylvie had granted the university indefinite consent, which meant that they could keep her as long as they wanted. It might be one year or it might be three. The university would notify the family when they were ready to release her remains, along with an invitation to their annual service of thanksgiving at the Église Saint-Louis, a modernist monstrosity, Delphine said bitterly, built after Brest was flattened in the war. The medical students from that year's class were also invited to attend the service. According to the university, it provided a wonderful opportunity for them to meet the families of their cadavers and express their gratitude. The way Delphine said it, it was like the words were bits of broken glass.

Tess pressed her fingers against her closed lids. Her eyes were gritty and her head ached. She hadn't slept. In the long raw hours after Mia had gone to bed, she and Delphine sat up talking in Sylvie's kitchen, except it wasn't Sylvie's kitchen because everything that made it Sylvie's kitchen was gone, the blackened espresso maker and the copper saucepans and the sticky jars and bottles on their tin trays and the herbs spilling from their pots on the window-sill, the piles of sketchbooks and dog-eared novels and newspapers turned inside out, the clusters of candles braided with drips of wax. In the harsh strip lighting, its Formica counters scrubbed and bare, the room was dingy and unfamiliar.

They drank Armagnac from Sylvie's small thick glass tumblers with the faceted sides. Sylvie did not own coffee cups or wine glasses. She drank everything from those tumblers, brandy, cham-pagne, espresso, sage tea from the silver-green bush by the back door, holding them up so that they caught the light like jewels, their sides scabbed with specks of clay.

'To Sylvie,' Delphine said, raising her glass.

'To Sylvie,' Tess echoed, trying not to cry. She had tasted her first Armagnac in this house, Sylvie laughing as she screwed up her face at the burn of it, but this was something different, rich and smooth. She took a second, deeper swig. Immediately Delphine poured them both another glass.

'The good stuff, thank God,' Delphine said. 'A present from Lucien.' Lucien was Delphine's second husband. He had telephoned earlier suggesting he drive out from Paris but Delphine told him there was no point, that there was nothing he could do. 'He bought her a bottle every Christmas, each year more expensive than the last, but she always said she couldn't taste the difference. It drove him to distraction. He called her a firewater socialist.'

'I imagine she rather liked that.'

Delphine twisted her mouth. She studied her glass, then drained it in a single neat swallow. 'Salt water and Armagnac, my mother's

14

keys to eternal life. Well, she was wrong about that, wasn't she? But then she was wrong about a lot of things. It's just that she would have died rather than admit it.'

Something passed over Delphine's face, irony or bitterness or grief, Tess couldn't tell. She wanted to protest but she bit her tongue. Sylvie was Delphine's mother, Delphine could say what she wanted. A daughter had that right. Tess took another gulp of brandy.

'Le feu dansant,' Delphine said. 'That's what the Gascons call Armagnac, did you know that? Not my mother. She called it phytothérapie.'

Herbal medicine. Sylvie had referred to marijuana the same way. Artist's elbow, she used to say to Tess, rolling her eyes in mock despair, it's a curse. Tess's mother had been one of those drinkers who claimed they barely drank, dismissing the gin in her hand as mostly tonic, surreptitiously stashing her empties under a blanket in the airing cupboard. Sylvie never pretended about anything. She rolled joints a dozen at a time, expertly, and kept them in an old pastille tin in the kitchen drawer.

'Do you know that old saying, that Gascony is so poor that even the crows fly over it on their backs so they don't have to see it?' Delphine asked. 'Fight the crow, Delphine, Sylvie used to say. My God but she was a hypocrite.' She raised her glass unsteadily to her lips and Tess realised to her surprise that she was drunk. She had never seen Delphine drunk before.

'No.' Tess shook her head. 'Sorry but that's not true. She was the opposite of a hypocrite, whatever that is. She never lied. She couldn't. She wasn't always right but she always told the truth, always, no matter what it cost her. Or anyone else.' She was drunk too, or she would never have said so much. Immediately she wanted to take the words back but Delphine only slammed her hands down on the table, a kind of triumph on her face.

'But that was precisely the nature of her hypocrisy, don't you see? Insisting on the truth, yes, the one and only, carved from stone, the Platonic ideal, but never allowing even for a moment that it might not be hers. I pleaded with her not to do it, Tess. I said I didn't think I could bear it, the thought of it, her like that, the students – and do you know what she said? That I was too sentimental. That it was barbaric to value ritual and ceremony over scientific knowledge. *Barbare*, like I was the savage.'

Tess could hear Sylvie saying it, her voice blithe and final at the same time, as though it was a game you both knew she would win, and immediately the kitchen was alive with her, her clutter jumbled back on the counters, the air stirred up as she padded barefoot around the table, her wild hair twisted up and secured with a rubber band, her hands sculpting sentences as she spoke. Her sudden fierce kisses, her mouth pressed against the top of Tess's head as though she meant to print the shape of her lips on the bone.

All this time, Tess thought, all this time she was here and I didn't come, and the thought sliced her like a scalpel, slick and deep.

Mia stretched lazily, her fingers grazing the sloping ceiling, and reached for her phone. Still nothing. She couldn't believe there was genuinely no Wi-Fi here. How did anyone live without Wi-Fi? She wondered if Yaz was awake yet, if she had already posted pictures from last night on Facebook. Sighing, she slumped back on her pillows.

The skylight above her was speckled with bird shit but the sky was very blue. Delphine had called the room she was sleeping in Sylvie's study but it looked more like a junk room to Mia. The bed was wedged in at one end by a chest of drawers and at the other by one of those old-fashioned desks with a flap you pulled down to write on. Where the ceiling was high enough to stand there was a huge table with a metal lamp on it and shells and pieces of seaweed and little clay sculptures and bleached-white animal skulls and stacks and stacks of paper weighed down with bits of pottery and big brown stones like potatoes. The walls were covered with bookshelves, so heavy with books that they bowed in the middle, and more books were on the floor, piles and piles of them, and canvases too, propped up between the piles. Delphine had apologised for the mess but Mia liked it. She thought if she ever had a study she would want it to be just like this one, so crammed with ideas that you couldn't help but breathe them in.

She yawned. She supposed she should get dressed and go downstairs but she didn't want to. It was too sad down there, it made her feel anxious, like whatever she did would be the wrong thing, and also bad for not feeling sad too, so instead she sat in Sylvie's chair and looked at all the things on her table. The little clay sculptures were all of pregnant women, lying down or kneeling or sitting cross-legged, their clay hands cradling their bellies. The clay was rough, like dried-out plasticine, and very fragile. Most of the women were broken. Mia picked up one of the potato stones and turned it over. Inside, instead of rock, it was a sparkling mass of ice-white crystals with a Ribena-purple centre. Charmed, she ran her finger over its jagged glitter.

It was only when she put the stone back that she noticed the framed photo on the wall. A close-up of a girl standing against a brilliant blue sky with her face painted blue and green, and on her back a huge pair of shimmery blue and green butterfly wings. Mia had seen it before, lots of times, especially since the Climate Camps had started and it was suddenly all over the internet. In the captions they always called her the Butterfly Girl, as though she didn't have a name, but actually it was Tess. She had her arms out and her head thrown back and her mouth was open like she was singing.

She looks wasted, Yaz said, laughing, when Mia showed it to her online, like she's on drugs or something, and it was true, she did.

When Mia asked her mum about it, Tess just shrugged and said it had been taken at a demonstration in the 1990s, a huge street party on some motorway in west London to protest against capitalism and cars. There had been music and dancing and actual sofas in the fast lane and bagpipe-playing stilt-walkers who walked slowly along the road in huge hooped skirts while, underneath and right in front of rows of unsuspecting police, protesters dug up the tarmac with pneumatic drills and planted trees in the holes. Her mum said the party was incredible but she didn't like the photo. She definitely didn't like that people still used it online. Once a journalist from some newspaper worked out that Tess was the Butterfly Girl and wanted to do a piece on her, but her mum refused.

'Because there's nothing to tell,' she said when Mia asked why. 'We made some costumes a hundred years ago. People wore them for a bit and then they stopped. Even those dismal rainbow fairies of yours have got better stories than that.'

Mia leaned closer. Another much smaller photo was folded and tucked into the Butterfly Girl frame. The smaller picture was also of her mum, only in this one she was wearing a red swimsuit and sunglasses and lying on a rug on the grass. She was pregnant, her belly round under the red swimsuit like a ball, and on top of her belly there was a hand. The hand was lean and brown. It had a thick silver ring on one finger.

Mia stared at the hand. Very gingerly she slid the picture from the frame and unfolded it. A man lay on the grass beside her mum. They were both laughing but, while her mum was looking at him, he laughed straight at the camera. He was slim with long tangled brown hair and a goatee and a line of silver hoops in one ear. His shirt was unbuttoned, exposing his tanned chest. As well as the ring, he wore a silver disc on a leather thong around his neck. The shadow of it drew a dark circle on his skin. On his right side, half hidden by the shirt, Mia could see the edge of a tattoo, much bigger than her mum's. It looked like a giant fish tail, though the shadow made it hard to be sure.

There was a noise in Mia's ears like the sea, only louder. On the back, in thick marker pen, someone had scrawled *T&D, Juin 97.*

D for Dave. For Dad. Mia had never seen a proper picture of him before, not up close. Her dad had left before Mia was born and died when she was only four so there weren't any photos of them together, and there weren't even any of him with her mum because her mum had thrown them away when she knew he wasn't coming back. The only picture Mia had ever seen of him was in an album at Grandpa Ivo's house: it had been taken at a party so it was dark and anyway he was only in the background and even when Grandpa Ivo pointed him out all she could really see of him was the side of his head. When she told her mum about it afterwards, Tess called Grandpa Ivo a fucking shit-stirrer. She didn't say anything about Mia's dad and Mia didn't ask her. The only things Mia could remember her mum saying about her dad was that he would have loved Mia more than anything and that being with him had been one of those ideas that seemed brilliant at the beginning but turned out to be impossible, like keeping a tiger as a pet.

Mostly, though, they didn't talk about him. It wasn't that they avoided it, more that he never really came up. Once, when Mia's mum's friend Ruth was over for supper, Mia overheard her mum telling her that Mia never thought about her father, that you couldn't miss what you had never known.

It was true, sort of. Except that recently Mia had found herself thinking about him, wondering what it might have been like to know him. At school her class had studied genes in science, how family traits were handed down through DNA. Until then, it had never really occurred to Mia to wonder how much she might be like her dad but Mr Mulvey said that, since nature favoured male genes, you were more likely to inherit traits from your father than your mother. So if your dad had dimples or bad teeth or webbed toes there was a stronger chance that you would have those things too. Also left-handedness. Mia's mum wasn't left-handed but Mia was. After that she thought about her dad sometimes when she did her homework, her hand twisted awkwardly around so that she didn't smudge what she had written.

Mia touched her dad's face with her finger, tracing the shape of it, the thought of him moving through her like a wave. His eyes were squinted up against the sun so she couldn't see what colour they were. She had always thought they would be blue like hers but Mr Mulvey said that wasn't how it worked. He didn't explain why, the bell went and there wasn't time to go into it, and she wanted to ask her mum about it when she got home, but somehow when the moment came she couldn't. It was like, somehow, without her realising it, her dad had become something they didn't talk about, that they didn't need to talk about.

'We're all we need,' her mum used to sing when Mia was little and they danced around the kitchen. 'Me and you, us two.'

Mia didn't know if the song was a real song or if her mum had made it up. In the photo her dad's hair was brown like hers, the ends bleached by the sun. She wondered if he got eczema in the crooks of his elbows in the winter like she did, if the soapy taste of coriander made him gag.

It was her in her mother's belly, not quite a baby yet but almost. Her dad's hand was on her.

His front teeth were just the right amount of crooked.

Tess picked her way down the narrow cliff path to the beach. The tide was going out. Near the water's edge the sand was smooth and cool, little bubbles breaking across its surface. Sandpipers skittered ahead of her, darting away from the shallow wavelets as they foamed and spread. The sand glistened with shells.

Tess crouched and picked one up. A razor clam, unbroken and still hinged, but when she picked it up it crumbled in her fingers, as brittle as old nail polish. Higher up the beach, where the sand was powdery, seaweed lay in lacy patterns and, entangled in it, brightly coloured bits of rubbish, cellophane wrappers, plastic bottle caps, fragments of frayed blue nylon rope. A battered pink flip-flop. She should have brought a bag. Sylvie always did. Her scavengings found their way into her sculptures, hammered or melted or woven together, reimagined as something unexpected and beautiful.

'How could he?' Tess's mother had shouted when Tess came home after that first summer at the end of the earth. 'That utter shit, how could he leave you like that with a total stranger?' and Tess thought of the ever-changing stream of babysitters that had flowed through her childhood, the homesick au pairs and the resentful cleaners and the children of her mother's friends who regarded her coldly and went back to their games, and she said nothing because it was the kind of question her mother always asked, the kind that didn't need an answer, and anyway Sylvie was a secret she wanted for herself.

The waves moved in and out. Tess watched a tiny crab skitter sideways into its hole. She thought it would be easier to think about Sylvie here, this stretch of sand that had always been hers, but he kept pushing his way in. The warmth of his sun-steeped skin as she leaned back against his chest, the salty, sleepy smell of him. The certainty of it, that there would never again be anyone or anywhere else she wanted to be.

'Happy as a clamshell,' he murmured, his lips soft against her ear.

Yanking off her towel, Tess scrambled onto the rocks. At the end, where a flat boulder jutted like a stuck-out tongue, it was deep enough to dive. Tess looked down at the waves slapping and bursting against the rocks. The water would be cold. It always was.

'Don't think,' Sylvie used to say. 'Just dive.'

It was Sylvie who insisted they come to Finistère. She wanted to meet him. To approve him, you mean, Tess corrected her, laughing, and Sylvie laughed too.

'You don't think it's a little late for that?' she said.

The two of them drove down in Dave's van. After all his talk of travelling the world they were finally abroad. Dave said France didn't count but Tess didn't care. It was June and the sun shone every day. The cliffs were a riot of flowers. Dave was more at ease than she had ever seen him, the tension all gone out of him. He danced around Sylvie's kitchen, singing tunelessly along to Joni Mitchell as he put the coffee on to brew. Sometimes Sylvie drank it with them, the three of them sitting at the table under the grapevine. She came to the studio every day but in the evenings, when her work was done, she walked back up the hill to the house of her friend Bertrand so they could have the place to themselves.

'We're chasing you away,' Tess said, but Sylvie only smiled.

'Darling girl,' she said. 'You will have plenty of time to be three.'

Tess was nearly seven months pregnant. She lay with Dave on the grass under the gnarled apple tree and watched the sky turn pink and gold between its branches. They swam naked in the starlit sea, their bodies fish-pale in the dark water, then ran back to soak in Sylvie's claw-footed tub. When he held her against him, his fingers threaded in hers, she told him about the bit in *Tess of the d'Urbervilles*, when Tess and Angel Clare wash their hands together in a basin of water, Angel asking *Which are my fingers and which are yours?*, and Tess's reply, *They are all yours.*

'Thank God for Thomas Hardy,' she murmured as his hands slid over her belly. 'If it wasn't for him I wouldn't know that fate is only ever bitter and unfair.'

She was so gorged with happiness she thought her skin would split.

On their last day they walked hand in hand along paths bright with yellow gorse to the tiny cove Sylvie called la Morsure, the bite. It was early, the sky still pale at its edges, the sea hushed and silken. At the top of the path down to the sand there was a small stone cottage with green shutters. An old couple sat close together on the front step, drinking coffee, a white dog sprawled at their feet.

'Let's never go back,' he said. 'Let's stay here at the end of the earth and grow old together.'

Could he sense it already, the darkness that was coming? So many nights she had lain awake and wondered what would have happened if she had listened, if they had stayed. But she didn't listen and they didn't stay. She laughed and kissed him and afterwards, when they had swum, they went back to the house and made love one final time and then they drove back to London.

Seven weeks later – but she couldn't think about that. Seven weeks later he was gone.

Should she have known? Sylvie had. One evening, walking up from the beach, Sylvie stopped. For once Dave was not with them, he had gone on ahead. The sun was low and their shadows were long in the golden light.

'I like your Dave,' she said. 'I like how happy he makes you.'

Tess smiled dreamily. 'Me too.'

Sylvie was silent, studying Tess's face as though she was painting her in her head.

'Be careful, my darling,' she said. 'He loves you but he is damaged, I think.'

'So?' Tess said angrily. 'I am damaged too.'

The sun was suddenly fierce on Tess's shoulders, the boulder rough beneath her feet. Beyond the bay, the ink-dark sea glittered like broken glass.

Don't think. Just dive.
She dived.

It was Tess who suggested the ceremony at sea. She took wood ash from Sylvie's kiln to scatter on the water and she put it in a pot Sylvie had made. The pot was a glossy brown with bluish streaks. Mia nodded when Tess showed it to her and said it was cool but actually she thought it was ugly. She didn't think brown was a good colour for anything.

At the harbour an old man was waiting for them. His name was Bertrand. Delphine said that he and Sylvie had been friends for a long time. Bertrand's boat was blue with a red stripe. It had been a fishing boat, he told Mia, but there were too many boats and not enough fish so the man who owned it sold it to Bertrand and learned how to fix computers instead. Bertrand had brought a shabby leather bag and a bunch of flowers wrapped in brown paper. The flowers were sparse and stringy, the tube-shaped petals curling back on themselves like they were half-dead already, but Tess put her hand to her mouth when she saw them, her forehead crumpling like she was about to cry, and gave Bertrand an awkward sideways hug.

Beyond the harbour the sea was rutted, the waves tipped with white. Huge boulders jutted out of the water. As they rounded a headland, Mia heard the sound of bells. Bertrand pointed up. A tiny church with a grey roof perched on the edge of the cliffs. The grass around it was hazed with purple.

'The chapel of Saint-They,' Bertrand said. 'In the local story, the bells ring to warn ships when they are in danger.'

'So we're in danger?'

'Nobody told you? The sea around here is full of monsters.' He smiled at Mia but Mia didn't smile back. Nothing was more annoying than grown-ups talking to you like you were a little kid.

Bertrand looked at her, his head on one side. His white hair made his face look even browner than it was.

'Either you are very brave or you know something I do not,' he said. Cutting the engine, he turned to Delphine. '*C'est bon, ici?*'

They stood together in an awkward half-circle at the back of the boat. Delphine read something from a piece of paper. It was in French so Mia didn't know what it meant. The wind blew her hair into her mouth. When Delphine finished reading Tess passed her the pot of ash. She had fastened a piece of newspaper over the top of it with an elastic band so that the ash could not fly away. It looked like a jar of jam.

'*Minute,*' Bertrand said. Fishing a bottle of champagne from his leather bag, he popped the cork. The glasses he had brought were all different colours. He handed Mia a purple one. Tess's was green. The champagne fizzed as he poured. Mia wished he would hurry up. The rocking of the boat was making her feel seasick. When he had filled everyone's glasses Bertrand looked at Delphine, who nodded. Mia looked at the horizon.

'*Il n'y a qu'un bonheur dans la vie, c'est d'aimer et d'être aimé,*' he said, holding his glass up in the air. His glass was blue. 'There is only one happiness in this life, to love and to be loved. Sylvie, *nous t'aimons.* We love you.'

He clinked his glass against Mia's. Tess clinked with Delphine. '*À Sylvie,*' she said.

'*À Sylvie,*' Delphine echoed and sipped her champagne. Mia sipped too, screwing up her face. Champagne didn't taste nearly as nice as she had imagined it would. Delphine took another bigger sip and, handing her glass to Tess, picked up the pot with Sylvie's ash in it. She didn't say anything. She just pulled the newspaper off the pot and shook the ash out over the sea but perhaps she didn't lean down far enough or perhaps the wind was too strong because, instead of scattering on the water, the ash whirled in the air and blew back into the boat. Mia tasted grit on her tongue. I am eating a dead person, she thought, before she remembered that Sylvie's body was not burned to ash but in a fridge somewhere, waiting to be cut up in a lesson. Mia wondered if it looked the same as it would have done when she was alive or if it was a completely different colour. She had never seen a dead body. The ash made her tongue taste burned. She took another sip of champagne, swilling it round her mouth like the pink mouthwash they gave you at the dentist. The champagne was still sour but she liked the feeling of it, the fizzy prickle on her tongue.

Delphine put down the pot. She was pretending not to cry. Tess touched her on the shoulder and gave her back her glass and Delphine drank the rest of the champagne in one swallow.

'I wasn't there,' Mia had heard her saying to Tess in the kitchen. 'I stepped out for some air and when I came back she was gone.'

Bertrand unwrapped the flowers he had brought and handed them out. Tess buried her face in hers, inhaling their perfume, so Mia did too. They smelled of honey and vanilla but fresh too, like lemon. It was hard to believe that something so ugly could smell so sweet. When Bertrand nodded they all dropped their flowers in the sea. Mia waited for someone to say something. No one did. They just stood there rocking with the boat, watching the flowers dancing on the waves.

A few minutes later Bertrand started the engine and they headed home.

When they were almost at the quay, Delphine went forward to the front of the boat and gathered up the mooring line, ready to jump ashore. Mia leaned against her mum. Tess slid an arm around her and pulled her close, kissing her on the top of her head.

'You OK?' she asked.

Mia nodded, biting her thumbnail. The engine was loud. No one could hear her but Tess.

'Can I ask you something?' she said.

'Sure.'

'What happened to Dad when he died?'

Dad. She liked how the word made her feel, like it was ordinary and shocking both at the same time.

Her mum stiffened. 'What do you mean?'

'I mean, was there a funeral?'

Tess shrugged, shaking her head. 'I suppose there must have been. Of a kind.'

'But we didn't go.'

'We couldn't. It was in Greece, remember?'

'So was he buried? Does he have a grave?' Mia's grandma was buried in a churchyard in Norfolk. Mia had only been there once but she remembered the grave. Under her name the headstone said GREATLY LOVING AND GREATLY LOVED.

Tess shook her head. 'No. He – he was cremated.'

'So what happened to his ashes?' Mia asked. 'Did someone scatter them for him like we just did for Sylvie?'

'I'm sure they did.'

'But you don't know where?'

'Mia—'

'Seriously, you don't know? How could you not know that? The woman who told you, Astrid, didn't you even ask her?'

Tess sighed. She tried to put an arm around Mia but Mia shrugged her off. The boat bumped against the rubber tyres that lined the quay.

'Well?' Mia demanded.

Tess hesitated. 'I don't think you should worry about that. Whatever happened to them, they're not him. They're just – remains.'

'How can you say that? And how can you not think it's a horrible idea, Dad having a funeral and us not there?'

'Mee, love. You were four years old.'

'So?'

'So you were four. And anyway I shouldn't think it was that kind of funeral. Apart from his brother he didn't really have any family.'

This time it was Mia who stiffened. She glared at her mother. 'He did have family,' she said furiously. 'He had me.'

3

Tess was eighteen when she met Dave Taylor. It was a Sunday in May and she was supposed to be revising for her A-levels. Instead she and her friend Lorna went to Camden. Lorna's boyfriend ran a stall in the market selling T-shirts and, not much more discreetly, weed. When they came out of the tube station, the street was in uproar. Two clapped-out old cars had crashed into each other in the middle of the five-road junction on Camden High Street. Traffic was at a standstill, gridlocked in every direction. Furious drivers shouted out of their windows and leaned on their horns but nothing moved. The drivers of the crashed cars made no effort to push them out of the way. Instead, in a frenzy of road rage, they were smashing the vehicles up with sledgehammers.

'What the hell?' Lorna said.

Then the music started. Immediately people started to stream from the subway and into the traffic-free space that the blockage had created. There were hundreds of them. Some of them were carrying scaffolding poles maybe twenty feet long. Like something from a circus, perfectly choreographed, the poles swung up into the air, making tripods, and suddenly people were climbing up them, balancing in the air. Around them crowds of people laughed and danced, their arms waving over their heads. At the crash site the drivers stood back, panting and grinning at one another as two men clambered onto the car roofs and unfurled a huge banner. **FREE THE CITY**, it read in giant black letters. **KILL THE CAR. RECLAIM THE STREETS.** Tess thought of Sylvie's photographs, the ones she took as a student in Paris in 1968, and her heart surged.

'Come on,' she said and, grabbing Lorna's hand, she dragged her through the clogged blare of traffic and out into the middle of the crowd. A girl with cropped blonde hair was sitting on someone's shoulders, reaching up to hang bunting from the lamp posts. Music was blasting from speakers mounted on an armoured vehicle, Louis Armstrong's 'What A Wonderful World'. Throwing her head back, Tess began to dance. Close to her a man in a sleeveless T-shirt was dancing too, his narrow hips rippling from side to side. He had honey-coloured hair and a drum under one arm. He ran his fingers across its skin, making a sound like rain.

'Fucking beautiful, isn't it?' he said, and his smile went all the way down her spine.

His name was Dave.

It didn't start then. Dave was already seeing someone. Astrid Osman was a PhD student and the first person Tess met when she dragged Lorna to one of the activists' Tuesday evening assemblies. There was no membership or requirement for entry to what they called the (dis)organisation, the meetings were open to anyone who turned up. There wasn't meant to be any hierarchy either, though it was clear to Tess that, along with a bloke called Jimmy, Astrid and Dave were mostly in charge. Lorna didn't get it, she said if you wanted to change the world you should go into politics, that principles were nothing without power, so the second time Tess went by herself. She had been living off and on at Lorna's house throughout sixth form, it was easier for school and much better than living with her stepfather, but the truth was they weren't really friends any more. Tess didn't know what she wanted but she knew she didn't want to live the way Lorna's parents lived, with drinks before dinner and bars on the basement windows. It thrilled her that London might one day be a place that was defined not by profit and pollution but by generosity and freedom, a place where it was normal to share food and make art together, to dance in the streets. It thrilled her that someone like Dave might want that too.

After the meetings, most of them went on to the pub. Astrid tutored hot-housed private school kids in the evenings and at weekends so most times she couldn't come but Dave was always there. A lot of the activists were skint, or said they were, they hung back when it was time to get a round in, but Dave was quick to put his hand in his pocket. He was a gardener, he told Tess, north London mostly but also one or two places out near the M25. He liked the rhythm of it, he said, the connection to the seasons, the earth. He liked how it coupled physical graft with skill and imagination. He volunteered in a community garden near Harlow where the vegetables they grew were given out free to local low-income families, but his passion was for flowers. There was something magical, he told her, miraculous even, in seeing a garden you had planted in full bloom.

He was twenty-eight. Tess told herself the age gap wasn't important but sometimes beside him she felt like a child. Dave knew so many things, he had experienced so much. He had been a hunt saboteur and part of the protest group that demonstrated against the 1994 Criminal Justice Act, the assault on public space that lumped together civil protesters and ravers and travellers, and criminalised them all. He had been at Twyford Down and the battle of Claremont Road. Though he had been arrested at least three times, somehow he had always avoided being charged.

'I was born lucky,' he said, and Tess believed him. There was an intensity about him, a glow like the Ready Brek kid in the old adverts. She felt its warmth whenever she was near him. She wasn't the only one. There was no fixed order to the Tuesday assemblies, anyone who wanted could pitch in with an idea, but when Dave spoke everyone listened. For all his laidback charm there was something powerful in him, a fierce streak that set him apart. He said it was his northern roots, Southport thrawn, he called it, which meant contrariness, defiance, but he made Tess think of the Pied Piper, him and his drum. People wanted to follow him.

After her A-levels were over and school had broken up, Tess was supposed to go to France. Instead she rang Sylvie and told her about the (dis)organisation. Sylvie didn't ask where Tess planned to stay or if she had enough money. At Tess's age Sylvie had been making performance art in Paris and sleeping with a famous and very married philosopher. Unlike Lorna's mother, Sylvie didn't consider someone of eighteen to be a child.

'Bravo, darling,' she said. 'The barricade blocks the street but opens the way. Come and see me when you have made the world a little better.'

Tess moved into her stepfather's flat in Chelsea. She was supposed to ask him first but Quentin was in London less and less, and on the rare occasions he did come up he always arranged for the cleaner to go in first so there was no danger of Tess being caught out unawares. She took a part-time job in a vegetarian café in Soho and threw herself into the (dis)organisation. It was like waking up in another world. She had never been political before, she had dismissed politics as bureaucracy, paper-pushing for old white men in ugly glasses and the freak of nature that was Maggie Thatcher. It had never occurred to her that it would be possible for a modern government to pass an act that, by its provisions against aggravated trespass, not only outlawed raves and squatting and the traveller lifestyle but somehow turned non-violent protest into a criminal offence. That made it actually illegal for more than ten people to gather and listen to rave music or, in the words of old white men in ugly glasses, 'sounds wholly or predominantly characterised by the emission of a succession of repetitive beats'. That allowed the police to take and log the DNA of anyone arrested on suspicion of a crime.

'I don't understand,' she said to Dave. 'It's like 1984,' and Dave shrugged.

'Yeah, well,' he said. 'Nothing gets the British establishment shitting its pants faster than a crowd waking up to the magic of its own power.'

Arrangements for a second street protest were under way, this time in Islington. Like in Camden, the idea was to bring the city to a standstill, to realise, if only for one afternoon, the utopia of an urban space that belonged to everyone, a commons reclaimed from the fat cat few and returned to joyful collective ownership. A protest, yes, but more than that, a celebration. The street stripped of its deadening weight of cars and commerce and transformed instead into a place to play, to dance, to eat and drink for free, without money and without permission. In meetings Dave was always challenging everyone to think laterally, theatrically. Bigger. It exasperated him how cautious everyone was. You had to risk to win, he said, and if you wanted people to listen you had to tell them a story. The greater the stakes, the more people cared about what happened in the end. There was something glorious in the scale of his vision, his refusal to be practical or prudent or afraid.

The result was Rave Against the Machine, a pop-up festival in the middle of Upper Street. It was like Camden, only bigger and better. Sofas blockaded the street at either end and all down the middle protesters sat like nesting storks on towers of scaffolding that could only be moved when they finally consented to come down. Dave wanted people in the bell tower of Angel Studios too, he said the place's connection with artists like Kylie and Robbie Williams would be catnip to the press, but Jimmy and the others were concerned about trespassing and criminal damage, and he was overruled. He satisfied himself with arranging for a dumper truck to empty tonnes of sand onto the pavement, creating an impromptu beach. Tess thought of the slogan sprayed across a wall in one of Sylvie's photographs from 1968: *Sous les pavés, la plage!* There was something gorgeous about the reversal.

London was in the grip of a heatwave and the sky was a bright hard blue. There were live bands, poetry, street food, paddling pools, toys and coloured chalks for the children. Techno blasted from a sound system mounted on an armoured truck and powered by bicycles. Wrong-footed once again, the police could do nothing. They watched, sweating in their uniforms, as two thousand people partied in the blazing sun. Tess danced exultantly, the music thumping through her, her head spinning with breathlessness and beer. The crowd was huge, she knew only a handful of them, but she had an overwhelming sense of being part of something grand and beautiful. Of belonging. Astrid was dancing with Karen and Nat. They caught hands and suddenly Tess was dancing, arms raised, inside the circle of their arms. She hadn't known it was possible for the world to feel so right.

It was evening when the rumours started. Someone had seen ranks of riot police assembling in a nearby street. Tess felt a tremor of fear go through her. Impatiently she pushed it away. The party was nearly over. The crowd had dispersed and the two hundred or so stragglers that remained were in a peaceable mood. People sprawled on the sofas. A few still danced, slack-limbed, in the golden light, their long shadows moving over the sand. The warm air smelled of weed.

Suddenly the roar of a police helicopter broke the calm. It buzzed low over the street, its rotors slicing the slanting sun. The dancers turned to look up at it. Then someone cried out, waving their arms. Behind the ordinary cluster of uniformed police, a column of officers in full riot gear was moving slowly towards them. Light glinted off their transparent shields, the lowered visors of their helmets. An electric charge ran through the protesters. Suddenly everyone was on their feet. People were shouting, punching the air with their fists. A woman snatched up a small child and wrapped it protectively in her arms. Someone threw a bottle. It hit a shield and smashed.

There was a pause like a dropped stitch. Then, drawing their batons, the riot police surged forward. Tess watched frozen as some of the protesters rushed towards them and others tried to get away. People were screaming at each other to stop pushing. In the confusion the police lashed out with their shields and batons, forcing the crowd back towards Angel. Tess was carried along with them, caught in the current. Looking desperately around her she tried to see a way out but the side roads were blocked with police vans, there was nowhere to go. Behind Tess a shirtless man fell. He thrashed as police grabbed him by the arms, dragging him backwards. There was blood on his face and in his dreadlocks. Beside him, visors lowered, the policemen in their riot gear looked like machines.

Tess stumbled, losing a flip-flop. She stopped but it was too late, she couldn't go back for it, the tide of people was too strong. The edge of a shield struck her back.

'Keep moving!' a voice barked from behind the visor and a gloved hand pushed her roughly. She staggered, losing her balance. The hand grabbed her upper arm as a metal baton came down on her thigh. Screaming, she curled herself into a ball, steeling herself for another blow, but it did not come. Instead she heard the thwack of a riot shield slamming into someone's body.

'This is a peaceful fucking protest, you pigs.'

Dave. Terrified, Tess hardly dared look up. The line of policemen kept coming, she was sure he would crumple, but instead he threw his weight against the riot shield, driving the officer backwards. Immediately two batons struck him with full force, one across his ribs, the other catching the side of his head. Doubling up he collapsed on the ground.

'Cunts,' he mouthed to Tess and grinned. There was blood running down his face. Then the kicking started and she couldn't see him any more.

Dave was arrested and held overnight but the next morning they released him without charge.

'I told you I was lucky, didn't I?' he said to Tess. He had a split lip, a black eye, an angry-looking gash above his temple. One of his ribs was cracked. At the meeting he lifted his shirt and showed everyone his bruises. The one in the small of his back was shaped like a butterfly. Tess had to clasp her hands together to keep herself from touching it.

'You're crazy,' Jimmy said. 'You'll get yourself killed.'

Dave smiled at Tess, a slow private smile that spread like a blush under her skin. The swelling on his lip twisted his mouth and made it crooked.

'I get overexcited,' he said, and it was like Jimmy wasn't there at all. 'No impulse control.'

When they went to the pub Astrid came too. They scored the big table by the window, there was lots of room, but Astrid squeezed onto the bench next to Dave, her shoulder against his. Everything she said was we: We loved that album! Of course we're in shock about Bosnia. We do miss bacon sometimes though, don't we? When he rested his arm on the table she leaned against him, playing with the leather thong around his wrist.

Tess downed her drink and went outside for a cigarette.

'Mind if I join you?'

He sat down next to her on the kerb. The darkness was warm, thick with exhaust fumes and chip fat. Tess offered him a cigarette but he didn't take it. She pulled her bare legs up to her chest. She was suddenly pricklingly aware of her body, the limits of it. In the silence the space between them pulsed like something alive.

'How's the rib?' she asked at last. Dave didn't answer. Instead he lifted the narrow strap of her top that had fallen from her shoulder and slipped it back into place. His knuckles brushed her bare skin as he ran it between his finger and thumb, smoothing it flat. Tess didn't dare look at him. She sat very still, her cigarette smouldering between her fingers as he ran the tips of his fingers very lightly along the line of her collarbone and into the dip at the base of her throat.

'These,' he said softly, his lips against her ear as his fingers drifted down her breastbone to graze the spatter of freckles above her cleavage. 'Do you have any idea how completely fucking crazy these have been driving me?'

Afterwards, when she knew he wasn't coming back, Tess told herself that he had taken advantage of her. She was so young then, hardly more than a child, she had been powerless to protect herself against him, but she knew it wasn't true. Even then, perhaps especially then, she had known her power precisely.

She felt no guilt about Astrid. All was fair in love and war and, besides, anyone could see that she and Dave made a terrible couple. It wasn't that Astrid was nasty or anything, just that she was so relentlessly, exhaustingly sensible, the kind of person who wore fleeces because they washed well and reminded people to drink water at parties. It was impossible to imagine her high or helpless with laughter or having sex. There was no hierarchy in the (dis)organisation, everyone was equal and Astrid pretended to be

37

chilled about it, but it was obvious to Tess that it drove her crazy not being able to tell people what to do. It was easy to imagine her as a librarian or local councillor, fretting about incorrectly shelved reference books or cars parked on double yellow lines. That kind of stuff bothered her. She couldn't help herself.

Astrid lived in Hackney, a flatshare with three other students. They would meet there sometimes, a bunch of them, before a protest or to collect flyers. The flat itself was a bit of a dump, dark and damp with dirty dishes piled up in the tiny kitchen, but Astrid's room was always immaculate. There were house plants and table lamps and a bedside rug and books arranged by size on a white shelf with no brackets and a perfectly made bed with a throw across the end of it and matching cushions. It looked like one of those show bedrooms in IKEA. Everyone in the (dis)organisation knew that Astrid and Dave were talking about moving in together, but by then Tess had seen Dave's bedsit, the mattress on the floor and the dirty backpack in one corner that did for a cupboard. As soon as she saw Astrid's bookshelf, Tess knew it was Astrid who was doing the talking.

Tess had no intention of making the same mistake. When Dave didn't break it off with Astrid, she said nothing. She let him pursue her. Sometimes she let herself be caught. More often she didn't. It did not come naturally to her; like him she was impetuous, prone to regret things later, but she knew her power lay in not needing. Dave wasn't interested in possessions or permanence. He talked often about travelling, getting away, taking a year or more to hitch across Africa or South-east Asia. Tess encouraged him. She didn't want him thinking she would hold him back. She had seen her parents' marriage fall apart, she knew how quickly men tired of women who demanded things they didn't want to give. And so she hid from Dave the longing he unlocked in her. She hid it from herself. Its ravenousness repelled her.

She offered him a different version of herself, the Tess she wished she was. A Tess who had been treasured all her life, who never doubted how dearly she'd be loved. That first night, as he led her by the hand to the back of the pub where the dustbins were, as he kissed her and slid his hand beneath the waistband of her shorts, as she gave in to a desire fiercer than anything she had ever felt, she took his hand and threaded her fingers between his. Nipping his ear with her teeth, just hard enough to hurt a little, she smiled at him and told him he would have to wait.

'I have to be somewhere,' she said, brushing her lips over his knuckles. 'Don't you?'

She lied a lot in those first few months but she never lied to him. Or rather she only lied about the little things, the things that didn't matter. She said she was busy when she wasn't, or that things didn't bother her when they did. That she needed time with her friends, that the (dis)organisation mattered to her more than anything, that life was too short and too full of adventures to spend it with one person. That she had meant to return his phone call but got distracted and forgot.

Not lies, then, so much as moves, her pieces slowly closing on his king. Whatever it was, it was exhilarating. She felt intensely, scintillatingly alive. Anything seemed possible. Something blazed inside her and she saw how it drew people and dazzled them, the light of her and the heat. So it did not surprise her, when she took the floor one Tuesday meeting to describe her plan for a butterfly protest, that a strange kind of excitement took hold of the room. Every pair of wings would be different, a particular and personal work of art. They could be sewn from scraps of silk, cut from coloured tissue paper or silver foil or cellophane. They could be painted in oils. As long as they were beautiful, Tess said, there was only one rule: that every pair had eyes. She showed them a picture of the peacock butterfly, its eyespots like a tiger's, blue-brown and glistening.

'No one knows for certain what the eyespots are for,' she said. 'They think it might be intimidation. Or distraction maybe, to disorient the enemy, buy time. I'd take either.'

The (dis)organisation distrusted the mainstream media, which mostly disparaged them as hippies or vandals, but Ivo had always had friends on Fleet Street and Tess made some calls. The first time a cloud of iridescent butterflies cycled slowly down Upper Thames Street, bringing the City's traffic to a standstill, there were pictures on the third page of the *Evening Standard*. **THE EYES HAVE IT**, the headline read. Policemen lined the pavements, red-faced beneath their helmets, but they let the protest through. A butterfly on a bicycle didn't raise people's hackles like an anarchist or a hunt saboteur. The second time, massed on Tower Bridge, they made the evening news. Only the local segment at the end, 'the news where you are', but still. Dave got someone he knew to record it on his VHS.

'Look,' he said, playing the tape back to her. 'This is you. This is what you've done.'

She had never felt so strong, so sure. There were times, it was true, that she had the sense of standing outside herself, like it was her own life she was watching on that screen, but it wasn't a lie. She was herself, only better, much better. It didn't feel wrong. It felt like growing up.

By the time she and Dave were officially a couple Tess had almost forgotten the girl she was before.

4

The iPad was the latest kind, a sleek white slice of sci-fi. Tess told Delphine not to lend it, she said it would do Mia good to have a day or two without the internet, but to Mia's relief Delphine just raised an eyebrow and handed it over.

'I feel your pain,' she said. 'I mean, no WiFi, really, who does that? It's like choosing to live without electricity. Or oxygen.' Her smile was so brief it might have been a trick of the light. 'The signal is better upstairs but still pretty slow, I'm afraid. Brittany remains resolutely in the dark ages.'

Delphine and Tess were going to see a lawyer in Quimper, something about Sylvie's will. Mia waited till they were gone, then took the iPad up to Sylvie's study. It was easier, not having her mum hanging around, pretending not to look at her screen while she scrolled. Tess was more normal than most of Mia's friends' mums about most things but she was weird about social media. When she found out Mia was on Facebook, she tried to talk her out of it and, when that didn't work, she came up with a bunch of random rules she made Mia promise to stick to: no information about her school or where they lived, no photos with their house in, no friends she didn't know in real life. It was like she had memorised the school presentation, Mia said to Yaz, the creepy stalker one they gave to parents in Year 7. Perhaps she had. Tess worked in the office at Mia's school so it was most likely her who typed it out in the first place. Mia thought she was fussing over nothing. Good luck to anyone who tries to groom me, she said to Tess, but Tess didn't find it funny. Yaz said it was single mothers, that they were always over-protective, but Mia thought it was the internet. She thought maybe there was something about the scale of it that freaked her mother out, like staring into outer space.

Delphine was right about the signal. It took forever for Yaz's Facebook page to load. The new photos unpeeled themselves in strips: Yaz, Lauren and Chloe striking poses, making Ls on their foreheads, holding up bottles of Smirnoff Ice, little curls of smoke twisting up out of Lauren's mouth. Someone had braided the sides of Yaz's hair, Yaz who got impatient waiting for microwave popcorn, who could barely sit through a five-second advert on YouTube. She was wearing loads of make-up and a crop top that showed her belly. Mia wondered where she had got it from. It wasn't hers, Mia didn't recognise it and anyway there was no way her mum would ever let her out of the house like that. Yaz's mum wanted Yaz to wear the hijab to school. Yaz leaned towards the camera, pouting her lips, her fanned-out fingers framing her chin. An ironic pose but at the same time not ironic. Her nails were electric blue.

Under the photos Yaz had written *D CREWZ IN D HAAAAAAS!!!!* Loads of people had already posted comments, friends of Yaz and Mia's from school but other names too that Mia didn't know. Yaz and Lauren's chat ran halfway down the page. *Yo ma gal yazza!!!* Lauren wrote at the end, and Yaz replied with *U D BESTEST* and a row of little black hearts. It was Mia who had shown Yaz how to add hearts to her posts. She hadn't known before.

Mia sat down on the bed. She tried to navigate back to her own page but the signal had dropped, it wouldn't load. Her throat ached and her head was full of white like one of those snowglobes with a plastic city inside. Pushing the iPad away she took the photo of her dad out of her pocket and it was like a cramp almost, the twist of him inside her, only without the pain. The way he laughed up at her, it was like he was looking right at her, like his laugh was just for her. So what if you missed Lauren's lame party, his laugh said. You're in France and the sun is shining and the sea is right there, literally right outside the window. If the others knew, if they could see you now, they'd be sick with envy. Who cares what's going on in boring old Palmers Green?

Her phone in her hand, Mia ran across the prickly lawn to the stand of pine trees at the edge of the cliff. Under the trees the shade was very black, the sand cool and powdery. Where the path went down towards the beach there was an old wooden bench with curved metal arm rests. The wood was silvery grey and rough with splinters. Mia leaned against the back of it, breathing in the hot herby smell of abroad. Tilting her head so the sea was behind her, she snapped some pictures of herself. In some she pulled stupid faces and in others she just looked at the camera. It was too sunny to see if any of them were good.

The photo of her dad was folded inside her phone case. An echo of the looking-at-it wave ran through her just knowing it was there. She didn't feel guilty about taking it. It wasn't as if it belonged to anyone, not now, not any more. She wondered if there was anything else of his in the house, books, maybe, or clothes he had left behind. Last year, after Mr Mulvey's lesson on left-handedness, she had tried to look for him online but she didn't find anything, or nothing to be sure of. Even when you screened out the snooker player and the American wrestler and the guy who played bass for Bryan Adams, there were just so many Dave Taylors, even more if you included

David, and anyway her dad had died in 2002 which was before social media properly existed, so most likely there wasn't anything online about him in the first place.

'*Bonjour*, Mia. How are you this morning?'

Mia turned round. It was Bertrand, the man who owned the boat. He was wearing a crumpled pink shirt and a straw hat which he lifted from his head, bowing at her like someone from a history book. His white hair stood up in a crown. It made Mia think of a dandelion clock.

'You are going swimming?' he asked.

Mia looked down at her bikini top and shrugged. 'Maybe later.'

Bertrand put his hat back on and sat down on the bench, looking out to sea. 'Myself, I have always preferred to be on the sea than in it. The idea of all those monsters – but I think you are not a person who believes in monsters, am I right?'

Mia shrugged again. She thought he was probably making a joke but his accent made it hard to tell, and anyway he didn't know her well enough to tease her. She opened her mouth to say she had to go but Bertrand was already saying something else.

'Or perhaps you are like Sylvie,' he said. 'Perhaps it is not so much that you do not believe than that you do not believe they would be so foolish as to pick on you.'

Mia smiled reluctantly, scrunching her toes in the sand.

'It's funny but when I first met your mother, I found it hard to believe she and Sylvie were only related through marriage. They were so much alike, not just to look at but in their spirit. You are like her too, like Sylvie, I mean. She said you would be and she was right.'

It hadn't occurred to Mia that Sylvie would ever have talked about her. She thought about her dying alone in the hospital, about her body being given to students so they could cut her up and look at her insides.

44

'Why did she fight with my mum?' she blurted out. She hadn't meant to say it like that but, once it was out, there was no point in trying to take it back. Bertrand was old and a stranger but he had already broken the rules by acting like they were friends, and anyway she really wanted to know the answer.

Bertrand shook his head. 'I don't know. Sylvie never told me. I do know she missed your mother's visits. The two of them had been very close.'

'My mum's like that. She falls out with everyone.'

Mia felt bad as soon as she said it, like it was a lie or a secret she had promised not to tell, but that didn't mean it wasn't true, or mostly true anyway. It wasn't just Sylvie. It was Grandpa Ivo and her dad's friend Astrid, and Quentin who had been her mum's stepfather, and all her friends from when she was the Butterfly Girl. It was Mia's dad. Her mum never talked about any of them.

Bertrand didn't answer. He leaned back against the bench and looked up at the sky. Suddenly his body tensed. '*Regardez là*,' he said softly.

Mia squinted upwards. A huge bird hung above them, the sun blazing through its wings, lighting up their elaborate patterns.

'A female,' Bertrand murmured. 'Can you see, her head is brown?'

The bird looked like a piñata, like she was made of tissue. She rose a little higher, riding the air. Then, swooping, she was gone.

'What kind of bird was that?' Mia asked.

'In French we call it *bondrée apivore*. *Apivore* means bee-eating, though in fact those birds eat mostly wasps. *Bondrée* I don't know in English. You will have to ask Delphine.'

'It was cool.'

Bertrand smiled. 'You're right, it was cool. These birds are not common in this region. If one were superstitious, which you do not need to tell me you are not, one might take it to be an omen. Perhaps even a good one.' He looked at Mia sideways, his smile pressing deep creases in his cheeks. She smiled back. He was funny, she thought, and his face was kind.

'Can I ask you something?' she asked.

'*Bien sûr.* Of course.'

'Were you here when my dad came? Did you meet him?'

'I did, yes.'

'So you remember him?'

The old man nodded. 'A little. It was a long time ago.'

'What was he like?'

'You don't think that is a question for your mother?'

'I want to know from you.'

Bertrand frowned, but not in a cross way. He took his hat off and ran his hand slowly through his white hair. 'He was handsome. Tall like you. I liked him. Sylvie did too.'

Mia waited for him to say more but he didn't. He put his hat back on, settling the brim. Then, leaning heavily on the arm of the bench, he levered himself up. He was about to say goodbye. He would walk away and she would be left exactly where she had always been, not knowing anything at all.

'Were they happy, him and my mum?' she burst out. 'Only I've seen photos and they look really happy.'

'Then perhaps they were.'

'You don't sound very sure.'

'Ah, Mia,' he said, shrugging in the Frenchest way Mia had ever seen. 'How can any of us presume to know of the hearts of others? We barely know our own.'

Aside from the legal complexities around the donation of her body, Sylvie's will turned out to be very straightforward. There were a handful of specific bequests, mostly her own paintings and sculpture. Otherwise everything went to Delphine. To Tess, who had not expected anything, she left her rosewood writing desk, the one that had belonged to Sylvie's mother. To Mia she left the sum of €3,000.

'"For the exclusive purpose of exploration and adventure",' the solicitor read. He smiled thinly at Tess and smoothed his moustache. 'Not, I should say, that there is any burden of proof.'

Afterwards Delphine and Tess walked back through the narrow streets of the medieval quarter towards the cathedral. Tess had forgotten how disorienting Quimper was, with its wonky-timbered candy-coloured buildings and its elaborately swirled cobbles. Like a Disney cartoon, she thought, or a hallucination. She wished she knew why Sylvie had left her the desk, if Tess was meant to understand some kind of message from it or if it was simply that Sylvie knew she loved it. Because she had always loved it, even when Sylvie teased her and called her a petite bourgeoise and said it was desks like that that started revolutions. In the square Delphine stopped, gesturing towards a cluster of tables shaded by orange umbrellas.

'I don't know about you,' she said, 'but I need a drink.'

She ordered white wine and olives and waited for the white-aproned waiter to withdraw. 'Actually I'm glad to get you alone. I have been wanting to speak to you.'

Tess stiffened uneasily. 'Have you? Why?'

'Please. There is no need to look so alarmed. I – I wished only to apologise. I realise now that I behaved very badly towards you. All those summers you should have been with us in Paris – back then, I didn't know what it meant to be a mother. Or to lose one for that matter. Perhaps I still don't. But being back here with you, with Sylvie gone, it is plain to me that I failed you. I am very sorry.'

Tess shook her head. 'It wasn't your fault. I had a father, remember.'

'Yes, but I permitted him to ignore his responsibilities. No, I encouraged him. I had no wish to share.'

The waiter brought the wine and the olives, green and glistening in their little white dish. They watched as he ceremoniously filled their glasses.

'My father is a self-absorbed vainglorious arsehole,' Tess said when he was gone. 'Don't look at me like that, you know it's true. You couldn't have changed him if you wanted to.'

'Perhaps not. But I could have tried. At the beginning and then later, after your mother died – I'm sorry. I should have done better.'

'Thank you. But it's OK. I was OK. I had Sylvie.'

'That's true, you did.' A shadow passed over Delphine's face. 'She was very proud of you, you know, of your work, your convictions. She was always telling me I should be more like you.'

'Then you were absolutely right to ignore her.'

Delphine smiled faintly. 'You are involved still, with the Verts?'

'No. Not for a long time.'

'I'm sorry to hear that. The Copenhagen summit was a fiasco. I was depending on you to save us from catastrophe.'

'Yeah, sorry about that, not sure how it slipped off the list,' Tess said, attempting lightness, and she felt the old ache of it, the ghost pain of a limb no longer there.

She had never imagined it would end. The (dis)organisation was part of who she was, who she and Dave were together. A foster family for the fucked, Dave joked, but fiercely, like it mattered. Dave had had a shitty childhood. His dad was an alcoholic and his mum Liz struggled with depression. Dave and his brother Paul had been mostly raised by their nan. She saved us, Dave said simply. By the time Dave and Tess met, Eileen was in a care home in Morecambe Bay. She had dementia. Dave was the only one who visited. Paul lived in South Africa, his dad was AWOL, and Liz was dead. An overdose. The doctors said it could have been an accident. He didn't know, Dave said, if that made it better or worse.

The Lone Sharks. Another joke that stuck. Tess on vocals, Dave on guitar, mandolin, banjo, piano, tambourine and drums. It was a lie, he said, that men could not multitask. Every photo of the two of them a potential album cover, except that Dave said they always looked too happy.

'Think of our public,' he said. 'They will never love us if we look like we don't need them,' and Tess laughed and leaned into him, this man who knew what she knew, that the heaviest part of loss was not grief but guilt because the grief was not just grief, because mostly it was anger and dread and a bitter kind of nostalgia for a past that might have been but never was.

She had not known how deep the rawness went in her until he matched it with his. The butterfly tattoo on her shoulder, people assumed she had got it because she was the Butterfly Girl, but that wasn't the reason. In ancient Greek, Ivo told her once, the word for butterfly was *psyche*, which was also the word for immortal soul, someone's essential self. Dave, the (dis)organisation, they were who she was, the best of her. They were her forever.

Except they weren't. After he left them, in the months after Mia was born, a crushing weight pressed down on her. It was hard to move, hard to breathe. Hard to want to. The doctor prescribed pills but Tess didn't take them. The weight was her punishment, for everything she had done or failed to do. She wanted to sleep and sleep, it was all she wanted, but her mind would not stop screaming. Mia screamed too. The broken windows were reglazed, the locks changed and the floor swept and scrubbed, but she couldn't banish the fear. The walls bulged with it. Wherever she was, in bed or at the kitchen sink or on the toilet, she kept seeing him, his face but not his, contorted, monstrous, his mouth a wide wet roar as he lunged at her. The sudden sickening certainty that he was going to kill her. And then a blank, a hole in time, before the slam of the front door brought her back to herself, hunched on the floor, her body juddering, her arms round her shins like a shield across her belly. His howl tearing through her like the howl of an animal.

Sometimes Mia screamed like that, catching his pitch, his anguish, and Tess had to put her down and lock herself in the bathroom, the taps at full blast and the shower on so she couldn't hear anything but water, until the sound of the water washed everything else away.

She didn't know what frightened her more, that he would come back or that he wouldn't. She was sure she saw him sometimes, the cut-out shape of him in the darkness between the street lights, the pale gleam of his face. On bad days he came in the daytime too. He was too clever to be caught but she saw how the leaves shivered in the hedge across the road, the streak of a cat from behind a parked car, and she knew he was there. She didn't answer the phone. The machine answered until it got full and stopped recording. Sometimes she heard Sylvie's voice or Nat's. Once she was sure she heard her mother. None of them made any sense. She was in a place beyond them, beyond time, where there was only her and Mia and the shadow of him like a sickness, sucking the meat from her bones.

Later, when she was better, she found it difficult to be certain of what happened in those months. Her memories were elusive, irrational, fragments of dreams. They didn't seem to belong to her. One Tuesday on impulse she took Mia to a (dis)organisation meeting but the old group had fractured and she didn't know anyone there. The new people were noisier, more militant. They wanted to bring down global capitalism through violent protest.

'No more hippy-dippy street parties,' someone said. 'This is class war.'

She didn't go back. She volunteered with Mind Matters, a group campaigning for better support for people struggling with mental illness. She marched against the Iraq War. Later, when the Climate Camps started, she thought about getting involved but by then it was too late. She couldn't risk running into people from the old days, people who had known Dave, people he might have stayed in touch with, not with Mia in tow. Once, on the tube, flicking idly through the *Metro*, she saw a photo of Astrid. She could still remember the panic that ran through her, the paper crushing itself in her hands as she hustled Mia off the train. They were in the street before it dawned on her that to Mia Astrid was only a name.

'I like the oak tree,' she said to Dave that day in the tattoo parlour, but Dave shook his head.

'Did you know,' he said, 'that the blue whale's heart is the size of a Volkswagen Beetle?'

'More?' Delphine held out the carafe. Tess blinked, looking down at her glass. To her surprise it was empty.

'Thanks.'

Delphine poured. 'Look, Tess, I wanted to say, I'm not sure what you were hoping for from this morning but I was thinking perhaps, if things are – if you were relying on her, financially, I mean, then I'm sure Lucien would agree—'

'I wasn't. But thank you.'

'My mother was a very stubborn woman. That doesn't mean we have to do things her way.'

'Actually I sort of think it does.'

Delphine bit her lip and didn't answer. Oh Sylvie, Tess thought. You're dead and I'm still siding with you against your own daughter. And then, how could you leave me too?

'What did she say?' she blurted. It was an effort to keep the childishness out of her voice. 'She must have said something, didn't she, when you told her I was coming?'

'She asked if you were bringing Mia.'

'That's it?'

Delphine frowned. 'You have to understand, by then, the morphine ... '

There was a long silence. Delphine picked up the carafe of wine. It was empty. She put it back down. The waiter showed a family to the table next to theirs. Tess watched as the mother shook out a napkin and spread it over the smallest child's lap.

'What happened between you two, Tess?' Delphine asked.

Startled by the bluntness of the question, Tess hesitated. 'She didn't tell you?'

'She wouldn't talk about it. She said it was between the two of you, that it was nobody else's business. One time only, the first summer you didn't come, what, eight, nine years ago? I asked her if everything was all right and she said – no, well. It doesn't matter.'

'What did she say?'

'No, really, forget it.'

'What did she say, Delphine?'

Delphine cleared her throat. 'She said you never really knew anyone. That even when you thought you understood someone completely, that you knew them inside out, they could do something and you would realise you didn't know them at all.'

Tess and Mia left the next day. Delphine was already gone. She said they could stay at the house as long as they liked but Tess said she had to get back, that she couldn't take any more time off work. She drove to Bertrand's house to say goodbye. They sat on the terrace under the old grapevine and drank lemonade. The lemonade had mint leaves in it and curls of lemon peel and cucumber sliced so thinly that it clung in cloudy circles to the inside of the jug. Grapes hung in clusters above their heads and the light was dappled with green.

When it was time for her to leave Bertrand took her to the greenhouse.

'*Chèvrefeuille*,' he said, gesturing towards a row of cuttings. 'Mia told me she liked the smell. I thought she might like to take some back to London.'

Chèvrefeuille, goat's leaf, one of Tess's first and favourite words in French. When she told Sylvie, Sylvie laughed and said that honeysuckle was better. The plants looked very fragile. Tess thought of the postcard Dave had found in a bookshop and stuck up on the fridge: *Gardeners, I think, dream bigger dreams than emperors.* She couldn't remember who was supposed to have said it.

'That's very kind,' she said. 'But I think they'd be safer here with you.'

'Mia has not inherited her father's green fingers?'

'The only thing Mia's ever grown is mould on the cereal bowls under her bed.'

Bertrand smiled. Tess looked out over the garden, at the bees drowsing in the lavender. Sylvie had always bought honeysuckle soap in thick slices from the market, wrapped in waxed paper like cheese. Tess could never smell it without remembering.

'Last night when I was sitting out here a hawk moth came and settled on this leaf, so close I could have touched it, and I knew,' Bertrand said softly. 'I knew she was at peace.'

Tess didn't answer. She sipped her lemonade, her heart tight with grief.

'You think I am a foolish old man,' Bertrand said.

'No. I think you're lucky.'

Mia lay on her bed and looked at the photo of her dad. She was supposed to be packing. She wasn't sure she wanted to go home, not yet, but her mum said they had to, that she couldn't take any more time off work. Of all the weird things about her mum working at Mia's school the weirdest was having to work in the holidays. Sometimes, when Mia was younger and there was no one else who could have her, her mum had taken her along too. Mia hated those days, all the doors locked and the deserted corridors echoing like the end of the world had happened and you were the only two people left still alive.

The photo was squashed from being in her phone case, the shiny paper already splitting at the folds. Mia turned over onto her stomach and smoothed it out on the pillow. Her dad laughed up at her, his hand cupping the bump of her like he already knew who she was going to be.

'Hey, Dad,' she said softly. Picking up her phone, she took a photo of the photo. That way, she thought, the photo could be somewhere safe and always with her, both at the same time. She opened her photo file, looking at his face in among all the other pictures. The ones Mia had taken on the cliff were rubbish, she had deleted them all, but some of the ones Tess had taken at the beach were all right. She wouldn't stop taking them, even when Mia told her to, even when she tried to grab her phone.

'One more,' she kept saying. 'Just one more.'

Mia sat up. Nobody took just one photo. She looked through the piles on the table and inside the desk, peering into the cubbyholes and opening the little drawers. The drawers were crammed with old cassette tapes and receipts and pictures torn from magazines and used envelopes with drawings on the back of them all jumbled up together. One of the drawers had a little key in it, a frayed green ribbon tied around its top.

The key didn't fit any of the locks inside the desk. It was only when she closed the flap that Mia noticed the big drawer underneath. When she slid the key into the keyhole, it turned with a satisfying click. Inside the drawer there was a brown envelope. The envelope had Sylvie's name and address typed on the front, only someone had drawn a line through those and written **TESS** in thick black capital letters across the front.

Mia took the envelope out of the drawer. There was another smaller envelope underneath, a white one, blank, torn open at the top. The white envelope had three photos in it, and a folded sheet of butcher's paper. The photos were all of her dad. None of them were as good as the one of him laughing but she still took pictures of them on her phone. There was one of him on the beach and one at a table drinking beer and one where he was squatting by a big green plant with a bandanna on and earth all over his hands. Her dad had been a gardener. Mia thought about it sometimes, what it would be like if their garden in Palmers Green was filled with flowers and not just dead grass and dandelions.

She unfolded the sheet of paper. A child's drawing in coloured crayon, three figures with swooping hair and triangles for skirts, two large and one small, and underneath them, in loopy handwriting, their names: *Momie*, *Sylvie* and *Mia*. Above them, squashed between a tree like a lollipop and a round yellow sun, there was a stick man in blue trousers with triangular wings. The stick man didn't have a name.

Mia put the drawing back in the envelope. She thought about putting the photos back too, but instead she tucked them inside the pages of her book and put the book under the clothes at the bottom of her bag. When her mum came back from saying goodbye to Bertrand, they would pack up the car and drive away. They wouldn't come back. Delphine was selling the house. Mia had heard her talking to her mum about having someone come in to clear it out. They would sell what could be sold, she said, or give it to charity but honestly who would want it? Most of it was junk.

Mia picked up the stone like a potato and touched the purple crystals inside. For a moment she wanted it very badly. She put it back on the table. The brown envelope with Tess's name on it was thin and light. Perhaps it was a will. Perhaps Sylvie had changed her mind at the last minute and decided to leave the house and the beach and all her money to Tess and Mia. Mia tried the flap but it was stapled shut. There was no way of opening it without tearing it so she held it up to the light, peering at the paper, and tried to imagine what it would be like to move here, to start all over again as a different person, a French girl with French friends and a French school and secret crystals on her desk and the beach every day like a holiday. Except she didn't speak French or even understand it and this place was just about the furthest you could get from real life before you had to be a fish.

Impatient at herself, Mia dropped the envelope on the bed. The brown paper was too thick to see through anyway.

Her mum had left her phone charging on the kitchen counter. Mia put the envelope next to it. If her mum asked her what she had been doing rummaging through Sylvie's desk she would say she was looking for a pen. Her mum was old enough to think you still needed pens for everything. The phone had two bars of signal. Mia picked it up. It was nearly 90 per cent charged. Unplugging it, she took it upstairs to the landing. A third bar flickered, then disappeared. When she leaned on the windowsill the third bar came back. The window looked out across the garden. When Tess came back from Bertrand's, Mia would see the roof of the car coming down the lane.

Quickly she thumbed in Tess's PIN code. Yaz had posted more photos of Lauren and Chloe on Facebook. She had friended lots of new people too, her wall was full of them. Tyrone was on there and Kai from the year above. It was like in the three days Mia had been gone, she'd become a different person, someone Mia didn't even know.

Unsettled, Mia clicked onto her own wall. On the crossing from Portsmouth she had posted a picture of herself standing at the front of the upper deck, her arms outstretched like the girl from *Titanic*. Underneath she had written: *I'm flying, Jack. Or I would be if my mum hadn't made me take this stupid ferry*. It made her laugh to think of Yaz laughing, Yaz loved *Titanic*, but when Mia checked her wall, Yaz hadn't left a comment. She hadn't even bothered to like the post. For a moment Mia stared at the screen, uncertain what to do. Then, quickly, furiously, she scrolled through her mum's photos of her on the beach and posted the best one to her wall. In the picture she was smiling and the sea was so blue it looked like something out of a brochure. *Livin my best life*, she wrote underneath it. *Wot u got, Palmers Green?*

It made her feel better, thinking of Yaz being jealous. Mia uploaded more photos, then opened her friend requests and scanned through them: her old babysitter, a couple of girls she'd met at sports club, a boy from the year below and a girl called Vanessa Morales whose name she didn't recognise. According to Facebook, they had five mutual friends. Curious, Mia clicked through to Vanessa's profile page. Her privacy settings meant you had to be friends with her to see her wall but there was a profile picture of her laughing with a fluffy brown dog. She looked nice. One of their mutual friends was Yaz. Mia wondered if Vanessa had been at Lauren's party, if Yaz had mentioned Mia. She accepted her request. According to her wall, Vanessa's relationship status was complicated. She lived in Crater Street, Sea of Clouds, The Moon. There weren't any pictures of the party but Vanessa had posted some pretty funny gifs. The best one was a penguin waddling up behind another penguin and knocking it over with its flipper. It made Mia laugh out loud. She clicked to like it. Yaz had liked it too.

Mia leaned on the windowsill, her mum's phone cradled in her hands. She breathed in the warm pine-smelling air and thought about the photos of her dad hidden inside her book, about all the questions she didn't know the answers to. The phone's screen went dark. Frowning, she re-entered her mum's PIN and quickly typed *david taylor cremation greece* into the Google search bar. It took a long time to load. When it finally did, there were lots of Davids who had died and lots of Taylors too but there weren't any David

Taylors and anyway all the names were from America. Apparently there was a town called Greece in New York state.

Mia deleted the search. She typed *Greece crematoriums* instead. She didn't know what she expected to find, maybe crematorium websites with lists of the people cremated there, but the first result on Google was a newspaper article. THREE YEARS SINCE CREMATION LEGALISED IN GREECE AND STILL NO CREMATORIA, the headline said. The article was dated 2009. There was a picture of a priest dressed in black with a white beard and a massive silver cross like a shield covering his chest. *For decades*, Mia read, *Greeks seeking cremation for their loved ones have been forced to travel to Bulgaria or beyond.*

From beneath the open window came the sound of a car engine, the crunch of tyres on gravel. Her mum was back. Clumsy-thumbed, her heart racing, Mia shut down Google, then reopened the browsing history and deleted the search. Outside the car door slammed. Flying down the stairs, Mia put the phone back on the counter, fumbling the charger into its socket, and went outside to meet her.

5

It was not quite true that in those first months Tess only lied about the little things.

Her age, for example. It was after Tess's third meeting that the subject of birthdays came up. They were in the pub. Someone asked Tess what her star sign was and she said she was a Virgo. Fuck, another control freak, someone said, laughing, and then Astrid leaned across the table and asked her in a clear sharp voice how old she was. It felt to Tess like a test she had to pass. Twenty, she said with a bland bright smile, and went outside for a cigarette. She didn't feel bad for lying. Tess had met girls like Astrid before: if she knew Tess was still at school she would treat her like a child. Two days later Tess sat her final A-level paper.

On the day her results came through there was an emergency meeting to discuss the Newbury bypass. The first stage of demolition had begun. Already there was a camp of protesters at Snelsmore Common. Dave wanted to join them. Astrid was against it. They argued. When Tess closed her eyes his voice crackled through her like an electric current. It was seventeen days since he had kissed her on the pavement. Since then they had kissed twice more, once after closing time in a side street near the tube station, the second time in a secret park Dave knew, a half-wild slice of nature reserve tucked in alongside the canal just north of St Pancras station. Despite the weeks of hot dry weather the grass of the wildflower meadow was still soft and green. They lay on their backs under a canopy of meadowsweet, white butterflies dipping and drifting above them.

'It's like magic, like we stepped through an enchanted door,' Tess said and, as Dave laughed softly, his lips grazing her neck, she knew that, whatever happened next, there would have always been a time when she was perfectly and completely happy.

The Newbury meeting dragged on. Somehow Lorna had convinced Tess to throw a results party at her stepfather's flat, so she left before it ended. At the party her friends talked about halls and grants and freshers' weeks, about the Oxbridge entrance exam. So, Bristol, people kept saying to Tess, and Tess didn't know what to say so she didn't say anything. She got high and thought about Dave. Someone burned a hole in one of Quentin's Persian rugs. The upstairs neighbours complained about the noise. Lorna was sick. None of it felt real. It was not until Lorna rang the next day and told her that Ivo had called that Tess realised it had never occurred to her to let him know.

Everyone said the heatwave had to break but it went on and on. London was desiccated, dazed with dust. Lorna brought round a letter from Bristol with details of Tess's accommodation. They smoked a joint on Quentin's balcony. Lorna told Tess she was going travelling. She said she would call when she got back but they both knew it was the end of something. When she was gone Tess didn't open the letter. She lay on the balcony and stared at the aeroplanes crossing the sun-bleached sky. They seemed to take her with them, carrying her further and further away.

Tess rang Quentin and told him about Lorna. He agreed she could stay in the flat till she went up to university. He asked her if she knew anything about a burn in the carpet. Later Lorna's mother forwarded another letter. By then it was September. This one had URGENT written at the top in capital letters. Some of the first paragraph was underlined. Cannot be guaranteed. Your immediate attention.

She didn't tell Dave where she was living. She was afraid of what he'd think if he knew, her childish dependence, her privilege. She said she was dossing on a friend's floor in Brixton, just till she sorted herself out. South London was far enough away to be safe. South London was another country.

In their secret park children were pond-dipping. Their high voices carried on the warm air. Dave crushed a leaf in his fingers. It was bee balm, he told her, also known as bergamot. The leaf smelled of spice and citrus and his warm skin. He said that the Native Americans used bergamot as an antiseptic and a hair pomade and to treat flatulence. When she laughed he laughed too but he swore it was true. The flowers were star-shaped and brilliant scarlet, like fireworks. She kissed his palm, the twist of scar tissue that puckered the base of his thumb. He had burned it as a toddler, he told her later as they lay in the long grass of the meadow. Entranced by the orange crackle of the bonfire his dad had lit in the back garden, he had tried to grab one of the flames.

'Like I said,' he said, his fingers sliding into her underwear. 'No impulse control whatsoever.'

On Tess's birthday Ivo rang. For years Tess had waited for his calls, hoping against hope that he would announce that he was in London, that she needed to get dressed immediately because he was taking her out. She ached for those rare glorious outings, the fierce brief blaze of his interest and affection. Now, to her surprise, she felt only a calm cold anger. She told him she wasn't going to university and, when he lost his temper, she put the phone down. It exhilarated her to realise that that was something she could do.

That evening Nat said they were going to the pub but, when the two of them arrived at Karen's flat, everyone else was already there.

'Surprise!' they cried and it delighted them, how shocked she was. There was bunting and a homemade banner that said **HAPPY 21st BIRTHDAY** in big brightly coloured letters. Nat had made her a crown out of silver paper with fruit pastille jewels. Tess wore it as they brought out the cake, as they sang to her. The smell of cream cheese icing and melting wax made her feel sick. She wanted to confess, to turn it into a joke against herself, *don't hate me, guys, but here's the thing*, but it was too late. They had taken too much trouble.

She blew out the candles, twenty of them anyway. One of them was the magic kind that went on relighting. She puffed at it dutifully while the others clapped and laughed. There was no way back, nothing she could say that wouldn't make them hate her. Someone opened a bottle of cava and the cork shot out so fast it hit the ceiling.

They went to join the protesters at Snelsmore Common. Dave drove everyone there in his van. They waited for him outside Astrid's flat, seven or eight of them, their sleeping mats in rolls at their feet. When Dave finally came down he said Astrid wasn't coming, that she wasn't feeling well. He didn't look at Tess. In the van Nat and Karen took the front seats. Tess sat behind them and looked at Dave's lean brown hands on the steering wheel. Just watching the bones move under his skin made her dizzy with desire.

Tess expected bulldozers, gouged-out weals of earth. Instead the place was wild and beautiful. Birds sang and the heather was hazed with pink. In the oak woods the protesters had built makeshift platforms in the trees. One of them, Jeannie, took Tess up. She told Tess that, if the bypass went ahead, one hundred and twenty acres of ancient woodland would be felled for nine miles of motorway, ten thousand trees lost to a road that would be redundant in five years. The platform was very high. When the wind blew it lurched, the ropes that secured it creaking against the branches.

'Don't look down,' Jeannie said. 'It's only when you see how far it is that you think about falling.'

Dave knew a lot of the people there. He sat with his old comrades around the fire, reminiscing about past battles, sharing ideas for the fight to come. There were plans to dig a network of tunnels under the site like the Viet Cong. Even a Tory government would think twice about driving heavy machinery over land that might collapse, burying people underground. Dave was excited. He wanted to know exactly where the tunnels would run, how deep they would be dug. He offered his van, tools, help with the construction. The talk grew louder, the plans more ambitious. Dave stared into the fire and his eyes shone.

He didn't look at Tess. But later, as the fire sank to red, he rose and, brushing her cheek with the back of his fingers, walked away into the woods. She made herself wait until he had completely disappeared from view. Then quietly she got up and followed him. She found him leaning against an old oak tree. He pulled her against him, his fingers in her hair, his mouth soft against hers. In the dark his eyes gleamed.

'Fuck, but you're beautiful,' he said and, taking her hand, he opened her fingers and slid a tiny tissue-wrapped package into her palm. 'Happy twenty-first, Butterfly Girl,' he murmured, his breath hot against her ear, and Tess's stomach pitched, liquid with desire and with shame.

She opened it. A silver chain with a tiny pendant. Dave sparked his Zippo, cupping the flame. The pendant glinted in the light, a delicate silver butterfly. She lifted her hair so he could fasten it around her neck. When he kissed her neck, she moaned, arching back against him. Then, unbuttoning her jeans, she let them drop.

He wasn't the first. At sixteen, oppressed by the burden of her virginity, she'd had sex with her then-boyfriend at a friend's party. The narrow bed had a racing car headboard and dinosaurs on the duvet cover. Afterwards she felt older, more definite, like she had finally cut the dotted shape of herself out of the paper. There had been other times since but not like this. Never like this, every nerve in her body exploding into light. Moments later, still breathless and loose-limbed, she reached for him again, the hunger in her sharper than before.

'What is it, this spell you've cast on me?' he whispered, and she wrapped her legs around him, pushing him deeper inside.

Sixteen months later, working as a receptionist in a doctor's surgery, Tess locked herself into a toilet cubicle and took a pregnancy test. On the back of the cubicle door was a framed information poster for the Domestic Abuse Crisis Centre. **LOVE SHOULDN'T HURT**, it said in big red capital letters, next to a picture of a bleeding heart. The blue line in the window of the test was dark and definite. When she closed her eyes it was still there, dividing the blackness in two.

She was twenty. Recently she had been thinking about reapplying to university. A lot of the activists were students, PhDs mostly, but some undergrads too. She listened to them talking and thought about the years she had given away. It was much too late to claim them back. The photos of her in Nat's fruit pastille crown were on Karen's toilet wall.

She and Dave were living together by then. Quentin had remarried and sold the Chelsea flat; from the proceeds he gave Tess just enough for the deposit on a one-bedroom in Crouch End. Tess put the test in a box with a ribbon round it and waited for Dave to come home. He and Astrid had travelled up to Liverpool to talk to the dockers sacked for crossing the picket line. Dave had grumbled about it, he had mostly managed to avoid being alone with Astrid since they split up, but Jimmy had insisted so he couldn't refuse. The plan was for a joint protest ahead of the upcoming general election, a two-day Festival of Resistance against a political system that was no longer fit for purpose, that, whichever party you voted for, offered only more of the same: more inequity, more exploitation, more ecological destruction. With the dockers alongside them, Jimmy said, they couldn't be ignored.

It was after eleven when she finally heard his key in the door. He looked knackered. She thought about asking how it had gone, then changed her mind. He didn't kiss her. He went straight to the kitchen cupboard and poured himself a whisky.

'For you,' she said, holding out the box. 'A present.'

She thought he would be over the moon. They had never really talked about it, not specifically anyway, but he had always made it obvious he wanted kids. In the early days, when he was drunk or feeling sloppy, he talked about the places they would go together. Now he speculated about the babies they would make, assembling them like a game of Heads, Bodies and Tails. Your eyes and legs and brains and my warm hands and hot dance moves, he said, or please God, not your cooking and my sense of direction. Once, at Newbury, Dave sat beside a boy of about five who was refusing to eat his porridge and, when Dave asked why, the boy claimed that in his house porridge was against the law, that he ate Haribos for breakfast every day. His mum rolled her eyes, she called him a terrible fibber, but later that morning Dave sneaked off to the local shop and bought the kid five family bags of Fangtastics. He told Tess that children would only learn to dream big if they believed that their dreams could come true.

'God help ours,' he said. 'They'll be the wildest dreamers of all.'

She didn't work up to it. She didn't look at him. She didn't want her uncertainty tainting the space between them, pushing its way into the gaps between the words. She blurted it out and she waited, breath curled in her throat, for his delight to break over her like a wave. For it to bear her forwards, drowning out her fear.

Even before he hurled his glass across the room, before it exploded into pieces against the wall, the horror on his face was ugly and unmistakable.

He left. He didn't come home the next day or the day after that. Tess didn't go into work. She lay in bed, stopped like a clock, staring at the ceiling.

When he finally returned on the third night, she told him to get out. She said it was over, that she had decided to have an abortion.

He cried. He said he loved her with all his heart, that he couldn't live without her, that he would never forgive himself for what he had done. He said that the fact that she was having their child, that together they had made a human that was half him and half her and yet already completely itself, was the single most petrifying and miraculous thing that had ever happened to him. He said that all he wanted was to spend the rest of his life with her, with her and their baby. He pleaded with her to give him another chance.

Tess let him lie down next to her on the bed. She said she didn't know what she wanted, what she was going to do. They lay there together, not talking, for a long time. At some point during the night, he held his hand out to her, the scarred one he had burned in the fire. He told her there was something he had to tell her, something he had never told anyone. His hand was shaking. He said that it wasn't true that he had put his hand into a bonfire. He said it was his father, that when he was six he had knocked over his glass of milk and, to punish him, his father had turned on one of the burners on the stove and—

Tess tried to put her arms around him then, but he wouldn't let her. He said she needed to know everything. He told her that as children he and his brother Paul were afraid all the time. That there were days when they could hardly breathe for the terror of it, that they would say or do something without thinking, something that woke the monster inside their father, that roused its horrifying rage.

'That fear,' he said. 'It went so deep in me. Years after he had left, it would come over me sometimes, this cold black panic, like I was drowning. That bastard, he – what if I'm like him, Tess? That glass, the way I lashed out at you, I . . . ' He turned onto his back, covering his face with his hands. 'I should have told you this before. When I was sixteen, this guy I knew, he – he forced himself on this girl and I lost it. This rage, I don't know, it came over me, I couldn't stop myself. They had to pull me off him.' His eyes brimmed with tears. 'What if I'm like him, Tess? What if that monster's in me?'

He let her hold him then. She felt ripped apart and overcome and fiercely, furiously protective, as though she was holding her newborn baby in her arms. The baby that until that moment she had not been sure she even wanted.

'It's all right,' she said. 'Everything is going to be all right.'

And for months, right up until they drove home from France, it was.

They were on the coast road. The autoroute was faster but Dave said motorways killed the soul.

'I like my roads like I like my women,' he drawled. 'Beautiful, a bit slow and absolutely free.' His American accent was awful but his laugh was loose and lovely. Tess laughed too. Her skin was salty, her hair still damp from their final swim. Behind them the sun sank in a blaze of pink and gold.

She had to tell him. The baby was due in two months and all

the forms required her date of birth. The GP already knew, and the midwife. It was on her passport, for God's sake. And in September she would be twenty-one. Sylvie had already suggested a party. Here on the beach, she said. Two celebrations in one. Bring the baby and stay a week, a month, as long as you like. It was only by chance that Dave was not there to hear. Twenty-one was a big deal. Even Ivo might decide to remember twenty-one.

Perhaps he would laugh. It wasn't like she was underage or secretly sixty. So she had added two years to her age. Two years was nothing. She thought of a story she had read in the papers, a woman whose ninety-eight-year-old husband only found out she was two years his senior when she got a birthday telegram from the Queen. He thought she was ninety-six.

'All this time my gran was a cradle-snatcher and we never knew,' her grandson told the journalist. He thought it was hilarious. His grandparents had been married nearly eighty years. What did it matter now, her sweet girlhood lie? It was such a small and silly thing.

It felt much bigger close up.

The outskirts of Saint-Brieuc were ugly, a sprawl of car dealerships and fast-food restaurants and clusters of blank-faced, lost-looking houses. It was getting dark.

'There's something I have to tell you,' she said.

She willed him to laugh. He didn't laugh. He swerved off the road and braked sharply, jerking Tess against her seat belt. A passing car blared its horn.

'Come on,' she coaxed. Outside, a half-finished house with blank holes for windows was silhouetted against the sky, metal struts sticking out of the concrete like bones. His face was hard, unreadable. 'I'm sorry, OK? It was stupid, stupid and childish, but it's just a number right? It doesn't change anything.'

This time he did laugh, a coughed-up bark with no softness in it. 'You think that's what this is about, how old you are? Jesus, Tess. Two birthdays and you never thought to tell me?'

'I did, I meant to, only—'

'Only what? It was easier to lie?'

'Don't say it like that.'

'Then how the fuck should I say it?' He twisted round, slamming his hands against the steering wheel. Tess shrank back against the window.

'I'm sorry, OK?' she whispered.

Dave gave a strange strangled roar and flung open his door. A pile of pale rocks was heaped beside a concrete mixer. Dave grabbed one and hurled it furiously at the unfinished house. Tess felt the crash in the pit of her stomach. She covered her face with her hands. There was another roar, another crash. A dog started barking.

Suddenly he was back in the van. He smelled rank and foxy, unfamiliar. She put her hand on his arm but he shook her off, jamming the key into the ignition.

'I never meant to lie to you,' she said, starting to cry. 'It just, it—'

'I don't want to talk about it.'

'Please, Dave, I—'

'I said, don't talk about it,' he snapped and, with a spitting skid of tyres, he jammed on the accelerator, jolting the van back out onto the road.

The message came through on Dave's pager while they were waiting to disembark at Dover. His grandmother had died. Dave dropped Tess in Crouch End and drove straight to Morecambe Bay. He was gone for two days. He came back with dark circles under his eyes and a brass carriage clock. He said the clock had been in his nan's living room when he was growing up. Otherwise he wouldn't talk about it. Tess didn't know if he was still angry at her or if it was just grief.

She didn't know how to comfort him.

They never talked again about Tess's age. She told herself that he had chosen to let it go, that, next to the death of his grandmother, it no longer felt important. She told herself that nothing had changed. Some days it was almost true. Some days she came home from work and it was just as it had always been, EMF blasting from the stereo and Dave dancing round the kitchen, tugging at her hands until, laughing, she danced too. *You're unbelievable!* One weekend he decorated the tiny spare room in a frenzy of enthusiasm. By then they knew the baby was a girl but he refused to make it pink. He painted white clouds on the pale blue walls and hung a mobile of paper air balloons above the cot. He said he wanted her to dream of flying. Some days he still pored over the book for expectant fathers that Jimmy had loaned him: today she is the size of a pineapple, he told her, or a cauliflower or a cantaloupe.

Me and you and Holly Blue. He wrote the song on a Sunday afternoon, a snatch of chorus really, and suddenly it was her name. Holly Blue Taylor after the butterfly with the blue wings edged in black, the butterfly inked on Tess's shoulder. His two beautiful butterfly girls, he said as they lay together on the sofa, his hands cradling her belly. And she leaned back against him, tears thistling her throat, because everything was going to be all right.

And then there were the other days. Raw red-eyed days when his fury hung in the air like burning plastic, when everything she did was wrong, when he stormed and raged and slammed his way out of the flat. The Tuesday meeting when, arguing with Jimmy, he had to be forcibly restrained, when he punched the wall instead and broke a knuckle. The time he kicked a hole in the bathroom door. The nights when he didn't come to bed, when he stayed up drinking or smoking weed, staring out of the kitchen window, rage crackling under his skin.

She didn't know what to do. She couldn't talk to him about it. She was afraid of his temper, of his shame. She was afraid of her own. Afraid that saying the words out loud would make them true. Afraid she was making too much of it, that she was making it worse, that it was her who was making him this way. Afraid that it was in his blood, that it would always be like this and there was nothing she could do to change it.

She didn't know then that anger like his might be a symptom of something deeper, that he might be ill. No one talked about mental illness then, or no one she knew. Perhaps if he had been unable to get out of bed, if he had wept or confessed to dark feelings she might have tried harder to help him, but he didn't. He raged at her and later, when he was calm, he said he was sorry, that it wouldn't happen again, and she believed him because not believing him was too frightening to think about. She told herself he was upset about his nan, that having a baby was stressful, that it was just a bad patch. That things would get better, that somehow, magically, he would mend. That she would too.

The last chapter in Jimmy's expectant fathers book warned of physical discomfort in the final weeks, of mood swings and anxiety.

Understanding how your partner feels, physically and emotionally, is key to supporting her through this final stage. Be gentle and follow her lead.

I love you, she told him, again and again, and she willed him to believe her, for it to go on being true. She was so tired and he was all she had. It was much too late to stop loving him now.

Near the end she started to get headaches. Her ankles swelled. The midwife said there was a risk of pre-eclampsia, that the baby might need to be induced. She made an appointment for Tess at the hospital. Dave was supposed to meet her there but he never turned up. When they called her name she left the waiting room. She couldn't do it, not on her own. She went home.

She couldn't remember the rest. Or she remembered only fragments, images like stills from a film. The kitchen table upended. The glitter of broken glass and crushed paper air balloons. The burn of metal on skin as he tore the chain from around her neck. The wet black hole of his mouth. His animal howl, its echo trembling in her like a bell.

Later, much later, she read about anger online. She read about the effects of violent abuse on children, the relationship between anger and fear, anger and grief. She discovered that, while anger was not itself classified as a mental disorder, it was associated with many mental health conditions from depression and anxiety to bipolar disorder and mania. No one knew exactly what caused these disorders but they thought heredity and biology played a part. So did psychological trauma: childhood abuse, perhaps, or a bereavement.

After his nan died, Dave never talked about her, or not to Tess anyway. He put a photo of her on the mantelpiece and wound her clock when it ran down. Tess hated herself for hating that clock, the neat tick that measured out their silences.

It was her fault.

She found an American study which found that in people aged thirty and over the unexpected death of a loved one doubled the risk of new-onset mania. In those with a family history the figure was higher still. His father, an alcoholic who terrorised him. His mother, a depressive who took her own life. A family history, born and then made. What chance did he have? What chance did either of them have?

There was still a small clear voice in her head that wouldn't be silenced.

You lied to him.

You were the one person in the world who he trusted and you lied.

It was you.

6

Mia stared out of the windscreen. People swooshed past in the opposite lane, their faces blurred behind glass. It was freaky to think that they were just like her, each one the main character in the complicated story of their life.

'You know your friend Astrid?' She tried to make it sound like Astrid had just occurred to her. 'Was she with Dad, you know, when he died?'

'Astrid? No, I don't think so. I mean, how could she have been? He was in Greece. Jesus, I can see you, you arrogant French prick. You don't have to drive right up my backside.'

Glowering into the rear-view mirror, Tess accelerated past the string of lorries in the slow lane and pulled over. Immediately a 4x4 overtook them. A little boy was strapped into a booster seat behind the driver. He stuck his tongue out at Mia. Mia gave him the finger.

'Mee!' Tess scolded.

'What? You started it.'

'He was just a baby.'

'So I'm keeping him from growing into an arrogant French prick. They give out Duke of Edinburgh awards for that.'

'You're an inspiration.'

'I bloody am.' Mia unwrapped a salted caramel and put it in her mouth. She waited for her mum to tell her off for not offering her one, or at least for the swearing, but she didn't. She didn't say anything at all.

'So?' Mia prompted.

'So what?'

'So how did that Astrid woman know about Dad? Who told her?'

Her mum blinked, shaking her head. 'I – I'm not sure.'

'She didn't tell you?'

'Maybe. I don't remember. It was a long time ago. Another activist probably, a mutual friend. Does it matter?'

'Are you serious? I don't get how you wouldn't have wanted to know something like that. Why you wouldn't have asked.'

Mia glared sideways at her mum, who sucked in her cheeks and didn't answer. It drove Mia up the wall when she did that, like she was this super-patient saint-mother who'd been driven to the very brink of endurance, when the truth was she was hardly ever patient at all. He was my dad, she shouted in her head. How can you not care what happened to him? She could hear her mum breathing, the sticky sound of her tongue in her mouth. There was something disgusting about it, like listening to someone on the toilet.

'What are you sighing about anyway?' she snapped.

'I'm not sighing.' Tess sighed. 'Please, Mee. I know the last couple of days have been hard and I'm sorry for that. But let's not fight, OK?'

Mia scowled. Her mum was always doing that too, making out like Mia was in the wrong when actually it was her who had started it. She jammed her tongue into the grooves of her back teeth, digging out the caramel. Behind her on the back seat, in a wooden box, were the plants Bertrand had given her. Her mum had wanted to leave them behind but Mia refused.

'He gave them to me, not you,' she said. 'What is it with you, anyway? Why do you always have to throw everything away?'

The silence grew longer. The sun flashed golden between the trees. There were hours of driving still to go.

'Shit!' her mum said, braking. 'Fuck.'

'What?'

'Nothing. They just – our number plate, it just came up on that screen we passed. Apparently I was speeding. Shit.'

Mia shrugged and didn't answer. Tess sighed again. 'Why don't you put on some music? Or we could do more Deadly Hallows.'

'Deathly.'

'What?'

'It's deathly. The Deathly Hallows.'

'Sure. Whatever. Shit. Do you think the French authorities can give me points?'

Mia didn't reply. It didn't seem like the kind of question that needed an answer. She frowned at the scatter of CDs at her feet. You guys are so retro, Yaz had said, laughing, the first time she drove in their car. Yaz's dad's car was new. You could stream music through the speakers straight from someone's phone. The picture on the *Deathly Hallows* box was the Gringotts vault exploding and Harry, Hermione and Ron all screaming in different directions.

'Astrid and Dad,' she said. 'Were they, like, a couple?'

'Mia, please—'

'What? I'm just asking was that how Astrid knew he'd died?'

'No. I mean, they were a couple once. Briefly. Before your dad and I got together. Long before. But not then, no. Absolutely not.'

'So they were just friends?'

'Yes. Like I told you. We all were.'

'So why aren't you friends with her any more?'

'Because. She moved. We moved. We lost touch. It happens.'

'What's her second name?'

'Mia, stop. Why all these questions all of a sudden?'

'Because I want to know the answers?' She glared at Tess, but Tess only looked at the road. 'I asked Bertrand about Dad,' she added and there was something satisfying about seeing Tess's face change, the skin pinching around her mouth. 'Bertrand said he liked him. He said Sylvie did too.'

'OK.' Tess's voice was pinched too.

'He said Dad had a tattoo. A big one, on the side of his chest.'

'Bertrand said that?'

'It's true, isn't it?'

'Yes, it's true.'

'So what was it? The tattoo, I mean?'

'It was a blue whale. Do you want to tell me what this is all about?'

Not a fish. A blue whale. A blue whale was way better. 'What was in the envelope?'

'Mia!'

'What? I'm just asking.'

'I don't know. I haven't opened it yet.'

'But when you know, when you open it, will you tell me?'

Tess was silent.

'We could talk about the envelope,' she said at last. 'But it might be better to talk about what's actually bothering you.'

'What's bothering me is that you never talk about any of it,' Mia said furiously. She was suddenly afraid she might cry, which made her more furious still. 'The past is real, you know. My dad was real. Why do you always have to make out like none of it ever happened?'

At Caen there was an hour until boarding. The food counter in the snack bar was closed so they bought chocolate and crisps from a vending machine. Mia put her headphones in and stared at her phone. Tess wished she knew what she was looking at. Facebook, she guessed, or texts – Mia and Yaz texted incessantly, texting was like hearts beating to them, life stopped without it. But still it persisted, the crawling fear that Mia was googling her father's name, that somehow she would find something, something Tess had never found, and she would look up from her screen and Tess would see it in her face, that she knew.

She should never have taken Mia to Finistère. It was years since she had asked about her father, since she had even mentioned his name, but Tess should have known it would bring it all back up. Memory was like that. You pulled one loose thread and suddenly everything started unravelling. He had been Daddy then, not Dad. Dad was new. On the ferry coming over Tess had asked Mia what she remembered about Sylvie and the house and Mia shrugged and said she didn't remember anything, but memory was not a straight line; just because you couldn't summon something didn't mean it wasn't there.

That morning, before Delphine left, they had gone down to the beach for a swim. Delphine had suggested la Morsure but Tess had refused, too vehemently perhaps because Delphine looked at her strangely, and they had gone instead to Sylvie's beach where Mia dived off the rocks and Tess and Delphine swam out into the bay and talked about *laïcité* and French attitudes towards the veil and carefully, firmly, not about Sylvie, and Tess looked down at her pale limbs beneath the clear blue water and thought about Mia at la Morsure in her swimsuit with the strawberries, her four-year-old face scrunched with concentration as she arranged stones on the sand.

'What are you making, little one?' Sylvie asked her.

'It's a picture for Daddy,' Mia said.

'A picture of what?'

'Just a picture. But I think it needs to be bigger.'

Sylvie smiled. 'How much bigger?'

'So he can see it from Heaven.'

Tess closed her eyes but Sylvie was still there, printed on the darkness like the red stain of the sun. The shock on her face, her mouth open as she turned stricken to Tess. The way it closed again when she saw Tess's expression.

All that afternoon they sat there in silence, watching Mia arrange her stones, and the words they didn't say were stones too, piling up between them. When they got back to the house Sylvie went to the studio. Tess bathed Mia and gave her her supper. Across the dark lawn she could see the light in the studio window. She took Mia up to bed. When she came downstairs Sylvie was in the kitchen. She handed Tess a glass of wine.

'Is she asleep?'

Tess nodded.

'Good,' Sylvie said calmly. 'So now you can explain to me what happened today.'

'I don't have to explain anything.'

'All right. So it's true. He's dead.'

Tess was silent.

'I see. So you lied to her.'

'It's not like that.'

'Then what is it like?'

'I did it for Mia,' Tess said. 'To protect her.'

'You don't protect a child by telling her lies.'

'Would you rather I told her the truth? Actually, sweetheart, the reason Daddy doesn't live with us the way Ruby's daddy lives with Ruby is because Ruby's daddy didn't smash up Ruby's house and assault Ruby's mother. Ruby's daddy didn't vanish into thin air before Ruby was even born. For fuck's sake, Sylvie! He never even knew her name.'

Sylvie sighed, staring down into her glass. There was paint on her hands, under her nails. 'So you thought it was easier to tell her he was dead?'

78

'Not easier. Jesus. Better. Kinder. She's four years old. Her friends at school, their daddies take them to the park, to the swimming pool, they pick them up from school. They're there, maybe not as much as they should be but they're in the picture somewhere, even the shitty ones. They exist. Dave . . . ' She broke off, shaking her head. 'He is dead. In every way that matters to Mia, he is.'

'Except that he is not.'

'You don't know that.'

'If he was dead you would know. Someone would have told you, someone who knew him, who knew you. You are not so impossible to find.'

Tess was silent. For four years she and Mia had stayed in Crouch End, in the flat that she and Dave had shared. It still frightened her sometimes that he knew where they lived, that he might try to hurt them. It frightened her more that he would come back and find them gone.

'Tess, my sweet strong girl,' Sylvie said. 'I know how much you have suffered, how hard it has been, but you have to listen to me. You cannot lie to your child, not about this. Bereavement, grief, loss, you know better than anyone, these things are not games.'

'You think this is a game to me?'

'I know it is not. But however honourable your intentions, they cannot justify what you have done. Dave has been a terrible father, not even a father at all, but he is not dead. One day Mia may want him in her life. What right do you have to take that away from her?'

'You talk like Mia has a choice. What choice does she have, exactly? How can she have him in her life when he refuses to be there, when he has always refused to be there?'

'And if that changes?'

'It's been nearly five years, Sylvie. Nothing is going to change.'

Sylvie was silent. The window was open and the air was suddenly cool. Outside, in the darkness, an owl hooted.

'This is very hard,' she said at last. 'But you have to think of Mia.'

'You think I'm not thinking of her? You think that I haven't been thinking of her the whole time?'

'So you would let her grieve a man who is not dead?'

'She's not grieving. She's fine. She's four, for Christ's sake.'

'You think four-year-olds have no feelings?'

Angrily Tess pushed back her chair and stood up. 'I'm going for a walk.'

'I think it would be better if we talked about this.'

'Why? What's the point when you don't listen, when you refuse to understand?'

'I understand that lies destroy people.'

'No. You know what destroys people? Hope. Hoping and hoping for something that's never going to happen, blaming yourself when it doesn't. I know what that's like and I won't let it happen to Mia. I won't. He's not coming back, Sylvie. He is never coming back.'

Sylvie placed her hands on the table, palms down, fingers spread. Her face was grave. 'Perhaps not. But you still have to tell her the truth.'

'No. I don't. And anyway I can't, not now. It's done. It's too late.'

'All right. Then I will.'

Tess stared at her. 'No.'

'Someone has to tell her.'

'No. They don't. You're not listening to me. I'm doing this for Mia.'

'As am I.'

'It's not up to you. She's my daughter, Sylvie. I decide.'

'Not about this. I'm sorry, Tess, but I won't lie to a child. For you or for anyone.'

'Not even to protect her?'

'Not even to protect you.'

*

They didn't talk about it again. There was nothing else to say. The next day Sylvie watched as Tess put the bags in the boot and buckled Mia into her car seat.

'Drive safely,' Sylvie said. And then, 'Tell her, Tess, or I will. I mean it. She's only little. She won't remember she didn't always know.'

The lounge on the ferry smelled of chips and stale beer. Around them the passengers slept bolt upright in the airline-style seats, mouths open, masks over their eyes. Mia slept too, her knees curled up to her chest. Tess looked inside her bag at the unopened envelope and the packet of cigarettes, sneaked furtively from the vending machine while Mia was in the toilet. She was supposed to have given up.

The door to the outside deck was heavy, Tess had to lean on it to push it open. She walked towards the stern, her feet echoing on the metal deck, until she found a window where she could see Mia through the salt-fogged glass. It was a cool, clear night. Leaning against the wall, she lit a cigarette, drawing the smoke deep into her lungs. Behind the ship, the wake unspooled over the dark water like silver lace.

She should never have used Astrid's name when she told Mia Dave was dead. She wasn't sure why she had, except that the story felt truer that way, with real people in it. It never occurred to her back then that she wouldn't control the story forever. That one day Mia would grow up.

The cigarette was making Tess's knees feel soapy. Crushing it out, she took the envelope from her bag. **TESS**. Sylvie's handwriting was like a familiar perfume, spinning her back into the past, to scribbled quotations and notes on the kitchen table and long letters with drawings doodled in the margins. Tess had kept them all, all but the one she never answered. She turned the envelope over. The flap was stapled. Tess picked out the staples one by one. Her hands shook.

The papers in the envelope were stapled together too. Tess stared at the top page. A birth certificate, a photocopy, a little grainy but still legible.

Harold David Taylor, born Seventeenth of March 1967 at Southport Maternity Hospital. The word *Seventeenth* written out in careful schoolgirl script, complete with a capital letter.

Father: Harold John Taylor, carpenter.

Mother: Elizabeth Taylor (née Lacey), housewife.

Usual address: 39 Chartwell Road, Southport.

Harold David Taylor. How was it possible that his name could still pierce her heart?

When Tess finally went to register Mia's birth, the registrar told her that it would not be possible to enter the father's name on the certificate, not without him present. It would be different, she said, if the two of them were married. She told Tess he needed to come in, either that or fill out a statutory declaration of parentage form. She took one from a shelf above her desk and pushed it under the glass. Tess pushed it back. The registrar shrugged.

'I'll leave that box blank,' she said. 'If you change your mind, you can always apply for re-registration.'

Tess had thought about it sometimes, late at night when her edges blurred and the darkness flowed through her like ink. His name on the certificate. His body in the bed beside her. Filling in the blanks. She wasn't sure when the empty box on the form became the true story, when she ceased to be sure that he had ever existed, that she hadn't invented him from the beginning.

Harold David Taylor. His parents called him David, to avoid confusion with his father. Though they could have done that making David my actual name, Dave said. He hated the name Harold. He felt the weight of it on him like a curse.

Tess looked at the certificate, at the familiar names and dates and places, and something that she thought had healed for good split open inside her. Blinking, she turned the page. Another photocopied certificate, clearer this time. Across the top, the words Certificate of Death.

Harold David Taylor on 28th July 1975 at Preston Royal Infirmary.
Cause of death: 1a. Septicaemia. 1b. Acute lymphoblastic leukaemia.
Father: Harold John Taylor.
Mother: Elizabeth Taylor.
Usual address: 53 Hilton Close, Preston.

Tess's mouth was dry. She couldn't think straight. It was like the ferry's engines were inside her, her brain and her heart juddering and roaring, filling her with noise. It was a mistake. There must be thousands of Harold David Taylors, probably hundreds of Harold and Liz Taylors too. It couldn't be her Dave. Her Dave had never lived in Preston. And, even if he had, it couldn't be him because obviously he hadn't died of leukaemia at the age of eight. The boy who died was someone else, another Harold David Taylor. It was a coincidence. It was a misunderstanding. Crossed wires. An administrative error. Those kinds of things happened all the time.

She looked back at the death certificate. It was a mistake, that was all. It wasn't him.

Date of birth: 17th March 1967.

Her hands were crushing the paper. A third sheet was stapled to the photocopies. She made herself turn the page. A letter addressed to Sylvie from a company called Benson Bourke Investigations in Croydon. The letter was dated 4th February 2003.

Dear Mme Pelletier,

Further to our conversation this afternoon, please find enclosed copies of the birth and death certificates as requested.

As we discussed on the telephone, the documentary evidence does appear incontrovertible. Harold David Taylor was born in Southport Maternity Hospital on 17 March 1967. He died in Preston Royal Infirmary on 8 July 1975, aged eight years. He is buried in Preston

Cemetery on New Hall Lane (plot #1152). I have attached the plan and a photograph of the headstone. He is survived by his parents, Harold and Elizabeth Taylor, currently of 23 Hilton Close, Preston, and by two siblings, Peter (b. 1971) and Lorraine (b. 1974).

It is our conclusion that, for reasons unknown, the man known to you as David Taylor intentionally and unlawfully appropriated the identity of the deceased.

I understand that at the present time you do not wish to pursue this matter further and enclose our invoice for payment. However, should you wish us to make additional enquiries on your behalf, we would be delighted to assist you.

Yours sincerely,

D. K. Bourke

7

It was very late when they finally got home. The street was silent, parked cars hunched along the kerb, the houses dark and heavy with sleep. A surveillance light snapped on in their neighbour's front garden as they drove past. Tess saw a dog fox staring at her, the gleam of its eyes. Then the light clicked off again and it was gone.

Mia went to bed. Tess sat on the floor in the kitchen, her back against the fridge. In the flat fluorescent light the room looked fake, flimsy, like the set of a sitcom. She closed her eyes, her arms tight around her knees. She had driven from Portsmouth to Palmers Green, nearly a hundred miles, but she couldn't remember any of the journey. She could have killed – but she couldn't think like that. She needed to stay very still. If she stayed still she might be able to hold things steady.

The fridge hummed. The electric shiver of it ran under her skin. She tightened her arms around her shins, shrinking into herself. She felt like she was coming apart. She rocked a little, banging her forehead again and again against the bones of her knees. There was something soothing in the rhythm of it, the regularity of the pulse, but it didn't stop the words from coming. It just kept them on the beat.

Dave Taylor is not real.

Dave Taylor has never been real.

Dave Taylor does not exist.

The words were soiled, so sticky with use that they had lost their shape and their meaning. They still tore through her like a vacuum bomb, sucking out the air, blasting through the gravitational field of the kitchen so that she was sent somersaulting into the infinity of space, only in space there were certainties, weren't there? Planets tracing their familiar orbits, constellations of stars drawing their unchanging patterns like cave paintings on the roof of the sky. So what happened when the certainties were gone, when the sun was burned out and the Milky Way sponged from the darkness like a wiped-up spill? What happened to the present when the past turned out to be a figment of someone else's imagination?

It didn't make sense. None of it made sense.

All this time Sylvie had known. Tess pushed the thought away but it only came back harder. For more than seven years Sylvie had known and she hadn't said. She had written Tess one letter, a letter she must have known Tess would ignore, and when Tess didn't answer – nothing. She hadn't come. She hadn't talked to Tess, tried to help her understand. She had put the photocopied certificates in a drawer and left them there, lumps of uranium leaking their poison into the air. Into Sylvie. She could have come. She hardly ever left the house in Finistère, she said the work never stopped talking to her when she was away from it, that it made her mad, but this was different. This wasn't a fucking social call. She could have come to London and she and Tess could have decided what to do. Sylvie was strong, stronger than anyone. She could have held Tess up.

But she didn't. On that hot July morning at la Morsure, when Mia was four years old, she laid down her terms. Tell her or I will.

Tess knew that she meant it, that, having staked her position, she would not back down. Sylvie never backed down. Tess had loved her for so many reasons but perhaps more than anything she had loved her for that, for her fierce unflinching faith in her own judgement. For the way she loved Tess as though Tess was someone special and extraordinary. And Tess loved her back, ardently, hungrily, because Sylvie *was* special and extraordinary and because being loved by Sylvie was not just a privilege but an honour.

Sylvie always chose the truth. But she hadn't, had she? Not this time.

For reasons unknown, the man known to you as David Taylor intentionally and unlawfully appropriated the identity of the deceased.

Tess buried her face against her knees. She couldn't think about that. If she let herself think about that the bolt of it would split her like lightning. It would turn her to ash. She clasped her hands together but the fight was in them too, her fingers finding the gaps between the bones, clamping them together, her thumb forcing them apart, pressing hard against the muscle, finding the ache at the centre of her palm.

The burn on Dave's hand, that was real. He told Tess that, in the hospital, his mother told the doctor it was an accident. They grafted skin from his thigh, two operations, but his fingers still curved in, he couldn't open them flat. A twisted rope of scar tissue ran across the base of his thumb. When you kissed that place, when you ran your lips over it, the raised skin was startlingly smooth.

On that last day, when he didn't come home, she rang the hospitals. No one had admitted a Dave Taylor. The police asked her if she wanted to register a missing person but he wasn't missing, just missing from her. She didn't know what else to do. His mother and grandmother were dead. Desperate, she tried to track down his brother Paul in Durban but there was no Facebook back then and Paul Taylor was an impossibly common name.

According to the letter written to Sylvie by D. K. Bourke, Harold David Taylor's brother's name was Peter.

Sylvie had known.

Sylvie was dead.

Tess would never forgive her for either.

It was almost dawn. Beyond the kitchen door the hem of the sky was paling, the last of the stars winking out. When Tess moved she could still feel the grinding roar of the ferry. She might have stayed where she was, only she was afraid that Mia would come down and find her there and she would have to try and explain. She couldn't explain. It took all the strength she had to stand up.

Upstairs she sank onto her bed. There were things you were supposed to do before you went to sleep but she couldn't remember what they were. She lay on her side with her feet still on the floor. Her eyes were gritty and raw. It hurt to shut them. Her face was very close to her bedside cabinet. She could see the faint lines the brush had left in the emulsion, the dried scab on one leg where the paint had dripped. The envelope had been in Sylvie's mother's writing desk. That was where Mia had found it. Sylvie hadn't left the desk to Tess because she knew she loved it. She had done it so that Tess would find the envelope when she was dead. She could have destroyed it, she could have burned those certificates in the sitting room fire, but she hadn't. She made sure that Tess would find out. Perhaps it was another form of Sylvie's fixation with the truth, but it didn't feel like that. It felt like vengeance.

Tess turned over, curling herself into a ball. There was another envelope at the very back of the drawer in her bedside cabinet, hidden inside an old sunglasses case. She hadn't opened the case for a long time but she knew it was there. A small cheap white envelope with a blue pattern on the inside, folded in half and then folded again. The removal man had slipped it into her hand as he left the Crouch End flat, like he was giving her a tip. He said that one of the guys had found it under the doormat on the landing. He thought it might have sentimental value.

She waited for them to drive away before she opened it. The butterfly was tarnished, almost black, the chain shrivelled where it had snapped. One of her hairs was caught in the clasp.

'You have all of me,' he said to her as they lay together in Sylvie's sagging bed, his breath in her breath, his skin against her skin.

She didn't know why she had kept the broken necklace. She hadn't kept anything else.

Harold David Taylor. The name on his driver's licence, in his passport. How could it not be his? His birthday too. He told her once that 17 March 1967 was a Monday, which explained why he was so incredibly good-looking. He said that, as a Pisces, he had the heart of a poet and the soul of a mystic and that if she didn't believe him she should read the limericks he wrote when he was on the toilet. He said that the only thing he dreaded more than his father's temper was that he might have it too.

But if Harold David Taylor was a boy who died, then it was not his name. His birthday was not 17 March. His father was not his father.

One night, one of their first in Crouch End, he woke them both with his screaming. She held him in her arms and told him he was safe now, that Harold Taylor would never hurt him again. Harold Taylor who had a dead son and two adult children and who lived with his wife in Preston in the same house they had lived in for twenty-five years. So who was the bastard who stalked Dave's nightmares, who had split his wife's lip and cracked her ribs and held his six-year-old son's hand over a lit gas ring to punish him for spilling milk?

Who was Dave?

The father of her child, the only man she had ever truly loved, and she didn't even know his name.

Why would I trust you?

She could hear him saying it, his coldness slicing chasms in the words, and she wanted to put her hands over her ears, only it was too late. The words were already a part of her. He was a part of her, in the water she drank and the air she breathed. When she died they would find traces of him in her bones and teeth. She curled herself tighter, her thigh bones hard against her ribs. All this time she had blamed herself. All this time hating herself for her stupid deception, for the irreparable damage it had done. All this time, when every single thing he had ever told her was a lie.

Mia woke late. Yawning, her eyes sticky with sleep, she fumbled for her phone and texted Yaz.

hey u

She felt both stupid and stupidly relieved when Yaz replied straight away.

u yeh

One of their longest-running jokes, ever since Year 7 when they finally both got phones and worked out that **u yeh** was **hey u** back. Mia waited for Yaz to ask how France was. She had her reply all planned: **Aw, u miss me?** and then the cute teddy bear face she'd copied from Vanessa's wall, but Yaz didn't say anything about France, just that she was home if Mia wanted to come over.

Tess's bedroom door was shut. Mia didn't think about it. Her mum was at work, she would have left hours ago. Grabbing her phone and her keys, she let herself out. If Yaz was OK with her sleeping over she would come back for her stuff later. She hoped Yaz would be OK with it. The last thing Mia wanted was an evening stuck in with her mum. In the car driving home from Portsmouth Tess hadn't said a word. Mia hadn't either. She was still angry, about Astrid a bit, but mostly about how her mum refused ever to talk about her dad – like he was something precious only Tess could look at, that if she let Mia look too he might get smudged or broken or spoiled. She thought about getting his photo up on her phone and forcing her mum to look at it, but she didn't know what would happen if she did so she hunched in her seat as Tess jerked at the steering wheel and jammed on the brakes, and tried not to think about what it would feel like to crash.

She was almost at the canal when Yaz messaged her again.

DO NOT come here

Startled, Mia stopped. An old lady with a trolley bag had to swerve to avoid her. She tutted at Mia as she passed, shaking her head. Mia ignored her.

?? she texted back and, when Yaz didn't answer, **?????**, jabbing at the keyboard as if she could poke it into answering. It didn't work. The screen stared back at her, oblivious. Mia thought wistfully of the beach in Brittany, the cold blue shock of the sea. Under the bridge the water was brown and slow. A white butterfly fluttered in the weeds. There were dark grey spots on its wings. Each time it landed it folded its wings neatly together so that the dots came and went like a secret message Mia didn't know how to decode.

Mia looked at her phone. Still nothing. She didn't know why Yaz would text her like that, it didn't make sense. Unless it wasn't Yaz who sent the message. She had a sudden image of Lauren snatching Yaz's phone, Yaz half-heartedly trying to get it back, laughing as Lauren pressed send. **Dont u no when ur not wanted?**

The white butterfly flew away. Another ping.

c u rec in 10

'Hey.'

Mia looked up. Yaz stood in front of her, typing something on her phone. Her nails were glossy yellow, like M&Ms. She gave the screen a final tap. Then, pulling out her earphones, she slumped down beside Mia on the bench. She was wearing Nike tracksuit bottoms with pink trainers and a cropped pink top Mia had never seen before. Perhaps it was Lauren's.

'Sick top,' Mia said and the words felt strange and clumsy in her mouth.

Yaz peered down at herself as though she had no idea what she was wearing. 'Oh, yeah. Primark. Like £5, not even.' She closed her eyes and sighed dramatically. She was wearing foundation, lots of it, and the sweat on her skin and the foundation mixed together, making her sparkle. 'My family, I swear to God, Mee. The drama, you would not believe it. All of them, Faizal and my dad and my uncle and my mum. My aunt's brother. Standing in the lounge literally screaming at each other. It was mental.'

Mia thought of the photos posted on Yaz's Facebook wall, the make-up and the Smirnoff Ices, Lauren with her menthol cigarettes. Yaz never worried about being caught out on social media, she said her mum didn't know the first thing about computers, that she couldn't even turn her phone on without Yaz helping her, but it wasn't exactly hard to look at someone's Facebook. Perhaps Faizal or one of her cousins had ratted Yaz out. Mia felt a small sharp stab of satisfaction.

'Shit,' she said consolingly. 'Are you in a ton of trouble?'

Yaz looked at her like she was an idiot. 'This isn't about me. It's Rash. He got into a fight yesterday. Broke someone's tooth or something.'

Rashad was Yaz's cousin. He was always getting in trouble. Last year he had been excluded for two weeks for damaging school property and verbally abusing a teacher.

'Not gonna lie,' Yaz said. 'I was kind of tempted to let you just come over. All of them yelling how this white boy's going to sue and who's going to side with the brown kid, and you walk in? It would have been beautiful.'

She laughed, her face scrunched. Mia didn't laugh back. She didn't like it when Yaz made a thing out of her being white. It had never mattered before, it was just the way it was, like Mia was taller and Yaz had nicer hair, but recently it was like Yaz thought being white was not just snobby but also kind of gross, like acne or athlete's foot. Yaz's phone buzzed. She looked at the screen and grinned, a private grin that had nothing to do with Mia.

'Gotta love him though,' Yaz said, still smiling as she tapped out a reply. 'Next to him, I'm an angel.'

Mia looked out across the rec. The grass was yellow with patches of brown dust. In the car last night, there had been a piece on the news about how the first six months of 2010 had been the hottest on record. The presenter interviewed two scientists, a man and a woman. The man kept saying that governments had to act now, before it was too late. The presenter asked him if he could prove the woman was wrong when she said that warming was a natural phenomenon, part of the earth's normal cycle of weather.

'No,' he said. 'But the chances of her being right just get smaller and smaller.'

'What, so you not speaking to me now?' Yaz demanded.

'Like you've given me the chance,' Mia snapped back.

Yaz sighed. She took a last sideways glance at her phone and placed it screen down on the bench beside her. A peace offering, kind of.

'Fine,' she said, shrugging. 'How was France?'

Mia hesitated. Ever since she had found out about her dad she had been waiting to discuss it with Yaz. Yaz loved mysteries. She would know what to do about Astrid-no-surname and there never having been any cremations in Greece. Once Yaz was a part of it, it would stop being something to worry over and become a story, an interesting puzzle for them to solve. Except Mia was no longer sure that was true. She looked sideways at her friend, at the foundation and the lip gloss and the mascara clumping her eyelashes into spikes, and it was like she was a stranger, someone Mia didn't know at all.

'It was OK,' she said shortly. 'You want to go for a walk?'

Yaz made a face. 'Why would I want to do that?'

'I don't know. For something to do.'

'I'm not that desperate.'

'OK. So come back to mine. My mum's at work.'

'Nah. I gotta go in a minute anyway.'

Mia looked at her, swallowing her dismay. 'Really? Why?'

'Ah, you know. This Rash shit, it's full fat kicking off.'

'I thought you said—'

Yaz's phone buzzed again. She picked it up, glancing at the screen, and put it in her pocket. There was something embarrassed in the twist of her mouth. Yaz who was never embarrassed about anything. 'Yeah. Sorry. I'll message you, OK.'

Mia shrugged.

'You annoyed?' Yaz asked.

'Why would I be annoyed?'

'You just seem annoyed, that's all.'

'Well, I'm not,' Mia said.

'All right then.'

'Yeah.'

Mia stared down at the cigarette butts under the bench, the bottle tops embedded in the dried-out earth. Yaz's phone buzzed again.

'You going or what?' Mia asked.

Yaz hesitated. She seemed to be about to say something. Then, pulling her phone from her pocket, she walked away.

Tess jerked awake as the front door banged. She hadn't known she had been sleeping. She didn't move. She kept her eyes closed, all

94

her attention in the unthinking parts of herself, her dry mouth, the stiffness in her limbs, but the thoughts came anyway, slipped like photos through the cracks.

The photos. It wasn't just the framed picture of his nan in the lounge. Dave had kept photos in his wallet, square and faded with thick white borders: his mum in a polo neck and cat-eye sunglasses with Dave on one hip, his nan and Paul building a sandcastle. Eileen, his nan, had dark curly hair and a wide smile. Paul looked like Dave, only blonder. The colours were faded. There was a third one too, much newer. Tess found it one night in the pocket of his coat when she was drunkenly hunting for cash to pay a taxi. A boy in a T-shirt with a J on it, sitting on a wall. Dave's nephew Jayden in South Africa. The photos were real, they had to be. Dave was himself, even as a baby. Jayden looked just like Paul.

Except there was no Paul. His name was Peter.

Except that it wasn't because Peter wasn't his brother. Peter was someone else's brother completely.

And like that she was back inside the madness, her brain a wild tornado spinning two hundred miles an hour, sucking up every scrap of debris in its path, turning it into a missile. All of those things he had told her about his childhood, the helter-skelter at Happyland and washing-up liquid in the Lord Street fountain and the day he and Paul and his nan went to see Red Rum given the Freedom of Southport Sands. If he wasn't Dave Taylor, if he hadn't lived at 39 Chartwell Road, Southport, then none of those memories were his. They belonged to someone else, a boy who was dead. She remembered how, in the early days of Friends Reunited, she had registered as a one-time pupil of Shoreside Primary just to see if he was there, if anyone still knew him. She had combed the message boards, pored over the fuzzily scanned black-and-white school photos, the rows of skinny gap-toothed kids, but she never found him. She assumed his class was missing, some of them were, but what if he was never there at all? And if he had lied about where he went to primary school, what else had he lied about? Was there anything he had told her, anything at all, that was true?

She squeezed her eyes shut, digging her nails into her scalp. How did a twister stop twisting, what made it stop? She had to make it stop.

Mia was in the garden. Tess could hear the tinny leak of music from her phone. In the distance a police siren shrieked. She had to get up. She had to be normal for Mia. She had to go to work. She rolled over onto her side, touching paper. The photocopies were on the bed beside her, the pages creased, moulded into a curve by her hip. Recoiling, she rolled back, her elbows together, her wrists over her face, burying her head. She stayed that way for a long time, breathing in her own used breath, the stale warm smell of her skin.

The room pulsed with them. Lumps of uranium, leaking their poison into the air.

Mia stood in the garden and looked at Bertrand's cuttings. She had thought they would be proper plants but they were basically twigs with a few leaves on stuck in pots of earth. It didn't seem possible they would ever grow. When she googled 'honeysuckle cuttings' the website said to create makeshift greenhouses for them by covering them with clear plastic bags, that the trapped heat would help rooting take place. It was so hot already Mia couldn't think how anything alive could stand to be any hotter, but she went back into the kitchen and dug around in the drawer for the bags her mum used for packed lunches. A fly was trying to get out of the window. The flap at the top was open but it buzzed and bumped against the glass, unable to find the gap. Mia watched it for a while. The sun burned through the window, painting a hot bright square on the floor. The kitchen clock ticked. This is what the house is like when no one's here, Mia thought. The thought made her feel claustrophobic.

Outside she put the bags over the pots. Then she read that you had to water the cuttings regularly and keep the soil damp till growth appeared, so she took the bags off again and went back into the kitchen for a jug. The fly was still buzzing in the window.

'It's open, you squid. If you want to go out, go out,' she said but the fly just went on bumping against the glass.

Squid. One of her and Yaz's words. So many of them, a private language almost, going back so long neither of them could remember how it had started. Mia clicked on her phone. Yaz still hadn't messaged. She scrolled back up through their thread, the non-stop stream of random comments, complaints, quotes and emoticons, the bubbles of their messages rising through their days, and it was like there was a space inside her like the space on the screen where the message should be, a sharp-edged square of nothing pushed up hard under her ribs.

She didn't want to think about Yaz. On Facebook Vanessa Morales had liked one of her posts so Mia scrolled down Vanessa's wall and liked a couple of hers back. One of them was of a whale half out of the sea with one of its fins raised and the caption WHALE, HELLO THERE! Mia didn't know what kind of whale it was but she knew it wasn't a blue whale because she had read about blue whales and they hardly ever breached.

There were loads of things about blue whales she hadn't known till she looked them up, like they were the biggest animals to have ever lived, bigger even than the biggest dinosaur. Just the tongue of a blue whale weighed the same as a whole elephant. Blue whales sang to one another in the ocean, songs with complicated melodies and variations and more notes than there were on a grand piano, and their songs travelled hundreds of miles. Her dad had written songs. There was one her mum used to sing to her when she was little, though later, after they had moved, when she asked her to sing it, her mum said she didn't remember.

The jug was too full. It splashed as she carried it outside. When she had watered the cuttings Mia put the bags back over them and arranged them in a shady patch along the wall. They looked good, professional. She almost took a photo. Instead she clicked on the photo of her dad. She wished she could talk to him about what she had done, ask him if it was right or if she should put the cuttings somewhere else. Something just between the two of them, that had absolutely nothing to do with her mum.

She typed it into the Google search bar idly, without expecting much. *Astrid Reclaim the Streets*. There were a few articles about the time they blocked the M41, pictures of banners and stilt-walkers and protesters sprawled on sofas under a blazing sun. Alongside the articles there were advertisements for greenhouses and plant food. Mia wondered how long it would take before they realised she wasn't the person they thought she was and stopped following her around. She scrolled down through the articles, scanning for an Astrid, but it was like those news reports with pixelated faces, none of the articles mentioned any names. Some of the photos showed activists being hauled away by policemen in old-fashioned helmets. They dragged them by the arms, roughly, their bodies trailing on the ground like they were rubbish left in the road, like they weren't people at all.

Mia clicked through to Images. There were a few more pictures of people getting arrested but mostly it was the Butterfly Girl, rows and rows of her all the same like a sheet of Christmas stamps. Next to the blurry black-and-white news photos, the ones of Tess looked fake, the colours too bright, the image repeated and repeated until it stopped meaning anything. Lots had inspirational quotes across the bottom in curly typography. HOPE IS A MUSCLE, one of them said in pink Comic Sans. Mia hated Comic Sans, it was her worst typeface, but it was true that, as well as looking wasted, Tess did look hopeful, her face tipped up to the sky like she couldn't wait to fly away, and Mia had a sudden plummeting feeling in the pit of her stomach that she couldn't explain, except that all her life it had always been her and her mum, the two of them against the world, and now suddenly there were other people too, real people who changed the story, only her mum wouldn't tell her who they were or even admit that they were there.

Then she saw it. A tag under one of the pictures: **CEREDIGION'S ASTRID OSMAN THE ORIGINAL BUTTERFLY GIRL**. She felt the crackle of the words going through her as she clicked. A local newspaper website, the *Ceredigion Chronicle*. A photograph of a woman with short grey hair standing by a wire fence.

The Butterfly Protests of the 1990s were the brainchild of Astrid Osman, Green Party candidate for Ceredigion and long-time environmental activist.

'The butterfly was then and continues to be our modern-day canary in the coalmine,' Osman told this correspondent. 'As both the victims and harbingers of global warming, their struggle to survive sounds a grave and urgent warning about the potentially catastrophic effects of greenhouse gases on our environment.'

Nearly twenty years on, Butterfly Girl remains one of the environmental movement's most iconic images.

Mia stared at the woman in the photo. In her mum's version of the story, the butterflies had been Tess's idea. Perhaps, she thought hopefully, this wasn't the right Astrid after all. But she knew that it was. It was all there in the article, the crashed cars, the stilt-walkers, the annoying brackets in the word (dis)organisation. Astrid Osman wore frumpy glasses and an anorak and a serious expression. She didn't look like the kind of person Mia imagined her dad going out with. She didn't look like a liar either.

It was easy after that. Mia typed *Astrid Osman* into the search bar and up it came: her postal address on the electoral roll, her email address on the Aberystwyth University website where Astrid was a professor of geography, her Twitter account. Her Twitter feed was filled with facts about the rising CO_2 levels and destruction of the Amazon rainforest and plastic in the oceans and species going extinct. As Mia scrolled down, a panicky feeling tightened inside her, squeezing out her breath. She looked at a satellite picture of Arctic sea ice in 2010 superimposed onto one taken in 1980. It looked like a stain on a handkerchief.

She closed the page. She didn't have time to freak herself out. She had to think about what to do next. She already knew what Tess would say if she tried to talk to her about it: 'None of this will bring him back,' or 'I know this is difficult for you but you just have to let it go,' or 'For Christ's sake, Mia, leave the poor woman alone.' Only Mia didn't want to leave her alone. She could email her. She could write a message right now. She could ask her about her dad, where he was when he died and what happened to him after. What he was like, his favourite films and books and music, the things that made him laugh. What his laugh sounded like. Whether he had talked about Mia sometimes, whether he missed her. Whether he had ever intended to come back.

PS Please don't think I'm some kind of weird stalker.

PPS Oh, and whatever you do, please please don't tell my mum.

Somewhere in another garden a child was screaming. The scream came in pulses, like a fire alarm. Astrid had been her dad's girlfriend too. She might know some of his songs. She might have letters he had written, stuff he had owned.

It gave Mia butterflies in her stomach just thinking about it.

Tess forced herself to breathe. A count of four in through the nose, then eight out through the mouth, her stomach rising with each inhalation, falling back with each exhale. Nat had taught her how to do it years ago, she said abdominal breathing calmed the central nervous system. Think of it like weed, she said, only it's legal and you don't need Rizlas.

Later Tess had tried to teach Dave. It might help, she said helplessly, but he just looked at her the way he always looked at her in those last weeks, his jaw clenched, and asked her to please just stop. All those evenings she had stood outside their front door, her key in her hand, steeling herself to face him, his anger clotting and crackling in the air like a storm about to break. The sweetness when she walked in to music blaring and Dave dancing around the kitchen. The reprieve of it.

You're unbelievable!

She breathed out. She didn't make it to eight. She needed to get up. She needed to go downstairs and fall over the trainers Mia had abandoned in the hall and hug Mia and tell her to put her bloody trainers somewhere they wouldn't kill someone and hum as she made them both a sandwich and laugh when Mia said did she even know that she was humming because only crazy people hummed like that, like they couldn't even hear it. She needed to be normal. She needed Mia to see her being normal. She needed to smile and talk and move around the kitchen like the ground wasn't opening in great fissures underneath her feet, like the world was steady. She needed to do all those things because if she didn't Mia would want to know what was wrong and she had no idea how to answer that question.

Don't think. Just dive.

I hate you, Sylvie, she whispered, or perhaps she just said it in her head. How could you leave me to face this all alone? And in her head Sylvie smiled, her arms outstretched like she could touch the edges of the sky, and disappeared into the water without a splash.

*

In the end Mia chose Twitter. Twitter was lame, a platform for middle-aged shouty people to argue IN CAPITAL LETTERS, but users on it were always reaching out to each other, it was normal to ask people you didn't know to follow you so you could DM them. She created a new email address, greenteen@gmail.com, and used it to set up an account, @GreenTeen. Quickly she clicked down the list of environmental organisations and activists Twitter suggested for her to follow. It didn't matter what platform you were on, you had to have a profile or you looked like a bot or a stalker. People checked. Then, before she could change her mind, she posted her first tweet.

@AstridOsman would you agree to be interviewed for a Year 9 project on global warming? We have LOADS of questions.

8

Tess sat at her desk in the school office. The pre-admission letters to new parents were supposed to have gone on Monday. It was a routine task, a template she filled out every year, but the thought of copying and pasting and printing and address labels suddenly felt overwhelming. She put her fingers on the keyboard, finding the ridges on the F and J keys. She put her hands back in her lap.

The room was sweltering. She had switched the fan on but, though the blur of its blades made her dizzy, it made no difference. It just stirred the soupy air in circles. Work was being done on the science block across the playground. Blue plastic sheeting hung from the scaffolding like it was a play about to start. Every few minutes, there was the screech of a circular saw. Each time it screeched Tess's heart screeched back. Tess wondered what Mia was doing, what she was thinking. She had made her a sandwich for her lunch before she left for work, tuna and sweetcorn, and left it on the counter. She made one for herself as well and wrapped it in silver foil, not because she wanted it but because it was what she would normally do. The smell of the tuna made her gag. She thought that maybe Mia was behaving strangely but she wasn't sure. Everything kept happening at half speed or much too fast, and there was something wrong with the sound. She said things or she thought she did and Mia didn't answer, either that or Tess didn't hear. She couldn't seem to keep track.

On her desk next to her keyboard there was a stack of headed paper held together with a paper band. There was also a green cardboard folder. The folder had the words **SAFER SCHOOLS INITIATIVE** printed on a white label on the front. Tess had stuck it there herself.

'Tess?'

Tess looked up to see Ruth Doukas leaning in through the door. Ruth taught art. She had wild red curls and a grin that split her face in half.

'Hey,' Tess said, forcing a smile. 'I didn't know you were here?'

'Ah, you know. No place I'd rather be and all that. How was France?'

'It was OK. She died.'

'Oh Tess, I'm sorry.'

'Yeah. Thanks.'

'You want to grab a drink later?'

Tess wanted to cry. She wanted to curl up in Ruth's lap like a child and tell her everything, right from the beginning. Ruth was funny and kind and a beautiful painter and she loved Mia like a niece. Perhaps Tess could explain it to her, why she had lied to Mia and told her Dave was dead. Why later she had also lied to Ruth.

'I can't, not today,' she said. 'Sorry.'

'No problem. Maybe on Friday if you're around? Oh, and by the way, I've got a big bag of bits and bobs from clearing out the art room cupboard. Would Mia want it or is she too cool for crafts now she's a teenager?'

'No, she – yeah. Thanks.'

'Great. I'll drop it off on my way out.' Ruth hesitated. 'You sure you're OK?'

'Yeah. Really. I'm fine.'

Ruth's frown deepened. Tess bent her head, straightening the already straight stack of headed paper. There was a silence and then the piercing shriek of the circular saw.

'All right,' Ruth said when the shrieking stopped. 'But call me, OK? Don't be sad all on your own.'

Tess made herself smile. Ruth blew her a kiss and disappeared. Tess looked at the green cardboard folder. She didn't open it. It wasn't him. She picked up her phone and looked at Mia instead. Her eyes were the same blue as the sea.

Mia was right about her throwing everything out. Back in Crouch End she had wanted to make photo collages like the ones in Karen's toilet but Dave said over his dead body, he said it was only one step from that to soft toys all over the bed, so she kept the photos in a shoebox instead. After he left she threw the shoebox out. She threw out his books too and his CDs and his nan's clock and the brightly coloured ceramic pots he had bought from the Turkish delicatessen which he lined up on the kitchen windowsill and filled with herbs. The herbs were dead by then anyway.

She leaned on her elbows, pressing the heels of her hands against her eyes. She could see the shape of the pre-admissions letters in her head. The address on the left and the date. *Dear [parent name/s].* *We look forward to welcoming [pupil name] in September.*

The door to the outer office banged. Hurriedly Tess pushed the green folder under the stack of envelopes in her in-tray, then, yanking out the paper drawer, slotted the stack of headed paper into the printer. When Shireen came in she was checking the first letter on her screen. *Dear Mr and Mrs Aydin.* Shireen noticed everything.

'The printer is on, right?' Shireen said. 'Christ on a bike, Tess. The heat in here, how can you stand it?'

Tess kept her eyes on her screen. *We look forward to welcoming Timur in September.* Shireen flapped a hand in front of her face and peered with mistrust at the white plastic fan on the filing cabinet. Tess knew she wouldn't touch it. Shireen had a phobia of germs. She wouldn't use door handles or other people's pens or the hand-rails on the staircases. She point-blank refused to eat in the school canteen. She brought in her own lunches and ate them at her desk, one paper napkin on her lap and a second spread on the desk like a tablecloth as she delicately sucked her chicken bones clean.

Abruptly the printer clattered into life and began to disgorge Shireen's pages, each one licking down on top of the next. Tess leaned closer to the screen, trying not to let its high-pitched whirr inside her. *Dear Ms Brown.*

'Well, then?' Shireen said encouragingly. 'Who is he?'

'Who is who?'

'You know. The mystery man you were on the phone to this morning. Benson somebody, was it? Oh, don't look at me like that. If you don't want people hearing, don't talk to them on the street.'

Tess bit the inside of her cheek. She had made the call on the corner by the church. When a woman answered, her first thought was that she had the wrong number. Is that Benson Bourke, she said, and when the woman said yes, how could she help, Tess pan-icked and hung up. Then she deleted the number from her phone.

'It wasn't anyone,' she said.

'I've always liked that name, Benson.' Using her nails as pincers Shireen peeled the top page off the stack on the printer. 'It's serious, you know, but smooth at the same time. Soulful. A lot more soulful than Ken anyway. Ah, bumbo, Tess! You put headed in here?'

Ken Rahimi was a maths teacher Tess had half-heartedly dated the previous year. He and Tess had worked together to set up a programme for pupils who were struggling or at risk of exclusion. Ken was a nice man, a good man. Shireen had never seen the point of him. The men she went for oiled their muscles for their profile pictures.

Tess shrugged. 'Pre-admission letters. Sorry.'

'Buggerama. In that case could you?' Shireen waggled her fingers at the printer. Tess considered saying no but she didn't have the energy, and anyway there was something strangely calming about being told what to do. She took the headed paper out of the paper tray and slotted a thick wedge of plain in its place.

'Did you see a man in Chicago ended up in the ICU from a paper cut? Blood poisoning, from a freaking paper cut. I'm serious, look it up. He nearly died.' Shireen plucked a tissue from the box on Tess's desk and wiped her fingers one by one. 'Benson and Tess, though. I like it. Goes together like, I don't know, Benson and Hedges. Bacon and eggs. Lung cancer or cholesterol, take your pick. So, go on then, how did you two meet?'

The phone rang in the front office. Shireen ignored it. She dropped the tissue in the bin and looked at Tess expectantly.

'Like I said,' Tess said. 'There is no Benson.'

'Come on, Tess. It's way too hot for games. Throw me a bone.'

The phone went on ringing.

'You might want to get that,' Tess said.

Shireen pouted. She looked like a child denied an ice cream. 'Just so you know, this conversation isn't over,' she said over her shoulder as she disappeared into the outer office. 'Not even close. Head's Office, how can I help you?'

Tess closed her eyes, resting her forehead on her hands. The tiredness was in her bones but the agitation was stronger, like a tic jumping in the corner of her eye, only everywhere, all over. The corner of the green folder was sticking out from her in-tray. Shireen was still talking on the phone. She pulled it out.

The photograph had been taken by the teacher on playground duty on her phone. She didn't confront the man, it was against school policy, but she reported the incident and emailed the photograph to Tess, who printed it and put it in the file along with a blurry shot caught by the CCTV camera at the front gate. In her accompanying statement, the teacher said that the man had his phone out, she thought he might be filming the children. That was over a year ago. No one had reported seeing him since. In the photo the man was looking through the playground railings. There was something in his hand that might have been a phone. He wore a baseball cap and sunglasses and the collar of his coat was turned up. It was impossible to make out his face.

She turned it over. She couldn't look at it. She put it back in the file. Then she took it out again. It could be him. She had thought it back then, the first time she saw it. Something about it, the way he stood perhaps, the tilt of his head, sent an echo through her. By then Tess was no longer afraid that he would hurt them. She was still afraid. Afraid he would confront Mia when she was alone, that he would tell her who he was. Afraid that Mia might go with him somewhere and not tell Tess where she was.

She was more afraid now.

The computer screen had gone to sleep. Spirals of colour twisted and furled across the screen, circling round on themselves, ceaselessly reforming, making new shapes. It was like watching the thoughts inside her head.

My daughter's father is [father's name].

Tess put the green folder in her desk drawer and locked it. As she walked through the outer office Shireen mouthed something at her, her hand over the receiver, but she didn't catch what it was. She walked away from the school towards the bus stop. At the corner she stopped and took out her phone. The telephone number was at the top of their website.

'Benson Bourke Investigations.'

The woman had the uninflected, unapologetic voice of an in-car satnav. She told Tess she was sorry but Ms Bourke was not available to take her call. She said she could not discuss a case opened by Sylvie Pelletier in 2003 nor could she comment on a letter purportedly received from the company, even if the addressee was since deceased. She was unable to confirm that Sylvie Pelletier had been one of Benson Bourke's clients or how much it might cost to trace a missing person. She told Tess that she needed to book a consultation with Ms Bourke. The consultation cost £150. The way she said it, it was like £150 was a drop in the ocean. She said that if Tess decided to progress the investigation, the fee would be deducted from her first bill.

Tess thought of the €3,000 Sylvie had left to Mia in her will. Exploration and adventure. She pushed the thought out of her mind. She asked if it was possible to have an appointment after work or at the weekend. The satnav woman offered her Monday morning at 11 a.m. Tess was supposed to be working on Monday. She said she would call the woman back. Then, flustered, she said she would take it.

When she hung up her phone was hot, the glass smudged from her cheek. Her cheek was hot too. The dread of Monday loomed over her, she felt sick at the thought of it, but at the same time she wished the appointment was today, now, so that she could get it over with, so that she wouldn't have to endure the days in between, the days and days of not knowing.

Later Tess received an email from Benson Bourke confirming her appointment. *We would ask that you bring with you copies of any documents or information that might be relevant to your enquiry*, the email said. *If your case regards a missing person, we ask that you also provide at least one good quality close-up photograph.*

She closed the email. She went home and cooked supper and folded laundry and tried to sound normal to Mia. She concentrated her mind on the details, the twisted hem of a T-shirt, the squares of diced onion like little baby teeth. In the night she woke up. The darkness swam with all the thoughts she was trying not to think.

She turned on the light. She had read somewhere that, when you couldn't sleep, it helped to write down what was bothering you. On her phone she wrote a list of the things Dave Taylor had told her about his childhood, his adult life. She put a cross against the ones she was no longer sure of. Shoreside Primary in Southport. North Hillingdon Secondary. His grandmother Eileen in Morecambe Bay. His brother Paul in South Africa. His date of birth. His name.

When she couldn't think of anything else to write she put the facts with no cross against them on a separate page.

1991(?)–1997 Activist + freelance gardener

1992(?)–1996 324a Hornsey Road N7

1996–1997 Flat 1, 185 Tottenham Lane, N8

Everything she knew about him, reduced to two addresses and a job description. Perhaps he had lied about the gardening too. She had never seen him working. She put a cross against it. Then she deleted the cross. He was a gardener. He had to be. A person could fake going to an office, there had been all those stories about Japanese businessmen who left for work every morning with their briefcases and sat in parks all day because they were too ashamed to admit to their families that they had lost their jobs, but Dave came home knackered and filthy and smelling of cut grass or woodsmoke, rings of black under his nails.

He was a gardener. Whenever they used the van for the (dis)organisation they had to unload all his gear from the back. And once or twice, if he had a big job, he offered a couple of the other blokes a day's labouring. Mikey, one of them was called. She couldn't remember the other one. One time, after they had done a garden clearance somewhere off the North Circular, she met up with the three of them for a drink. She remembered how tired

Dave was that evening and how happy. He couldn't stop talking about the wisteria, how the thick vines twisted up and over wooden frames along the length of the house. He thought it had to be fifty years old at least, maybe more.

'And Chinese,' he said. 'Chinese twists anticlockwise in case you're wondering. Japanese wisteria goes the other way.'

Tess smiled when Mikey and his mate teased him, calling him Percy Throw-up or Alan Tits-Much, but, when he explained about the wisteria, tracing the twist of it on the pub table, her heart swelled with love. There was something beautiful about the scope of his knowledge, the limitlessness of his curiosity. His favourite garden was in Essex. It made no sense really for him to travel that far but he had worked for the owners for years in north London and, when they moved, they asked if he would continue. They paid for his petrol, the extra time it took to get there and back.

'They've adopted you,' Tess said, laughing, and Dave frowned and said it wasn't like that, they were just too old to get used to someone new.

Dave loved that garden. He had talked about it so often that Tess could still picture it in her head: the stone terrace with its clematis and climbing roses, the broad lawn and herbaceous borders, the vegetable garden beyond the wall with its twisted apple tree, its pea vines and currant bushes and rows of fragrant herbs. It wasn't grand, Dave said, but a garden had no business being grand. He hated National Trust formality, the straight-backed ranks of colour-coded tulips, the sharp-cornered box. He thought a garden should be artless, abundant, an almost-jumble of different coloured flowers and foliage. Chaos with a plan, he called it. A garden for butterflies, he said, touching his lips to the ink on her shoulder, butterflies and bees. He had spent nearly five years making that garden, planting and pruning, staking and cutting back, crafting its beguiling haphazardness, its voluptuous prodigality. The previous owners had let it run to seed.

'Take me there,' she said once, towards the end. 'Let me see it.'

'You know I can't do that.'

'Of course you could. I'd be very quiet. Old Mrs Whatsit wouldn't even know I was there. What is her name anyway?'

'Stop.'

'You're ashamed of me. No, you're fucking her. Octogenarian sex. That makes sense, actually. She's not paying your petrol for you to mow the lawn. She's paying for you to take her roughly under the apple tree.' Tess giggled, twisting around in his arms to kiss him, but he pushed her away.

'What the fuck is wrong with you?' he shouted as he slammed out of the room. 'Why won't you ever fucking shut up?'

Tess dropped her phone and walked over to the window. The dog fox was back. He stood in the middle of the street, his head cocked, ears pricked forward like he knew she was there, that she was watching. Over the months she had learned to endure Dave's anger. Sometimes she soothed him and sometimes she raged back at him and sometimes she closed her ears and walked away. She pretended to believe him when he said it wouldn't happen again. What she had never admitted to anyone, not even to herself, was that, by the time he left, by the time of that last terrible outburst, she wanted him to go.

9

The office was a modern glass-and-metal block with a revolving door. Sun glared off the windows. Tess put a hand to her forehead, shielding her eyes, and stepped back into the shade. She was early. She could see someone moving through the glass reception area, the flash of light as the revolving door turned and two women came out. One of them was crying.

'And none of your skinny latte bollocks either,' the other woman said, tucking her arm through her friend's as they walked to the pedestrian crossing. 'A proper drink.'

Tess couldn't hear anything else after that, the roar of the traffic drowned out the words. When the lights beeped, they walked away, the car exhausts shimmering around them. It looked like they were walking on water. At the doctors' surgery where Tess worked before Mia was born, she was told to advise patients referred to a specialist to take someone with them, a relative or friend, especially if the conversation was likely to be difficult. Partly it was for emotional support but mostly it was because stress short-circuited the brain. You thought you were listening but afterwards you couldn't remember a word.

'What are you up to this morning or is that a stupid question?' she had asked Mia earlier as she checked her bag for phone and keys. 'How is Yaz, anyway?'

'She's fine,' Mia said impatiently, like she was annoyed at being interrupted. She was reading a cookbook of all things, Mia whose idea of gourmet cooking was making toast, and when Tess peered at the page over her shoulder she snatched it up and marched out of the kitchen, slamming the door behind her. Tess didn't move. She stood very still in the sudden silence, listening to the glasses in the cupboard singing softly to themselves.

Denise Bourke was tall with sharply cropped hair and glasses on a chain around her neck.

'Thanks for seeing me, Ms Bourke,' Tess said.

'Please, call me Dee. Coffee?'

The office was squeezed into the corner of the building, two glass-doored cubicles with a wooden door in between. The desks in the cubicles were piled high with folders and stacks of paper. There was no sign of the satnav receptionist. Tess waited while Dee fetched coffee from a machine on the landing.

'We're in here,' Dee said when she came back, gesturing at the wooden door. Tess opened it and Dee put the coffees on the table. The room was tiny, with barely room for a chair and a two-seater sofa. Tess sat on the sofa. The window behind her looked out over the main road. Dee lowered the metal Venetian blind halfway, blocking out the sun, and closed the door. She put a laptop and a cardboard folder on the table.

'Right,' she said, folding her hands. She wore a steel watch and a bracelet of plastic beads, all different shapes and colours, strung together on elastic. 'Why don't I give you a brief rundown on me and my background? Then, if you're happy, we can talk about your case and what we might be able to do for you.'

When Tess nodded, Dee told her that she had worked for the Metropolitan Police for sixteen years, first as a uniformed officer and then as a detective with the CID.

'Why did you leave?' Tess asked.

'You mean, was I sacked?' Dee smiled dryly, revealing a gap between her square front teeth. 'My third kid was born with cerebral palsy. Apparently some forces out there really do walk the talk on flexible working. Mine wasn't one of them.'

'So now you do this.'

'So now I do this.'

'And your kid?'

'He's lovely, thank you for asking. He was nine on Saturday. The point is, private investigation and police work are not the same thing but there's a reason why most successful PIs have been in the force. On-the-job detective experience is invaluable, but what counts for even more are the contacts I still have on the inside. Most of the time we do a way better job than they do, but once in a while it helps to have access to their bells and whistles.' She opened the folder on the table and took out a slim bound document with the Benson Bourke logo on the front. 'This is our introductory pack. You'll find my credentials in there along with more information about the agency and the work we do. Take it away and have a read. You can always come back to me if you have further questions.'

'Thank you.'

'Yours is a missing persons case, is that right?'

Tess nodded.

'Ray Benson, my partner, is increasingly involved in personal and commercial fraud,' Dee said. 'We do some covert surveillance too but our bread and butter is still missing persons. You should know that as an agency our success rate is over ninety per cent.'

'That sounds good.'

'It is good. The thing to remember is that no one really disappears.

They just disappear from view.' Putting on her glasses, Dee opened her laptop. 'Let me show you something. I'm going to put your name in here. Tess, is that your full name or is it short for something?'

'Esther.'

'We'll put in both.' Dee tapped the keys. 'This subscription database gathers intelligence from open sources, which means the information is all in the public domain. OK, so here we are. Your date of birth, two addresses, current and past, your email address, another email address, landline and mobile number, your current employer.' She turned the laptop round so that Tess could see the screen. 'And down here, see, details for your parents too, Ivo and Angela, is it? Divorced, let's see, 2006.'

'Angela was actually my father's third wife but yeah, wow. That's kind of terrifying.'

'That's only the start. After that we start drilling down.'

Tess looked at the information on the screen, then down at her lap. She picked up her plastic cup of coffee. A thin skin floated on its pale surface. She put it down again. 'What if you don't have a name?'

'What do you mean?'

'What if the only name you have turns out not to be theirs?' Tess reached into her handbag and took out the brown envelope Mia had found in Sylvie's desk. She slid out the birth and death certificates and put them on the table. She handed Dee the covering letter. 'This was you, wasn't it?'

Dee scanned the letter, glancing at the documents. 'May I ask how you came by these?'

'Sylvie Pelletier was my father Ivo's mother-in-law. His second mother-in-law. He married her daughter Delphine after he and my mother divorced. Weeks after actually, not that that's relevant. It's probably all there on your database.'

'And Madame Pelletier gave these to you?'

'She . . . she left them for me. Sylvie died last week.'

'I'm sorry.'

'Thanks.'

'So is there a particular reason why she wished to involve you in this case?'

Tess shifted on the sofa, looking out of the grimy window. Beyond the bus stop a camera fixed the traffic with its hard unblinking eye. 'Dave Taylor, the man who claimed to be Dave Taylor, he was – he is my daughter's father.'

'How old is your daughter?'

'Twelve. Nearly thirteen.'

'And you split when?'

'He walked out on us the week before she was born.'

'And when did you last see him?'

'That was the last time.'

'Right. So his name isn't on your daughter's birth certificate?'

'No.'

'Forgive my bluntness, but there's no question about paternity?'

'None. He was the one – he wanted her. Right up until he left he wanted her.'

Dee nodded slowly. 'All right then. Why don't you tell me everything you know?'

It did not take long. Dee listened intently, occasionally interjecting to clarify a point. From time to time she typed a note on her laptop. When she was finished Tess took the file she had prepared from her bag and gave it to Dee.

'I'm sorry. It's not much.'

Dee scanned Tess's list. 'No photographs?'

'Not yet, sorry. I'm trying to track one down.'

'Can you give me a description at least?'

'Five foot eleven, light brown hair, blue eyes. Slim build. Then, anyway.'

'Any distinguishing features?'

'He burned his right hand when he was small. He had a graft but the scars are still there. Also a tattoo. A blue whale on his side.'

'Anything else I should know?'

Tess thought of the butterfly necklace in her purse. She didn't know why she had brought it. The thought of it, tarnished and broken, flooded her with shame. She shook her head.

'OK. So I just have a few questions I need to ask you,' Dee said, scrolling down her screen. 'Did Dave have a bank account?'

'He had a debit card but he hardly ever used it. His work was all cash in hand.'

'Do you remember which bank?'

'Lloyds, maybe? Yes, Lloyds, because there was a branch at the end of our road.'

'Did he ever fill out a tax return?'

'I don't know.'

'What about rent, a mortgage?'

'He had a bedsit when I met him. Hornsey Road, the address is on my list. It was a dump actually, single room, shared kitchen. No bed even, just a mattress on the floor. A mattress-sit. When I bought my flat he moved in with me.'

'So you shared the bills?'

Tess nodded.

'Any direct debits, that kind of thing?'

Tess thought of the leather pouch in the kitchen drawer, the roll of notes secured with a rubber band. The smell of them, earth and tobacco. She shook her head. 'Anything that needed a bank account I paid for and he paid me back. Like I say, his jobs were all cash.'

'What was his work?'

'He was a gardener. He looked after people's gardens. North London mostly. One in Essex.'

'So he had transport?'

'A Ford transit. White.'

'I don't suppose you remember the registration number?'

Tess shook her head.

'And this was what, '96, '97, so no phone, I assume?'

'He got a pager when I was pregnant, one of those one-way ones for emergencies. But no, no phone.'

'What about his clients? Any names, addresses?'

Tess looked helpless. 'I'm sorry. It sounds awful but I – I never thought to ask.'

'Why would you? We assume the people we love will tell us the truth.'

Tess didn't answer. It was a relief when Dee turned to Dave's involvement in the (dis)organisation. At least that she could be sure of.

'So he was arrested on three occasions but never charged?'

'That's right. He always said he was lucky.'

Dee nodded slowly. She typed something on her laptop and closed the screen. Her gaze was level. 'You say you told your daughter her father was deceased, that you wanted her to be able to grieve him and move on.' Tess was grateful for how reasonable she made it sound. 'So why try to find him now, after so long?'

Tess stared at the table, the box of tissues.

'I thought I knew my story,' she said at last, and her voice was so soft it was as though she was talking to herself. 'It was a shitty story but in the end it was OK because I had Mia. Dave, the way it ended was a mess but something wonderful had come out of it, something he couldn't take away. But now? Now it's like everything I went through never happened. This man I was so mad crazy in love with, who for years I was terrified would harm us or harm himself, this man who I couldn't stop thinking about, who broke my fucking heart, who is he? He doesn't exist. He never did. Everything he told me, everything I thought I knew about him, it was all a lie. His life, our life together, none of it was real. He made it up. When I think back I think surely I must have known something, that I must have suspected, even if I didn't want to admit it to myself, but I didn't. I believed him. And all that time he was lying about everything. I don't know anything about him. I don't know his name. How can I trust my judgement after that? How can I trust anyone? I can't even tell myself I'm being paranoid because I'm not. That's what happened and I don't know how to deal with that. I don't know what to do.' She put her head in her hands. 'Sorry.'

'Don't be. Would you like some water?'

Tess shook her head. She took a tissue and wiped her eyes. Dee waited until she had composed herself.

'You're OK? You're sure you don't want some water?'

'I'm fine.'

'Fine enough to talk about what this might involve?'

Tess nodded.

'OK. I'm going to be upfront with you. This is not a simple case. For one, it's thirteen years since there was any trace of your MP. That's not only cold, it's pre-internet cold. So, unless he's still using the same false name, which is possible but frankly unlikely, that means no social media, no email records, nothing in the public domain. Second, we don't have much to go on. No date or place of birth, no leads on relatives or employers. No records with the Revenue. No phone. A white Ford van but no reg. Add to that the possibility that the search is international and, well, you get the picture. You're looking at a very big haystack.'

'So you can't help me?'

'I didn't say that,' Dee said. 'But it'll take time. And the issue with time is it costs.'

'How much?'

'My basic rate for simple investigative work is £60 an hour.'

'Wow. OK.'

'Surveillance, interviews, that stuff is more expensive. Then obviously there's travel and out-of-pockets on top.'

Tess winced. 'So what would that mean for a job like this?'

'It's hard to guesstimate but, looking at what we have here, unless we get unbelievably lucky, I'd say a minimum of five grand. It could be significantly more.'

'Five grand?'

'Like I say, it could be more. I won't know for sure till I start digging.'

'But I don't have that kind of money.'

'We could look at a structured repayment plan if that worked better for you,' Dee said. 'Spread the costs. We've done that before.'

'However you spread it, it's still five grand I'm never going to have.'

'I understand that. It's entirely your decision.'

Tess shrugged. 'I don't have the money. What's left to decide?'

'How badly you want to know the truth.'

'Except it doesn't matter how badly, does it? I can't afford to know. Although—'

'Although what?'

'What could you do in two and a half hours?'

'I beg your pardon?'

'If I wanted to hire you for two and a half hours. What could you do in that time?'

'I'm not sure I follow you.'

'It doesn't matter.' Fumbling together her papers, Tess stood up. 'Do you send me a bill or do I need to settle up with you now?'

Dee leaned back in her chair. 'Right. You're talking about today's fee.'

'It was stupid. I just – forget it. I'm sorry. Thank you. You've been really helpful. I'll see myself out.'

'Sit down.' When Tess hesitated, Dee pointed at the sofa. 'Sit down.'

121

Tess sat down.

'In this business it is all about evidence, proof and more proof,' Dee said. 'So you need to understand that what I'm about to say comes with every disclaimer in the book. I do have some initial thoughts about your case but I'm talking about instinct here, not data. It's impossible to know if any of it would stand up to further investigation; I may be on entirely the wrong track. Do you want me to go on?'

Tess nodded.

'OK. Based on what I know about appropriated identities, I'm guessing your David Taylor falls into one of two categories. Number one, he was evading the authorities. He was wanted by creditors or, more likely, by the police. Perhaps there was an outstanding warrant for his arrest or he'd broken his bail terms. Either way he would have wanted to keep a low profile, stay under the radar.'

'So he would never have risked travelling abroad?'

'That depends. Why, did he?'

'We went to France together. June 1997.'

'For a demonstration?'

'No. Just a holiday.'

'And he travelled under his assumed name?'

'I think so. No, he did, definitely, because I remember laughing about the photo in his passport. How different he looked with short hair.'

'So his passport was in his false name?'

'I think so, I mean, he let me see it so it must have been, but how? Is that even possible?'

Dee grimaced. 'I'm afraid so. But it does make my second option much more likely.'

'Which is?'

'That he was some kind of covert agent. Either in corporate espionage, which back then wasn't much of a thing, or . . . ' She hesitated. Tess felt a shimmer of fear.

'Or what?'

Dee frowned, folding her hands together in her lap. Or what, Tess wanted to shout. Dee looked at her. Her gaze was steady.

'Or he was Special Branch. An undercover police officer.'

10

An undercover police officer. All night the phrase went off in Tess's head, jolting her awake. She threw off her sheet but her body still chafed; she wanted to throw that off too, to be free of her jittery limbs, the endless questions in her head.

Her first response in Dee's office was to laugh. Not from amusement but disbelief.

'Special Branch?' she said. 'But why? That doesn't make any sense.'

It wasn't the first time she had heard it, of course. There had always been people in the movement who distrusted outsiders, who regarded every newcomer as a potential infiltrator. Tess thought they were being paranoid. The Cold War was over. The Berlin Wall had come down. There weren't any spies any more. And even if there were, it wasn't like the (dis)organisation was the IRA or some psycho skinhead Far Right hate group. They didn't have bombs or guns. They were a ragtag bunch of (more-or-less) idealists exercising their democratic right to (mostly) peaceful protest. Why would anyone consider them a threat?

The cynics thought she was naive. They checked plug sockets for listening devices and muttered darkly about the surveillance state and corporate totalitarianism. But even the most paranoid ones never doubted Dave. He was one of them, an old-timer and brother in arms. Once, at a meeting just before the M41 protest, Jimmy announced that he had reason to believe that someone in the room was an infiltrator. In the stunned silence that followed, Dave stood up and looked at one of the guys sitting on the other side of the room, a bloke called Dario who had only been around six months or so, and said in a fierce quiet voice, 'It's you, isn't it?'

Dario denied everything. They still kicked him out. When Tess asked Dave how he had known he shrugged. It was the little things, he said. Dario had no experience of activism, there was so much he knew less than nothing about, yet he was always angling for more responsibility. He asked too many questions, pushing for detail on stuff that he didn't need to know, but he was the last person to volunteer for the grunt work. He didn't like getting his hands dirty. It just didn't smell right.

'And if you're wrong?' Tess asked, and he shrugged again and shook his head.

'I'm not.'

An undercover policeman. It wasn't possible. She thought of Upper Street, the police officers sweating in their riot gear with their Perspex shields, their batons slicing the sky. The blood on Dave's face as they dragged him away. They blacked his eye that day and broke his rib, left a blue and purple bruise on his back in the shape of a butterfly. When she kissed it a quiver ran underneath his skin.

'I'm hurting you,' she said, and he shook his head.

'Only if you stop.'

He wasn't a copper. He couldn't be. Dave loathed the police. After Wayne Douglas died in police custody, it was Dave who persuaded them all to join the pickets outside Brixton police station. There were ugly scenes that night, shops smashed up and cars set on fire, a lot of people thought it had got out of hand, but Dave defended the rioters. He said peaceful protest had its place but, when the police acted like a man's life had no value, how could you expect anyone to value the rule of law?

The sultry night wrapped itself around her, stifling her. She pressed her fingertips against her closed eyelids, massaging her eyeballs. In Crouch End, on hot nights, she and Dave used to climb out of the window and lie on their backs on the flat roof, looking up at the sky. Dave pretended to know the constellations. Up there, see, that's the electrocuted jellyfish, he would say. Or, that one, that's the Cheddar ploughman's. Long after midnight, the asphalt-scented roof was still warm from the sun. Afterwards, when she touched him, the skin on his back was pitted all over from the grit.

An undercover cop. His hands, his tongue, his dick, they were the hands, tongue, dick of a policeman. All those times he was inside her, moving inside her, all those times she was being fucked by a policeman.

Sitting up, she switched on the light. She had to stop thinking. She reached for the radio, the World Service. A man with a German accent was talking. His voice was low and very calm. Until recently, the man was saying, scientists had assumed that gravity would slow the expansion of the universe over time. Instead experiments had shown that expansion was getting faster all the time. It was like throwing a set of keys up in the air expecting them to fall back down, only to see them flying to the ceiling.

'We believe this expansion of the universe is driven by a kind of repulsive force generated by quantum fluctuations in otherwise empty space,' he said. 'The more the universe expands, the stronger it seems to grow. We don't know why. We call this force dark energy.'

Tess turned off the radio. She was afraid she might be sick. Maybe she should have a shower. When she was pregnant, showers were the only thing that eased the nausea, the water as cold as she could stand it, pounding on the top of her head. That and ginger chews. She had bought bags and bags of them from the Asian grocery on Topsfield Road, stashing them like a junkie all around the flat. She had never been able to face them since.

Like a slow sulphurous bubble a memory rose and burst. A grey April morning in 1997, two weeks before the general election. Tess huddled in a dressing gown at the kitchen table, the ginger fiery in her mouth. Dave has already gone. She will go too, just as soon as she can trust herself not to throw up. Today they are marching. This time it is not like Islington or Shepherd's Bush. It is not a celebration. Hundreds of Liverpool dockers have been sacked, hospital workers are on strike. Perhaps once an election might have meant something but everyone knows that the political parties are all the same, that a cross in a box won't change anything. Only direct action can force transformation. **NEVER MIND THE BALLOT!** the posters shout. **RECLAIM THE STREETS!**

They are starting in Kennington Park. They know the police will try to cut them off so they start the same way they started in Camden, in Islington. They buy four bangers at auction. The most expensive costs £200. Abandoned strategically, blocking the surrounding streets, the cars will act as barricades. The police vans will not be able to get through.

Dave volunteers as a driver. Tess wants to go with him but he refuses, she is five months pregnant, he worries she will get hurt. She lets it go. The last few days have been good days, she doesn't want to spoil it. She mainlines ginger sweets as she rattles south on the tube.

There are thousands of them. They fill Trafalgar Square. When the speeches are over, they dance to heavy techno under banners slung between the lions. The bass shakes the water in the fountains and thumps in the stones beneath their feet. Someone has spray-painted a slogan on the National Gallery: **ART FOR EVERYBODY OR FOR NOBODY**. Tess can feel the baby moving. She throws back her head, straining for the old joy, for the exhilaration of Islington and the M41, but, despite the crowds, the mood is tense. There are riot police everywhere, hundreds of them, faceless behind their visors and their shields. They bristle blackly across the pavements, blocking the roads out of the square. Armoured vehicles line Whitehall. Later Tess will learn that a group of DJs have been charged with conspiracy to murder for driving their van too close to police lines. Beneath the music the air vibrates, a string pulled too tight. Around her people dance like they are fighting. They headbutt the night and punch the sky with their fists. They swarm over the plinths. There are mounted policemen in the arch leading to the Mall. The horses wear visors too. Tess is suddenly afraid. She looks around for Dave, for a way out. She cannot see either. The riot police are moving forward, the horses too. As the cordon closes scuffles break out. The police strike protesters, force them to the ground. There is something triumphant in the way they drag them away.

Most people leave peacefully. When the crowd is mostly dispersed the mounted police storm the square. Close up the horses are much bigger than you'd think. Tess goes home. She doesn't know where Dave is. She leaves a message on his pager. On the news Michael Howard congratulates the police for their swift response to the violence. He is proud, he says, that this government acted to give them the powers to deal with this kind of lawlessness.

A little before dawn, Tess wakes. The bed is empty beside her. Dave is in the kitchen, sitting at the table. He has a glass cradled in his hands. Whisky, the bottle is beside him on the table. It is almost empty. She thinks of the night he threw the glass at her and a cold fear spikes through her, she wants to run. But when he turns to look at her he is not angry. His face is the face of a drunken child, bereft.

'I fucked up, Tess. I totally fucked up.'

Tess puts his glass on the table and takes his hands in hers. He tells her that, when he abandoned his car, he made a catastrophic mistake. He left the window open. When the police arrived they simply reached in, released the handbrake, and pushed the car aside. The police vans drove straight through.

'So you made a mistake,' she says. 'People make mistakes,' but he shakes his head. Pulling his hands away, he reaches past her for his whisky glass and drains it. He tells her Jimmy and Phil got arrested. Because of him, he says, because of his fuck-up. They don't know it was him, not yet, but, when he tells them, once they know, he'll have to leave. He can't stay in the (dis)organisation, not once he's lost their trust. Tess knows he is right. Dave is popular but he doesn't pull his punches. There are a lot of people who would be glad to punch him back.

'So don't tell them,' she says.

He looks at her.

'Why does anyone have to know? So you fucked up, so what? What's done is done. What matters is keeping on. There's so much still to do. We can't do it without you.'

He resists, a little. But he lets her persuade him. He lets her take him back to bed.

That was it. She was the only one who ever knew about the window and she never told a soul. It never crossed her mind that he might have done it on purpose.

Outside, in the darkness, foxes screamed. Mating or fighting, Tess didn't know. The screams scraped down her spine. The pump of the shower screamed too, if she turned it on now she would wake Mia.

In the kitchen the light from the alley painted bright squares on the kitchen floor. There had been a local petition to have it installed, someone had put a letter through her door urging her to consider the risk of drug deals and burglary. The light blazed above the back fence, unshaded and blinding white, like a floodlight in a football stadium.

When she filled the kettle the water caught the light, a twisted rope of silver.

If he was a police officer, then nothing that had happened between them was real. She was a tactic, collateral damage in his plan to penetrate the movement. *Penetrate.* The word danced around her head, mocking and malevolent. Dave had always refused to call what they did fucking. She teased him about it, the last of the old euphemists, she called him, but he just smiled and shrugged and said that it was true, all the words anyone had thought of were wrong: making love was coy and screwing robotic and shagging boorish and bonking ridiculous and fucking, fucking was transactional, for money. He said that what they did together didn't have a name yet because the people who made up the words didn't understand it, not properly. No one did but them.

But if he was a police officer, an infiltrator, then all that fucking, all that *penetration*, did have a name. It was work. A perk of the job. Did it give him a thrill, is that what that face meant when he came, the sheer sick joy of getting paid to fuck? Perhaps there was a special box for it on his time sheets. *Project*: Fucking for Britain. *Hours*: And the rest, mate.

He had fucked her because it was his job.

Water poured over the top of the kettle. Tess looked at it uncomprehendingly, at the water spilling over her hand and into the sink.

Once, just after he ditched Astrid, Tess had nearly broken it off. She had held herself back for so long, squashing down her feelings until she scarcely remembered the old shape of them, and suddenly he was hers and it was too much, too bright, like staring straight into the sun. It frightened her, how fast and deep she could fall. It wasn't that he was perfect, just that he was perfect in all the ways she needed, the precisely engineered prototype for the partner she had not even known she wanted. But what if that was the point? What if the man she loved was an algorithm, if he was made entirely from the manipulation of her own data?

If you liked that, you'll love this.

He had invented himself to delight her and she had been delighted. He had said what needed to be said, done what needed to be done, to make her love him. She had no idea why. None of it was real.

The water was still running. Tess turned it off. She could feel the darkness closing over her, pushing her down. Perhaps it wasn't true. Dee had no proof, she said so herself. Yes, she was an ex-police officer. She knew that world, its subterfuges and secrets. But she didn't know Dave. She had not seen the force with which he hurled himself against the police shields that day in Upper Street, the hatred with which he stared at the ranks and ranks of them clustered like cockroaches in the pipes of Trafalgar Square.

Some of the protesters refused to take the police seriously. They laughed at them sweltering in their uniforms, their faces blank and stony under their stupid helmets. Some even tried to get the officers to dance, pulling them by the hands out of their line, cheering and clapping as one or two of them jigged half-heartedly from foot to foot before scuttling back to their ranks. Tess couldn't do that. She couldn't bring herself to touch them, to look at them even. She thought of the faceless helmets bearing down on her in Upper Street, the glint of the riot shields, the batons slicing the air, and she thought, that's who you are. You're not human. You couldn't be.

'We did it,' he said to her as they lay together on the roof after the M41 protest, staring up at the sky. The sun was rising. Tess didn't think she had ever been more tired or more proud. 'We turned a six-lane fucking motorway into a wood. Whatever else happens, however it goes from here, we'll always have that. No one can take it away from us.'

And nobody had. Till now.

Dee had walked with her out onto the landing. She shook her hand and wished her luck. They waited together in silence for the lift but, as Tess stepped inside, Dee jammed a finger on the button, holding the doors open.

'Call me if you change your mind,' she said, and she let the button go. Then, as the doors were closing, 'It is a kind of torture, not knowing. Don't let it make you mad.'

Outside the sky was changing, a pale orange-pink bleeding upwards from behind the dark line of roofs, and above it, a thin scurf of grey cloud like lint from the tumble dryer. It was almost morning. Encased in the pale bubbles of their plastic bags, Mia's cuttings looked like ghosts. Tess pressed a hand to her forehead, her gaze moving mechanically over the clutter on the table, Mia's trainers discarded on the floor.

Another memory. Dave sitting in their kitchen in Crouch End, cleaning his old leather walking boots. He had his back to the door and there was music playing, he didn't know she was there. Leaning forward, his elbows on his thighs, he hummed as he worked, his brush moving in a brisk, practised motion over and around the toe, Dave who didn't know one end of a duster from another, and, in that moment, she felt a jolt of panic, as though she had stumbled on an intruder sitting there, someone she had never seen before. And then he looked over his shoulder and smiled at her and it was like a switch had been flipped, he was himself, as familiar as her own face, and whatever it was that had frightened her was gone.

She never mentioned it to anyone. She pushed it out of her mind. It wasn't long before she forgot all about it. It was so brief a moment, and anyway it was stupid, a trick of the eye, of the heart, one of those strange brief out-of-body moments that stop you in your tracks for no reason. They happened. They meant nothing. When Tess was young, after Ivo left and she hardly saw him, she was always glimpsing him out of the corner of her eye, her heart leaping as she turned to look again. It was never him.

He cleaned his boots like he had been trained to clean them. Like a squaddie in the army. Like a policeman.

11

Mia waited in Yaz's lounge while Yaz's mum went to the kitchen to fetch her a glass of water. The windows were shut and an angry stripe of sun scorched the end of the couch. Mia sat as far away from it as she could. The doors that led to the kitchen were shut too. It looked cooler in there but maybe it was just the wavy glass. It was like looking into water.

For the twentieth time she took her phone out of her pocket. For the twentieth time she felt a sick twist in her stomach. Where was Yaz? On the doorstep Yaz's mum had frowned at Mia, her eyes huge behind the thick lenses of her glasses like they could see right into Mia's head.

'Mia? So where is Yazmeen?'

It was horrible, like being in a dream where you were on stage with everyone looking at you and you had no idea what your lines were or even the story of the play.

'I told her quite clearly, if she slept over at your house she had to be back here by ten. We have family coming, I need her to help with the preparations. Where did she go anyway? What was so important that she couldn't even make a one-minute phone call to her mother?'

Panicked, Mia had mumbled something about Yaz wanting some fresh air. She cringed remembering it. Yaz hated fresh air and, anyway, if that was true, why would Mia have come to her house? It would serve Yaz right, Mia thought, if, when Yaz's mum came back, she just blurted out the truth. Sorry, Mrs Nazeer, but Yaz wasn't with me last night, I don't know where she was. The thought of all the trouble Yaz would be in then made her ears burn.

She looked at her phone once more, panic fizzing up in her again. What if something bad had happened to Yaz? What if she was in hospital or dead? She pushed her phone under her thigh as Yaz's mum appeared at the glass doors. The wavy glass broke her up into random blobs of colour. She smiled at Mia and put a glass of water and a plate of nankhatai biscuits on the table.

'Pistachio and rosewater,' she said. 'Freshly baked this morning.'

'Thank you,' Mia said faintly. The thought of eating made her queasy but she took one anyway. She waited for Yaz's mum to go back to the kitchen, but she didn't. She just went on standing there. Mia broke off a bit of biscuit and put it in her mouth. Tess hated cooking. The only cookbook they owned was her dad's. Mia had found it by accident years ago, she wasn't even sure her mum knew it was there. The book had grease spots on the cover and *For DT, happy birthday + all my love A xx* written very neatly on the flyleaf. She had looked at it a lot since they got back from France. A for Astrid. It felt like a clue. One page had its corner turned down. Thai Red Curry. The recipe was covered with orange splatters. It was stupid but she couldn't help wondering if they were also a clue, that, if she cracked the code, there would be a message in them just for her.

Yaz's mum cleared her throat. Mia tried to swallow but the biscuit clogged her mouth. She took a gulp of water. Where was Yaz?

'So, Mia, I wanted to ask you,' Yaz's mum said. 'Mr Rahimi, the maths teacher, I think your mother—'

The front door banged. Yaz's mum stepped out into the hall.

'Yazmeen! Is this what you call ten o'clock? Where on earth have you been?'

Yaz. The relief was like dizziness, Mia had to close her eyes. There was the thud of a bag being dropped. Yaz muttered something Mia couldn't hear and stamped into the lounge. She was still rolling her eyes when she saw Mia. Her expression froze.

'What the – Mee? What are you doing here?'

'I messaged you.' Mia glared at her, willing her to understand. 'That Mario game, remember? I brought it back.'

'My phone,' Yaz mumbled. She looked like she was going to say more but, though her lips moved, the words didn't come. Her face was blank, stunned.

'Let's go up to your room. Thanks for the biscuit, Mrs Nazeer.'

Grabbing Yaz's arm, Mia dragged her upstairs, slamming her bedroom door and then pushing the armchair against it to be sure. Yaz was not allowed to have a lock. Her mum said the only people who wanted privacy were people who were doing something wrong. Once or twice, Yaz had caught her listening at the door. Mia took Yaz's iPod from the dock and put on the first song she saw, 'Paparazzi' by Lady Gaga. She turned up the volume.

'So?' she hissed. 'What the fuck?'

Yaz threw herself down on the bed, her laugh harsh and sudden. 'Shit. When I walked in the lounge and saw you, I thought I was so dead. You sat there like some kind of zombie guest from outer space, I swear to God you almost gave me a heart attack.'

'I didn't say anything.'

'Yeah, but still. Fuck. You could have, you know? You could have just blurted it right out. Can you even imagine the tsunami of shit I'd have been in then?' She bugged her eyes at Mia, blowing another laugh out through her lips. 'Man, it's so hot, I can't stand it.'

Rolling onto her stomach, she pushed open the window. Everything about her was so familiar to Mia, the slip and jangle of her bracelets as she raised her arm, the fuzz of black hair under her ponytail. It made Mia want to cry.

'Fine, I get it,' Yaz said without turning round. 'I should have asked.'

Mia said nothing. She waited for Yaz to say sorry or thank you, to smile at her even.

'Fuck,' Yaz said. 'If I don't sleep my head's gonna explode.'

I'm your biggest fan, Lady Gaga sang. *I'll follow you until you love me.*

'Where were you?' Mia asked and her voice was small and hard. 'Were you at Lauren's?'

Yaz gave a half-shrug, half-nod like she was and she wasn't. Her face was blank. She might have been feeling everything or nothing. Mia wondered how many other times Yaz had told her mum she was at Mia's house when she was somewhere else completely. She watched as Yaz took her phone out of her pocket and plugged it into the cable on her bedside table. The screen was smashed, a curved pattern of cracks sweeping up from the bottom corner.

'Like today of all days I had to run out of charge,' Yaz said. When Mia didn't answer she rolled her eyes. 'What's up with you, anyway?'

'What's up with me?'

'That's what I said, isn't it?'

They stared at each other. Mia could feel the heat spreading under her skin.

'I don't get it,' she blurted. 'Are we even friends any more?'

Yaz shrugged. Like they were and they weren't. Like it wasn't really Mia's concern either way. Mia bit her lip, afraid she might cry.

'Because you know what?' she said. 'Right now it doesn't feel like it.'

Yaz sucked in her cheeks. Her face was cold. 'You know why? Because you can't stand me being friends with other people. Like you think I should be friends with you and no one else. Like that isn't totally fucking weird.'

'That's not true.'

'Actually it is. Ask anyone.'

'What's weird is wanting to be friends with Lauren and Chloe when you've always said they're skanks,' Mia said, her voice high and thin.

'No, what's weird is you acting crazy jealous the minute I even talk to someone else. Like, I dunno. Like you're freaking in love with me or something.'

Mia gaped, winded. She waited for Yaz to laugh and tell her how easy she was to wind up, but Yaz wasn't laughing. She didn't even look like Yaz.

'Fuck off,' she said doubtfully.

'You think I'm making it up?' Snatching up her phone Yaz started scrolling through the messages. '**Where are you? You OK? Can I come over? Message me. Why aren't you answering?** I mean, seriously. You're like my fucking stalker.' There was something triumphant in the way she glared at Mia, her phone held out like a prize. Mia glared back. She wouldn't cry. She wouldn't give Yaz the satisfaction.

'Where I come from it's called being friends,' she said. 'Answering messages, making sure the other person's all right. But what would you know about that?'

The Lady Gaga song had given way to Usher. *Baby, I can break you down, there's so many ways to love ya.* Dragging the chair away from the door, Mia stumbled downstairs. Yaz didn't come after her. When Mrs Nazeer saw her fumbling on her trainers, she came to the kitchen door, wiping her hands on a tea towel.

'You're not staying?'

Mia shook her head.

'In that case.' Yaz's mum disappeared back into the kitchen and returned with something wrapped in a green paper napkin. 'Spinach and potato. Your favourite, right?'

The package was warm, the napkin stained dark with oil. 'Thanks,' Mia managed.

Yaz's mum nodded. 'Thank your mother for having Yazmeen last night, won't you? And come again soon. We're always happy to see you.'

Mia walked until she reached the weeping willow beside the canal. Inside the curtain of its branches the light was green and still. There was litter scattered on the smooth hard earth, empty bottles and scrunched-up beer cans, polystyrene takeaway boxes, a torn Tesco carrier bag. One of the bottles had a red plastic lid in the shape of a Mexican hat. Once, when Mia was much younger, her friend Elif had produced a bottle like that from a cabinet in their lounge and showed her the fat white worm that lived inside. The worm had brown feet and a pug's brown squashed-in face.

At home later, when she and her mum looked it up on the internet, it turned out that the worm wasn't a worm at all but a caterpillar who lived in the plant they made tequila from. The caterpillars made no difference to the drink but they put them in the bottles anyway because the tourists thought they were funny. Left alone, they would have turned into butterflies.

A burst of sun came through the leaves. It made a dappled pattern like water on the earth by her feet. Mia watched the light moving and thought of how, when she was little and she asked a question her mum couldn't answer, Tess would sit her on her lap at the computer and put her arms around her and Mia would lean forward and put her hands on top of her mum's as she typed.

Why is water wet?

How big is the world?

Do birds sleep?

She could still remember the way the bones in the backs of her mum's hands moved up and down as she touched the keys, the humming noise she made as she clicked and scrolled. The pattern of the hums told Mia how close they were to finding an answer.

Where is Daddy now?

At school they said when people died they went to Heaven. Her mum didn't say that. She put her hands over her face. 'I don't know,' she said. 'I'm sorry.'

It frightened Mia to see her crying. After that she didn't ask her about her dad again. You know you can always ask me anything, don't you, her mum said once, and Mia nodded and it was like they had shaken hands on it, that this would be the agreement between them from then on, that there was nothing they couldn't talk about, even though they knew it wasn't true.

The roots of the willow tree crisscrossed out over the dusty ground. Mia sat down on the fattest one, her knees pulled up against her chest. She was still holding the wrapped-up samosa Yaz's mum had given her. She opened the napkin, even though she wasn't hungry, and maybe it was the triangular shape or the golden-brown colour with its darker bubbles at the edges or the green napkin like foliage underneath it but, instead of Yaz, she found herself thinking about a video on Astrid Osman's Twitter feed, a butterfly that with its wings closed looked exactly like a dead leaf, not just the shape but the stalk running up the middle with the leaf veins running off it, its battered edges and speckles of mould. In the film it was on the ground, other fallen leaves trodden into the sand around it, and Mia couldn't work out what she was supposed to be looking at, and then suddenly it opened its wings and it was the most beautiful butterfly she had ever seen, a dazzling jewel, blue with golden stripes like something out of a picture book. The fuck-you sass of it took her breath away.

Mia wanted the samosa to open its pastry wings and fly away too but it just lay on the napkin in her hand, greasy and unmoving. Yaz didn't like spinach. She preferred the sweet samosas, filled with sugary coconut and almonds, which Mia thought were gross. Just the thought of desiccated coconut made Mia gag. There were so many things Yaz loved that Mia didn't. Liquorice. Japanese anime. Rollercoasters. The smell of petrol. Sleeping without any covers on. And Yaz hated things that Mia couldn't imagine hating like dogs and mayonnaise and swimming in the sea and butter icing and board games and karaoke. Mia knew already the face Yaz would make if she tried to talk to her about butterflies or climate change. Yaz thought Mia got too worked up about things and she didn't really care about nature. She liked the funny animal clips on YouTube but she didn't see how animals had anything to do with real life. Perhaps she wouldn't even have liked the butterfly video. Perhaps Mia would have shown it to her and she would have watched it once and shrugged and clicked onto something else, something that made her laugh, and forgotten about it straight away.

Maybe they weren't really meant to be friends. Maybe Yaz belonged with Lauren and Chloe and Smirnoff Ices and *America's Next Top Model*, and Mia belonged with – other people. People who liked the same stuff she liked. Maybe all this time Mia had been like the dead leaf butterfly with its wings closed, blending in with her surroundings and pretending she wasn't really there, and now suddenly she would open her wings and she would be something else altogether, something brilliant and magical.

Or maybe it was Yaz who was the butterfly.

Dropping the samosa onto the ground, she put her hands over her face.

'Barney! Barney, come back here!'

There was a frenzied rustling and panting, the scrabble of claws on hard earth. Mia looked up to see a brown and white dog gulping down the samosa, its plumed tail wagging in greedy delight.

'Hey Barney,' she said softly and the dog grinned at her, panting, his pink tongue stuck out of his mouth like the pellet from a Pez machine. When she stroked him he jumped up at her, licking her face like she was something to eat too. His breath smelled of onions. Mia wanted to put her arms around his neck and cry into his soft brown and white fur.

'Barney!'

The voice outside the tree was closer and louder. The dog hesitated. Then, wheeling round, he crashed back out of the tree. Mia looked at the hole that it had made in the branches and then down at the ground. Then slowly she stood, sliding her phone out of her pocket.

Astrid Osman had replied to her tweet.

@GreenTeen, I've followed you so go ahead & DM me, happy to answer your qus if I can. And check out my website, loads of links there to useful sites.

Mia stared at the tweet, a bubble of something stirring in her stomach. Astrid Osman was willing to talk to her. There was no point in hoping, not yet, it was a big jump from talking about climate change to talking about her dad, but still. It was a start.

She was still looking at her phone when a new tweet pinged up. The original tweet was a picture, the words CANDLELIT CLIMATE VIGIL with the 'i's drawn like candles, and underneath, SATURDAY 30 JULY. Astrid had retweeted it with a comment: *Want to change the world? It starts here. #ClimateCrisis #TrafalgarSquare #SeeYouThere.*

The bubbles in Mia's stomach fizzed and popped. She clicked on the link. The march was scheduled to start at 11 p.m. with a church service at St Martin-in-the-Fields. At midnight there would be a candlelit procession down Whitehall and then an overnight vigil at Old Palace Yard outside the Houses of Parliament. For the 'Climate Vigilistas' who made it through the night, there would be a communal breakfast at 6 a.m.

Mia read it again, this time more slowly. Bring a candle, the website said. Bring a costume. Bring banners, music, coffee, homemade cake. Bring your families and friends.

SeeYouThere.

She swiped the screen and there he was, her dad, his eyes squinted against the sun. She was getting used to it, almost, the jolt of seeing him laughing up at her. His hand cradling the bump that was her.

He looked proud.

12

Nat looked at Tess over her shoulder, a glass bottle of milk in one hand, a dripping teabag balanced on a spoon in the other. 'Sugar? Or there's Canderel?'

Tess shook her head. 'Just milk's fine.'

Nat flipped open the pedal bin with one foot, eyed the overflowing contents, and dumped the teabag in the sink. A clear crystal hung on a string in the window. When it caught the sun, streaks of colour darted across the wall like fish.

'Someone told me recently that any day now all the sweetener in the water table is going to trigger plants to stop photosynthesising,' she said, clicking a tablet into one of the mugs. 'Which I get would be an existential catastrophe but frankly, till it's official, it's Canderel all the way. I swear, one look at sugar and I put on half a stone.'

Tess smiled. Nat had gained weight, it was true, but it suited her. She looked substantial, stately even. 'You're looking good.'

'I'm looking middle-aged is what I'm looking. The three Fs, my friend Angie calls it: fat, fraught and fucking knackered.'

Sweeping cereal boxes and school books to one side, Nat put

the tea in front of Tess. Tess had steeled herself for discomfiture, coldness even, but it was like they had stepped straight back into the past, into their old selves. She half expected Karen to walk in through the door. She didn't want to think about Karen. She took a gulp of tea, burning her mouth.

'Talking of putting on weight, let's see what sorry crumbs the kids have left in here,' Nat said, unclicking the tabs on a large plastic box. 'A client's sister gave me a stack of these boxes, she must have been a rep or something because the entire time we were timing contractions, she was banging on about locking technology and BPA-free plastic and how a properly airtight seal keeps biscuits fresh for millennia. I wanted to say you know what works even better? Eating the whole packet in one go. And we have – let's see – three broken custard creams and the wrapper from an Orange Club. If you really, really want the wrapper, I'm willing to go halvsies.'

'You go ahead. I've already exceeded my daily packaging allowance.'

'Such discipline. There's a reason you're a size ten and I'm a—' Nat coughed ostentatiously. Fishing out two of the broken custard creams, she clamped them between her teeth and picked up both mugs of tea. 'Let's go into the lounge. If I stay in here I'll look at the floor and want to put my eyes out.'

Tess followed her down the passage. Her legs were shaky. She wasn't sure what she was doing here, only that she had to stop going round and round in her head or she would go mad. She had to talk to someone who had known him, someone who would say, yes, you're right and this is why, or better still laugh and tell her she was crazy, that Dave was still Dave and there was an explanation for everything.

She'd thought Nat and Karen might be hard to track down. In fact it took all of five minutes. When she put *Karen Knox Save the Children* into the search engine the second entry that came up was her JustGiving page, even though she worked for Oxfam now. Nat was on Facebook. Tess had to set up an account to send her a friend request. Afterwards she tried to delete it but it turned out you couldn't do that on Facebook. Tess hadn't known that. She had always stayed off social media, right from the beginning. If he ever decided to try and find them, to spy on them, she wanted him to search as she had searched for him, in vain. She would not let him press his face up against the window of their lives, watching them from his own private darkness like a detective behind a one-way mirror. Being invisible was the only power she had left.

'If you're wondering,' Nat said, pushing open the lounge door, 'the vibe we're going for in here is bombsite chic.' Most of the cushions had been pulled off the sofa and a box of Matchbox cars upended in their place. On the only one still in place a ginger cat was sleeping. There was a half-finished Lego spaceship on the coffee table, shipwrecked in a sea of scattered Uno cards and magnetic building sticks and different-coloured felt-tip pens. Tess skirted a wonky tower of Jenga blocks and stepped across the plastic Twister mat laid out on the rug. Right foot yellow. Left foot blue. When Tess had arrived, Nat's husband and her two boys were getting ready to go to the park. The silence when they left was unnatural, like the air had been sucked inside out.

Nat cleared a space on the table with her foot and put the mugs down.

'You take the chair,' she said, fishing the Twister spinner and an orange Nerf gun from its depths. The Jenga tower swayed. 'I'll sit on the cat.'

'He's gorgeous.'

'Only to look at.' Scooping him up, Nat dumped him unceremoniously on the floor. 'When we went to the shelter, the boys wanted the mangy, friendly one but I overruled them. You can teach personality, I said, but ugly, that's forever. It'll make a fabulous TED talk, just as soon as he stops being the worst pet ever.'

'How long have you had him?'

'Ssh. Two years. Which is only about a fortnight for cats, right?'

Tess had forgotten the honking way Nat laughed, like a strangled goose. She had forgotten so much. In her memory those years belonged to Dave; when she thought of them it was like the aura before a migraine, distorted and shimmering, staticky with the pain to come, but she had spent at least as much time in Nat's tiny basement flat, the three of them, Nat, Karen and Tess, sprawled on the floor, aching with laughter. It was Nat who told them about the plump: a V of flying geese was called a skein, she said, but if they were flying close together they were a plump. After that they didn't even have to say anything. Just hearing Nat honking was enough to set them off again.

The cat rubbed itself along the side of her chair, then stretched, arching its back. Tess held out her hand towards it. The cat eyed her disdainfully and, tail waving, picked its way through the debris to the other side of the room.

'So,' Nat said. 'First things first: how's Holly, I mean, Mia? Sorry. Old habits.'

Mia had been Holly to everyone right up till the day she was born. Afterwards, when Tess came home from the hospital, a parcel arrived from Nat and Karen. A card with *Welcome to the world little Holly!* scrawled inside and, wrapped in pink tissue, HOLLY in big brightly coloured letters sewn from stuffed felt and strung together like bunting. Tess couldn't bear to look at it. It made her think of those arrangements at funerals with NANNA spelled out in chrysanthemums.

Tess shook her head. She was nervous, she realised, her hands were shaking. 'Before we get to that there's something I have to say. I was a horrible friend and I'm sorry.'

Nat made a face, batting the words away.

'I'm serious,' Tess insisted. 'When I phoned I half expected you to tell me to fuck off. Karen did.'

'Yeah, well.'

'She told you?'

Nat shook her head. 'Karen and I aren't really in touch any more.'

'Really? Oh.'

There was a silence. The cat stretched and settled in a square of sunlight. Tess took another gulp of tea. She thought of the way Karen's voice hardened when Tess told her who was calling. The sharp snap of her consonants as she informed Tess that she had nothing to say, that she would be grateful if she didn't call again.

'Good tea,' she said. 'Strong enough to trot a mouse on.'

Nat smiled. 'Hark at you and your good old Irish ways. My nan would be proud.'

'It's still one of my favourite expressions. Mia's too, now.'

'And does she act the maggot too?'

'She's nearly thirteen. The maggot's all there is.'

Nat grinned. Tess grinned back and gulped more tea. 'So anyway, I'm sorry,' she said. 'I just wanted to say that.'

'Again.'

'Again. Sorry.'

Nat rolled her eyes. 'Would you stop? Unless this is one of those AA things and you only get your certificate when you've apologised twenty times or whatever, I think we can consider ourselves done. Are we done?'

'We're done. For the record, though, my name is Tess Campbell and I am not an alcoholic.'

'So you claim. I would however draw the court's attention to Exhibit A, namely that night we did tequila shots for Lee's birthday and you were sick in the kitchen sink. Just saying.'

'And this from the woman who passed out in a complete stranger's bed after Carnival, what was that guy's name?'

Nat honked. 'Oh God. I don't know. I deny everything.'

'Denial. The first sign of an alcoholic. Just saying.'

'Shit, you're right. Fancy a drink?'

Tess laughed, giddy suddenly, like the altitude had changed. This is how it was, she thought. This is how it always was.

'For what it's worth, I'm sorry too,' Nat said. 'I should never have left you to deal with that Everest of crap all on your own.'

'You didn't leave me to anything. I pushed you away.'

'So I should have pushed you back, only harder. What are friends for if not some mutually supportive common assault?'

Tess wanted to laugh but she was afraid she might cry instead so she bent her head, staring down at her empty mug. She wanted to say something about the past, about how she thought it was fixed, solid, only all of a sudden it was like Jenga, one by one the blocks were being pulled out and she didn't know how long it would be before the whole tower fell down, but she didn't know how to say that or whether it was even true so she looked at her mug and said nothing. Perhaps tea stains were like tea leaves, she thought. Perhaps if you knew how, you could read what was coming in the brown circles around your cup.

'You done with that tea?' Nat asked. 'Only there's a bottle of rosé in the fridge that's got our sorry alcoholic names all over it.'

'Thanks.' Tess held out her mug. Nat smiled. Leaning down she planted a kiss on Tess's cheek.

In its patch of sunlight the cat stirred, stretching itself long.

Nat came back from the kitchen with a bottle and two glasses.

'It's midday, or near enough. And we can always google the serenity prayer after.' She raised her glass. 'To us.'

'To us.'

'I'm glad you called. It's good to see you.'

Tess nodded, sipping her wine, swallowing the knot in her throat. 'You too.'

'I tried to get in touch once, you know, years ago, but you'd sold the old flat and I couldn't find any trace of you. I kind of assumed you'd got married, changed your name. Moved away.'

'Seriously? You thought I wouldn't keep my name?'

Nat shrugged. 'You weren't any of the Tess Campbells on Facebook.'

'No, well. I never really got into social media.'

'What?' Nat looked aghast. 'So how do you glory in the dead-end lives of the girls who made your life a misery at school? What about cats that look like Hitler?'

'Every great life demands sacrifices, Nat. For me, it's the Hitler cats.' Tess put down her glass and clapped her hands together. 'Right. The last thirteen years, starting now.'

'Speed updating? I like it. OK. Husband Rob, CBT therapist, kids mostly, though when I look at our two I'm pretty sure he down-loaded those diplomas from the internet. Married ten years. Two boys, Ryan eight, Joe five. Both a bit of a disappointment, frankly. Neither of them has achieved anything of note. They're not in Team GB or running their own digital start-ups or doing a PhD at Oxford. That fucking tandem's going straight back on eBay.'

She sloshed more wine into both of their glasses. Tess's was too full to pick up without spilling, she had to lean down and slurp it, sucking the wine from the surface. Nat laughed.

'Your turn,' she said, pretending to look at her watch. 'And go.'

Tess nearly said there was nothing to tell. A habit from child-hood, her mother's sharp admonishments ringing in her ears: *No one is the least bit interested in you.* She wondered if now was the moment to ask about Dave, to find out what Nat knew, but it was too much, too soon, she didn't have the courage. So instead she told Nat stories she had forgotten she remembered: Mia pretending to be a dog in the park and getting her head stuck in the railings, the catastrophe that was Mia and Yaz trying to pierce each other's ears, Mia aged six explaining furiously to Ivo, 'I'm crying, Grandpa, because I am so *fuckerstrated*.' As Nat laughed her honking laugh, Tess laughed too.

'What about Dave?' Nat said. 'You're still in touch?'

The laugh shrank in Tess's throat. She shook her head.

'Not even for Mia?'

'No.'

Nat frowned. 'Is that what you wanted?'

'None of it is what I wanted.'

There was a silence. Tess looked at the framed canvas above the fireplace, a giant photograph of Nat and Rob and their two boys, hugging each other and grinning fit to bust.

'I haven't heard from him since that night he walked out,' she said quietly.

Nat stared at her. 'No way. So Mia . . . '

'He never saw her. He never came back.'

'Fuck.' Nat puffed out her cheeks, releasing the breath in a slow incredulous hiss. 'I mean, *fuck*. Jesus, Tess. So what, he vanished into thin air?'

'Something like that.'

'Fuck. How do you *do* that?'

'You stay off Facebook for starters.'

'That's not what I meant.'

'I know.'

Nat shook her head, rubbing her forehead like she was trying to rub away her disbelief. Tess stared into the pink gleam of her glass.

'How much do you remember about that time?' she asked. 'About him?'

'Specifically, you mean?'

'I don't know, it's just, when I think back – after he left I threw everything out, not just photos and letters but everything, anything that had anything to do with him, I just wanted to forget, and now, it sounds stupid, I know, but when I try to remember, it's almost like I dreamed the whole thing. Like I made him up in my head.'

'And Mia? If you made her up in your head you should be in the *Lancet*. Or the Bible.'

Tess tried to smile but her face was too stiff.

'I remember him being crazy about you,' Nat said.

'You do?'

'Yeah. I mean, we'd seen him with Astrid and, OK, Astrid was about as sexy as a lentil, but with you? He was head over heels. Back then I didn't doubt him for a second.'

'And now?'

Nat looked uneasy. 'What's this about, Tess? What is it you want me to say?'

Tess leaned forward on her elbows, her hands over her face. She wanted to rewind, to go back to the silly stories and Nat honking. The wine was starting to give her a headache.

'I met with a private investigator last week,' she said at last. 'There were – it turns out Dave Taylor wasn't his real name. He stole a boy's identity, a boy who died.' She didn't look up. She was afraid that if she saw Nat's face she would not be able to go on. 'I can't afford her, the private investigator, but she said she thought Dave, or whatever his name really was, there's no proof, not yet, it's all speculation but from what I told her, she thinks – she thinks there's a chance he was an undercover cop.'

Nat was silent. Tess looked up.

'Oh my God,' she said. 'You knew.'

Nat shook her head. 'No. I didn't, I mean, I guess I wondered, you know, with everything that happened afterwards, it occurred to me, of course it did, but I never . . . '

On the path outside the window, the clatter of football boots. Someone laughed. A face appeared abruptly at the window, mouth and nose squashed against the glass, palms clawing. The face made monster noises.

'Shit,' Nat said. 'Sorry.' Twisting round, she stuck her tongue out, her fingers wiggling at her ears. 'Rrraaaahhh,' she growled back.

Tess heard the front door open, voices rushing in like water. The face vanished, leaving a ghostly smear of itself on the glass. 'I should go,' she said.

'Take off your boots,' Nat yelled. 'I mean it. No studs in the house.' And then in a different voice, 'No. You absolutely shouldn't.'

The lounge door banged open and a boy burst in. He had Nat's wide-set eyes, her wide, easy grin. 'Mum, Mum, you're never going to guess what happened—'

'Hello, Mum's friend Tess, my name is Ryan, how do you do?' Nat prompted.

'Hi. So we were playing at the top, you know, by the road, and—'

'Ten minutes,' Nat said firmly. 'I'll be done here in ten minutes. Then you can tell me from the beginning.'

'But, Mum—'

'Ten minutes. Tell your dad. By the time you've drunk your squash I'll be through. Go. And shut the door behind you.'

Ryan gave Tess a narrow look.

'Ten minutes,' Nat said firmly.

The door closed.

'Sorry,' Nat said again.

'Don't be. He's lovely.'

'He's a pain in the backside is what he is. Look, Tess, I don't know what to tell you. After you vanished like that, both of you pretty much overnight, yeah, sure, there were theories. Activists are a paranoid bunch, you know that. People said all sorts of shit. That he'd turned you, that you'd turned him, that you were both

153

in it together. That you were never even pregnant, that it was all just part of some master plan.'

'What? They thought *I* was an infiltrator? But I was a kid.'

Nat shrugged. 'Only some of them thought it. And most of what they thought was bananas. Crazy conspiracy shit, stuff that got twisted or made up.'

'And the rest? Please, Nat. You said yourself you wondered. So why? What made you wonder?'

'You're sure you want to do this? It's not going to just make things worse?'

'It couldn't.'

Nat looked at Tess. 'OK.' Her tone was flat, like she was giving evidence in court. 'Like I say, most of it was off-the-charts stupid but there were a couple of things for me that always felt – off. The car at that march before Blair was elected, you know, Never Mind the Ballot. The open window.'

'You knew about that?'

'Of course. We all knew. But Dave made us promise not to say anything.'

'He told you about it?'

'He was worried about you. You were pregnant, that awful morning sickness, he said it wasn't fair to blame you, you felt terrible about it and we should cut you some slack. That we should think of the baby.'

Tess stared at her. 'He said it was me who left the window open?'

'He said it was an honest mistake. Was it?'

'How the fuck would I know? I wasn't even in the car that day. Dave wouldn't let me go with him. He said the car wasn't roadworthy, that it wasn't safe. He made me take the tube.'

'What, so – ?'

'So he was the one who opened the window. It was Dave. He said it was a mistake, that he fucked up. He was distraught. He made me promise not to tell.'

'That fucker.'

'Yeah.'

'That fucking fuckhead fucker,' Nat said. 'Sorry, but sometimes there aren't enough fucks for all the fuckery.'

Tess tried to smile. 'What was the other thing?'

'What other thing?'

'You said there were two things that made you wonder. What was the other one?'

'Really? I mean, on top of that, are you sure?'

'I'm sure.'

Nat exhaled. 'OK. Well, the second one was something Karen told me Astrid told her, so I can't be sure it's true. I mean, Astrid was always so weird about Dave anyway, wasn't she? The way she talked about him, even after you two moved in together, even after you were pregnant, it was always DT this and DT that. Or worse, Deets. Remember that? Deets, like he was a hamster or something. Anyway, it got even weirder after he left. Everyone else wondering what the hell was going on with him, with both of you, but she just had this kind of Zen smugness about her, like she knew exactly what was going on.'

'And did she?'

'Who knows? All I know is that she told Karen that when she and Dave drove up to Liverpool that time, to meet with the dockers, do you remember? Anyway, Dave left his jacket somewhere and for some reason it was Astrid who went back to get it and she claimed when she picked it up a bank card fell out of one of the pockets. I mean she was obviously going through them, wasn't she, you can see her doing it, but that's not the point. The point is that the name on that card wasn't Dave's.'

Tess felt her stomach turn inside out.

'I don't know what the name was. All I know is that when Astrid asked Dave about it, he told her he'd found it in your flat.

That when he confronted you with it you said you'd picked it up in the street, that you were going to hand it in. He told Astrid that it might be nothing but he wasn't sure, that he was afraid it might have something to do with your man – Dario, was it, the one who got kicked out? He asked her not to say anything to anyone, to let him handle it.'

Tess's mouth was dry. The day Dave had driven to Liverpool, the day he told Astrid he thought she was an infiltrator, that was the day Tess told him she was pregnant. The day he threw a glass at her head.

'But it wasn't anything to do with you, was it?' Nat said. 'That card, it was his.'

A burst of loud music exploded from the kitchen, one of Nat's boys shouting the words. Rihanna's 'Umbrella', one of Mia's old favourites. *When the sun shines, we shine together, told you I'll be here forever.*

'I have to go,' Tess whispered, but she stood up too fast, that or the wine had gone to her head, because the room tilted and she was so dizzy suddenly she thought that she would fall.

'Wait till I get my hands on that motherfucker,' Nat said, wrapping her tightly in her arms, and Tess laughed though it was more like crying, her face buried in her friend's shoulder.

13

The cemetery was quiet. The sun blazed. The zinnias fixed him with their flat hard gaze. He should go home. There were roadworks on the M6. If he left now he might beat the rush hour.

He didn't want to go home.

In Loving Memory of Harry Taylor
An Angel on Earth and an Angel in Heaven
Rest in Peace

Again he looked over his shoulder. Again there was no one there. He was still angry at himself, though, at his stupidity. Shaken too, that he could make so obvious a mistake. The boy's father had died a few years back but the mother still lived nearby. Of course she still came to put flowers on his grave. It was only thirty-three years since she had lost her son. When it came to your children, thirty-three years was nothing.

The first time, twenty years ago, he had been more careful. He had watched the entrance for half an hour before he allowed himself to go in. It was February then and bitterly cold, the leafless trees cracking the icy sky. White tulips in the memorial vase, their heads drooping, and, beside them, a bedraggled-looking teddy bear in a Liverpool scarf. That was the week of the report into the Hillsborough disaster, the Liverpool strip was everywhere. Ninety-six Liverpool fans crushed to death because of failures by police. The teddy bear had stared at him forlornly, its eyes crossed.

His feet were frozen solid but he didn't care. He was excited, buzzed from his trip to Southport. It was belt and braces, he knew, but it was something he had to do, to walk the streets one more time, to imprint them precisely, indelibly, into the putty of his brain. He wanted all of it there without thinking, the everyday details of an ordinary childhood: the walk to the bus stop, the red-brick chapel with its cracked concrete forecourt, the sweet shop that sold pineapple cubes by the quarter in white paper bags. The slap of the wind off the sea as you turned the corner onto the main road. In three days the two most senior officers in the unit would interrogate him on his legend, backwards, forwards, upside down, and, whatever way they shook him, he would have to be solid. After that any last connection he had to the police would be wiped from the record. His mates in Special Branch had already thrown him a big leaving do, speeches, a card, the works, like he was emigrating or something. In less than a week he would hand in his warrant card. In exchange he would get a passport, a driver's licence, a bank account, a national insurance number. After five months of painstaking preparation, he would finally be Harold David Taylor, christened Harold for his father but always David to his parents and, to everyone else, just Dave.

You picked a child who had died. The Jackal Run, they called it in the squad, after the film. You went to St Catherine's House and you went through the records till you found a kid that ticked your boxes, a kid who could be you. That way, if a suspicious hairy got off their activist arse to check you out, they would find a registered birth certificate. Name, parents' names, date and place of birth, it would all check out, just the way you had told them. In those days of paper copies deaths were registered separately, they wouldn't find a death certificate unless they were looking for it, and who looked for the death certificate of someone who was alive? Two cardinal rules, that was all: a birth date close enough to yours and your first name. No matter how sharp you were, how vigilant, you could never quite rid yourself of the instinct that made you turn round when someone called your name.

Better still, you found a Harold David Taylor, a dead kid with your first name as their middle name. It wasn't unusual for a family to call a kid by his second name so it wouldn't raise any flags, but it made it just that bit more difficult to join the dots. It bought time. There were systems in place, flags on the documents, warnings triggered the moment anyone started nosing around. That way you had half a shot at getting out before some bastard blew your cover.

He knew Harold David Taylor was the one as soon as he saw him, a jolt of recognition like the kid had been waiting for him, like something broken had been put back together. Taylor was a sound surname, ordinary enough to be unmemorable, not so ordinary it rang alarm bells, but he couldn't explain why it felt so particularly his. Taylor-made, Andy joked, and he couldn't deny it. Right from the start it was a perfect fit.

Once you had your name, it was your job to find out everything there was to know about your duff, where he had lived, where he went to school, what his parents did for a living, their birthdays and wedding anniversary, where they had grown up. That was how you built a legend, from the ground up. You took the documented facts, the fixed points, and constructed an entire existence around them, blending the stuff you made up with your own lived experience until you could no longer see the joins. Dave Taylor even had a false criminal record, inserted into the Police National Computer. Nothing serious, some juvenile stuff, an arrest for affray and criminal damage. The paperwork had to be solid, you never knew what your activist colleagues would have access to, but more than that you needed plausibility, a life story that made sense of your decision to get into activism but also one you already knew how to live. The best legends took things that had happened to you in your real life and wove them in to the pattern. A little brother. A bathroom cabinet full of Valium. A childhood accident on Bonfire Night. The familiar scuffs and scars of twenty-five years put together in a different order to tell a different story.

By Any Means Necessary, the squad's unofficial motto.

When he wrote Dave Taylor's legend, he cut the parents from the story. It was easier that way, less messy, but there was also a kind of satisfaction in it, like he was setting his own record straight. Of course he knew the dead kid's parents were both still alive, still living in the house in Preston they had moved to a year before their son died, the dad an optician, his wife a part-time administrator at Lancashire County Council – fuck, he knew the registration of their Vauxhall Cavalier – but somehow, until he stood there freezing his arse off at the boy's headstone, they had never felt to him like real people. He had a sudden vivid picture of Elizabeth crouching stiffly down to arrange the tulips, Harold hauling her to her feet when she was done. The two of them, heads bowed in silence, remembering. *Rest in Peace.* What peace was there for a boy stripped of his skin so that a stranger could wear it as his own?

Jayden was only two back then. He thought of the solid soap-scented weight of his son in his arms, the abandonment with which he slept, blanket kicked off, his arms thrown out above his head. He walked quickly back to the car, stamping his feet to warm them, but the discomfort clung to him, he could not shake it off. *Rest in Peace.* On the M6 he stopped at a service station and called home.

'No reason,' he said when Kim asked why he was calling. 'I was just thinking about you both, that's all.'

Back then he hadn't had a clue. He was just a bloke with a wife and a son and a new job that required him to pretend to be someone else. No one told him how it would go, how it always went, how the truth wove itself into the story, or the story into the truth, until you could no longer remember which memories were yours and which were duff, until the legend you had painstakingly put together was at least as real as the life you had lived before. Your own DNA entwined with your duff's, a double double helix.

Nobody ever told the dead kids' parents what they had done.

His head was aching. He needed water, a Nurofen. The night before, after closing time, Andy had produced a bottle of whisky. He didn't know what time they had finally got to bed, only that when he came down in the morning the bar was still a mess of torn-open crisp packets and dirty glasses. He didn't stay to clear up. He said he had to get home, that there was stuff he had to do.

'Come back again soon, mate,' Andy said reluctantly, pumping his hand. 'When you've got your head round all this shit. Don't leave it too late, though. This is going to blow, it has to. Make sure it's you that lights the fuse.'

He was glad to be back on the road, to put some miles between them. He had hoped seeing Andy would sort out his head but Andy was not the man he had expected him to be, not the man he remembered. When he started in the squad, Andy had been top dog, the one everyone looked up to. He had infiltrated Militant Tendency after their expulsion from the Labour Party, had worked himself right into the centre of things. Every field officer sent in regular reports, or blue bags, to HQ and Andy's were the best in the squad. In those days there was no training and no written rules. You learned on the job, by watching, and, during his first six months as a back-office boy, as he processed the blue bags and followed up on requests to check number plates or call in phone records, he watched Andy. When he finally made it out into the field, they met most weeks at the safe house in Gunnersbury. Everyone came. It was a way of letting off steam. They laughed, drank beer, swapped stories. Andy brought his mutt of a dog. He spent a lot of time slagging off Maggie Thatcher. In all that time there was never the slightest indication he would go on and do what he did.

Standing here twenty years ago, stamping in his boots to keep his feet from freezing solid, he had felt uneasy. He had had misgivings, of course he had. But mostly what he had felt was pride. Everyone knew Special Branch was the Met's elite unit, its secret weapon, but the squad, that was another level. It wasn't rogue exactly but it was very well hidden. Even within SB only a handful of officers knew of its existence. They worked for the Met but also directly for the security services. So what if it was the poor man's MI5, spying for squaddies, as a senior dickhead once drunkenly told him? MI5 could go fuck themselves. The day they told him he was in was the first day in his life that he finally felt like someone.

The tinny jangle of a bell made him jump. A small girl in a pink helmet was bicycling along the path behind him. The bicycle had stabilisers and the girl wobbled from side to side as she pedalled. Bunches of foil streamers glittered on the handlebars. A woman with a pushchair followed after her. Too young to be the sister, he thought quickly, and anyway Lorraine Lacey Taylor's children were both boys.

'Wait for us at the corner,' the woman called, but the girl didn't answer. She pedalled harder, her face screwed up with concentration. Once the little ones had stopped his heart. These days it was the schoolgirls giggling on the bus that did for him, the teenagers in jostling clusters outside McDonald's. The skinny ones with wavy brown hair and thick dark eyebrows and blue eyes that tapered at the corners. He watched them, with their made-up women's faces

and their gawky child bodies, their self-consciousness and their
bravado and their heart-breaking vulnerability, and it made him
giddy, all the years that were gone.

Jayden was only twenty but already he had a little flat and a full-
time job and a fiancée. When they argued about college, Jayden
said it was pointless, that all students were wasters. He wanted to
tell Jayden that a waster was a piece of pottery that had warped or
cracked during firing but of course he didn't. It was second nature
by then, to edit himself before he spoke, snatches of his duff life
blacked out like redacted phrases in a document. Jayden was used
to his silences. Like Kim, he took them as an admission of defeat.

Jayden worked at Stansted Airport in passenger services. Every
day, watching other people taking off and never going anywhere,
but then Jayden had never liked having his feet off the ground.
Other kids tightrope-walked across the climbing frame and took
their skateboards to the top of the slide. Jayden screamed if you
tried to put him in the swing. Kim had always babied him. She kept
him off school on the days he didn't want to go. She let him sleep
in their bed. He wasn't home enough to stop it. He came back every
other week, and each time the two of them seemed to have slipped
a little further away from him. Sometimes, sitting watching TV in
the lounge, he would catch Jayden looking at him and he knew he
was wondering when this strange man would leave so that things
could go back to normal.

When he moved up to Birmingham he bought a settee that
pulled out into a bed. *You know there's always a place for you here if
you need it*, he wrote to Jayden in an email, but Jayden never replied.
He went on emailing, once a month or so, friendly dashed-off messages he took hours to compose. Jayden never answered. Perhaps
he would, one day. When he looked at Jayden's wall on Facebook
it was all pictures of his fiancée Bianca looking over one shoulder
and pouting. He supposed it happened to all girls at some point,

that they stopped pulling silly faces for the camera and tried to look sexy instead. Twelve wasn't young these days, not for London kids anyway, but it hadn't happened to Mia, not yet. He told himself that it wasn't over, that as long as she was still sticking out her tongue in photos, there was still time.

'Abby, come on, it's time to go,' the woman with the pushchair called. He turned around. The little girl had abandoned her bike on the path. She squatted beside a bench, staring intently at something in the grass. There was a butterfly on the back of her T-shirt, its wings flecked with glitter.

Holly Blue. They had called her that from the start, from the moment they found out she was a girl, but on her birth certificate her name was Mia. *Mia (Latin): my or mine*, it said when he looked it up online. *Also: wished-for child; rebellion; bitter.*

Her middle name was Holly.

He saw holly blues everywhere that summer, not just in their garden at home but in the clumps of forget-me-nots around the playground, the brambles at his brother-in-law's place near Blake Wood. Dozens of them, darting and drifting in the periphery of his vision.

It shook him up. Sometimes he looked at them and wondered if he was the only one who could see them. He felt like the edges of himself were fraying. Several times he drove to Crouch End in the middle of the night, just to be close. He was gone by dawn but still. Rule number one: whatever the temptation, you stayed away from bandit country. It wasn't only about protecting yourself. It was about the safety of the squad. Your blood brothers, your amigos, your comrades in arms, most of them still undercover. Your tour might be over but they were still your family, the only people in the world who could ever understand.

He was careful. He followed squad protocol, not just the everyday dry cleaning – circling roundabouts twice, changing his route, diverting through side streets — but the same rituals he had followed every time he went home to Kim and Jayden. Andy used to joke it was like stepping through those disinfected footbaths in public swimming pools, you walked back through your front door verruca-free. He thought of it as more like that TV show he and Paul had watched as kids, *Mr Benn*. *Suddenly, as if by magic, the shopkeeper appeared*, except, instead of a fancy dress shop on the High Street, his changing room was the Welcome Break at South Mimms motorway services. However circuitous his journey, he always stopped there and, as he headed back up the A12 with his wedding band back on and a different wallet in his pocket, it was as though he had folded Dave Taylor up and handed him back.

It was always difficult. When it was finally over, his tour complete and five months' leave to get through before he could go back to work, it became impossible. In the old days, whenever he came home, he worked in the garden. It calmed him, the way it changed all the time but also didn't change at all. Now, for the first time, he couldn't summon any interest in it. He couldn't concentrate on anything, couldn't sleep. He got up late or not at all. Somehow the rage he had cultivated for his duff had taken root in him, he was always losing it. He drank too much. Eventually Kim took Jayden and went to stay with her brother. It was both better and worse without them there. He sat in a chair on the patio, a beer in his hand, watching the holly blues flicker in the phlox. *Torn love letters that flutter and float*, someone had said to him as they watched the butterfly protesters massing on London Bridge. It was one of the occupational hazards of activism, overeducated postgrads spouting pretentious bollocks, but that line stuck in his mind. Holly blues were the flimsy grey-blue of airmail paper, their wings blackened at the tips like they had been burned. He had never seen so many.

Years later, lost in one of those labyrinthine rabbit holes that lure the sleepless online, he discovered that it was part of an established pattern, a cyclical struggle with a particular parasitic wasp. The female wasp pierced the living holly blue caterpillar with its syringe-like sting, injecting a single egg inside. The wasp larva developed inside the caterpillar, biding its time as the caterpillar grew fat and spun its chrysalis and digested itself into the caterpillar soup that was the first stage of its transformation into a butterfly. Then it fed. When the pupa split open, instead of a holly blue butterfly, it was an adult wasp that emerged, its black head striped with poison yellow. The wasps were very efficient parasites. They killed almost all of the caterpillars. Those years there were hardly any butterflies. But when the wasps ran out of caterpillars and had nowhere left to lay their eggs, their own numbers collapsed and the holly blues returned.

The year he read that article, he didn't see a single holly blue. Perhaps they were all wasps. Or perhaps he wasn't looking. It was the year he moved out. The flat in Chelmsford was on the third floor. It didn't have a garden.

The morning Tess went into labour she paged him five times. It gave him a jolt to see her number on the screen, like a letter arriving from someone who is already dead. He had flown in from Berlin the day before. He was supposed to stay two weeks but he couldn't stand being so far away. He didn't tell his handler he was coming back. He didn't tell Kim either. He walked around London all day, hardly noticing where he was going. When evening came he went to the safe house in Gunnersbury. It was against the rules to bunk there when you weren't on a job but everyone did it. There were times when you needed to be nobody at all.

He sat in the chair by the window for a long time, drinking and watching the sky darken, the wink of the planes descending into Heathrow. Later he went out to the phone box on the corner. Fumbling drunkenly with the coins, he punched in the hospital's number and asked to be put through to the maternity ward.

'Name?' the woman who answered asked, and for a second he

couldn't remember. His passport was in his jacket pocket, his green paper driver's licence folded inside. He opened it. *Harold David Taylor. Date of birth: 17th March 1967.*

'Not yours.' The woman had a warm voice, he could hear the laugh running through it. 'Who are you trying to reach?'

As he gave her Tess's name he thought he heard a baby crying in the background, and his heart turned inside out. Holly Blue.

'I'm the father,' he said. 'I just want to know she's OK, that's all. That they're both OK.'

She put him on hold. Outside the phone box the street was deserted, the houses dark. He supposed it was late. He did not have a watch. They had taken it back at the last debrief, before he left for Berlin. There was a pale stripe on his wrist where it had been, a Casio, standard squad issue, adapted to function as a recording device. He had shown it to Jayden once. He hoped he might be impressed. Like James Bond, he said, playing Jayden's voice back to him, but Jayden only shrugged. James Bond has a Rolex, he said dismissively. It detonates bombs.

Folding the driver's licence into a small square he slipped it into his jeans pocket. There was a click on the line as the woman came back.

'The midwife's asking if she can call you back,' she said in a different, crisper voice. 'Can you give me your number?'

He thought of the midwife, the way she rubbed Tess's back like she was rubbing the marks of him off it. He had forgotten about the midwife. He hung up.

It was five weeks before Tess finally registered the birth, another twelve before he was able to access the certificate at the Family Records Centre. He looked at it for a long time, at the name of his child, the blank box where his name should have been, and it winded him, that even now, after everything that had happened, she could still see straight into his soul. That somehow, he didn't know how, she knew that, when he handed Dave Taylor back, there was suddenly no shopkeeper, no real-life clothes to put back on. That instead they had left him stranded, naked and nameless, trapped in an in-between that was neither there nor here. A blank box on a form, missing in action, unable to find his way home.

Tess never understood why people trussed their kids up in fancy names. She said a name should be loose enough to fit a child whatever shape it was they decided to become.

Missing in Action.

MIA.

It took another six years for him and Kim to split. They should have done it sooner but they had stopped talking by then and neither of them had the heart for it. Packing up in the garage, he opened the strongbox he kept there and found, among the other bits and pieces, Dave Taylor's driver's licence, folded very small. It was supposed to have been handed in with the rest of his documents at the end of his tour, but he told his handler he had put it through the washing machine by mistake. His handler made a joke about taking dry cleaning to the next level and gave him a docket to sign. Harold David Taylor, RIP. It felt strange writing his own name.

When he was finally settled in his flat in Birmingham, he unfolded the licence and sent it off to the DVLA. Paper licences were being phased out, it was all photocards by then. When the licence came back he felt an echo of the feeling he had had the first time, the intoxicating buzz of being someone else, someone new. Back then he had taken his new credit card to a Covent Garden bar.

'I'm Dave Taylor,' he said that night to a bunch of strangers as he bought them drinks. Later, on a lumpy futon in Kensal Rise, he looked at the naked stranger asleep beside him.

'My name's Dave Taylor,' he murmured, and the rush of it made him hard all over again.

He never used the driver's licence. He put it in his wallet. He almost forgot it was there. Then, driving up to Andy's two days ago, he had stopped at a pub for lunch.

'Name?' the kid behind the bar asked, scribbling down his order.

'Taylor,' he said. 'Dave Taylor,' and the taste of it was sweet on his tongue.

Andy's undercover tour ended in 1993. He extracted himself without incident but the following year he assaulted a DS. He was suspended pending an inquiry. They told him to instruct a lawyer. Instead he went to the senior brass. He said they couldn't hold him responsible, that his undercover work had left him with severe PTSD. He said either they reinstated him or he would go to the newspapers and tell them every dirty little detail. According to Andy, the brass tried to frighten him out of it. He received anonymous phone calls, veiled threats about his kids. Andy refused to cave. A month later the assault charge disappeared. Andy signed an NDA and a settlement was reached. With the proceeds he bought himself a pub with rooms on the edge of the Lake District. The Pig and Whistle, he called it. A joke, but only just. A show of defiance. It was like the K in knife, he said with a hard laugh, or the H in whistle. The blower was silent.

'Pete? Pete Taylor?'

A cold wave rolled through him. Slowly he turned around. The woman with the pushchair bent over awkwardly on the path behind him, holding the little girl's bike by its handlebars.

'Oh,' she said. 'Sorry. I thought . . . but. You're not – are you?'

He shook his head. 'No. Sorry.'

'So you a relative? I mean, sorry, it's none of my business, only you've been standing there a while so I thought maybe . . . '

'No, I . . . ' I'm just browsing, he almost said, as though he was looking at shirts in a department store. 'I was just walking through. But I got distracted.'

'Well, you do, don't you? When they pass so young like that. I do anyway. There but for the grace of God and all that.' The little girl tugged at her mother's skirt but the woman ignored her, loosening her fingers absently as though she was unknotting a tangle in her hair. 'We lived down the street from the Taylors when I was a kid. Harry had passed by then, obviously, but Pete Taylor, the brother, oh, I thought the world of him. Went off to college when I was nine years old and broke my heart.' She laughed, shaking her head. 'Anyway. You're not him. Lucky for you, really, in the circs. I'm going to stop talking now. Sorry. Not enough adult company. You think kids won't change you, then one day you wake up and discover you've turned into your nan. Nice to meet you, Not-Pete. Enjoy your afternoon.'

'Thanks. You too.'

He watched her walk away, the little girl pedalling beside her. Suddenly he wanted to be somewhere else, anywhere but here. He thought of Andy, banging bottles down behind his bar. By any standards Andy had hit the jackpot, the lump sum settlement, the pension, the medical cover, the works, and all of it without betraying a single UCO. Andy had won. And yet he was raging. You could hear it even when he wasn't talking, the fury inside him hissing and spitting like fat in a pan. He seethed with it. It wasn't enough that he had what he wanted. He wanted the ones who were left held to account. He had signed the gagging agreement, he had consented to their terms, he would never have got what he got without that, but it tormented him all the same. He couldn't stand it, those dogs still sleeping where he'd let them lie.

'You could do it, mate,' Andy kept saying. 'You could blow those bastards sky high.'

He didn't say what would happen after that.

14

Tess sat at Nat's kitchen table and looked at the packets of photos. Despite her exhaustion, she couldn't keep still. Her arms and legs fizzed. Her thoughts fizzed too, sharp little bubbles zigzagging up through her brain.

'This is literally what Twitter's for,' Nat said. 'We say we're working on, I don't know, a documentary about the birth of eco-activism, that we're trying to track down those involved. We post a bunch of photos, not just of him but all of us, and ask for anyone who recognises anyone to be in touch. OK, we might get nothing. But what have we got to lose?'

Only everything, Tess thought, but Nat didn't wait for an answer. She said there had to be someone out there who knew him. Everyone lived somewhere. There would be neighbours, friends, people who knew him from the gym or the pub or picking kids up from school. They just had to put the word out there. A good tweet was like a snowball: with luck and a decent shove, it not only grew, it gathered speed.

Tess nodded. Nat was saying something about tagging people but she didn't listen. Somewhere, maybe not even that far away, Dave was someone else. Someone with friends who knew his real name, who invited him over for barbecues and asked him about his job. What did he tell them about his job? What if all that time he was married? What if all those days when he said he was going to work he kissed her and went home to his wife?

If she found him, if she could show Mia that he was never who he said he was, would his lies justify hers? Would his betrayal cancel hers out? Or would Nat's giant snowball just hurtle through their lives and leave everything Mia believed in smashed to smithereens?

Nat's phone rang. She was still talking about Twitter.

'Sorry, Ryan's playdate,' she said to Tess, grimacing as she answered the call. Ryan's friend had just thrown up. The boy's mother asked if Nat could pick up Ryan and take him home.

'You start,' Nat said, grabbing her keys. 'Or don't. Whatever you'd rather. I'll be back in ten minutes.'

The photos were jumbled together, a thick wedge in one envelope, three or four in another. Tess took them all out and put them in a pile. Some of them were of Nat's wedding. In one of them Nat and her mum were waltzing together, their arms around each other's waists. Tess wondered what it was like to have a mother you wanted to dance with at your wedding, who wanted to dance with you. She felt flimsy, jagged, like she wasn't really there.

The night before, in the supermarket, she had taken a tin of tomatoes from the shelf and, as she put it in her basket, she was overcome with a feeling of terror so sudden and intense that her legs gave way beneath her and she fell. Shaking, sweating, her heart pounding so furiously she thought it would explode, she scrabbled on the floor but her legs were useless, she couldn't get up. A man standing near her had tried to help her but she lashed out at him, screaming at him to get away from her. She couldn't remember what happened after that. The next thing she knew she was sitting on a bench in the car park and a middle-aged woman in a black trouser suit was holding out a bottle of water.

A panic attack, the woman said. Shelagh Healey, Deputy Store Manager. Her name was on a plastic badge on her lapel. She told Tess to sit tight, asked if there was someone she could call to come and fetch her, and Tess said there wasn't because all she wanted was for it to be over, to be somewhere else. The car park was busy, cars honking, people clattering trolleys. She kept her eyes on the woman's badge. Shelagh Healey, Shelagh Healey. The words were like a mantra, like a song. She walked home, her lips moving silently, laying the syllables down in front of her one step at a time. Shelagh Healey. She felt hollow, scraped out, scoured not only of what had happened but of whatever was supposed to come next. Shelagh Healey, she said, over and over, but she could still hear it under the words, like a mosquito, the high thin whine of fear.

Tess rubbed her face and looked down at the photos. Most of the (dis)organisation ones had been taken on the day of the M41 protest. Less than fifteen years ago but they all looked like children, the boys bare-chested, full of skinny swagger, the girls with flowers in their hair, and behind them the policemen stiff and sweaty in their uniforms. A more innocent time, wasn't that what they always said about the past, as though it was the internet and mobile phones that corrupted people and not the other way around. In the photos people had cameras and Walkmans in their back pockets, headphones slung round their necks. Only airlines used headphones like that these days.

She told Mia she thought she might be coming down with something. Later, sleepless, she had googled the NHS website. *Panic attacks are a natural response to stressful or dangerous situations*, it said. *You may start to avoid certain situations because you fear they'll trigger another attack. This can create a cycle of 'living in fear of fear'.* Tess wanted to know if there was a way she could stop being afraid and learn how to be really fucking angry instead, but there wasn't any information on the NHS website about that. They recommended she talk to her GP about counselling and anti-depressants. She closed the laptop and cried. Then, afraid that Mia might see what she had been looking at and be frightened, she opened it again and clicked to clear her history. Her search was the only one listed. Everything else had already been deleted.

Six of Nat's photos had Dave in them. Tess laid them out on the table, a circle with one in the middle, like tarot cards. Only one had her in too, a group shot taken with one of the bagpipe-playing stilt-walkers, Dave in the middle and Tess in her butterfly costume on the end. Tess was laughing, her wings glittering in the sunlight, but Dave must have moved as the shutter snapped: his face was a blur. It hurt Tess's throat to look at it. She turned it over.

A child deleting their browsing history might simply want privacy. Or it might be a warning sign. The school distributed a booklet on internet safety to parents at the start of Year 7. *Talk to your child,* the booklet advised. *Make sure you regularly check in with his or her online adventures.* She and Mia had always talked about everything. Tess was proud of that, of the casual unconcern with which Mia discussed things that Tess would have died rather than raise with her own mother. But since they had got back from France, she realised, they had hardly spoken at all. There had been no walks together to the corner shop for milk, no card games or cups of tea. Mia was out with Yaz or she was up in her room. She told Tess she was working on an art project – which made sense, Oakfield was big on summer activities – but usually her projects took over the whole length of the kitchen table, paints and glue and snipped-off bits of coloured card strewn everywhere, her iPod speaker blasting out Katy Perry and the biscuit tin open beside her. This time she took the materials upstairs and closed the door. She took the laptop too, she told Tess she needed it for research. When Tess tapped on the door and asked her to remember to put down newspaper, she heard a metal scrape as Mia slid the bolt.

You cannot lie to your child, not about this. Sylvie's words on a loop in her head. *Bereavement, grief, loss, these things are not games.*

She hadn't thought Mia would grow up. It made no sense when she said it like that but it was true. Alone with a small child, trapped in a permanent present tense, the future was unimaginable, an alien language in a script Tess could not decipher. It had no meaning. And so she rewrote the final paragraph, closed the book. And then he died, THE END.

The new version was better, neater, no loose ends. Mia would never blame herself the way Tess blamed herself, for Dave leaving, because he hadn't left. He was dead. When Tess said it, it felt true. Like her mother, he was gone, irreversibly, and there was no point in wondering about what might have been or wishing it was different. If she felt a flicker of unease, if sometimes Sylvie's voice niggled in her head, she closed her ears. She never pictured herself like this, listening to the bass thumping in the ceiling, waiting for the moment when her daughter walked in and looked at her like she was a stranger, like she would never not be a stranger again.

Tess looked down at the photos. They were useless, all of them. The only close-up was taken in half profile, his hands cupped to light a cigarette. Two others showed him playing the drums, his head thrown back. He could have been anyone.

'Fuck but I love you,' he said to her that day on the M41, hope and happiness blazing off the sun-baked tarmac like a mirage. Later that night he suggested they move in together. He said it might be too soon but he couldn't help it, she had turned him upside down.

Tess's fury came suddenly, violently. Blindly she snatched up the snapshots, crushing them as she rammed them any which way back into their envelopes, knocking a slither of pictures to the floor. There was nothing left. He had destroyed everything, every shared moment, every treasured memory stamped in scarlet: **VOID**. His arms raised, eyes closed, he played the drums in an ecstasy at her feet. Furiously she kicked at him, then, dropping to her knees, grabbed at the photo, crumpling the glossy paper, tearing it again and again until he was nothing but scraps of shiny colour.

She sat back on her heels, fists clenched, her breathing ragged. She needed to clear up the mess before Nat came home. She leaned forward, scrabbling up the photos from under the table. One of the pictures was of her and Nat, laughing on a sofa made of hay bales. Tess picked it up. It must have been taken right before Mia was born, her bump was huge, but they looked so young. So blithely, blindly happy. Tess bit her lip. Behind them, in the background, barely visible behind a bloke in a Nirvana T-shirt, a couple were kissing. Tess peered at them and the breath went out of her body. The girl had her back to the camera but Tess knew her from the shape of her, the cropped line of her hair. Astrid Osman. The man's shirt was unbuttoned. On his torso, barely visible in the shadowy light, she could just see the tail of a blue whale.

The front door banged.

'We're back,' Nat called. Tess heard Ryan's feet pounding up the stairs as Nat came into the kitchen. She put her hands on Tess's shoulders, leaning over to look at the photo.

'Ah. Look at us.' Her smile faded. 'Hang on. Fuck. There, at the back, is that—?'

'Yeah.'

'Fuck.'

'Yeah.'

'Fuck,' Nat said again, pressing her thumbs into the base of Tess's neck. Tess closed her eyes, yielding to the pressure. How could it possibly matter that this stranger who had deceived her about every single thing, whose whole life had been a lie, had all the time been betraying her in the most banal and humiliating way, with his ex? She hadn't thought there was any pain left to find. And yet.

Shelagh Healey, she intoned in her head. Shelagh Healey.

'Oh my God,' Nat said, pressing harder. 'So all that time she was actually telling the truth.'

'She *told* you?'

'No, not then, of course not. It was later, after he'd gone – not that I believed her. She used to get drunk and go on about Dave and her starting a new life in Durban, how he was sorting it out and she was going to join him when he was settled. We all thought she was nuts. But maybe . . . ' Nat shrugged. 'Eventually she moved to Aberystwyth. Which I'm pretty sure wasn't in South Africa, even back then.'

Tess hugged her arms over her chest and stared at the table, the jumble of photos. Karen holding up a painted placard: **CARS CAN'T DANCE**. I had a panic attack in Tesco, she wanted to say. I screamed on the floor and kicked a man who came to help me, but even as the words gathered in her head, they seemed to splinter apart, other words pushing through the spaces in between. *Panic attack. You know that was a dream, right? I feel like I'm going mad.*

'Of course you do,' Nat said. 'How could you not?'

Tess felt the panic rising in her. She hadn't even realised she had said the words out loud. 'I need to sleep. Maybe I should get some pills. Do you know which pills? Because I have to sleep. I have to stop thinking and thinking about it.'

'Pills is one way. Or maybe you need some answers. Maybe it's only the truth that'll let you put this thing to rest.'

'You think I can ever put it to rest?'

'Process it, then,' Nat conceded. 'Decide what you want to do next.'

'So we find out his name, where he lives. How will that change anything?'

'Because once you know who he is you can do something. Press charges, prosecute him, I don't know. Make sure he's punished. Tess, we're talking about a man who deliberately and systematically violated you. A man who pretended to be someone else the whole time the two of you were supposedly in a loving relationship, who lied to you about every single thing. That's abuse, Tess, pure and simple. That bastard abused you. Fuck, some people would say it was rape. Can you honestly let him just walk away from that?'

I was raped. He raped me. The words hammered into her, spiking saliva into her mouth.

'And what about Mia?' Nat said. 'Sooner or later, she's going to want answers too.'

Tess fled to the bathroom. Dropping to her knees, she vomited violently into the toilet bowl. The force of it brought tears to her eyes. She took a ragged breath, trying to steady herself, and heaved again.

'Here,' Nat said gently, holding out a plastic cup of water. The cup had tractors on it and white streaks of toothpaste. Tess took a sip, tasting mint. Nat stroked her hair. Sinking down onto the floor, Tess rested her head against the wall. Shelagh Healey. Shelagh Healey. Nat took the cup from her and flushed the toilet.

'I'm so sorry,' she said quietly. She sat down next to Tess, their shoulders touching. 'I was out of order.'

'It's OK.'

'No. It's not OK at all. Next time I try telling you something that makes you want to hurl, tell me to shut the fuck up.' She reached for Tess's hand, sliding her fingers between Tess's. 'Top marks for the excellent shot, though. The boys have a habit of redecorating when they chuck. I once found a lump of old sick in the pocket of my bathrobe. Too soon? Sorry. I'll shut up.'

Tess leaned against Nat, looking down at the weft of their fingers, the pale skin and the dark. It should be weird, she thought, sitting on a bathroom floor with someone I've hardly seen in thirteen years, but it isn't weird at all. It's the safest place I've ever been.

The doorknob rattled. Someone thumped at the door.

'Mum?' Ryan's voice was urgent. 'Mum, I need the toilet.'

Nat sighed. 'Shit. Sorry.' Hauling herself up on the side of the bath, she extended a hand to haul Tess up too. 'All right, love,' she said, unlocking the door. 'It's all yours.'

'Eww!' Ryan scrunched up his face. 'It stinks in here.'

Nat pushed open the window. 'Not any more.'

'It does so. It's gross.'

Nat bugged her eyes at him. Opening the bathroom cabinet, she took out an aerosol can of deodorant, spraying it liberally around the room. 'Fine. There you go. Dry confidence, forty-eight-hour protection. Aah, Bisto. Because you're worth it.'

Ryan glared at her. 'Can you just *go*?'

Downstairs Nat put the kettle on. 'Tea?' she said.

'I should go home. Make sure Mia's not being groomed by paedophiles or burning the house down.'

'Ah, the joy of teenagers, I can't wait. Come here then.'

Tess let Nat put her arms around her. She was shaking. She hadn't realised she was shaking.

'You sure you don't want tea?' Nat asked. 'Or, I don't know, some of the Christmas brandy? The kids don't get through that nearly as fast as the biscuits.'

'I'm OK.'

'No. You're not. But you will be. I promise.'

Tess nodded. She was still shaking. She tried to disentangle herself from Nat's embrace but Nat didn't let go.

'And Mia will be OK too. She's got you, after all. Not many kids get that lucky.' Nat leaned back to look at her, her gaze so soft Tess couldn't bring herself to meet it. 'Have you said anything to her yet? Does she know what's going on?'

Tess looked past Nat's shoulder at the table, at the photo of Nat waltzing with her mum. Was that why Nat was such a good mother, because her mum had shown her how? She pressed her lips together, shaking her head.

'It's only, I wanted to say that when you do, when you're ready to do that, I'd be happy to talk to her, you know?' Nat said. 'If you wanted me to. Not straight away, obviously, but if you thought it would help, you know, to understand that it wasn't just you, it was all of us, that he fooled us all right from the start. That we believed him just like you did. That we all loved him too.'

Tess wanted to speak but her mouth was too dry and there was something stuck in her throat that wouldn't go down. Nat squeezed her arm.

'You can tell me to sod off if you want but you shouldn't have to do this by yourself.'

I understand that lies destroy people.

Tess looked at Nat's hand on her arm and then at Nat.

'I told her he died.'

Mia sat back on her heels, wiping her hands on her jeans. Her back ached and her feet had gone dead but she felt a rush of triumph. Without a sewing machine or money for proper materials, she had been afraid they wouldn't come out how she wanted, that they would end up looking super lame, but they didn't. They looked cool.

She had made lots of mistakes at the beginning. Like using wire coat hangers for the frames, only a single hanger was too small and, when she googled it, the only way to join wire hangers together properly was to solder them, so she lost heart a bit until she realised that there were people all over the internet sharing tips about this kind of stuff. Wire was one of their favourite subjects.

It turned out she needed green garden wire because it came in different strengths and it was also super-cheap. At the B&Q on Dearsley Road she found a huge roll, metres and metres, for £2.99 so, on top of the double-layered edges, there was enough wire left over to crisscross back and forth so that the insides had something to attach to. She thought her mum would notice she had taken the money so she invented a story about ice creams from the van in the park (they didn't give receipts there) but she never had to use it because Tess never asked. Perhaps it was Sylvie dying but recently it was like her mum had a podcast playing in her head, she would start speaking and then just tail off in the middle of a sentence, and one time she forgot the pasta for so long that by the time she remembered it was still cooking it was basically sludge in the bottom of the pan. Mia could dance stark naked on the kitchen table and she wouldn't even see.

Her distraction had its advantages. She didn't say anything when Mia told her she would be staying over with Yaz on Saturday night. She just nodded. Mia hadn't told Yaz, not yet, though she would. Some time. That way Yaz would have to cover for her if her mum ever said anything. That way Yaz would know Mia was fine without her, that she wasn't sitting around waiting for her to come back.

The Butterfly Girl's wings had been made of silk but Mia didn't have any silk. There were some offcuts of coloured cellophane in the box Ruth had given her mum when she cleared out the art room, leftovers from the stained-glass windows she did every Christmas with Year 7, but they were too small and, when she taped them together, the joins looked rough and ugly. Mia thought maybe she could slide the pieces inside two layers of clingfilm, that the clingfilm would be sticky enough to hold them, but it wasn't sticky at all. The cellophane kept sliding out of place.

It was the clingfilm that made her think of the art project she had done years ago in a school summer camp. You took those paints that came in squeezy bottles and squiggled them onto a large sheet of card. Then straight away, while the paint was still wet, you stretched a piece of clingfilm over the whole thing and squidged and smudged all the paints together with your hands. When you peeled the clingfilm away, you were left with an abstract picture, except what if it wasn't the card you kept at the end but the clingfilm? It wouldn't dry but that wouldn't matter, not if the paint was trapped between layers of the film. That way she could use glitter too and snippets of coloured cellophane.

It took a few tries. The first time the paint was too thick but, by diluting it and then working it gently with her fingers between the plastic layers, she created a streaky, semi-translucent bluish-green. She didn't know why her mum had chosen that colour for her wings as the Butterfly Girl when the real peacock butterfly was mostly dark red. The real peacock butterfly used to be rare in northern England but it wasn't any more. Because of global warming there were now peacock butterflies on the Shetland Islands, which were only 400 miles south of the Arctic Circle. Mia had been watering the honeysuckle cuttings and she had sort of hoped that, when they grew, they might attract peacock butterflies to their garden but, when she looked it up, it was white admiral butterflies who laid their eggs on honeysuckle. Peacock butterflies preferred nettles. Mia wanted to tell her mum that, she thought it was funny that all this time Tess had been doing peacock butterflies a favour without knowing it, but she couldn't. It got harder the more she learned. She worried she would blurt something out by mistake and give herself away.

The two sets of eyespots took her almost a day to make. She experimented with various materials but in the end she decided on toilet paper because it was absorbent and very light. She copied the eyes from photos online, the vivid blue-purple of the centres, the dark pupils, the delicately feathered circles of white that surrounded them. Studies had shown that, confronted by a peacock butterfly's eyespots, blue tits made the same alarm calls they made when faced with a predator of their own. Even big birds like chickens were intimidated by them. Mia googled the weight of a chicken (average two and a half kilos) and the weight of a peacock butterfly (average half a gram). She rated the peacock butterfly even more after that. The eyespots on a peacock's wings had a white streak at the edge of the iris, like they were catching the light. The eyes were already weirdly realistic but it was the streak that made them come alive.

When the eyespots were finished she put them on the windowsill to dry. All that was left to do was to work out how to attach the wings to her back. In a crafting forum online someone suggested the straps of an old backpack, with the backpack part cut off. Mia still had the old Pokémon one she had used in primary school, the one Yaz had given her for her eighth birthday. Grabbing the scissors, she hacked at the nylon fabric. She didn't know how to stop it happening, the way whatever she did, whatever she thought, everything kept looping back to Yaz. The night before on Facebook, Vanessa Morales had posted a meme of SpongeBob and Patrick jumping over each other in party hats with the caption *THERE'S NO FEELING QUITE LIKE ACTING CRAZY WITH MY BEST FRIEND*, and it was such a small thing, not even funny, but she couldn't help herself, suddenly she was crying.

Abandoning the straps she picked up her phone. Astrid Osman still hadn't replied to her tweet but she didn't care. It was better this way. There was no way Astrid wouldn't notice her at the Candlelit Climate Vigil, not if she was dressed as the Butterfly Girl. Mia would go and talk to her and tell her it was because of her that she was there and then they would have all night to talk, or they would when they weren't actually protesting. According to Astrid the Liberal Democrats had promised that, if they won the election, they would cut UK carbon emissions to zero by 2050 but, even though the Lib Dems were now in the coalition government, they hadn't yet done anything to keep that promise.

We have to hold our leaders to account, Astrid tweeted with her third link to the vigil website in a week. *There is no Planet B.*

Mia knew about global warming, of course. People were always making jokes about it like I don't know what the problem is, decent British summers at last, but she had never really thought about it, or not as something to worry about. It was a problem science would have to solve when it got serious. No one said that it was serious right now: the worst ever droughts in the Amazon, the worst ever floods in Pakistan, the highest ever temperatures across the world, all in 2010.

On Astrid's website there was a link to a film of an Arctic glacier falling into the sea under the headline: **ALREADY TOO LATE?**

As the permafrost melts, millions of tonnes of greenhouse gases will be released, tripling the carbon dioxide in the atmosphere and massively accelerating global warming. Three million years of ice could disappear within five years. The resulting rise in sea levels would wipe out hundreds of island nations and leave world cities like New York, London, and Mumbai underwater. It would also cause the total collapse of the Amazon ecosystem, converting it into the single greatest emitter of carbon dioxide in the world. Even if it were possible to cut global emissions to zero, many scientists believe it is already too late to stop global warming. But it remains our only hope for averting total climate catastrophe.

When Mia let words like that get inside her, she crackled with a fierce dread that made the inside of her skin feel like it was burning.

The eyespots were dry. Fishing a bottle of Tippex from her pencil case, Mia painted a few strokes with the white liquid on each eyespot. The Tippex dried almost immediately but she blew on each one to make sure. Then, very carefully, she slipped them under the top layer of clingfilm, smoothing them out so they floated on the gleam of paint beneath.

She took some pictures with her phone. The clingfilm gave the wings a glistening silvery translucence that made Mia think of the dragonflies at the canal. Not many people knew that it wasn't just dragonfly wings that were transparent, butterfly wings were too, only because of the way the light reflected off the tiny scales that covered them the human eye saw only patterns and beautiful colours. That was the thing about butterflies. No matter how much you discovered about them, there was always something else that blew your mind.

Mia looked at the pictures, then tilted the wings towards the window so they caught the light better, and took some more. She wished she could forward one to Yaz and show her what she had made. The old Yaz would have known how to appreciate them. Maybe. Yaz had never been much into making stuff, not the way Mia was. She was too impatient to do anything properly, she got bored. Most likely Mia would send them and Yaz wouldn't even reply. Mia hadn't heard anything from her since she left her house, not even when she posted a meme on her wall of Megan from *Drake and Josh*:

I have dreams . . . And sometimes in those dreams, things happen to you.

Drake and Josh had been one of her and Yaz's favourite TV shows. They still quoted lines from it to each other, it always cracked them up. Mia wanted Yaz to see her post and know it was for her, but she hadn't even liked it. Vanessa Morales had, though, **LOL ow just twisted my liver** which was really funny if you knew *Drake and Josh*. Mia liked her comment. Underneath it she typed **;) did she just call us Drink and Juice?**

The picture of her dad was on her bedside table. Mia picked it up. Her dad had been an activist long before her mum, it was how they met, because her mum ended up at a demo by accident. In the 1990s the protests were mainly about roads, the ecological damage of more and more concrete and cars, but also about how greed was swallowing the planet. There were loads of articles and blogs about it online. In the photos the protesters had their fists in the air and their mouths open, like they were shouting or singing. They looked young and scruffy and angry and excited. They looked like her dad. There were other pictures of them being arrested, the police dragging them by the arms so their shirts were pulled up, exposing their bare chests. Mia studied all the photos, looking for her dad's blue whale. She never saw it but she knew he was there somewhere, shouting and singing and not being afraid of the police. If he had not been on that motorbike in Greece, if he hadn't died, he would still be fighting, lying down on airport runways and in front of power stations and at the mouths of rivers where plastic rubbish poured in an endless vomiting wave into the sea. Mia was sure of it. He would never just have given up.

Her phone pinged. **Vanessa. that episode when they switched D&J's boss for a random black lady LOL.** Mia grinned. Over the years she and Yaz had compiled many lists ranking the most important qualities in a human, but an encyclopaedic knowledge of *Drake and Josh* had to be in the top five. She wished she could say that to Vanessa. There were other things she wanted to say too, like did she know her name was actually a genus of butterflies, that the Vanessa genus included the red admiral and the painted lady which sounded to Mia like characters in Cluedo, but she was afraid Vanessa would think she was a crazy stalker, so she posted a meme of a sealion clapping its flippers instead. She thought about asking if Vanessa knew whether sealions were threatened by climate change, but she didn't because that was probably even weirder than the thing about Vanessa being a genus of butterflies, and anyway she wasn't sure she wanted to know the answer.

Downstairs the front door banged.

'Mee?' her mum called up the stairs. Mia checked the bolt on her bedroom door.

'Yeah?'

'I'm back. You want a sandwich?'

'No, I'm OK.'

She waited for her mum to tell her to come down anyway, that Mia needed to eat, but she didn't. Mia imagined her frowning into the fridge the way she always did, like there wasn't anything inside. Tess didn't eat meat and she didn't fly and she bought soap rather than shower gel because of the packaging, but she still drove a car and she never went to protests and she didn't talk about melting glaciers or rising sea levels or any of the other terrible things that were pushing the world towards catastrophe. The (dis)organisation was like a family, she once heard her mum say to Grandpa Ivo, except we liked each other. But if Tess had liked the others so much, then how come she never saw them? Perhaps the only one she really liked was Mia's dad. Perhaps that was the only reason she had got involved in the first place, because she wanted to be his girlfriend and not because she cared about the planet. Perhaps if she had actually wanted to do something, if she had been as serious about it as Mia's dad and not some stupid eco-groupie, the two of them would still be together.

Perhaps then he would have wanted to stay.

15

After his undercover tour was over, when he had completed his compulsory leave of absence, they reassigned him. A desk job at Scotland Yard, routine intelligence duties. He had only been out seven years but it felt like a lifetime. The systems had all changed. No one knew who he was. He turned up to his interview with HR and they couldn't find his file. He wasn't even allowed to drive a squad car because his clearance had expired. The people, the jokes, the pointlessly hi-tech coffee machine, everything was different. It was like walking into the house you had owned for years to find all your furniture gone and a bunch of strangers sprawled in front of the TV.

He let it go, mostly. He was so tired. His work was slapdash. He drank too much, came in late and hungover. Occasionally, spectacularly, he lost it. A red mist came down and he couldn't stop himself. The brass cut him some slack. It was not unusual, after a tour. Dark moods, a short fuse, excessive alcohol consumption, they all went through it. The advice was the same, handed down from officer to officer: go down the pub, mate, have a few drinks. They laughed about it. No one talked about what it did to you, seven years of living two lives, the constant fear of betraying yourself, blowing your cover. Seven years of attending meetings as a trusted member of the group and then going home to transcribe the recordings off your watch. Of offering to drop your mates home in the van so you could memorise their addresses, of collating details of their workplaces and contacts and conversations for the dossiers that went back in your weekly blue bags. Of living six days a week with a woman who never thought to doubt you and on Thursdays going home to your wife.

When all that ended, when the adrenaline that had powered you for seven years finally stopped, all that was left was the fear. Fear and the backwash of your duff. It was like those Method actors, the nutters who went so deep into the part that they couldn't leave it behind, who went on talking in the accent and wearing the costume even after the cameras stopped rolling. In the last months of his tour he had stoked his fury like a fire. He had no choice, his rage was his only ticket out, and so he cut deep, opening the old scars, drawing out the buried anger like bad blood: anger at his stepfather for being a bastard and at his mum for her inability to protect any of them and at Paul for leaving and at the brass who wouldn't listen when he said he needed more time, who wanted to tear him away from the only life in which he had ever been himself, pouring petrol on the blaze until it exploded inside him and all he could see was the flames. It had frightened him, if he was honest, how easy it was to find it, how real it felt. That last morning in the flat, when Tess came back too soon—

Every officer preparing to go undercover had to have an off-plan, a detailed strategy that would allow him to extract himself at the end of his tour without arousing suspicion. They grilled you on it relentlessly before you went in. It wasn't enough for your explanations to seem probable. Probable left loose ends, it put other officers in danger. By the time you activated your off-plan your activist mates needed to know that you had no choice but to go. The off-plan had to make it inevitable.

The off-plan he went in with was textbook. It took four key threads of Dave Taylor's story – the death of the grandmother who raised him, his abusive alcoholic father turning up again out of the blue, his brother in South Africa, his abiding desire to travel – and wove them together into an overpowering urge to get as far away as possible, to start over. The brass singled it out for specific commendation.

Then Tess got pregnant. The baby changed everything. When he first found out he was incandescent. He couldn't believe she'd been so careless, that she had so recklessly compromised his position. She would have to get rid of it. He couldn't see how else it could be managed. He stormed out, holed himself up in a cheap hotel, drank too much, called clinics. His heart felt like it was being clawed out of his chest. It was only on the third day, hungover and miserable, that it dawned on him that he couldn't do it. That perhaps this was what he had been waiting for all along. That, by having a family, it wouldn't just be the child who was born brand new into the world but Dave Taylor. That it was the only way to keep hold of who he was.

And so he went back. Tess agreed to keep the baby. He didn't tell anyone at HQ about her or the child. He was happier than he had ever been. And yet, at the same time, in another, separate part of himself, he understood it was a catastrophe. He couldn't stay, not after the baby was born, but he couldn't just go either. It wasn't just the legal paper trail a child brought with it. It was Tess. She believed in him. She wouldn't let him walk away. If he was to exit effectively, in line with squad guidelines, he had to be sure she wanted him to go. It was the only way to make sure she didn't come after him, that she never tried to track him down.

He planned it rigorously. For weeks he timed his outbursts

carefully, making sure they happened in public, that everyone saw him lose his shit. To start with it was an agony, behaving that way towards Tess, but as the deadline for their parting drew closer and the dread of losing her intensified, to his surprise it grew easier. She moved through those last weeks dreamily, folded in on herself in a way that left no place for him. He had been afraid that, with no family of her own to support her, his departure would overwhelm her. Now he saw that he no longer mattered. She and the baby were a whole on their own. He could vanish and they would still be complete, an unbroken circle of two. The only one who would be destroyed was him. Forced into silence, tormented by bitterness and guilt, his anger blazed and blazed.

Two weeks from her due date there were complications. He agreed to go with her to the hospital. On the morning of the appointment he refused to talk to her. When she asked if he thought the milk was off, he hurled the carton against the wall and walked out. Later, when she was gone, he went back.

He knew what he had to do, he had gone over and over it, but once he started to break things, it was like something inside him broke too. The list in his head – break crockery, upend table, kick hole in wall, pull clothes from the wardrobe – melted into a red-black fever of fists and fury. Even now he could remember almost nothing of that morning, only the excruciating lack of relief as he punched and smashed, and a single moment that replayed again and again in his memory, that he could never stop from playing: Tess's face as she stood in the hall, her keys falling from her hand, and afterwards, outside on the landing, his hand opening and inside it, smeared with his own blood, a little silver butterfly on a broken chain.

They're not your friends, they're your targets. The squad mantra, drilled into them all from the moment they walked through the door of the scruffy office in Putney. He had mentioned Tess in his blue bags. He had to, she was the Butterfly Girl. A relationship with her counted for something, it proved he was doing his job. But he had never said anything about the baby. The baby wasn't anyone's business but his.

'Rule number one, always use a condom,' Andy said, like it was the Green Cross Code. 'Rule number two, whatever you fucking do, don't ever fall in love.'

When he had been back at Scotland Yard six months, his old boss from the squad took him out for a lunchtime curry. Brian Richards was matey, solicitous even. It still felt oddly like one of the pre-tour interrogations he had put him through, prodding for weak spots in his legend. A test to pass or fail. He wanted to tell Richards the truth. That, after seven years in the squad, he hated the police with a vengeance. That on the other side he had seen it all too clearly and too close: the brutality, the bigotry, the verbal abuse. He wanted to grab the man by his lapels and demand to know how, after he had been punched, kicked, slapped, choked, spat on, beaten, and held face down in a police van with a boot in his back, he was supposed to go back to being one of them, to pick up where he had left off.

He drank four pints, one after the other, and said nothing. It was only as he gestured for the bill that Richards asked him casually if he was still in touch with Andy. When he shook his head, Richards leaned across the table, punching him lightly on the arm.

'Look, we all know what it's like, mate. Coming off tour, you miss it, right? The challenge, the stimulation. So if you want to take some time to get your head together, travel the world, I could have a word with the DCS, fix you up some sick leave. You've earned it.'

Afterwards he wasn't sure how he had managed to keep a hold on himself. It was all he could do not to punch Richards in his patronising mouth. It was Dave Taylor who had itchy feet, you prick, he snarled in his head. My duff, remember? I gave up being Dave Taylor six months ago. Instead he swallowed his beer and bit his tongue. Afterwards he didn't know if it was the habit of silence that kept him from speaking or just that he knew it wasn't true.

When the job came up at GenSync he jumped at it. John McLeod, who had started the company, was ex-Special Branch. West Midlands, so their paths had never crossed, but for more than fifteen years Mac had run a team of UCOs in the animal rights movement. GenSync Risk Management was his bid for a profitable retirement. The company offered corporate security crisis risk management solutions, which in English meant spying for hire. There had always been a flow of information between the police and big business but, as the internet flourished and the potential for disruption grew, vulnerable sectors were crying out for more. Boards flinched at the corporate sabotage, the ugly news footage, the persistent harassment of senior executives. They wanted protection. They wanted security audits of vulnerable premises and advice on anti-protest defences. They wanted future-proof intelligence, in-depth risk analysis, twenty-four-hour warning systems in case of an emergency. After Shell's nightmare with Brent Spar, they wanted more than anything to safeguard their brand image and, with it, the price of their stock. If activist groups were permitted to take control of the public narrative, they could create a public relations nightmare. GenSync's client list included a pharmaceutical company, an airport authority and a fast-food chain.

It meant moving to Birmingham. The pay was the same and he was walking away from the full police pension, but he and Kim had split by then and Jayden wasn't talking to him and what else was there to keep him? He needed to be out of the force. He couldn't take it any more, the rigid hierarchy, the petty rules, the pride in the uniform. The desk wankers with their procedures and their protocols. The seething shame of being one of them.

He thought about getting out entirely but he didn't know what else he could do. Gardening, maybe, but gardening was a young man's job and the money was lousy. The other UCOs he knew who had quit the police had all struggled to find work. One was a train driver, another an executive chauffeur. A couple did security for events management companies. None of them used their old skills or were paid anything close to what they had made in the police. At GenSync he would be doing a version of his old job. He would also continue to have access to the police databases, to the DVLA and HMRC and mobile phone records and council tax registration and the electoral roll. Eight years on he could still remember the panic that took hold of him when Tess and Mia moved and it was like the power being cut, everything dark, until he found them again in Palmers Green. If he had been a gardener and not a police officer, he might have lost them forever.

At GenSync he ran the environmental desk. Their biggest client by some margin was AED Power, an energy giant with a huge UK business. 9/11 and the war in Iraq had pushed the climate campaigners temporarily out of the spotlight but things were gearing up again. AED had plans for thirty new coal-fired power stations across Europe. They knew they were a target. Officially GenSync was employed on an ad hoc basis to provide information on threats to AED's reputation or safety. In truth the team was on a retainer, its remit to get on the inside track, to report not only the dates and locations of future protests and the tactics proposed by their organisers, but minutes of meetings, confidential briefing documents, computer passwords, bank details, activists' names and addresses. Off-the-record comments made by one activist about another. Personal emails. Anything at all that could give AED an advantage, put them on the front foot.

By Any Means Necessary. He knew the drill.

'This isn't Special Branch,' Mac told him when he started. 'We're a business, you understand me? No police budgets here. So yes, you'll need eyes and ears at public meetings, boots on the ground at the big actions, for sure, but only freelance and only when you can bill it straight on. Day to day, it's all about virtual surveillance. Cheaper, less compromising and, most of the time, frankly, no less reliable than an embedded UCO. Best of all, and much to the aggravation of our old pals still in uniform, for agencies like us it's pretty much a regulation-free zone. Special Branch is dead. Long live the Wild Wild West.'

It was 2004, the year of the Blackwood road protests in south Wales. The next G8 summit was scheduled for Gleneagles and already activists across the country were planning their campaign. The scale of the operation drove organisation online. Private password-activated chatrooms started to spring up to sort everything from catering to compostable toilets. Once you were in and in active contact, you could load a protester up with cookies so precise you could trace pretty much every stroke of their keyboard, but you had to get in the door first. Many of the activists knew one other. They were suspicious of strangers. You could get your email address on a circulation list, no problem, but there was no way they were about to get intimate with anyone who didn't come with a warm body attached.

So they did it the old way, the squad way. Every email address got its own comprehensive legend, created from the bottom up: a family, friends, interests, a job. They trawled overseas networks for redundant accounts and scraped them for images from which they built social media accounts and photo albums and convincingly inexpert websites for house painters and dog walkers and tree surgeons. They set up answering services to respond to enquiries. Raff, his number two, joked that he was seriously considering moonlighting as a window cleaner, that as Micky Griffin he was fighting customers off with a stick.

The dogs, they called them, after a New Yorker cartoon Vijay found and stuck to the bulletin board: a drawing of a dog sitting at a computer and the caption, *On the internet no one knows you're a dog.* He had the team set up a wall of their photos, tagged with their names. He wanted everyone in the room to remember they were real. Over time the dogs' faces grew familiar, their personalities too. Vijay and his team managed the tech, updating profiles and harvesting their data. The rest ran the dogs day to day. He ran a bunch himself. He claimed it kept his hand in but the truth was he loved the work. For a day or two each week, he got to be someone else. He had forgotten how unguarded people could be, the things they said to strangers when they thought they were on their side. When they thought no one else was listening.

In time the technology became more sophisticated. Demand grew and so did his team. New recruits got pretty much the same spiel his old boss at the squad had given him when he was first deployed. Don't be deceived by their media profile, he warned them. Deep in their bleeding hearts these people are anarchists, rabid anti-capitalist fanatics whose violent tactics put lives and livelihoods at risk. These people aren't pushing for policy change, he said. They're out to bring down the state. They're domestic extremists and they're dangerous.

Not that he believed it. Sure, there was a hard core of crazies who wanted to bring the global economy screeching to a halt. But most of them weren't like that. Most of them made a lot of sense. It terrified him, the crazy unsustainable acceleration of human consumption, human destruction, human waste. The protesters' demands might not be easy to meet but they were reasonable. They didn't plant bombs or incite hatred. If anything, they were too cautious, too few of them doing too little. Back in the days of the (dis)organisation he had argued in vain for bigger stunts and disruptions, technical climbers to scale power-plant fences and chimneys, to break into airports and occupy control towers or the roofs of planes, criminal damage that went beyond inconvenience and actually closed shit down. It had driven him up the wall, the effort the (dis)organisation had wasted on actions that they all knew would never change a thing.

He didn't say that to his team at GenSync. He said that organisations like AED had the right to pursue their legitimate business interests without violent disruption from activists, that it was their corporate responsibility to do everything they could to protect their stakeholders, whether they were shareholders or customers or employees. Raff was a believer. He took the protests personally. As for the others, he wasn't sure if they swallowed it or even if they cared. Perhaps for them it was no different to being a window cleaner. Perhaps they went home in the evening and didn't think about any of it until they came back in the next day.

Sometimes he listened to them joking around in the open-plan space outside his little office and he couldn't be sure if the tightness in his chest was anger or envy.

It was late when he finally stuck his head round Mac's door.

'You wanted a word?'

Mac looked up. He didn't smile. 'Right, yes, come in. Drink?'

He shrugged, his arms crossed, waiting for Mac to tell him why he was here. Everyone knew the company was for sale. Cyber security was a boom business and several big security firms were sniffing around, looking to beef up their offering. When Mac sold, and for all his bullshit about being carried out in a box he was going to sell, he was screwed. Despite vague promises over the years about equity and a seat on the board, Mac had never come good. Five years on and he hadn't even agreed to a contractual notice period.

I wouldn't dream of pinning you down, Mac had said lightly when he demanded to know why. I've seen the way you fight when you're boxed in, you're like a bear with a fucking migraine, and his smile had steel running through it.

Mac took a bottle from the cabinet and rummaged for glasses. Outside the July sun was finally setting, a stripe of vivid gold lighting the Beetham Tower like a filament.

'There might be some ice if you want it?' Mac said vaguely, holding out a glass. When he didn't take it, Mac's mouth hardened. Slowly, deliberately, he put the glass down on the desk and walked over to the window, looking out over the city.

'Tony Skinner called me.'

'OK.' He kept his voice casual, concealing his relief. If this was just about Skinner it would go away. Skinner was a bump in the road.

Mac didn't turn around. He went on looking out of the window.

'Don't worry about Skinner. I've got him.'

'Is that so?' Mac said flatly. 'Because that's not the way Skinner sees it.'

'You know what Skinner's like. He gets these dumb-arse fixations. I'll sort it.'

'And how exactly do you plan to do that?'

'We can't cave on this one, Mac. What Skinner's asking for goes way over the line. We're not fucking vigilantes.'

Mac frowned at his glass. 'What Skinner's asking for is a new direction. Fresh eyes.'

'Fresh eyes? Jesus, Mac. What he wants is a team who'll drop their trousers and let him take them up the arse.'

'And?'

'And we're not fucking doing it.'

Mac drained his Scotch. 'Your principles are commendable. They are also entirely irrelevant. AED is our biggest and most profitable client. You won't bend over for him, fine. I'll give him someone who will.'

There wasn't much left to say after that. He walked out of Mac's office and out of the building and along the street towards the canal, faster and faster until his anger streamed out behind him, chalking the darkening air like a vapour trail. When he came back, Mac was gone, his office dark. He went in, not bothering to turn on the light, took the whisky bottle from the cupboard, and sloshed some in a glass. In the dark sky beyond the window a plane's lights winked. Planes always made him think of Jayden. Swallowing the whisky in one gulp, he poured himself another.

There was still a chance, he thought, that Skinner might back down. According to their intel, the protest at AED's Northford power station would go ahead in two weeks. There were plans to scale and occupy the chimneys, to spray slogans, to incapacitate coal conveyors, all the stuff Dave Taylor had pushed the (dis)organisation towards more than a decade ago. The protesters wanted to get arrested. They wanted their day in court, a public platform from which to denounce AED and its catastrophic effect on the environment. In response his team had put forward a programme to disable the threat: newspaper briefings to discredit key activists, injunctions to prevent access, agreements with police that anyone arrested would later be released without charge.

It was a solid plan and Skinner approved it, but afterwards he asked for a word. In his office, the door closed, he said he had been reading about civil rights activism in America in the 1960s. What he found interesting, Skinner said, was that when the state used violence against peaceful black protesters, white moderates supported the blacks. But the moment the protesters themselves turned violent, that support evaporated. Suddenly what those moderates wanted was Nixon, and law and order, and the agitators safely behind bars.

'So here's the question,' Skinner said. 'Why are we focusing on damage limitation when we could get the moderates to support Nixon?'

'Your model doesn't apply here. Climate protesters aren't violent.'

'Maybe not so far, but we both know how it goes. A couple of troublemakers, some petrol bombs, a police car torched. Before you know it, all hell's broken loose.'

Provocateurs, thugs for hire shipped in to kick things off. The more he thought about it the angrier he became. The activists would be unprepared, unarmed, unable to protect themselves. Skinner said nothing directly, he was too canny for that, but he made it pretty fucking clear that the police could be relied upon to stand off long enough for the violence to take hold.

'You want war, go somewhere else,' he told Skinner. And Skinner had gone to Mac.

He staggered a little as he stood up, knocking the receiver from Mac's monster of an executive phone. He didn't put it back. He stared out of the window at the Beetham Tower, neon purple against the brown-black sky. Years ago, when he had first moved up here, his then-girlfriend Heather had come for the weekend and he had taken her there for a drink. Heather worked at Scotland Yard, one of a tiny group of officers there who had kept hold of her soul. For some reason he thought the bar was on the rooftop but it turned out to be on the first floor. The only view was of the offices opposite. The next morning Heather told him it was over. She said she was OK with a relationship that was going nowhere but not if she had to go to Birmingham to get it.

'We had fun,' she said as she kissed him goodbye. 'And nothing is forever, right? That's why they invented martinis. And Gloria Gaynor.'

Perhaps it was the whisky that made the lights of the city slip and streak. Go home, he thought, but instead he went into the team room and sat down at his computer. Nothing is forever. On the wall, shadowy in the darkness, the dogs stared down at him, rows and rows of them. They were what mattered, the officers in the field, them and the kids on their computers, pumping out lines of code. Their stories were the ones that held. He was no one. He had written himself out of the script.

Go home, he told himself again. You're drunk. Nothing good will come of doing anything tonight. The thoughts were clear, they cut cleanly through his brain, but the need was sharper. He opened her page. She had changed her profile picture. In the new one she was sitting on some rocks, the sea bright blue behind her. He knew those rocks. He had sat there himself. Sylvie's beach at the end of the earth. He rubbed his forehead, an ache in his chest as he looked at her, and she looked back steadily, her hair falling over her face.

Mia Campbell. CEO of Haribo. In a complicated relationship with green apple Sour Gold-Bears. Yes, all of them.

The ache spread its fingers, poking the gaps between his ribs. When he found out where she went to school he had to fight the urge to go there. His need to see her pulsed like a second heart inside him but he never went. Schools had security cameras these days and anyway he didn't trust himself to keep his distance. In the photo Mia wore a bikini top and cut-off denim shorts, her pale gawky body caught halfway between childhood and adolescence. Her eyes were very blue. When he zoomed in, he could see the darkness of her eyelashes, the scatter of freckles across the bridge of her nose. He reached out, touching her cheek, and the futility of the gesture made him feel both ridiculous and bereft.

She looked just like Tess.

'So what now, Holly Blue?' he said, though perhaps he didn't say it out loud. He knew Tess must hate him, that she had probably taught Mia to hate him too, but hate was different when it was just an idea, when there was no one real to attach it to. Wasn't it? He was still her father. Surely she thought of him sometimes. Perhaps sometimes she even looked at his photo the way he looked at hers, as if the force of his looking could shock her into life.

'You don't owe anyone anything,' Andy said to him, standing in the bar the squad had paid for. 'You know this. Fuck, I *taught* you this. You don't win by sticking shit out. You win by picking the best exit.'

His bad hand was aching. As he worked his thumb into the palm, a comment appeared underneath Mia's photo. *Nice tan LOL.* Chloe Breslow. No doubt Chloe Breslow would insist it was a joke. He still wanted to send her a message and demand to know why she had to be such a little bitch.

'It's all right, I won't,' he said to Mia's profile picture and she smiled back at him. Her eyes were so blue. It had taken him years to find her. If he left GenSync and the dogs, he would lose her again. He couldn't lose her. He scrolled down her wall, his fingers hovering over the keyboard. He wasn't sure why he hesitated. He knew the rules. Fuck, he had written the rules. Keep it light. Encourage them to talk. Avoid the personal. Don't get into something unless you're sure you know how to get out.

So pretty, he typed. It was the kind of anodyne compliment girls on Facebook scattered like confetti but almost immediately a reply pinged up on his wall.

Awww shucks, thanks Vanessa 🖤

He closed his eyes, letting the warmth of it spread through him. Nothing was forever. Nothing except Mia. His Holly Blue.

16

Tess lay in bed and stared at the ceiling, at the white paper lampshade that gleamed in the grainy darkness like a moon. She felt shrivelled, emptied out, a skin without its snake. And still the voices jostled inside her head, plucking at her: *And what about Mia? You have to think of Mia. I won't lie to a child. Someone has to tell her. Sooner or later, she's going to want answers too.* Except the answers she wanted, the answers Tess wanted to give her, were not the answers Tess had.

Your father's alive.

Your father is not Harold David Taylor.

Your father was not an activist.

Your father stole the identity of a dead child.

I do not know your father's name or his age or his place of birth.

It is likely that your father was a police officer.

It is likely that your father was paid by the state to have sex with me.

I did not consent to sex with a police officer.

Your father raped me.

He was a rapist.

You are the child of rape.

What was it Ivo claimed Oppenheimer said after he watched the detonation of the first atomic bomb, his atomic bomb, in New Mexico? *Now I am become Death, the destroyer of worlds.* Tess stared up at the lampshade moon and in her mind she saw the bomb falling, its apocalypse curled tight inside its smooth grey shell.

Mia will be OK, Nat said, she's got you. But how could Tess protect Mia when the ground she walked on could no longer be trusted, when the heat and the blast knocked her sideways and the walls that held her roof up were nothing but dust?

She had to tell her. She knew that. She had to find a way to tell her, not all at once but piece by piece, so that slowly, inch by inch and edgeways, Mia could find her way towards the truth. It was like Nat said. She had to trust that somehow, together, they would make it through, that Tess would hold Mia steady, that she would be enough. That Mia would be all right.

She just didn't know how to begin.

17

She started at the beginning. A name. If she found his name she would have options. Mia would have options. They could decide together what they wanted to do next.

It was Friday afternoon. The builders had left and the science block was silent behind its blue plastic sheeting. Earlier she and Ruth had taken their coffee outside. They sat on the bench and surveyed the empty playground. To absent fiends, Ruth said, raising her mug. When Ken Rahimi came outside, she told Tess to budge up so he could join them but Tess said she had work to do and went back inside.

Astrid Osman was all over the internet. LinkedIn, Twitter, Facebook, shaking hands and making speeches and marching in the rain. Tess looked at a photo of her at the Blackheath Climate Camp beside a banner that read **ECO NOT EGO** and underneath, in green type: *To all of you who have lost patience with the government and big business, who can take no more denial and delay, join us. Climate change is a global emergency. We must act now.* Behind her there were hay bales and tents and protesters in hoodies and, in the distance, against a grey sky, the glittering glass towers of Canary Wharf.

The printer clattered, spewing out pages. The head insisted on circulating the school's statutory policies in hard copy ahead of the annual review, he said it focused minds. The paper would all end up in landfill, Tess knew, hardly anyone bothered with the recycling bins in school, and the stupid unnecessary waste of it flooded her with shame. On Facebook Astrid was friends with Karen and Jimmy Haynes and at least six or seven others from back then. A new post popped up on her wall, something about a Candlelit Climate Vigil. The 'i's were drawn like candles. Underneath, in the comments, someone had written *'Reality is one of the possibilities I can't afford to ignore': Leonard Cohen*. And under that, someone else had added, *There's a crack, a crack in everything, that's how the light gets in.*

The words were like a familiar perfume, an instant time machine. Inhaling them, Tess was sixteen again and barefoot in Sylvie's kitchen, her mother dead and her father in Paris and Cohen's gravelly voice filling her head.

'Listen,' Sylvie said. 'He is speaking to you.'

'I don't get it,' Tess said, and Sylvie put her arms around her, pulling her close.

'You do,' she said. 'Listen again,' and for the rest of that summer Tess listened as Leonard sang to her about brokenness, his bleak voice somehow, miraculously, still shot through with hope. *Ring the bells that still can ring. Forget your perfect offering.*

After that, when Tess was back in London and at school, Sylvie often sent her cassettes, recordings of songs and poems she wanted Tess to know, and in between her own voice, warm and rough with cigarettes, explaining to Tess what to listen for, how to hear. Tess loved those tapes. She felt like Sylvie was fitting the pieces of her together, like she was showing Tess how to be herself. It wasn't till much later that she wondered if Sylvie might just have been trying to make her into the person Sylvie wanted her to be. And when she refused to be that person, when she defied Sylvie, Sylvie cut her out. Except perhaps that wasn't true. Perhaps it had been the other way around.

'Mightn't you be happier,' Ruth asked her once, 'if you didn't run away every time someone tried to get close to you?'

A message pinged on her screen. Astrid had just reposted the Candlelit Climate Vigil graphic, this time with *SEE YOU TOMORROW!* written across it in capital letters.

The door to the outer office banged. Hurriedly shutting down her screen, Tess took the still-warm stack of papers off the printer and began to staple them together.

Policy and procedures: staff discipline, conduct and grievance
Policy and procedures: allegations of abuse against staff
Policy and procedures: safeguarding and child protection
The words struck Tess like an axe, splitting her in two.

'It's modern-day slavery.'

Shireen stood in the doorway. She was wearing a tight-fitting leopard-print skirt and gold stilettos. Gold bangles jingled on her wrists.

'I'm serious. What kind of psychopath makes their assistant come in at five o'clock on a flipping Friday, a Friday by the way which they explicitly arranged to have off, just to email them some bloody documents? The man's a maniac.' Tess waited for her to go back to her desk but she went on standing there, working an antibacterial wipe into the gaps between her fingers. 'So go on then, what wild and crazy plans do you have for the weekend?'

'None yet. But Mia's sleeping over with a friend tomorrow, so . . . '

Shireen looked at her, bugging her eyes. 'So it's Benson-time.'

'Right, a date with my imaginary boyfriend. No, actually I was thinking of going for a drink with an old friend. You don't know any bars near Trafalgar Square, do you?'

'Sugarpops, you know I do. Now let's see . . . '

Just a drink, Tess thought, as Shireen tapped at her phone. She could message Astrid, tell her she wanted to get involved again. She would say she had some ideas, that she would love to buy her a drink and catch up. Half an hour tops, if she could spare it. Or thirty seconds. The question required only a two-word answer.

Whose name was on the bank card in his jacket, Astrid? Tell me the name.

'I've texted you some suggestions,' Shireen said. 'The last one's my top pick. Oh, and check out this evening's dish of the day.' She turned the phone round so Tess could see the screen. 'No touching, thank you. But ain't he a booty beauty?'

Shireen was a dedicated user of online dating sites and went out conscientiously every Friday and Saturday night, almost always with a different guy. Tess supposed she had sex with some of them, though she couldn't imagine the protocols. Perhaps they sold full-body antibacterial wipes online. The man on Shireen's screen had a leopard crouched on his bicep. Tess nodded at her skirt.

'Dressed to match,' she said. 'I like it.'

'Grrr,' Shireen growled, clawing the air with her nails. 'And I'm feline good. Call Benson. Get yourself a load of his tattoos.'

'Bye, Shir.'

'I'm serious. Call him. It shouldn't be me having all the fun.'

Tess was halfway across the playground when she saw Ken Rahimi and a woman in a sari talking by the gate. The woman had her back to Tess but it was clear that she was agitated. She gesticulated angrily at Ken, her fingers raking the air. Tess hesitated. She had no desire to intrude on a confidential conversation, less still to be stuck with Ken for the walk home. The woman threw her hands up and stalked away. Ken stood for a moment, his hands in his pockets. Then he too walked away.

Tess waited until he was out of sight before slipping through the gate.

'Tess?'

She turned. The woman in the sari waved her phone. It was Zenab Nazeer, Yaz's mum.

'That's so strange,' Zenab said. 'I was literally just about to call you.'

'Oh?'

'It's about Rashad. I tried talking to your Mr Rahimi but he wouldn't listen. Said he couldn't discuss someone else's child, as if Rashad isn't as good as a son to me.'

He's not my Mr Rahimi, Tess wanted to say. Instead she shrugged. 'He's right, I'm afraid. The rules are very clear.'

'And the rules that protect my nephew, where are they?' Zenab retorted. 'This club Rashad goes to, the one your Mr Rahimi recommended, the one you yourself told us was so great, are you aware that it is paid for by the government? That the police come there all the time, that they are spying on the boys?'

Tess sighed, rubbing her forehead. The school had referred Rashad to a local youth programme when it became clear that he had behavioural issues, that he struggled to control his temper. The club ran a regular evening programme for boys at risk of exclusion. Zenab's brother, Rashad's father, had supported the idea. So had Zenab.

'I'm pretty sure no one is spying on anyone,' she said wearily. 'I told you the club was great because it is. We send lots of kids there.'

'No. You send only the Muslim ones. The ones you think are trouble.'

'We send Muslim boys because it's a Muslim club, because that's why Shaf and Adeel set it up in the first place, to help boys from their community. You told me yourself that you thought it was helping, that Rashad was settling down, doing better at school.'

'And he was, until he got in a fight with a white boy who told him to his face that he must be a terrorist because all the boys at that club are terrorists, that's why they are there, so the police can spy on them. Rashad was arrested, Tess. He was cautioned. Now he is angrier than ever. He has done nothing and now suddenly he is a terrorist? How can that be right?'

'It's not, of course it's not, but Rashad has a temper, we both know that. Isn't it possible that this boy was just winding him up, pushing him for a reaction?'

'No. Because Rashad knows the boy is right. He has seen it with his own eyes, policemen hanging around the club, asking questions, taking away papers. Can you explain that?'

'No, but Shaf or Adeel probably could. Did Rashad even ask them?'

'Why are you defending them, Tess?' Zenab demanded. 'Why are you on their side?'

'I'm not on anyone's side. But Rashad lashing out doesn't help. It never has.'

Zenab bowed her head, her hands palm to palm against her lips as though she was praying. When she looked up, her eyes were fierce with fear. 'My nephew caused some trouble at school. If he was a white boy they would not send him to a club like this one, but Rashad? In their minds he is already making the bomb.'

'Zenab, I really don't—'

'How can we protect him when they have already decided he is guilty? How are we supposed to keep him safe?'

Tess promised Zenab she would talk to Ken Rahimi. As they walked back together towards Hampden Way, she thought about Rashad Haq, his belligerent swagger and reflexive resistance to authority. He was exactly the type to take a half-baked conspiracy theory and swallow it whole. Two weeks ago she would most likely have dismissed Zenab's accusations as absurd, but now? She glanced sideways at Zenab, at her rigid back and pinched lips, and she wanted to hug her close. Not just for Zenab but for herself.

At the corner where their routes diverged, she stopped. Cars roared by them, sunlight flaring from glass and metal. The warm air was acrid with exhaust fumes. Zenab raised a corner of her scarf, covering her nose and mouth.

'I'll call you, OK?' Tess said. 'And look, Zenab, if it's too much, Mia doesn't have to stay over tomorrow. It's not like there won't be other chances.'

Zenab frowned. 'Mia is staying over with us tomorrow?'

'You didn't know? I'm sorry, I assumed – from what Mia said, it sounded all arranged.'

'Oh, I am sure it is. Between the two of them. My daughter doesn't always like to tell me her business. Even when it is also my business.'

'I know what you mean.'

A huge lorry with wheels as tall as they were thundered past them, swallowing them up inside its noise, its clattering dust.

'She is welcome, of course,' Zenab said when it had passed. 'I am happy she is coming. That they have made up. Mia is a good friend to Yazmeen.'

'I didn't know they had fallen out.'

'Oh yes. We haven't seen Mia all week, not since she came round the day after Yazmeen slept over at yours, when was that, last Saturday? Still, it was obviously nothing to worry about. If they are arranging sleepovers, they must be friends again. Look, I have to go. I'll see you, OK? And we'll see Mia tomorrow.'

The sun caught the gauzy fabric of Zenab's scarf as she hurried away, lighting it like a flame. Tess stared at the roaring river of traffic, the grimy buildings shimmering in the oily air like reflections of themselves. The choke of the exhaust fumes made it hard to breathe. She thought of Mia slipping past her on the stairs, disappearing into her bedroom or already halfway out of the house. I'm meeting Yaz, Mum, we're going to the park. Yaz came over while you were at work. Yeah, Yaz and me hung out at hers.

She should be angry, Tess knew she should be angry, but all she felt was a kind of vertigo. She thought of the platform lurching and creaking in the tree at Snelsmore Common, the gasp of the ropes as they tautened. Don't look down.

Slowly, dizzily, she walked home.

18

'So I bumped into Zenab outside school this afternoon.' Tess picked at her pizza crust, her eyes on her plate. 'She seemed surprised about you staying over tomorrow.'

Mia's stomach pitched. Carefully she drank some water and put the glass back on the table. 'That's weird. Yaz said it was OK.'

'She also thanked me for having Yaz to stay over last Saturday.'

Mia was silent.

'Why would Yaz tell her mother she was here when she wasn't?'

'I don't know.'

'The truth, Mia.'

'That is the truth,' Mia said fiercely. 'Yaz never even told me she'd said that. I found out by mistake.'

'So where was she really, when her mum thought she was here?'

'She wouldn't say.' Mia glared at her mother, Yaz's betrayal fresh and hot inside her. 'So does she know now, Yaz's mum, I mean, about her not being here, did you tell her?'

There was another silence.

'No,' Tess said at last. 'Not yet.'

Mia looked down at her plate, the pizza crusts like thin-lipped smiles, smeared with tomato sauce. She couldn't make a mistake, not now, or all her planning, all her work on the butterfly wings, would be for nothing.

'Zenab also told me you and Yaz haven't seen each other since last weekend,' Tess said. 'Which means that every time you told me you were with her you were lying.'

A line from *Drake and Josh* flashed up in Mia's head: *Are you calling me a liar? Well, I ain't calling you a truther.* There was a difference, though, between lying and not telling the whole exact truth. Her mum knew that better than anyone.

'I tried to see her,' she said. 'I wanted to. I went to her house but ...'

'Mia, you can't lie to me about where you are! You're twelve years old. What if something happened?'

Mia stared at her plate and didn't answer.

'So where were you, when you were supposed to be with Yaz?'

'I don't know. Walking around.'

Tess covered her mouth with her hands. Mia wasn't sure if she was furious or about to burst into tears. 'Mee, for God's sake! Why didn't you say something? Why didn't you tell me?'

'I wanted to. It's just, I don't know, recently whenever I tried – it's like you're not even here.'

'What do you mean, not here? I'm here the whole bloody time, I'm always here!'

'No, you're not. Not properly. Not since we got back.'

Her mum opened her mouth to protest. Then she closed it. When Mia looked at her again she was staring at the table.

'You're right,' she said quietly. 'You're right, I'm sorry.'

'It's OK.'

'No. It's not.'

Mia hesitated. Then, slipping out of her chair, she went round to her mum's side of the table. Tess put her arms around her, hugging her close. Mia hugged her back. She knew better than to mention the sleepover now. She would message Yaz later, tell her to tell her mum that Mia was coming. That way, if Tess called, and she probably would now, it would all be OK. Tess squeezed her tighter, squashing the air out of her body. Mia thought of the song her mum used to sing to her. We're all we need, me and you, us two.

'You know, there's something I meant to tell you,' Tess said. 'Sylvie left you some money in her will. Three thousand euros, that's almost £3,000. To use for exploration and adventure.'

'Are you serious? No way.'

'Way.' Tess smiled. 'I mean, I don't think you should have it till you're a bit older, but . . . '

'Cool. That's – that's amazing.' Mia let her mum hug her a bit longer, then gently pulled away. 'Sorry, but is it OK if I go upstairs now?'

Tess nodded. She didn't say anything about clearing up. Mia picked up her plate and glass anyway and put them on the counter by the dishwasher.

'Thanks for the pizza,' she said, and fled.

Upstairs she messaged Yaz: **u need 2 tell ur mum im staying over at urs 2moro**. She pressed send, watching the text swallow itself up into a speech bubble. A moment later she typed again: **2moro u can say i cancelled but not b4 6 earliest ok**. And again: **that way we r even**. Her thoughts like sour burps, belched up from her brain. She dropped the phone on her bed, then picked it up again: **do this rite or im telling ur mum**. Her thumb hovered over the send button. Then quickly she deleted it. She hated Yaz, she hated her more than she had ever hated anyone, but she couldn't threaten her like that, and anyway she didn't need to. Yaz already knew.

The wings were in a black bin bag under her bed. If her mum saw the bin bag she would say it was something for Yaz. Her mum might be curious but she wouldn't ask to see. She said it was important to respect each other's privacy. Knotting the handles, Mia pushed the bin bag back out of sight and took her backpack from its hiding place in her cupboard. Unzipping it, she checked again that everything was there: black school swimsuit, black leggings, black plimsolls. A candle, one of the tall white ones her mum kept in the top cupboard and never used, and a circle Mia had cut out of cardboard to put the candle through, like they did at the Christmas carol service, to keep the melting wax from burning her fingers. The box of face paints with two brushes, one thick and one thin, and the square of sponge her mum used to apply the base. Tess had painted Mia's face all the time when she was little, for dressing-up days at school and at her birthday parties but also just for fun. Help, help, Mia, there's a tiger in the house, Tess would cry, and Mia would growl and squeal and squirm into her arms, torn between delight at fooling her and the fear that Tess didn't recognise her, that she no longer knew who she was.

Mia zipped the backpack and put it back in the cupboard. After that she didn't know what else to do, so she took the cookbook from its hiding place and lay down on her bed. She wished it was tomorrow already. The closer it got the more her certainty seemed to rub away. What if they refused to let her join the vigil because she didn't have an adult with her? What if it turned out Astrid hadn't come or wouldn't talk to her? There were so many things that could go wrong.

Mia had never been out by herself at midnight. She wasn't frightened, not really. Trafalgar Square was always busy, even at night, and eco-activists weren't exactly the kind of people who abducted children or mugged them for their phones. It was perfectly safe. She still wished she had someone to go with. Maybe Yaz would have been the wrong person; she wouldn't have taken it seriously enough or even understood what they were doing there, not properly, but at least they would have been in it together. Mia sighed, shaking the thought out of her head. She was going to do it whatever, she had to. She had made up her mind. It was just an awful lot of responsibility to carry by yourself.

Turning onto her side, Mia hugged the cookbook against her belly. She had taken it down to the kitchen, she thought her mum would recognise it, but if she did she didn't say so. The photos of her dad were inside it, and the folded-up list she had made the night before when she couldn't sleep. Mia didn't need to look at the paper to remember what was written on it.

Why did he leave before I was born?

Do you have any photos or anything at all that once belonged to him?

Did he ever talk about me?

Perhaps when she was older, with the money Sylvie had left her, she could go to Greece, to the place where he died.

Tell me every single thing you remember about him, from the beginning.

Tess stacked the dirty plates in the dishwasher. She put what was left of the salad in the fridge and wiped the counters and folded the empty pizza box so it fitted in the recycling bin. She rinsed out the water jug. She moved slowly, mindlessly, like one of those robot vacuum cleaners advertised on TV. The robots were programmed so that, when they were finished, they returned to the socket automatically to recharge. Mia was in the bathroom. Tess heard the toilet flush, then the high-pitched shriek of the shower pump.

There was a bottle of white wine in the fridge. Tess poured herself a glass and took a gulp. A second and the glass was half empty. She topped it up, leaning against the stove.

It bewildered her now, how she had ever thought she would be able to do this. It hadn't even started yet and already she was getting it wrong. She should have been tougher with Mia about the lying, she knew that, she should have made it clear that trust was something to be earned, but how could she? How could she say those words and not choke on her own hypocrisy?

She drank more wine. She thought of the physicist on the radio talking in his calm voice about dark energy, the way it grew stronger and faster the more space it opened up. The idea of all that powerful emptiness made her want to weep. She refilled her glass. Behind her, behind the wall, water gurgled noisily in the downpipe. She thought of the bathroom fogged with steam, Mia softening like soap, dissolving to a sliver as she slipped away from her and down the drain.

Her phone rang. Zenab. Tess drained her glass. She didn't answer it. When she touched her screen Mia grinned up at her before a voicemail notification masked her face. There was a new text message too. Astrid Osman.

Wow, Tess Campbell, quite the surprise to hear from you of all people. It's been a long time. Shocked to hear you're back in touch with Nat (& Karen?) & v curious indeed to hear what you have to say. 9pm Compton Liquor. Don't be late. AO

Mia lay on her bed in her pyjamas, looking at her Facebook wall. Yaz had liked the dead leaf butterfly video. She hadn't commented; the only comments were from a couple of girls in their class who no one was really friends with and who always commented on everything, but she had liked it. Surely that meant something. Mia had only posted the video an hour ago. She twisted over so that she was lying on her front, her elbows hard against the tingle in her chest, and opened messages. Still no reply. Her messages clustered one on top of the other, filling her side of the screen.

I mean, seriously. You're like my fucking stalker.

It wasn't stalking when you didn't expect a reply, Mia retorted in her head, when all you were doing was making things quits. She opened the video of the dead leaf butterfly, watching as it quivered on the sandy ground, brown and dry and shrivelled, and then suddenly opened its wings, a blaze of sapphire and gold. There were other animals that were brilliant at camouflage like stick insects and chameleons, she had seen videos of chameleons on YouTube, but all they did was blend in, make themselves invisible. They weren't like the dead leaf butterfly. They didn't have a secret self hidden inside them.

Her mum tapped on the door. Mia slipped the photo of her dad under her pillow.

'Yeah?'

There was a pause. The door handle turned in its fitting.

'Mee, can you unlock the door?'

When Mia opened the door, her mum was standing closer than she expected. She smelled of wine. Mia stepped backwards, wrinkling her nose. 'Are you drunk?'

'What? Of course I'm not drunk. Come here.' She tried to pull Mia into a hug. Mia squirmed away.

'You smell like you're drunk.'

'I've had one glass of wine, thank you, Mrs Killjoy.'

Mrs Killjoy was the name Grandpa Ivo teased Mia with when she was little and disapproving, only in her mum's mouth it didn't sound like teasing. Mia scowled. She had forgotten how horrible it was when her mum got drunk. It hadn't happened for a long time.

'Go to bed, Mum,' she said.

'You're not going to say good night?' Tess's face was creased, her eyes pulling downwards at the edges, her mouth too, like they were too heavy for her skin.

'Good night,' Mia said fiercely. She got into bed and pulled the duvet over her head.

'Sleep tight,' her mum said at last. She sounded defeated. Mia waited till she heard the click of the door closing, then got up, locked the door, and picked up her phone. Phones were like the wardrobe in the Narnia books, Yaz said once, only better because you weren't stuck with the White Witch and eternal winter, you could go anywhere you wanted, anywhere at all.

Mia rubbed her eyes roughly, wiping her nose on her pyjama sleeve. Vanessa Morales had commented on her dead butterfly. *WOW!!* in capitals. Mia hesitated. *ikr,* she replied. There was a pause, then Vanessa's reply. *u seen this?*

Mia clicked on the link. A huge tree covered all over in butterflies, hanging down in thick tassels, overlapping one another like scales, layers and layers of them, their orange wings patterned with black and white, like some vast and elaborate dress. As Mia watched they all rose up together, exploding upwards in an orange butterfly firework, filling the sky. Mia gaped. *omg,* she replied.

<3, Vanessa answered.

Mia watched the video again. It was even more incredible the second time. She tried to think of something to say to Vanessa in return but it felt awkward, like the heart marked the end of the conversation. She wondered where Vanessa lived, if she was somewhere close by. In her profile picture she was laughing, her dog licking her face, it was hard to see what she looked like. Her pink hoodie looked just like the one Mia had. Perhaps they had sat on the upper deck of the same bus or queued in the same corner shop after school. Perhaps if Mia looked out of her window she could see Vanessa's house, the light in her bedroom window.

It was getting late. Mia touched her phone screen. Her dad laughed up at her.

'Good night, Dad,' she said softly. She wished he could see the wings she had made but he didn't look sideways towards the other photos on the screen. He looked straight at her, laughing and laughing like nothing could ever go wrong.

Quickly, before she could regret it, she opened Facebook Chat.

Clicking on the two best photos, one wide and one close up of the eyespots, she attached them to a message.

butterfly envy, she typed and pressed send. Then, before Vanessa could reply, she shoved her phone under her pillow. Already, perhaps, somewhere under the same brown north London sky, Vanessa was looking at her wings. Mia hugged the duvet around herself and tried not to wonder what she was thinking. It was scary, stupid even, to take a chance like that. What if Vanessa thought she was weird or pushy or totally lame? What if Astrid Osman thought that too? What if she took one look at Mia in her stupid butterfly costume and told her to get lost? What if all of it was for nothing?

Faced with a predator, the peacock butterfly didn't just show its eyespots. It made a hissing noise. The hissing was aggressive enough to scare off rats.

Scrambling out of bed, Mia dragged the wings out from their hiding place and, pulling off the bin bag, propped them up against the wall. She stared at them for a long time after she had switched off the light, watching as they took shape in the darkness, the spots resolving themselves into eyes that held hers.

Somewhere in the distance a dog was barking. She hoped it was afraid.

Under her pillow, her phone buzzed.

19

He sat in the car, windows down, working himself up to go in. A one-storey building of yellowish brick with dark-stained window frames and a low tiled roof, Orchard Court was flanked on both sides by the neat blank houses of the modern estate. A narrow strip of terrace at the front of the building was marked off from the car park by a line of desiccated dwarf conifers in wooden planters and two dusty stands of pampas grass. There were benches on the terrace, not that he had ever seen anyone sit there. A single spindly cherry tree stuck out of a round brick-walled bed in the middle of the car park. It looked like a stick in a sandcastle.

Back when he created his legend he'd located his nan's care home in Morecambe Bay. She needed to be far away, too far for anyone to suggest visiting, and Lancashire made sense. It pleased him to settle her in a deckchair in the sunshine, looking across the sweep of the sea to the mountains. Back then she still lived in Hillingdon, in the terraced house where he and his brother had spent much of their childhoods. He still missed it sometimes, the sound of the planes going over, the promise of them, like the world was bigger than you could ever imagine. Eileen lived alone and he worried about her. When Jayden was born he had tried to persuade her to move closer to them but she refused even to think of it.

'Why would I want to be moving at my age?' she said. 'This is my home.'

She had been the one steady thing in their lives, him and Paul. That part of his legend was true. It was one of the first bits of tradecraft they taught you in the squad: undercover, what mattered wasn't the facts. It was the feelings. If in your duff life you were going to claim an abusive father or a mum who had died of cancer or a disabled sibling, you couldn't rely on faking it. You would meet people who knew that pain, who had lived through it, and you needed to know it too, really know it, in the bone. His own father was never violent but he liked drinking and fucking other men's wives. When he finally left, his mum was a mess, pills and booze and never any food in the house, wild rages followed by weepy declarations of remorse. Then she met Geoff and promptly had two kids with him. Geoff only hit him and Paul at the beginning, until they got bigger than him, but he never stopped telling them they would never amount to anything. It wasn't exactly a leap, then, for him to imagine himself into Dave Taylor's skin, to inhabit his stubborn self-reliance, his fury and his fear.

His nan's illness was the only stretch. He had never known anyone with dementia. He borrowed that from a mate, a bloke he had trained with at Hendon, whose Polish grandma kept slipping back to Łodz before the war, querulously demanding to know if Jan had chopped the wood yet or tended to the horse. It was impossible to imagine Eileen like that, not knowing what was going on. Eileen had never let him and Paul get away with anything. When he asked her if he could have her brass carriage clock, that he needed it for work, she gave it to him, but only after she had told him most people had the nous to come up with a better excuse and the manners to wait till someone was dead.

He had been out of the squad five years when Eileen's neighbour called to say he had found her stranded on a traffic island on Long Lane, clutching the metal railing like she was afraid of falling in. She didn't know where she was or how to get home. He told the neighbour he would come straight away. Then he put down the phone and cried. It was stupid but he had the weirdest feeling that it was his fault, that somehow as he turned himself into Dave Taylor, as that became the person he was, he had turned her into Dave Taylor's nan. That the Alzheimer's was because of him.

She managed at home for a while but, two years later, when she could no longer be relied upon to remember to get dressed or eat meals or use the toilet, they had moved her in here. Paul paid the top-up fees. It was the least he could do, Paul said, his synthetic Aussie lilt turning the sentence into a question, and he wanted to snap back that it was, it was the absolutely fucking least, but he remembered the warning look his nan used to shoot him when they fought, and he said nothing. The deal worked well enough. Paul paid the bills and he paid the weekly visits, bringing flowers from the community garden and boxes of her favourite After Eight chocolates. Paul had gone to Brisbane two weeks before his twentieth birthday and never come back. He had a wife and three children and a business selling air conditioning. The pictures of his house on Facebook looked like something from a magazine.

The sun burned through the windscreen. The sweet peas he had picked that morning were already wilting. He sighed, gripping the steering wheel. Then, throwing open the car door, he went in.

She had been here for five years. It still hit him every time, how much it resembled the place he had imagined in Morecambe Bay: the blond wood veneer of the reception desk with its metal skirting, the wiry blue carpet tiles, the flowery curtains and the flowery coffee mugs and the flowery prints on the wall. The artificial ferns in their rattan baskets. The signs (No Smoking, No Unauthorised Access, Fire Exit Keep Closed) that ensured no one would ever really think of it as home. All of it, just the way he had described it in his legend. As though his legend made it happen.

'Sonya's asking if you could just give them a few minutes,' the woman at reception said brightly. Sonya was his nan's main carer. 'Perhaps you'd like to wait on the patio?'

On the patio the two tables with their flimsy umbrellas were already occupied. He appropriated a couple of white plastic chairs and tucked them into a narrow slice of shade by the wall. He never usually came on a weekday but he had called in sick this morning, the second day in a row. He couldn't face Mac, not yet, not until he'd decided what he was going to do next. It played in his head on a loop, Skinner's bland expression as he talked of petrol bombs, the breeziness in his voice run through with steel. He had seen Tess fall the day they stormed Upper Street, the terror on her face as the riot police knocked her to the ground, and suddenly he was filled with a furious rage not just at Skinner's indifference but his unquestioning certainty that, no matter the damage, he was always and inexorably on the side of righteousness.

At the table next to him a shrivelled-up old woman huddled in a wheelchair while her visitor, her daughter maybe, talked loudly about a holiday in Cornwall. He clasped his fists in his lap and looked out over the garden. You could do something with it, if you gave it some time, got rid of the crappy planters and dug some proper beds, but there was no one here who cared enough to bother. By the fence, where the grass grew long, nettles were flowering. If he was closer, perhaps he would see the tiny tents that the red admiral caterpillars made to conceal themselves, the nettle leaves folded edge to edge and sealed with silk. Red admirables they had been called once, two hundred years ago, before people got too lazy for four syllables. Or in Latin, *Vanessa atalanta*.

He had not looked at his phone all morning, had made a point of not doing so, but his hand slid into his pocket now, finding its corner with his thumb. He could see Mia's wings, every time he closed his eyes they glistened in the darkness, their eyes gazing back at him. *Butterfly envy*. Tess had been the same way, the things she said casually, like he was a peach she split open to take out the stone.

He could still feel it in the pit of his stomach, the shock that went through him when he realised she had messaged him directly. At work they called it the breakthrough, that moment when a dog moved from open platforms to private chat, from the general to the personal. The rush of it could make you careless, it was easy to come back too hard, so he did what he trained his teams to do, he followed the protocol. He waited an hour before replying and, when he did, he kept his message scrupulously generic, a cookie-cutter compliment and some exclamation marks, nothing more. It was late, he thought she would have gone to bed, but she replied straight away. Like she had been waiting for him. He told himself to close it down, to sign off with something friendly and final – **gotta go, ttyl!!** – but he couldn't do it. To know she was there, not just somewhere in the ether but really there, in real time – it felt unreal, a wonderful impossible mistake. He wanted to put his hand to his screen the way visitors reached out to prisoners in movies, their palms meeting against the Plexiglas. He knew it couldn't last. So he messaged her back and she answered and suddenly it was one in the morning and their conversation was forty messages long.

He slid his phone from his pocket, cradling it in his palm. Last night, when he finally went to bed, he had deleted the app. He didn't trust himself to stay away from it. But before he deleted it he took screenshots of the chat. He liked the way they looked, her messages slotted into his. **the wings r 4 a climate march**, one said. And underneath, **not sure itll change anything but?** The question mark brought a lump to his throat. All these years and she was still Dave Taylor's girl. She had her mother's eyes and her father's activist heart beating in her chest. He looked again at the photos of her wings. She had sent him a close-up of one of the eyespots. He touched the screen, enlarging it. She was good, he thought, the pride leaping in him. The way the paint caught the light, the gleam of it—

And then he saw it. The gleam was not a gleam of light. It was a skull. It grinned at him, its tiny empty eye sockets fixing him with the same intensity as the eyespot itself. She knows, he thought, panic clawing his throat. She is telling me she knows.

A beat and then it was gone. He rubbed his forehead, embarrassed at his foolishness. The skulls meant nothing. They were a flourish, a teenager's stab at profundity. Of course she didn't know. How could she? He had given nothing away. In all of her messages there was not one word to indicate that this was a challenge or a warning. It was the stress of the last two days finally getting to him, that was all. He had forgotten how it took you, the fear. Sweating on the inside, Andy used to call it, that heart-stopping moment when you were sure they had you cornered. The meeting when Jimmy Haynes announced out of the blue and in front of everyone that he had proof that one of the people in the room was an infiltrator. The day he walked into a lobby in Liverpool and found Astrid staring at Kim's bank card. The moments every officer in the squad knew to be prepared for, when all those interrogations and rehearsals kicked in, but which still struck you like a sledgehammer when they came, the fear closing down your lungs and your brain, sucking the spit from your mouth.

'Well, this is a nice surprise! You'd better come on through.'

He looked round. Sonya was smiling at him from the doorway. He smiled back. He liked Sonya. She was kind. She teased Eileen but gently, like a daughter.

His nan was sitting in her chair, her eyes closed. She looked smaller and frailer than he remembered, her hair so sparse he could see the blotched skin of her scalp. The room smelled stale. He fiddled with the window but it had a special safety latch, it only opened a crack. He looked out at the staff car park, a cluster of cars with silver foil reflectors glaring on their dashboards, a bank of giant plastic wheelie bins. Other rooms had better views but, when he suggested moving her, Sonya said that change was challenging for Eileen and it might be best to leave her be. When he sat down, his chair crackled. He slid his hand into the space between the cushion and the arm. Dozens of shiny black After Eight envelopes, tucked away out of sight.

Eileen opened her eyes.

'Hi, Nan,' he said but she shook her head at him, her tongue working stickily in her mouth.

'Where you been?' she said querulously. 'I need the – the, you know, Stan, the – it's Mother. She's been asking.'

It was a new thing, her calling him Stan. Stanley, his grandfather, Eileen's husband, had been dead for twenty years. In the early days, back when she first came to live at Orchard Court, he had corrected her mistakes. Stan's gone, he said, or you're not at home any more, remember? You live here now. But after several visits Sonya took him to one side. It distressed Eileen, she said gently, to be told she was wrong. It made her feel frightened and ashamed. Sonya knew it was painful but it would be kinder to Eileen if he went along with her, let her believe.

'It's OK,' he said. 'Don't worry, everything's sorted.'

He stayed for an hour. It was not one of her good days. She couldn't stay afloat in the present tense, she kept slipping under. She made him fetch the digital photo frame that Paul had recently sent her from Australia. He forced himself to watch as it cycled through its slideshow. Eileen eyed him sideways and slid the box of chocolates into her lap. He could hear the rustling as she rummaged inside but he pretended not to notice. The pictures all had Paul in them: a portrait of Paul and Michelle on their wedding day morphing into Paul as a toddler with Eileen and again into Paul grinning on a ski slope, a kid in goggles at his side. When had Paul become a person who skied? The photo dissolved and became a picture of Paul and Jayden beside a statue of a giant koala. A sign above them read LONE PINE KOALA SANCTUARY. Jayden who never went anywhere, who hated to fly. Paul had his arm around him. They were both laughing. Jayden in Australia with Paul. Then they were gone and it was only Paul in swimming trunks, driving a boat.

'I know him,' Eileen said, gripping his arm. He turned the device face down, pushing it away from him on the table. 'He comes here.'

'He never comes here, Nan.' He didn't mean it to come out so harshly.

'But I thought . . . ' Her face crumpling, she looked down at the shiny black envelope of chocolate in her hand and dropped it on the floor. He sighed.

'Look, Nan, I'm sorry but I have to go.' He could see the chocolate under her chair but he didn't pick it up. On the table the light from the changing photos leaked from under the edges of the frame. 'I'll see you next week, OK?'

Leaning down he kissed her on the cheek. Eileen caught his hand. Her grip was surprisingly strong.

'She came though,' she said, and her voice was hard. 'Walked right in here.'

'Who came?'

'You know who. That girl of yours, bold as bloody brass. You need to see me, that's what she said. To know I'm real.'

He stared at her. Eileen glared back, like she was daring him to say something, but he didn't. He didn't trust himself. He thought of Mia sitting in the chair where he had sat, her long legs tucked up under her, her hair falling over her face. Her butterfly wings with their skull eyespots glistening on her back. He had never told Eileen about Mia. He could tell her now, show her the picture from France, let the fact of her great-granddaughter stream through her like water through a sieve. She wouldn't remember. He didn't know if he could bear that, that she wouldn't remember.

'But it's me who's real, Stan, me.' His nan's voice rose, agitated, distressed. 'I'm your wife! That girl? She's no one, you hear me? No one at all.'

20

It was a long time since Tess had been in the West End on a Saturday night. It was still light as she walked up Charing Cross Road, the deep blue of the sky bleached pale at the edges, lavender shadows drifting in the spaces between the buildings. Above her the low sun burnished the roofs, turning them gold.

The theatres were quiet, locked up, the dramas inside already halfway towards the interval, but in Soho tables spilled out over the streets and clusters of laughing drinkers crowded the pavements. At Compton Liquor, the bar Shireen had recommended, the plate glass doors were pushed back. Tess looked around at the girls in scarlet lipstick smoking cigarettes and sucking the olives from their martinis. She couldn't see Astrid. Inside she took a stool at the bar and ordered a gin and tonic. The barman slid a coaster in front of her.

'Bombay Sapphire, Tanqueray, Hendricks?'

'Just regular gin's fine. A double please.'

The barman put her drink in front of her. Tess took a gulp, feeling the cold alcohol sliding into her bloodstream, smoothing her edges. That morning, when she had apologised to Mia, Mia had hugged her and told her it was fine.

'It's OK, right, that I'm going to Yaz's?' she said and, when Tess nodded, Mia hugged her again and disappeared into her room. Tess heard the slide of the bolt as it closed. Perhaps, she thought, she should unscrew it. Back when Mia was eight, it seemed reasonable that she should have private space, secrets of her own. It was different at almost thirteen.

'Almonds?'

'Thanks.' She smiled vaguely as the barman placed a silver bowl beside her. Everything was different at almost thirteen.

Astrid was late. Tess checked her phone but there was no message. She should have called Zenab on her way, told her about her conversation with Ken, but she couldn't face it, not tonight, not while Mia was there. There was no way Zenab would take it calmly and that wasn't fair on Mia, on either of the girls. It would be easier for everyone if Zenab and Ken could sort it out between them but she knew already that Ken would never bend the rules. So it would have to be Rashad's father, which Tess worried would only make things worse.

She had been sure Ken would dismiss Rashad's allegations out of hand. Instead he sighed.

'Look, it's tricky,' he said. 'It's true that the club is state-funded, that making money available for initiatives like this one is part of a wider strategy by the government to prevent extremism. So yes, there's a support officer, an ex-copper attached to the council, who comes in and out, signs off expenses, keeps an eye on things. You can call it mutual support or you can call it surveillance but either way it's the price of doing business. Without it the club would have to close and where does that leave kids like Rashad? If he ends up excluded from school, well, you know the stats as well as I do.'

'So Rashad's right, the government is spying on them.'

'I mean, yeah, sort of, but you have to realise, the club has nothing to hide. As you know, it's all about encouraging the kids to make the best of themselves, to take responsibility, programmes the government is fully behind. Programmes the parents of these kids are – or should be – totally behind. OK, so there are compromises, but Shaf and Adeel are very open about that and it doesn't help kids like Rashad to get angry about it. Too many angry young men die early in this country. Too many of them are angry young Muslims.'

Ken's grandfather had come to England from Pakistan in the early 1960s. It was five years before he could afford to bring over his wife and two daughters. Now he was a respected elder at a mosque in Birmingham. At the end of the call Ken said maybe they should go for a pizza sometime and Tess mumbled something noncommittal in return. She knew Ruth would tell her to go. There were much worse men than Ken. There was every possibility that Kendall Rahimi was his real name.

'Tess Campbell, as I live and breathe.'

Tess looked up. Astrid Osman stood beside her. She wore a T-shirt with some kind of logo on it and baggy khaki trousers. Her watch strap glowed, fluorescent green.

'Astrid,' Tess said, slipping off her bar stool. She thought about shaking hands but Astrid just stood there, her hands on her hips, so she smiled awkwardly instead. 'Thanks for coming. How are you?'

'Yeah, all right. Not sure about this place, I've got to say, but ...'

'We can go somewhere else if you want?'

Astrid glanced at her watch and shook her head. 'No time.'

'Well, can I at least get you a drink?'

'OK. A glass of water, thanks. Tap, not bottled.'

'Really? Nothing more exciting?'

'Thanks, but I'll get my thrills elsewhere.'

Not rude, exactly, but not quite a joke either. Tess gestured at a table and told Astrid to sit down. She ordered Astrid's tap water and a second gin and tonic, not because she wanted it so much as for the small satisfaction of defiance. When she returned to the table with the drinks, Astrid was looking at Tess's phone. When she saw Tess's expression she shrugged.

'Just checking you're not recording our conversation.'

Tess took back her phone and sat down. 'Why would I record it?'

Astrid ignored the question. Pulling a Tupperware from her backpack she peeled off the lid. 'We could do it that way,' she said. 'Or we could cut to the chase. We both know this isn't about you rediscovering your eco-credentials, so why am I here?'

'I don't think I—'

'OK then, let me guess,' Astrid interrupted. She took something brown from the Tupperware and put it in her mouth. 'You're going back to full-time corporate espionage and you're looking for a reference?' The same tone again, like she was defying Tess not to get the joke. Tess smiled uncomfortably.

'And don't give me that butter wouldn't melt shit,' Astrid snapped. 'You really think I don't know, that DT didn't tell me everything?'

'I'm sorry?'

'I know all of it, Tess. The car window you left open and Dario Lombardi and GSS and Sir Quentin Brooke and the bonus that paid the deposit on a one-bed flat in Crouch End.' She counted them off on her fingers. 'Or does none of that ring a bell?'

Tess frowned. Dario Lombardi was the infiltrator Dave had confronted at a meeting and kicked out of the movement. GSS was a huge multinational security services company which Tess had only heard of because a Nigerian deportee had recently died on a flight to Lagos with three GSS guards and the story had been in the news. Sir Quentin Brooke was Tess's stepfather. She had no idea how they might connect together.

'In that case let me help you,' Astrid said. 'DT and I – he always knew it was dodgy, the way you joined us out of the blue like that, knowing absolutely nothing. When he found out your stepfather was on the board of GSS, he was devastated. He wanted you kicked out there and then. He'd have done it too. But you were the Butterfly Girl and you were already going behind our backs to the press and we really didn't need that shit, and anyway corporate infiltrators are like cockroaches, aren't they, you can stamp on one but there'll always be another scuttling out from under the skirting. No, better to keep your friends close and your enemies closer. Move in with them if you have to. Everyone needs a useful idiot. We got a kick out of it, actually, most of the time anyway, knowing every drop of misinformation we fed you was being piped pretty much directly and unfiltered straight to the Minister for Transport.'

Tess swallowed some gin and tonic. Her head was swimming. Nothing Astrid said made any sense. The idea that she had been a spy in the pay of her stiff stranger of a stepfather, that he had paid the deposit on Crouch End not because he wanted her off his hands but as a bung from the DfT for services rendered, it wasn't just crazy. It was hilarious.

'So let me get this straight,' Tess said. 'Dave told you I was spying for the government?'

'He told me everything. We had no secrets from each other.'

'Right. So he told you his real name?'

'His name was Harold David Taylor. Harold for his father.'

'Except it wasn't, was it?' Tess took Dee Bourke's letter to Sylvie out of her bag and pushed it across the table. 'You can keep that, it's a photocopy. I've got a copy of the death certificate too if you're interested. I assume you're interested.'

Astrid glanced at the letter and pushed it back. Her face was pinched. Jamming the lid on her Tupperware, she shoved it back in her bag. 'You know what? I don't have to listen to this crap.'

'OK,' Tess said. 'But didn't you ever wonder why you couldn't track him down after he left? How, no matter hard you looked, there wasn't a trace of Harold David Taylor anywhere?'

235

It was a guess, more provocation than certainty, but it hit clean. Astrid froze.

'He said he'd come back,' she said shrilly. 'If you hadn't trapped him by getting pregnant, if he hadn't been terrified of what you might do . . .'

'Is that what he told you?'

'I mean, was it even his? Because Dave was never sure. He said he wouldn't put it past you to lie about it to his face.'

Tess shrugged. To her surprise it didn't hurt. 'He was the one who was lying. Don't you get it? That whole time, it was him, he was the infiltrator. Not Dario, not me. Him.'

'I don't have to listen to this—'

'What was the name on the bank card you found in his pocket, the one he said was mine?'

Astrid stared at her, her backpack hugged against her like a child.

'Look, I get you don't like me,' Tess said. 'If it helps, I don't like you either. But don't you want to know the truth? You obviously looked for him. Wouldn't it be a relief, finally, to know where he went, who he really is?'

'I've told you. I already know who he is.'

'And you're sure about that?'

'I'm certain.'

'Fine. So all this time you knew he was an undercover police officer?'

The words struck Astrid like a punch, knocking the air out of her. It frightened Tess to look at her. It was like looking at herself.

'I'm sorry,' she said quietly. Astrid shuddered, a convulsion going through her like she was about to vomit, then drew herself up. Her cheeks were flushed, twin round spots of red like a cartoon doll.

'Dave was right,' she hissed. 'You're poison. Stay away from me, do you hear? You contact me again and, I swear, I'm taking you all down, you and GSS and the Department of Transport and Sir

Quentin fucking Brooke. You think it could never happen, that people like you are above the law, but you're wrong. You don't think the press wouldn't bite my arm off for a story like yours, the whole stinking system rotten all the way to the top?'

Her chair lurched backwards as she stormed away. In the semi-darkness the crush of drinkers on the pavement merged into a single organism, a giant many-legged monster, barring her way. Then suddenly it swallowed her and she was gone.

Tess sat at the table. She sat there for a long time. She knew it was her fault. Somehow, wilfully, she had blown it. There was no way Astrid would ever talk to her again, no way Tess would ever discover whose name was on that bank card.

It was over. Unless she could magic up five grand, it was over. There was nowhere left to go, no other way of getting to the truth of who he was, the man who had called himself Harold David Taylor, who had told her she turned him upside down and asked her to grow old with him at the end of the earth.

She knew she should feel frustrated with herself, angry even. She knew she had let Mia down. But instead she felt – how did she feel? Not relieved exactly, but quiet and empty and very still, as though the wind had dropped and the stinging, pelting, lashing sandstorm that had pounded her since France, scouring the skin from the inside of her, had finally subsided. It would come back, she knew it would come back, but for now there was only silence and a landscape newly made.

Mia stepped onto the up escalator at Charing Cross station. Her hand was sweaty from carrying the bin bag. On the other side, going down, the escalator was crowded with people, groups of teenagers, couples holding hands, tourists manoeuvring wheelie suitcases, families with kids. Mia felt like she was caught up in a riptide, everyone else riding the waves in to shore while every minute she was being pulled further out to sea. She had to fight the impulse to turn, to run back down, outstripping the steps that kept making and making themselves underneath her feet.

She changed in the public toilets in Trafalgar Square. There was a mirror there, its corners tagged with graffiti, but her hands were shaking and she couldn't get the face paint to go on right. The colours smeared together and the glitter stuck to her fingers. Both the soap dispensers were empty so she had to wipe the mistakes off with wet toilet paper which melted into little lumps when she rubbed it. She had to do her cheeks three times before they looked anything like her mum's in the Butterfly Girl photo. She put on her wings and stared at her reflection. 'Ta-da!' her mum used to say when she was done, lifting Mia up to look at herself in the mirror. The same every time, *ta-da!*, but to Mia it was always new, the shock of the face that looked back at her, the face that suddenly wasn't hers at all.

When she came out it was night, the last of the pale summer light sucked from the sky. She was still too early. She sat on the low stone wall of one of the waterfalls and looked at the lit-up pool, the shifting glint of silver coins on the bottom. The water smelled of chlorine. Leaning down, she trailed her hand through it. When she moved her fingers, bits of glitter flashed in the water like sparks.

People were starting to gather under the street lights outside St Martin-in-the-Fields. Some of them had placards that they leaned on like walking sticks, their messages upside down: **STAND UP FOR PLANET EARTH** and **THE WORLD IS NOT FOR SALE**. They didn't look like the people in the pictures of the Reclaim the Streets protests on the internet. They didn't have bongos or dreadlocks or tattoos, or not that Mia could see. Mostly they looked middle-aged and sensible, like people on a tour of a stately home.

Mia straightened her wings. Slowly, trailing her backpack by its handle, she walked towards the protesters. As she got closer, a woman smiled at her. She had long grey hair and a heavy-looking camera on a strap around her neck.

'Wow, fabulous outfit!' she said, lifting the camera to her eye and adjusting the focus. As the flash burst, some of the other people in the group smiled too and a bony-legged man in a bucket hat gave her a thumbs up.

'Who was it who said that the caterpillar does all the work but the butterfly gets all the publicity?' he asked, laughing at his own joke. Mia looked around at the other groups. She had thought she would know Astrid straight away but she was no longer so sure. Most of the women standing around had greyish hair and glasses. Mia was just working up the courage to ask the woman with the camera when Camera Woman turned away. Stepping out of the group, she touched a smaller woman on the arm.

'What's up?' she murmured. 'Are you OK?'

The other woman had her back to Mia so Mia didn't catch her reply. She was wearing a blue T-shirt with a blue-and-green planet Earth on the back. Camera Woman rubbed Planet Earth's shoulder and handed her a tissue. Planet Earth blew her nose. She was wiping her eyes when she turned and saw Mia staring at her. Mia ducked her head, looking away, but not before she had seen the way Planet Earth's face changed as she saw her, her eyes stretched with shock and something else, something like fear. Not before she had seen that Planet Earth was Astrid Osman.

Mia backed into the shadows. It was like something had passed between them, the shock and the fear were suddenly inside her. When she looked back, Astrid was hurrying up the stairs towards the church, a dark outline against a pale slice of stone where the light spilled out of the open doorway. She had dropped her tissue. It lay forgotten on the pavement, a twisted blur of white.

'Astrid Osman!'

Mia didn't mean to say her name, not like that, out loud. It was like a sneeze almost, something her body needed to get rid of. Astrid turned. So did Camera Woman, and quite a lot of the other people too.

'Ignore her,' Astrid commanded. 'It's just a stunt. A cheap stunt.'

Suddenly Mia saw herself through Astrid Osman's eyes, a child in makeshift fancy dress, a tacky imitation Butterfly Girl, and every part of her shrivelled with embarrassment and shame. She wanted to tear off her rubbish homemade wings and run. She would never be able to face Astrid now, not ever again. She thought of her dad laughing up at her, his hand on the bump that was her. The moment Astrid Osman walked away, the last flimsy thread that tied Mia to him, the real him who real people had known, would be broken.

'Astrid, please,' she begged, her practised lines forgotten. 'I have to speak with you. Please.'

'About the existential threat of global warming?'

'About Dave Taylor.'

Astrid Osman stared at her. Mia felt it again, or an echo of it, a crackle of connection between them. She took a step forward, then another. Astrid Osman shook her head but she didn't stop staring.

'You're the kid,' she said, and there was recognition in the way she said it, like all this time she had known Mia would come. Like she had been waiting for her. Mia felt the earth shifting beneath her, plates grinding as they jolted into place. She nodded. Slowly, carefully, she took another step.

'Oh my God,' Astrid said. 'You poor – how old are you? What kind of monster – a cockroach double act! That woman literally has no shame. None.' Her laugh was sour, sharp with disbelief.

'Keep her out of the photographs or I won't use them, she's not one of us,' she said to Camera Woman, and she walked into the church without looking back.

Tess walked down Wardour Street and into Chinatown. On Gerrard Street plucked rows of ducks hung headless and shiny-red from their ankles in the windows of the restaurants, and the sky was strung with red paper lanterns. Tess looked up at them and she thought of the balloons that sometimes drifted across the sky when she was a little girl, strings trailing as they crested the line of the trees, the grief that opened up in her as they coasted higher and higher, a vanishing dot, as if she was the child who had somehow let them go, and she wondered if it had changed a long time ago without her noticing or whether it was only now that she had stopped thinking of herself as the child in the story and become the balloon.

She didn't want to go home. She kept walking, down Lisle Street, through Leicester Place. In Leicester Square there were jugglers and human statues and a cart selling candy floss and teenagers smoking in huddled groups and a busker with a broken amp playing Leonard Cohen's 'Hallelujah'. Bare-legged girls in six-inch heels queued behind scarlet ropes. Families ate ice creams. Police officers clustered together by their patrol cars, their walkie-talkies crackling. A monumental Shrek grimaced down at her from the giant illuminated billboard of the Odeon cinema. **SHREK 3D, THE FINAL CHAPTER**, it trumpeted. **IT AIN'T OGRE ... TIL IT'S OGRE**. It was a jolt to step out of the neon spill and into the dark tunnel of the side street that led back out on to Charing Cross Road. She skirted the shadowy bulk of the National Portrait Gallery, its black railings pinstriping the darkness, following the curve of the pavement towards Trafalgar Square.

Outside St Martin-in-the-Fields a small crowd had gathered. Some of them had banners. Keeping her distance, her face averted,

Tess crossed the road towards the square. There was hardly anyone there, it was too late for tourists, but the light was dazzling and solid: the gleaming gold façade of the National Gallery, the white-light plumes of the fountains, the blaze of water in the low pools like bubbled glass. Around the perimeter the moving cars drew circles with their lights, loops of white and red. Tess walked down the shallow steps towards Nelson's Column. To her left, a lion gazed down Whitehall towards Big Ben. A street lamp spilled light over its back, picking out the tumbling curls of its mane. Its face was in shadow. She had half turned away when, between its outstretched front paws, something moved. The darkness flickered, a curved scatter of silver like the start of a migraine. She blinked, then turned to look again.

She saw the wings first. They seemed to unfold as she watched, blue-green and glistening, a shimmer at first and then suddenly alive with light. The eyespots pierced her. A hallucination, she thought, or a dream or a slippage in time, the barbed wire of the past tearing a hole in the present. Whatever it was, it didn't frighten her. It was hers, the arch of the forewing, the margin of the hindwing, the pattern of the wing veins, the dark shape of the narrow thorax dissolving into the lion's shadowed head and then abruptly separate, poised on the lip of the plinth. She waited, breath stopped, for it to fly. Instead it turned, its face a smeared jewel, cerulean blue. Tess stared.

'Mia? What the – Mia, is that you?'

The butterfly ducked, tucking herself into the space beneath the lion's open jaws. Tess broke into a run, circling the plinth just as she scrambled to the edge and jumped down. It was Mia. She carried her backpack in one hand, the blue one Tess had given her for Christmas with the furry monkey hanging from the zip. She stumbled a little as she landed, her weight tipped forward as though she meant to make a run for it.

'Mia, come back here!'

It was too late for fear but that didn't stop it pouring through her, fear and rage and exquisite relief. She caught Mia's arm, expecting her to try and twist away, but instead Mia sagged, all the tautness going out of her. Tess wanted to shake her, to demand what on earth she was doing here, a twelve-year-old girl alone in London in the middle of the night, but she didn't. She looked at the wings and the smudged face paint and she knew.

'Christ, Mia,' she said. 'What the hell were you thinking?'

Mia stared at the ground and didn't answer. The light from the street lamp caught in her wings. She looked like she might fly away. She looked like Tess.

'I'm so angry with you right now, Mia. I can't believe you'd do this, that you'd be so – so irresponsible. You could have – anything could have happened. Do you understand me? Do you understand how dangerous this was?' When Mia didn't answer, Tess caught her shoulders, turning her round so that they faced each other. 'Look at me.'

Mia glared briefly up at her mother, then back at the ground. Her jaw was hard.

'You lied to me, Mia. You lied and you put yourself in danger and that's not OK, none of that is even a tiny bit OK.' Tess hesitated, biting her lip. 'But look, I also – I get why you did it, why thought you had to come. You came to see Astrid Osman, didn't you?'

Mia's head jerked up. She eyed her mother warily. Tess thought back to the long drive home from France, the questions she had refused to answer. *The past is real, you know. Why do you always have to make out like none of it ever happened?*

'This is my fault too,' Tess said. She tried to sound calm, authoritative, like she knew what to say, what came next. 'You were right. I should have answered your questions. I should have talked to you about what happened. About your dad.'

'You could talk to me now.'

Inside Tess a flurry of wind eddied, spitting grit. She had never felt so afraid. She took Mia's hand, threading their fingers together. Mia did not pull away. She stood there, her blue face smudged where she had rubbed it, her shining wings gloriously spread.

'Your wings are amazing,' Tess whispered.

'Fucking hell, Mum.'

'OK. You're right. Sorry.'

The grit blew harder, scouring her chest. Whatever was coming, she couldn't stop it now.

21

He drove back to Birmingham too fast but the ache was lodged in him, he couldn't shake it off. He thought of calling Jayden, of Skyping Paul in Australia. Instead he went out, a bar he knew in Digbeth with a roof terrace. Somewhere he could breathe. It was Saturday night, the place was busy. Beyond the glass parapet, the city glittered.

She was with a group of women, dressed up and drinking fancy cocktails. Mid-thirties, he guessed. A birthday, not hers. There were presents in gift bags under one of the chairs. A waitress brought a dessert with a firework in it and a woman in sequins hid her face while they sang. When he went to the parapet to smoke, she came and stood beside him. He offered her a light. A pink cocktail ring on her left hand but no wedding band. Above the neckline of her dress her skin was sprinkled with freckles.

'Tell me you hate birthdays,' she said.

Her name was Nikki. She had a big smile and toned gym bunny arms. She stayed for another drink when the others left. They had babysitters to get home to, she said, early starts. 'Do you have kids?'

'Two. A boy and a girl.' He had never said it aloud before. 'Twenty-one and twelve.'

'So you're married?'

'Not even slightly.'

People were dancing. There were fairy lights in the potted trees and candles in bowls on the tables. Spotlights lit the bottles behind the bar. Moths fluttered in the vertical columns of light, banging their wings against the glass.

'The ghosts of dead butterflies,' she said. 'That was my theory about moths when I was little. Sinister little beggar, I was. Wednesday Addams's missing twin.'

They were playing Leonard Cohen when he kissed her. She smelled familiar, cigarettes and citrus. He pulled her closer, breathing her in. Then and now folding in on themselves, corner to corner. His hand on her back, in her hair.

Later, on the street, he kissed her again. She hailed a cab.

'I could come with you,' he said as she opened the door.

'Or you could call me.' Cadging a pen off the cab driver, she scrawled a number on the back of his hand. 'The old-school way, but then I'm an old-school kind of girl.'

'You know this means I'll never wash again.'

'Right. In that case maybe don't call me after all.'

He smiled. 'You sure you don't want me to see you safely home?'

'What, to protect me from strange men?' She kissed him one last time and, laughing, climbed into the taxi. 'Good night, you. Dream of me.'

He watched her tail lights disappear into the night. Then, crossing the road, he started the long walk home. A couple of cabs passed him with their lights on but he let them go. Away from Digbeth the streets were deserted, shops metal-shuttered. Alcohol and arousal powered his legs, pushing the blood through his veins.

'It's not you,' Heather said dryly when she broke it off. 'It's my crappy taste in men.'

When Astrid presented him with Kim's bank card, he freaked. Not that it showed. A quiet part of his brain spoke to him calmly, slowly, from a great distance. He put his hands over his face. He sighed. It was important she knew how hard it was for him to talk about.

'It was folded inside a sweater in Tess's drawer,' he said at last. 'She told me she found it in the street, that she was going to hand it in, but—'

'But you don't believe her,' Astrid said, and he shook his head.

'I don't know,' he said helplessly. 'I want to believe her but so many things she tells me, they don't add up. I'm so afraid, Astrid. I don't know what to do. What if she has been lying all this time, what if she isn't who she says she is? She's having my baby.'

Astrid put her arms around him.

'It's OK,' she said, and then she started to say something else, something about telling Jimmy, and he had to stop her talking so he kissed her. She looked at him, her eyes round, and then she kissed him back. It was too late after that to regret what he had started. He needed to be sure she would stay silent.

In those last weeks he met with Astrid twice a week in the afternoons, in a flat she borrowed from a friend. He hated himself for fucking her but it wasn't the worst part. He and Astrid had been a couple for two years. Having sex with her again was like watching a film he had seen many times before, any change it might make in him had already happened. The worst part was the things he said to keep himself safe. I don't love her. Perhaps I never loved her. She trapped me. What if the baby isn't mine? It's you, Astrid, it was always you.

A blaze of self-pity flared in him. Andy was right. Those fuckers in Special Branch, they turned you inside out and then they screwed you. No one ever talked about the price you paid, how you sacrificed one life going in and another coming out. That for the rest of forever you would be trapped in the wrong man's body, in the wreckage of the wrong man's life, unable to go backwards, unable to move on, missing your daughter like a limb. Missing your son. Knowing you had betrayed every single person who ever trusted you, and for what? So you could subvert legitimate protest and undermine public faith in the persistent minority of obstinate fuckers who considered it their responsibility to keep the world from eating itself alive? So you could stand trial under a false identity and perjure yourself, the moment someone asked you your name?

'I promise you one thing,' Brian Richards said to him the first time they met. 'When this is over you'll tell me these have been the best years of your life.'

He walked faster, past the mosque. They lit it at night, the dome and the minarets, it looked like something from outer space, like any minute great doors would open in its side and an army of aliens would step out. On top of the minarets crescent moons reclined on their backs, points upwards like they were smiling. Perhaps on the aliens' planet everything was rosy. Too bad for them they had landed on Earth. There was fuck all to smile about here.

And suddenly he knew exactly what he had to do. He wouldn't go for Skinner. Skinner was an arsehole but he wasn't stupid. There was nothing on the record, no proof of any kind that their conversation had ever taken place. If he took it to the wire, it would be a case of his word against Skinner's and Skinner would win. The machine at AED would kick in, GenSync too. Mac wasn't exactly the type to sit by while a disgruntled employee blew up his company and his chance of a home on the Four Oaks estate. The problem with an agency that provided corporate security crisis risk management solutions was that they knew precisely how to neutralise a threat.

But then Skinner wasn't really the problem. He was the thin end of the wedge, the embodiment of the fuckery that was Special Branch and its hidden cabals. Men like Skinner thought the law didn't apply to them, that they could act with impunity, because for the whole of their careers it had been true. Nothing they ordered had been documented so none of it had happened. The citizens who they spied on, whose lives they filed away in secret dossiers, would never know. Questions wouldn't be asked in the Commons because the Commons had no idea there were questions to be asked. The units did not officially exist. There would be no justice until men like him spoke out, until everyone in the country knew that for decades, unregulated and uncontrolled, a rogue squad of spies had been covertly infiltrating politically troublesome organisations across the country, by which, of course, they meant organisations whose politics they didn't like. That, funded by their taxes, undercover police officers had repeatedly lied to activists, subverted legitimate protest, incited violence and resisted arrest. A private police force that deliberately concealed itself from Parliament and the judiciary, run by men whose roles had never been publicly acknowledged but who were now busy profiting from their experiences in the private sector. Men like Skinner and John McLeod.

Bring down the squad and you brought them all down, the whole stinking house of cards.

Of course you had to be careful, play it right. What you needed was a media agent, or so Andy said, one of those Max Clifford types who stepped in to handle the press. Without their protection, you would be eaten alive. Andy had files on his computer, lists of agencies and their clients, the stories they had placed. The fees they had negotiated. Andy had even offered to act as his manager, oversee the whole thing on his behalf. There was a shit ton of money to be made, Andy said, if you knew how.

It wasn't about the money, though, not for him. It was about the truth. About finally holding those bastards to account for the wreckage they left behind them, the bodies they stepped blithely over every day. Having said that, he wouldn't turn down an offer. A wise man didn't jump out of a plane at thirty-six thousand feet without a parachute.

He walked for a long time, until the night sky faded and the dawn crept in, clean and new. He had forgotten how it felt to give a shit. To believe that what you chose to do could change things, that a man really could move mountains. He thought of the first butterfly protest, hundreds of them gathered on their bikes on London Bridge, the music and the crazy colours and the backed-up cab drivers leaning on their horns, and underneath it all the river tumbling and flashing in the sun like it was laughing itself stupid. Tess had cried, the tears streaking the blue and green patterns on her cheeks.

'We did this,' she kept saying. 'Look at what we've done.'

Fuck but he envied her then. He knew it was messed up, he was a UCO for Christ's sake, but he did. Whatever else Tess did, she would always be the Butterfly Girl. He wanted that. To be remembered as someone who mattered, who had made a difference. He had buried that urge for years, along with all the other parts of himself that had no place in his life any more, but perhaps now, more than a decade later, he finally had his chance. If Skinner's past was exposed, if he could get the press to ask enough awkward questions about his secret history, he could bring that fucker down. It wouldn't be the end of AED.

They would go on building coal-fired power stations, belching Olympic-class emissions, but it would hit them where it hurt. They would never again be able to pretend that they were the good guys, greenwashing their filthy laundry, mouthing platitudes about targets while behind their high security fences they pulled the pins from their grenades. Their boardroom wouldn't be full of men like Skinner, playing golf on manicured lawns while the ice shelf melted and the seas rose and the forest fires they had set raged across Australia like the blaze of Hell.

not sure itll change anything but?

He could do it. It wasn't too late. Fuck the Official Secrets Act and loyalty to the squad. He owed it to the British public to tell the truth. He owed it to Mia. If GenSync got caught in the crossfire, well, Mac knew better than anyone that in this business there were always casualties. As for him, he couldn't lie any more. He was so tired of hating himself, of always being on the wrong side.

Once, for a time, he had been a good man. A man who wanted to make the world a little better. If he stepped up to the microphone, if he said that he was sorry, that he regretted everything, that when he left Tess and Mia he lost everything, his identity, his happiness, his sense of purpose, that the work he once thought of as a service to his country had destroyed not just him but everyone who knew him, that he meant to start making amends, could he finally put that man back together? If he brought down Skinner, if he stopped AED in their tracks, if he was the kind of father she could be proud of, the kind of father she deserved, would Mia be listening? Might she start, just a little, to understand?

Outside his flat he stopped. The rising sun spilled over the rooftops and the glass front of the building burned gold. He was filled with a fierce elation. Tipping back his head, he held his arms out wide.

My name is Dave Taylor and I am an activist.

22

My dad's alive.

Mia sat on the toilet, her elbows on her knees. Outside her cubicle, the hand dryer roared. It felt like the noise was coming from inside her head. She pressed her fingers hard into her eye sockets. Her eyeballs pressed back. He wasn't buried or cremated or anything because he didn't die in Greece in a motorbike accident. He didn't die at all. It was a lie. He told everyone his name was Dave Taylor but that was a lie too. Her mum didn't know his real name or where he was now or why he pretended for years and years to be someone else, but she knew he was alive and that, wherever he was and whatever he was called, he was still Mia's dad. His eyes were blue and his teeth were crooked and he was out there somewhere talking and laughing and walking around because he was alive.

I have to tell you something, her mum said when they sat down. The words came out in clumps, like hair. You can ask me anything you want but first you need to let me tell you, OK? She was trying not to cry. They were upstairs in McDonald's at a table by the window. When Mia turned her head she could see herself reflected in the glass, her smudged blue face and, above it, a winking red light. When she looked up she saw it was a security camera. She wondered who was watching them. Her mum had bought a Coke and some chicken nuggets for Mia and a cup of tea for herself. She said they couldn't sit there without buying anything, that someone might ask them to leave.

Mia didn't eat her nuggets. Her mum had forgotten to get ketchup and she didn't like them without ketchup. She sucked up some Coke and watched her mum turning her paper teacup round and round on the table, the yellow arches of the logo flashing between her fingers. It was late, the restaurants at street level were closed, but McDonald's was busy. Drunk people laughed too loudly and pushed each other and spilled their French fries on the floor. Her mum didn't look at them. She didn't look at anything but the cup with its plastic lid, the little square hole going round and round as she turned it, like time going by.

'I thought – I think I thought that it was worse for you, to have no answers, to always be wondering why, somehow thinking it was your—' Her mum stopped, the sentence stuck in her throat. She put her clenched hand to her mouth, pressing her knuckles hard against her lips. 'I should have – I don't know how to explain, when I look back now – I had no right. I don't know what to say except I'm sorry.'

It was horrible. It wasn't just the words, the terrible choking words, but her mum, hunched over, pleading, like each one was breaking her. Mia wanted to run away, to stick her fingers in her ears and scream at the top of her voice. She didn't know what she was supposed to do with the feelings inside her, how to breathe. Her mum said she was not asking Mia to forgive her, she said she knew she never could. The lie was too big. But if that was true, what was supposed to come next?

There was a hole in the knee of Mia's leggings. She worked her finger into it, feeling the scrape of her nail against her skin. Beneath her trainers the floor of the toilet was dirty-wet like melted snow, sodden twists of toilet paper trodden into the slush. She wished she had her backpack. Her phone was in it and the photo of her dad. She needed to look at him, to see him laughing up at her, his hand on the bump of her, holding her steady. He was alive. The thought was like a sea inside her, the waves coming and coming, knocking her down. Somewhere, every single day of her life, her dad had got out of bed and brushed his teeth and eaten his breakfast and gone outside and, when he looked up at the sky, it was the same sky as hers.

'Shut up, he never? He *never!*'

'I'm serious!'

There was laughter from outside the cubicles, then silence as the doors banged shut either side of her. Mia heard the clunk as the plastic locks were turned, the soft hiss, in stereo, of pee.

'Mia? Are you in here?'

Mia hugged her knees. Half of her wanted more than anything to unlock the door. That half wanted her mum's arms around her, the familiar shape and smell of her. The other half knew that the cubicle was the only safe place left, that to leave it would be like being sucked down into the earth, the pressure would crush her. She dug her finger deeper into the hole in her leggings, watching as it grew, the fabric shrivelling away like something burned.

'Mee?' Her mum's voice was sharp, stretched tight. 'For God's sake, if you're in here, answer me. Please.'

On either side of her the toilets flushed. The cubicle doors opened.

'I'm gonna tell him,' one girl said, and the other squealed.

'No way!'

'Yeah, I am, I'm gonna tell him. I'm serious.'

'No way, you are not!'

Perhaps they saw her mum then because suddenly they stopped talking. There was the sound of water running and the roar of the hand dryer, then, in an explosion of giggles, they were gone. Mia bit the insides of her cheeks. There was a poster on the back of the cubicle door with a close-up photo of a headlight. *We recycle our used cooking oil into bio-diesel to power our delivery fleet*, the poster said. The headlight stared at Mia with its silver eye.

'Mia, please, is that you?' her mum said again, her voice high and strange, and she banged on the door of Mia's cubicle with her fist. The bang made Mia jump.

'Go away,' Mia said.

Outside the cubicle her mum took a ragged breath.

'Mia, please, listen to me. You have to come out. We can go home, we can ... '

'I said, go away.'

'I can't.'

It was Mia who found him. Her mum didn't say it like that but it was true. The envelope Mia had taken from Sylvie's desk in France, the one with her mum's name on it, there were papers in that envelope that changed everything. It sounds stupid, her mum said, but until I saw those papers there was a part of me that really believed he was dead. It was only when I saw that little boy's death certificate that I understood how awful the lie was. My lie, I mean. There was a long silence. Mia stared at the table. I'm sorry, her mum said, and her voice was very sad and tired. You don't need to hear this. I'm sorry.

Mia's eyes were prickling. She pulled a length of toilet paper out of the plastic dispenser and blew her nose on it. The paper was too thin, her snot went through it and round it, stretching in silvery strings and sticking to her fingers. She pulled more paper out, then more, wadding it into a ball in her hand. Her mum had tried to find him too. That's why she was here, to talk to Astrid Osman. It made Mia feel dizzy to think of it, both of them thinking about Astrid at the same time, in the same room even, checking her Twitter feed

255

and waiting for a message. Both of them thinking and thinking about her dad. Mia closed her eyes. There were goosebumps on her arms, on the bare skin of her thighs.

'I mean it,' she said. 'Go away.'

There was a long silence.

'I'll wait outside,' her mum said. Mia listened to her footsteps walking away, the clunk of the closing door. Then she put her hands over her face and cried. At the table, twisting her tea, her mum said that no one knew her dad's real name, not even Astrid Osman, and then she said, perhaps that's OK. Perhaps it's OK not knowing, if knowing doesn't change anything. The way she said it made Mia's throat hurt. She looked at her nuggets in their box, the grease stains on the cardboard, and she thought about the dead leaf butterfly samosa, about the worm in the tequila bottle and Bertie with his feathery tail. Her mum put a hand on her arm, then took it away again. Whatever you want, she said. It's up to you.

Mia twisted the wad of toilet paper. How could she know what she wanted? Her dad was alive. He was alive and out there some-where, his sky the same sky as hers, and in all that time he hadn't once tried to find her, not even when she was born. I'm sorry, her mum kept saying, like they were the only words she had left. I'm so sorry.

Someone was in the bathroom. Mia could hear them going in and out of the other stalls, flushing the toilets. They pushed at Mia's door so it rattled in its socket. They ran the taps. Over the noise of the water, Mia could hear them humming. The humming made Mia hum too but silently, in her teeth. She put her hands over her ears. The water stopped. Then suddenly whoever it was was standing right outside Mia's cubicle.

They pushed the door again, harder this time. 'You come out?'

Mia held her breath and didn't answer.

'Only you not come out I go tell manager. This is rule.'

Mia hesitated. Then, pulling up her leggings, she flushed the toilet and pushed open the door. The cleaner was wearing a black baseball cap. When she saw Mia her eyes widened in surprise and Mia wanted to ask her what her problem was, only she caught sight of her face in the mirror, the blue patterns smeared and smudged. Yanking a paper towel from the dispenser on the wall, she walked out of the bathroom, her face buried in its rough folds.

Her mum was waiting in the corridor. She tensed when she saw Mia. There was a moment when everything froze, before Tess smiled at her and carefully held out her arms. Mia stood stiffly in the circle of them and closed her eyes. It frightened her, how badly she wanted to go back to the before.

'You didn't have to do that, you know,' she said, pulling away. 'I'd have come out on my own.'

'I'm sorry,' Tess said. 'I was worried.'

Mia shrugged. 'So are we going?' she said, and her mum bit her lip and nodded and they left.

Charing Cross tube station was closed, heavy metal gates drawn across the top of the stairs.

'It doesn't matter,' Tess said. 'There's a night bus that goes pretty much the whole way.'

They walked in silence towards the bus stop. Tess carried Mia's wings in their black bag. She wanted to say something but she didn't know what to say, if she was even allowed to say anything. How did you comfort a child when you were the source of her pain? She wished Mia would shout at her, cry, something to break things open, to force things back to how they were before. At the table, when Tess asked Mia if there was anything she wanted to know, the only question Mia asked was if her dad had ever tried to contact them since she was born. When Tess said he hadn't, Mia went to the toilet. She didn't come back.

Mia could see her mum trying to think of things to say. She willed her not to say them. It was easier when there weren't any words, then you could just look at stuff, things that weren't your responsibility, that had nothing to do with you, and let the pictures run through your brain without them having to mean anything. She wanted to tell her mum to chuck the bag with her wings in, that she never wanted to see them again, but she knew Tess would do it, that she wouldn't even ask Mia why, and she couldn't bear that, so she walked faster and tried not to look down.

There were cars on the road and taxis with their lights on, but hardly anyone else on foot. They passed a Tesco Metro and a Pret A Manger, both dark and shut up. In the window of Pret the tall stools were stacked on the long counter, legs up. They looked like the sticking-up legs of people buried upside down.

They were standing at the pedestrian crossing when Mia saw them. A swaying snake of people carrying candles and banners making its way down the middle of the road. There was a bus behind them and some cars but they didn't move aside. One of the banners was so wide it took five people to carry it. It was white with the words **CLIMATE EMERGENCY** on it, only they were walking away so the letters were backwards and the street lamps made the white look orange. Under the trees there were pools of darkness where the street lamps didn't reach. In those places the candles seemed to move by themselves, like they were floating.

The green man on the traffic light flashed. Mia let the numbers count backwards down to nought. She could feel her mum waiting, watching her. She thought of Astrid's pinched face, the hiss in her voice. *Ignore her, it's a cheap stunt.* She hesitated. Then, without saying anything, she turned and started to walk towards the marching protesters.

'Mee, it's so late, don't you think we should go home?' her mum called after her, but Mia kept walking. She could hear the hum of voices and, faintly, music. It sounded like a bird singing. Pulling the backpack off her back she unzipped it and reached inside for the candle.

'I brought one too.'

Mia turned. Her mum was right behind her. She held out a thick cream-coloured candle, like the ones they had in church at Christmas. 'Hold this, would you?'

She gave it to Mia and, taking a matchbox from her pocket, struck a match. Mia held out her mum's candle and then her own, touching the wicks to the flame. The candles lit Mia's face like a tribal mask, familiar and very strange.

'Mine's better than yours,' Tess said, and when Mia shrugged she shrugged back. 'I feel like – I feel like we have to start saying normal things. Before we forget how.'

Mia nodded. She wasn't sure she was ready for her mum to know how glad she was, that she had said that and not something else. She stared at the flame of her candle until the brightness burned itself onto the backs of her eyes, until it was there when she blinked.

'You want to swap?' Tess asked, and Mia shook her head even though she did want to, a little. The procession was further away now, the lights flowing around the sombre hulk of the Cenotaph.

'Are you scared?' Mia asked. Speaking made the flame of her candle kink. Already wax was dripping down the candle, spreading over the circle of cardboard. She could feel the heat of it on her fingers.

'Yes,' her mum said quietly. 'I'm scared.'

'I don't mean about – I mean about what's happening, you know. To the planet.'

'I know.'

'People say we have time but we don't. They're like, we'll do something later, but it's already happening. What if it's already too late?'

'Mia, I don't think . . . '

'I'm serious. Don't they see that if nobody does anything, there won't be a planet to live on any more?'

'People are doing things,' Tess said. 'You're doing something right now.'

'I'm carrying a stupid candle that's probably polluting the environment. And anyway what difference does it make? Most people don't even care. Or they give up. You gave up.'

Tess was silent.

'I don't understand it.' Mia's voice rose. 'You knew what was happening, back then you could have done something, something that would have changed things, but you gave up. How could you do that? How could you just give up?' Her eyes shone in the candlelight, spilling over. She scrubbed at them roughly with the heel of her hand.

'Mee,' Tess said, her heart cramping, but Mia shook her head.

'You say Dad wasn't who he said he was, that all the time he was pretending to be Dave Taylor he was someone else, someone with a completely different life. Well, that picture of you on the internet, the Butterfly Girl. You're just as much of a fake as he was.'

'No.'

Mia wasn't sure why but that one word was like the match striking all over again, only this time the flame was inside her. She wiped her nose on her sleeve. Her cuff was streaked with blue, and the palms of her hands.

'That's not true,' Tess said, and suddenly she sounded to Mia like she was used to her sounding, like she was sure. 'I was that girl, then, the Butterfly Girl. After your dad disappeared, I don't know. It's hard to explain. I suppose it was sort of like a butterfly in reverse. I was in a pupa for a long time and when I came out I was a caterpillar.'

'It doesn't work that way.'

'I know. But I think that's what happened.'

'So you gave up.'

'Yes, and I shouldn't have. I wish I hadn't. It was a mistake.'

'So why did you?'

'Because it made me so sad. Because after your dad disappeared I kind of fell apart and for a long time it didn't feel like there was anything left that mattered or made any sense. Except you.'

Mia bit her lip. The flame inside her was very small. It would take nothing to pinch it out, the way Grandpa Ivo used to do, with his fingers. Instead, very carefully, the movement so small it was hardly a movement at all, she let her body soften towards her mum's, shoulder against arm.

Tess felt the touch like a kiss. She felt dizzy, like she had just stepped back from a cliff edge, her heart skittering against her ribs like stones towards the sea. She shifted her weight, leaning into Mia's shoulder, deepening the pressure, and it was as though every part of her was concentrated into that place, the small warm square where her daughter's skin met hers.

'I love you so much,' she said softly.

'I know.'

'And I'm sorry, I mean it, I'm so so sorry . . . '

'Mum.'

The sharpness in her voice was a warning. Tess bit her lip. It was so close, the cliff edge, the drop, but, if she was careful, if she held on tight and listened, really listened, she could still keep them from falling. Perhaps Mia could too.

The protesters had reached Parliament Square. Whitehall was deserted. Delicately, like a struck glass, Big Ben chimed the quarter hour.

'We should get marching,' Tess said. Mia nodded. She didn't move. She stared at her candle, the drips of clear wax hardening to white.

'Will it make a difference?' she asked. 'This vigil, I mean.'

'I'm sure it will.'

'Are you?'

Tess hesitated. 'I think that if we're serious about changing things, there are better ways.'

'And are you? Serious, I mean.'

'Yes.'

'So if I was serious too, you'd help me, you know, to find a better way?'

'I would, yes. Absolutely.'

Mia was silent. Tess looked at her and her heart was hot and clear like molten wax, spilling over.

'In that case,' Mia said, 'is it OK if we go home?'

23

He rang Andy. He told him that he had been thinking it over, that he was ready to go to the press. It was time somebody stood up and told the truth. His heart was big in his chest. He waited but Andy didn't answer.

'That thing you said, about acting as my manager,' he prompted, his stomach prickling. Fear or exhilaration or both. Perhaps they were the same thing. 'Because I think I'm going to need someone like that. You know, to keep control of things.'

Andy laughed, a hard snort through his nose. 'Control. That's funny. No, really, when you think about it, it's fucking hilarious.'

He heard the distinctive hiss of a beer cap, the gulp as Andy swallowed. It was not quite ten in the morning. Credit where cred-it's due, someone in the safe house had remarked sardonically when they heard about the Pig and Whistle. Andy might be a treacherous cunt but he's the only fucker in the squad who got the brass to stand him drinks for all eternity. Sitting with him that night in the pub the police paid for, after the punters had gone home, he watched as Andy drank doggedly, fixedly, like a man staring down the barrel of a gun. My life for a boozer in the middle of butt fuck nowhere,

Andy announced at one point, toasting himself. The bargain of the century.

Another swallow. There was a muffled curse, then a crash as something fell.

'For fuck's sake, Andy,' he said angrily. 'This was your idea, remember? It was you who said to light the fuse.'

'And boom!' Andy laughed again. 'No, you're right. You should go for it, mate. Blow yourself sky high.'

'Fuck off. You make me sound like a suicide bomber.'

'Yeah, well. Like we're not dead men walking anyway.'

'What, so now you're saying I shouldn't do it?'

'I'm saying do your worst,' Andy said. 'Go out in a blaze of glory. I mean, they'll hunt you down and fucking destroy you but they'll never forget you. The Dick'll be picking bits of your brain out of his hair for the rest of his days.' The Dick. Andy's name for Brian Richards.

'So you'll help me?'

'Fuck, no. You seen today's News of the Screws? You want to end up rotting in a holdall, that dick of a Dick's all yours. I'm planning on dying of monotony and alcohol poisoning in an Area of Fucking Outstanding Natural Beauty.'

Andy was still laughing when he hung up.

He went to the newsagent. It was raining. The air tasted of metal and wet dust. Nikki's phone number was still on the back of his hand. A faded blue zero circled the vein that ran from between his knuckles to the strap of his watch like it was the destination on a map.

Back at the flat the TV was still on. Football, Inter Milan v Man City. He didn't check the score. He stared at the sodden front page of the *News of the World*. **SECRET LIFE OF S&M SPY**, the headline blared. The story had been kicking around all week, the body of a junior MI6 codebreaker discovered inside a padlocked sports bag in the bathtub in his flat. He had been dead for eight days. In the photos he had a high forehead, wide-set brown eyes. His co-workers described him as quiet and conscientious, someone who kept himself to himself. There were rumours of Russian connections. Now suddenly Britain's biggest-selling tabloid had a different story. In an exclusive interview, a source close to the investigation disclosed that the victim was in fact an aficionado of autoeroticism, a secret transvestite with a taste for male prostitutes and Class A drugs. The police had found cocaine and women's underwear in his flat. His death was most likely an accident, a kinky sex game gone wrong.

A source close to the investigation. You didn't need to be a codebreaker to know what that meant. Someone had fucked up and MI6 were furiously covering their tracks. And so a diligent junior analyst was transformed into a scumbag, a filthy pervert who had deserved, asked even, to come to a sticky end. The *News of the World* gave the story six lascivious pages. What did MI6 care for the reputation of a dead man, the anguish of his grieving family? Their job was to protect the institution. The people who gave their lives for it, who remembered them?

On the television the commentator was shouting, his voice rising with excitement as players clustered round the goal. He didn't look up. He looked at the dead man's face, his trusting brown eyes. If he stood up and told the truth, if he threw Skinner and Mac and Brian Richards under the bus, how long before they came for him? MI6 murmured their libels in oak-panelled gentlemen's clubs but Special Branch were squaddies. They fought dirty. He had kept Tess's pregnancy out of his blue bags, it served no one to know about that, but he had logged her as his girlfriend. She was the Butterfly Girl, a feather in his cap. In his back-office days they stored the live files on site. Everything else was archived.

Nothing was ever thrown away. How long before they dug her up and threw her to the tabloids? How long before they found Mia?

Control. That's funny. Andy's bitter laugh echoed in his head. It wasn't just Special Branch. It was the press. Since when did they give anyone a fair shout? They might make out like they wanted his side of the story. They might even write a cheque. It wouldn't stop them from printing exactly what they wanted. There might be bits of his version in it, if he was lucky. But it wouldn't stay his. No one kicked the hornet's nest and got away with it. Sooner or later, like the poor trusting fucker in the sports bag, they would take him down. He wouldn't be the courageous whistle-blower with a conscience, the Special Branch high achiever who thought he was serving his country. He would be the love-rat copper who betrayed two women, who left his son without a father and his daughter without a backward glance or a penny of support. The Judas who screwed the activists by going undercover and his colleagues in the squad by speaking out. They would doorstep Tess and Mia, Kim, Jayden and Bianca, his dad if they could track him down, his bastard of a stepfather. They would lie their way into Orchard Court and harass his nan. Andy was wrong. There wouldn't be bits of him everywhere. The press wouldn't give up on him until they had devoured every last scrap. Until there wasn't a single fragment left with which to identify the body.

A roar from the television. Someone had scored. Clicking it off, he walked over to his desk and slid open the drawer. Everything was in there, the photos of Tess he had taken in France, and the grainy printout from Mia's twenty-week scan, and the baby book with each week of development marked with a vegetable, and the shabby old Led Zep T-shirt of his Tess used to wear in bed, and the song he had written for Holly Blue with Tess's illustrations in the margin. He had taken the items one by one, in the last week before he left, sneaking them out of the flat and stashing them under his tools in the back of the van. He took out the T-shirt and buried his face in it but it was years since it had smelled of her. He looked at it, at the figure of Lucifer on the front, or perhaps it was Icarus. Whichever. The ending was the same either way.

Rain ran down the window, the drops merging as they met. In the street a woman in a windcheater was walking a dog. He took his wallet from his pocket, sliding the driver's licence from its slot. Harold David Taylor. The card changed colour as it caught the light. A repeating motif was stamped into the laminate, two interlocking wavy strands like the double helix of DNA.

They would crucify him for that too, the unlawful appropriation of a child's identity. They would never understand that his Dave Taylor was someone else entirely. Not a grave robbing or a paper doll cut from someone else's documents, but a part of who he was, grafted like the skin on his burned hand till there was no difference between the new skin and the skin that came before.

He opened the baby book at random. *27 weeks. Your baby is now the size of a cauliflower.* Tucking the driver's licence between the pages he closed it and put it back in the drawer. The drawer had a lock, though he had never used it. He locked it. He put the key onto his keyring. Then, twisting it off again, he took it into his bedroom and slid it under the mattress. It made him think of a story Jayden was always on at Kim to read him when he was little, *The Princess and the Pea.* Jayden liked the pictures best, the princess with her pink dresses and long blonde hair. He watched his son stroking the pages of the book, enchanted, and he couldn't stop them playing in his head, the things his own father would have said if he had seen it. In the story the princess slept on dozens of mattresses but, because she was a princess, she always woke up black and blue because she could still feel the pea hidden underneath them. He wondered if the time would come when he forgot the key was there.

If he could cut out all that, if they would let him keep the half that was Dave Taylor, he would do it. Start again somewhere else. Or better still, pick up where he left off, if they would let him. But no one would let him. They would never understand. They would rip away Dave Taylor and discard him as a costume, a disguise to hide behind. They would claim that everything Dave Taylor ever did was a lie. He would never be able to explain to them that they were wrong, that Dave Taylor was the only true thing he had ever been, the only part of himself worth keeping.

His laptop was on the settee. He opened Facebook. Mia was not online. He checked her wall but she hadn't posted anything since Friday. Jayden had posted a picture of Bianca holding a puppy. When he scrolled back there were pictures of Australia, of Jayden and Bianca and Paul and Michelle and the children jumping in the swimming pool. The photos were three months old. For three months he had never thought to look.

He closed his eyes. The euphoria that had filled him a few hours ago felt like a kind of madness. Mia would not forgive him. By the time the squad were done with him, any possibility of reconciliation would be gone forever. At least if he stayed with GenSync he would still have Vanessa Morales. If he walked away what little contact he had would be severed completely and forever. He didn't know if he had the strength to do it all over again, to walk away from her and never go back.

He looked at the number on the back of his hand. He could call Nikki, suggest they go out. He imagined them sitting in an Italian restaurant, one of those too-small tables where there wasn't space for the side salad. They would drink wine and she would laugh and tell him stories about her life and later outside on the pavement they would kiss and perhaps, maybe, it would be the beginning of something.

He touched the screen of his phone, meaning to put her number into his contacts, but his thumb found the Facebook app instead.

Mia was the only name in his chat. Never initiate a conversation. Let them come to you. His fingertips itched.

hey u wassup?

He pressed send before he could change his mind.

24

N at rang on Monday morning as Tess was walking up the road to work.

'So?' she asked. 'How did it go?'

It was such an enormous impossible question that Tess almost laughed.

'Oh Nat,' she said, exhaling, and it was like she had been holding her breath forever.

The last thirty hours were a blur. She and Mia had hardly slept. In her bedroom, side by side in her double bed, it was like being in a plane or a hospital ward, the outside world disappeared. Time lost its sense. Every now and then, when Tess thought they should be hungry, she brought something upstairs on a tray. Sometimes they talked. Sometimes they lay side by side, and stared out of the window. The light was flat and grey. Outside the rain came down in sheets, the clouds so low the house felt like it was floating.

At one point, without saying anything, Mia got up. Tess watched from the bed as she padded across the landing and went into her bedroom. Her hair was tangled at the back, standing out from her head the way it used to get when she was little. She closed her bedroom door. Tess waited for the scrape of the bolt sliding shut. Instead the door opened again and Mia came back. She was carrying a book. She put the book on the bed. Then, like she had decided something, she opened it. There was a photo tucked into the pages. She held it out to Tess. Dave laughing up at the camera at Sylvie's, his hand on Tess's belly. Tess stared at it.

'I don't understand. Where did you get this?'

'It was in my room at Sylvie's house. She had it on the wall above her desk.'

Tess hugged her arms over her stomach. She couldn't make sense of it. Sylvie knew, she knew Dave was not who he said he was, and yet she had kept a photo of him and Tess on her wall, where she could see it every day. A crease ran down the centre of the photograph, so deep it was almost a tear. She touched it with her thumb.

'I didn't do that,' Mia said. 'It was like that when I found it. So you could only see the half with you in it.'

Tess nodded slowly, rubbing her forehead. She didn't know if that made it better or not.

'I'm going to keep it,' Mia said. 'I know you think I shouldn't but I'm going to.'

'I never said that.'

'You didn't have to.'

'Mee . . . '

'You don't get to tell me what to keep. Not any more.' Mia looked at the photo. 'He looks so happy. Do you think he was pretending?'

Tess shrugged helplessly. She felt like she was fainting, only she didn't faint. She didn't regain her balance either. She just went on spinning. 'I don't know.'

'How could you not know? How could you let him pretend like that and not know?'

All night and all the next day they danced this terrible dance, a step forward, a step back, except it wasn't like dancing because dancing had a shape to it, an equilibrium. The steps led somewhere. This was something else, like juggling knives, Tess torn between her own pain and Mia's, between inflicting hurt and assuaging it, between the knowledge that it had to be endured and the impossibility of enduring it.

Later Tess took the white envelope out of her bedside drawer. She unfolded it, tipping the butterfly necklace out into Mia's palm. 'I should have given you this before.'

'What is it?'

'Your dad gave it to me for my twenty-first.'

Mia's eyes widened. She held the necklace up by its broken chain. 'When you were pregnant with me.'

Tess hesitated. 'Yeah. It doesn't look like much but we could clean it up. Fix the chain.'

Mia watched the tarnished butterfly turning slowly in the light. At some point in the night, Tess had wiped her face clean with a flannel but there were still streaks of blue at her hairline, in the whorl of her ear. Whatever he had done to her, to both of them, he had done this too. Tess had Mia because of him. How could she ever wish that undone?

'Do you remember it, him giving it to you?' Mia asked.

'Of course I do.' We were in these beautiful woods. There were plans for a road that would destroy it. People lived in the trees there to keep the developers from cutting them down.'

'Did you?'

Tess shook her head. 'I wish I had. Perhaps if there had been more of us we might have stopped them.'

'So they built the road.'

Tess nodded.

'What about Dad?'

'What about him?'

'Did he sleep in a tree?'

'Maybe. He went a few times, more than I did.'

'Why?'

'They had this idea for a network of tunnels under the ground, they thought if people were down there the contractors wouldn't risk heavy machinery that might crush them. For a while the tunnels were kind of an obsession with your dad—' She broke off.

'What?'

'It doesn't matter.'

'*What?*'

'I was just – I suppose I was wondering if he wasn't trying to protect the trees. If maybe he was feeding back what he found out to, I don't know, the government? Or the police.'

'And you just let him? What was wrong with you? You lived with him. How could you be so *stupid?*'

Over and over again Tess struck it, the point where Mia's pain was abruptly too much to bear. Over and over again she wrestled with her impulse to soften the truth, to smooth away its sharp edges, agonising over her choices as Mia readied herself to begin all over again. To Tess's exhausted confusion it was not her lie that Mia could not leave alone. It was Tess's credulousness, her naivety. Again and again, Mia came back to it, biting open the wound like a dog, then lashing out in fury and in pain.

'How could you have believed him, how could you?'

'I don't know.' Again and again, from the bottom of her heart. 'I don't know.'

'How can you not know?'

Because he loved me. Because with him I was someone who was loved.

'You know what, I'm glad,' Tess said suddenly, when Mia's back was turned towards her. The dawn was coming and the room was full of grey. 'I'm glad I believed him.'

Mia twisted round to glare at her. 'How can you even say that?'

'Because if I hadn't, there would be no you.'

A pause, no more, hardly longer than a breath, and then another storm of words, as it all began again. To Tess it seemed that they might be there forever, stranded like space travellers in the frowsy unmade bed, the weight of the questions that would always be asked and never answered tipping the room sideways on its axis and spinning it giddily further onwards and away, while the world beyond their walls went indifferently on with its business.

'What time is it?' Mia said much later, when more greyness had gone and the sky beyond the window was blank and black.

Tess rummaged for her watch. 'Half past seven. Blimey. Almost bedtime.'

Mia didn't smile. She didn't bite Tess's head off either. She pushed back the duvet and sat up, turning her head from side to side so that Tess could hear the bones in her neck cracking.

'Can I say something?' she said without looking round.

Tess tensed. Her body ached from tensing. 'OK.'

'From now on, like now this minute, can we not talk about this any more?'

'You don't think we're going to have to?'

'Maybe sometimes. But only if there's a reason. Please?'

Tess hesitated. She could feel the cool wash of relief moving through her and, at the same time, the fear that relief was the wrong reaction, that to feel relief was somehow to fail Mia.

'If I want to know something I'll ask you,' Mia said.

'You promise?'

'Mum.'

'Promise me.'

'Fine. I promise.'

Mia pushed back the duvet but she didn't get up. She went on sitting on the edge of the bed, her shoulders hunched, twisting the hem of her pyjama top around her finger. The tangles in her hair tangled Tess's heart.

'I thought he was someone else,' she said softly and, as Tess took her in her arms, she began to cry.

Tess cried when she told Nat.

'Come over later,' Nat said. 'We can drink too much wine and look at kittens on the internet.'

'I can't. I don't want to leave her.'

'Then bring her. We have Coke too. And everyone likes kittens.'

Tess laughed despite herself, wiping her eyes. She thought of the picture of Nat and her mum, dancing at Nat's wedding. One day Mia would be as old as Nat was then. She wanted to ask Nat if it was her mum who had taught her how to be a mother or if she had just worked it out on her own. 'Maybe another day. But thank you.'

'Oh sweetheart. Any time. Whenever you're ready.'

The head was in his office with some of the staff. Through the narrow strip of glass in the door Tess could see him talking, gesticulating with his hands. She frowned questioningly at Shireen, who stopped typing long enough to draw an imaginary zip across her mouth.

It was late morning before the meeting broke up. They filed out towards the corridor, talking in low voices. Ken was among them. When he saw Tess he held his hand up to his ear, thumb and little finger extended. Call me, he mouthed, and Tess nodded. When she turned round, Shireen was grimacing at her in disbelief.

'Er, this is your captain speaking,' she said, imitating Ken's hand gesture. 'Tell me you're not thinking of sliding back into that abyss?'

'You're mean, did you know that?'

'Mean? I'm the Good Samaritan. Here you are on the side of the road, half-dead from boredom and, let's face it, shame, and do I leave you there? I do not. I save you from yourself.'

275

'You're a saint.'

'Honey, you know it. I suppose this means you still haven't called the soulful Benson?'

'Shit.'

'Tess, you're breaking my heart. You gotta call him. Promise me you'll call him.'

Tess thought of Mia, the expression on her face when Tess said perhaps it didn't matter that Astrid Osman didn't know her father's real name, that perhaps it was better not to know. She hadn't told Mia about Dee Bourke. What good would it do her, to hanker after something she could never have?

'Sorry,' she said. 'I can't promise anything.'

She left school at lunchtime. She told Shireen Mia had a temperature, that she needed to get home to check on her. She walked the long way round towards the High Street. She would buy strawberries, she thought, and a tub of the expensive ice cream Mia loved.

A girl was sitting at the bus stop outside Superdrug, picking polish off her fingernails. Only as Tess got closer did she see it was Yaz. When she stopped and said hello, Yaz eyed her warily. Her eyebrows looked like they were drawn on with felt tip. Yaz was a November baby, which made her older than Mia by nine months. Looking at her, it could have been nine years.

'It's good to see you,' Tess said. 'It's been a while.'

'Yeah, well, I haven't really – I saw Mia though. When she stayed over at mine. You know. On Saturday.' Yaz chewed her lip unhappily and craned her head to look down the road, her whole body taut as though, if she only concentrated hard enough, she could will her bus to materialise. Tess felt a sudden rush of tenderness for her, for her thickly made-up face and her puffy trainers, her beauty and her swagger and her agonising self-consciousness.

'Yeah,' she said. 'Mia said.'

There was a silence. Yaz stared down at the phone cradled in her hands. Tess could see the top of a bus as it turned the corner into the High Street. Even in this traffic it would only be a few minutes before it reached the stop.

'Look, Yaz, I don't know the right way to say this, Mia would probably kill me if she knew I was even talking to you, but would you call her? Please? Or message her or whatever. I think she really misses you.'

Yaz was silent. Sucking in her cheeks, she pushed one chipped banana-yellow thumbnail down into the cuticle of the other. Tess put out a hand to touch her shoulder, then changed her mind. The bus was at the pedestrian traffic lights.

'I realise it's none of my business, it's just, the two of you, it's, I don't know.' She frowned, trying to arrange the words, the thoughts, into something that made sense. 'I suppose what I'm trying to say is that if I was having a bad time, if I was Mia and things were hard, if that was true, I'd want you around. You know. If I could.'

Yaz's eyes slid sideways. The bus was pulling up beside them, its brakes wheezing as it slowed. The doors sighed open. An old woman with a wheeled shopping bag hustled past Tess and hauled herself on board. Yaz gestured at the bus with her phone.

'So – um – I gotta . . . ' she said. She didn't look at Tess.

'Sure,' Tess said. 'Well, it was good to see you, Yaz. Take care, OK?'

Yaz nodded. Stepping onto the bus, she touched her Oyster card to the reader. The driver was staring up at the CCTV screen above his head. Yaz hesitated. Frowning, the driver jerked his head at Tess.

'She getting on or what?'

Yaz shook her head. Biting her yellow thumbnail, she disappeared out of sight.

25

Mia turned over in bed. She could hear daytime noises, a lawnmower and traffic and children playing outside, but she buried her face in the pillow. As long as she was asleep, she wouldn't have to think. Except that the problem with thinking about not thinking was that it made it impossible not to think. She could feel it starting up again, the crawl of anxiety in her scalp, in the pit of her stomach.

The evening before, while her mum drifted from room to room, unable to settle, she and Vanessa had chatted for hours online. It helped, not thinking about her dad, not thinking about anything. Vanessa was funny and nice. She liked the same stuff Mia liked and she knew every silly gif on the internet and she didn't keep looking at Mia with that awful crease between her eyebrows or ask her every ten minutes if she was OK. She just went on messaging like everything was normal, like it was an ordinary boring Sunday night. Mia didn't want it to stop. She was afraid that if she left it too long without messaging back Vanessa would say she had to go. So she went upstairs and brushed her teeth and got into her pyjamas and said good night to her mum and saw the way her mum looked at her phone and bit her lip and didn't say anything, and all the time she and Vanessa kept chatting, the messages stacking up on top of one another like stones in a wall.

In her bedroom she knelt on her desk chair and looked out of the window over the city. Somewhere out there, maybe even somewhere close, her dad was walking around or sleeping or watching TV. She had no idea how that made her feel. But she liked it when Vanessa sent her a video of a dog in the passenger seat of a car with its head out of the window, its tongue lolling and its ears turned inside out. The dog had its paws up on the dashboard and a blissed-out smile on its face.

this is literally pepper, she wrote. **how come dogs r so good at being happy??**

It was almost midnight when Mia said she had to go to sleep. She didn't want to stop but her eyes smarted and her body was so tired it kept twitching.

Vanessa messaged back. **talk 2moro??**

Mia smiled as she typed. **u know its 2moro in 2 mins rite ;)**

nooooo + i have maths test 1st lesson im so gonna fail!!!

Mia stared at the text and it was like the Chronicles of Narnia when the White Witch touches the wolf with her magic sword, all the twitchy exhaustion inside her froze instantly to dread.

?????? she messaged back.

im serious I suck at maths argh SCHOOL

er doesnt yr school have holidays??

She waited but Vanessa did not reply. There wasn't even the little bubble that showed she was typing. She put the phone down on the bed. It was stupid to worry. Vanessa would have an explanation. In the morning it would feel like nothing. But her mind still kept jerking back to that dumb online safety presentation they had been made to sit through in Year 7. *Be careful who you trust. If someone seems too good to be true, they usually are.*

Her phone buzzed. Vanessa.

its that stupid summer school i told u about starts 2 moro :(

Mia didn't think Vanessa had told her anything about summer school. Although that didn't make it a lie. She stared out of the window, at the roofs of the houses stretching away into the darkness. Every one of them full of people she would never know. Her thoughts seethed through her head, crawling over themselves like flying ants. She swiped her phone screen. Her dad laughed up at her, his eyes squinted against the sun, and she was gripped by the sudden dread that it wasn't him at all, that the man in the photo was just a random man. She knew even as she thought it that it made no sense but knowing didn't seem to make any difference. Her phone buzzed again.

2 solid wks of maths + science TORTURE while u get 2 hang out + watch tv :°(

And again.

wot can i say my parents r STRICT if they even knew i woz on FB theyd go mental

And, after another long pause, **mia??? pls tell me my tragic life story didnt send u 2 sleep?!?**

Mia curled up on her bed, her knees drawn into her chest. The ants were all over her now, swarming in the roots of her hair, under her skin. Curling tighter, she pressed up against the wall. It comforted her somehow to feel the firmness of it pushing back against her knees. In the dark it looked like it was made of dust.

She must have slept. When she looked at her phone again in the morning, the battery had died.

In the shower Mia cranked the hot water up until she couldn't see for the steam. When she finally got out her skin was scarlet and the air on the landing was thin and cold, like opening a fridge, but inside she was still the same. Her phone was on the bed, plugged in to the charger. It kept twitching like a dog dreaming in its sleep. Every time it twitched she twitched too.

Downstairs in the kitchen she watched YouTube videos on her mum's laptop. Each time one finished, another one came up. Floods in Pakistan. Forest fires in Russia. An iceberg in Greenland calving into the sea. A mudslide in China five kilometres long and five storeys high. Plastic choking the Ganges. It made her feel worse but also better, like the panic was being sucked up out of the deepest parts of her and onto the surface, where she knew what it belonged to and exactly what it meant.

She was watching a video about an oil spill in the Gulf of Mexico when she heard the front door open. The spill was the largest in history. An American policeman in a bunchy uniform watched a pelican flailing in the sludgy surf. The pelican looked like someone had dunked it in brown paint. Her mum pushed open the kitchen door, her hands full of supermarket bags which she deposited on the floor.

'Shit,' her mum said, looking at the pelican over her shoulder. 'That poor thing.'

Mia paused the video. Freeze-framed, the pelican fixed her with its round unblinking eye. 'What if we went to the police?'

'About the pelican?'

'About Dad. What if we went to the police about Dad?'

'I'm not sure I ... '

'If we told them what he did, mightn't they try and find him?'

'They might. Or—'

'Or what?'

'Or they might do everything they could to make sure they didn't.'

Mia was silent. Tess put her arm around her. Mia didn't pull away.

'What about a – you know – a private detective?'

'Mee—'

'They're real, aren't they? Private detectives. I mean, they exist, right? I bet if I googled it right now we could find one.'

'Mee, sweetheart, you need to stop . . . '

'It'd cost money probably but I could pay. I have Sylvie's money. Exploration. This would be exploration.'

'Mee, no!'

Mia's mouth hardened. 'You said we had to talk. If there was a reason, you said. You made me promise.'

Tess closed her eyes. She looked old, Mia thought. There were creases Mia hadn't noticed before around her mouth.

'You're right,' Tess said. 'I'm sorry.'

'Yesterday you said it might be better not to look for him, that he would have found us if he wanted to be found. But it's different for you. You have the real him to remember.'

Tess bit her lip.

'You think I can just forget about him, but how can I? He's half of who I am. If I don't know who he is, then who am I?'

Vanessa had posted a Snoopy cartoon on her Facebook wall. *Don't try to figure me out*, it said. *I'm a special kind of twisted.* Lots of people had liked it, including Yaz. She had also messaged Mia on Chat. The time stamp said 8.17 a.m.

guessing u fell asleep on me last night LOL

At 8.26 a.m. she sent a picture of her dog Pepper with a cut-and-pasted maths book shoved into his mouth. *stupid dog why wont he eat my homework????*

And then, at 8.41 a.m., *maybe msg me l8er*?? *if I havent died of maths*

Mia read the messages. They seemed – ordinary. The terror was still inside her somewhere, she could feel the echo of it in her when she moved, but it wasn't Vanessa's fault. It wasn't Vanessa that was all wrong. It was everything else.

K, she messaged back. But later, when she went to the shop to buy the bread her mum had forgotten, she left her phone at home. It felt weird, being out without it, as if she had forgotten to bring a part of her body with her. But it felt good too, light somehow, like she had shed a heavy skin. Like finally, briefly, she could be completely free.

Mia and Yaz walked slowly along the canal. It was cooler finally, the harsh glare of the sun softened to buttery gold. Children were playing under Mia's willow tree. They squealed as they ran in and out, pushing through the curtains of the branches.

'How are Lauren and Chloe?' Mia asked casually, like it was just something to ask.

Yaz shrugged. 'Chloe's in Spain with her dad. Lauren – I don't know. She's around. She claims she's got this new boyfriend, some crazy rich eighteen-year-old with a BMW. So that's nice.'

'You don't believe her?'

'Come on. She's thirteen, you know? Like an eighteen-year-old wouldn't want someone his own age. Or closer anyway.'

'Maybe he's madly in love with her.'

'Or maybe she's full of shit.'

'It might be him who's lying. Maybe he's twelve and just really tall.'

Yaz grinned, sucking in her cheeks so it didn't show. Mia wanted to ask if that meant she didn't like Lauren any more but she didn't want to break something that wasn't mended yet, so she fished a crumpled pack of gum out of her pocket instead. There were two tablets left.

'One each,' she said.

'But you like two.'

'Maybe I've changed.'

'Have you?'

'Maybe. A bit.'

At the bridge they leaned on the parapet and looked down into the water. A tattered Tesco bag drifted in the weeds. There was a part of Mia that wanted to tell Yaz about her dad but she knew she wouldn't. Not yet. It felt good to have a bit of her life that didn't have her dad in it, like that was a different story, a show on another channel.

'Wanna hear a joke?' Yaz said.

'Only always.'

'OK. So, thanks for explaining the word "many" to me. It means a lot.'

Mia grinned. 'I *knew* that one would make you laugh.'

'You heard it before?'

'Vanessa Morales posted it on her wall.'

'Oh. Yeah. Who is she, by the way?'

Mia frowned, a flicker of the old fear moving inside her. 'I thought you knew her.'

'Nah. Don't think so.'

'So how come you're friends with her on Facebook?'

'I don't know. How come you are? You're always on her wall.'

You noticed, Mia thought, and she hugged the bridge parapet, the wood sun-warmed against her stomach. 'I guess I like her posts. She's funny. Plus her dog's really cute.'

'I thought your mum had some big rule about not being friends with anyone you didn't know in real life, like she's afraid they're all crazy paedo groomers or something?'

'What, like your mum has a rule about you not being friends with girls who smoke and drink alcohol and have sex in imaginary BMWs?'

Yaz looked at her and Mia looked back and something passed between them, fierce at first and then not, like that bit in *Harry Potter and the Half-Blood Prince* when Ron Weasley threw a knife at Fred and, without saying anything, Fred turned it into a paper aeroplane.

'Also this,' Mia said, fishing in her pocket for the fiver she had pilfered from the kitchen drawer. 'You know what time it is, right?'

'Don't toy with me, Mia Campbell.'

'Never. It's Magnum o'clock.'

*

Later, when they were licking the last of the chocolate from their fingers, Yaz looked at Mia. 'I'm still going to be friends with them, you know. Chloe, anyway.'

'I know.'

'Maybe not Lauren. She's – I don't know. Her mum and dad are splitting up so she's probably going to have to move. Essex or somewhere, I'm not sure.'

'That sucks.'

'You don't think that.'

'You're right. I don't think that.' Again, Mia looked at Yaz and Yaz looked back and whatever it was, a knife or a paper aeroplane, it was steadier this time and less scary.

'What about your crazy paedo groomer?' Yaz asked. 'Still going to be friends with him?'

'Why, you jealous?'

'No way. I'm happy for you. Maybe he'll turn out to be the crazy paedo groomer love of your life. I can give the speech at your big fat crazy paedo wedding.'

Mia laughed uneasily but she felt her heart squeeze. Yaz wanted to give the speech at her wedding. 'You wouldn't be nervous in front of all his made-up Facebook friends?'

'You know me. I like people. The really cute made-up dog, though?' She pulled a disgusted face. Mia laughed again. It was weird being back together, both exactly the same and not the same at all. She wondered if maybe it was kind of what dating a boy you liked felt like, when every nod, every laugh, was a sort of victory.

And then Yaz had to go. It was the day before Ramadan and her uncle and his family were coming for dinner.

'How's Rash?' Mia asked and Yaz shrugged.

'Oh, you know. On some police watchlist as a potential terrorist but apart from that, great.'

'A terrorist? But why, what happened?'

'Nothing happened.'

'I don't understand—'

'No, well, why would you? You're not brown and Muslim and probably carrying a bomb in your school backpack.'

It was like an iceberg calving, the sudden void between them. Mia felt sick.

'That doesn't mean I don't get it,' she blurted. 'Being white doesn't make me an idiot.'

Yaz looked at her, snapping her gum with her tongue. Then slowly she smiled. 'Fair point. What's that thing Mr Mulvey's always banging on about? Correlation is not causation.'

'Fuck off,' Mia said, laughing a little despite herself, and Yaz laughed too and bumped Mia with her elbow. She didn't say sorry, not in so many words, but Mia knew that's what she meant.

'You want to meet tomorrow?' Yaz asked.

'OK.'

'I should warn you, I'll be hangry.'

'I can take it.'

'OK then,' Yaz said. 'Tomorrow.'

'Bye.'

Mia bit the insides of her cheeks as she walked away but she couldn't stop the corners of her mouth from turning upwards. Her phone pinged. A message from Yaz.

hey u

A dimple pressed itself into Mia's cheek. Already the muscles in her face were starting to ache. Muscles need to be used all the time, their PE teacher at school was always saying, otherwise they get out of practice. She turned round but Yaz was already out of sight.

u yeh, she messaged back and the smile escaped her teeth and curved upwards, pressing itself into her cheeks.

*

Tess watched from the living room window as the girls walked away together down the street. Perhaps it was all right if she was not enough for Mia, if there were things she couldn't be. She wasn't the only person who loved her. Perhaps Yaz would be able to help Mia in ways a mother never could. You are only ever as happy as your unhappiest child, one of the other mothers at school said to her once, and Tess had been glad she only had one. Now she carried Mia's anguish wrapped up in her own, a rock inside a rock.

Sylvie's desk had been delivered that morning, a lump of plastic and packing tape, bubble wrap bulging under its skin. The delivery men had had to push the armchair to one side to make room for it. They had delivered a cardboard box too, FRAGILE printed on its side in Delphine's careful capital letters.

Tess opened the box first. An envelope was taped to the inside of one of the flaps.

My dear Tess,

It feels a little foolish to be FedExing the enclosed but Sylvie left very specific instructions that you were to have both the desk and its contents and I mean (for once) to respect her wishes, even though Lucien tells me you will only throw it all away. As I think I told you, we have decided to sell the house but the agent here has advised that we wait till spring when demand will be strongest. Till then please know that it is yours to use whenever you wish. It is bleak at the end of the earth in winter but also very beautiful.

Affectionately,

Delphine

Tess tipped the box's contents out onto the floor. If Mia had not found it, the envelope with her name on would be in there still. Their lives intact, ordinary, about to be smashed to smithereens. Tess poked warily through the pile, afraid there might be more, but it was only detritus of the kind Sylvie had always accumulated: dog-eared snapshots and blank cassette tapes and sketchbooks secured with rubber bands and bundles of receipts and stubs of the thick pencils she loved and sharpened with a knife, and, right at the bottom, the wire of its headphones wrapped around its belly, Sylvie's old Walkman, the one Tess gave her that first Christmas so she could have music wherever she went. Tess untangled the wire and ran her thumb over the scabs of paint on the case, the buttons indented like old steps. She thought of Sylvie in the studio, her hips moving with her brush and a hum rising off her like an incantation. The feeling of privilege and exclusion as Tess watched her work, oblivious to Tess at the window, belonging to no one but herself. In those long summers she had shown Tess so much she had not understood before: the joy of being alive to her instincts, the exhilaration of living in the present tense. The irresistible physicality and openness of love, whatever its nature. If she understood anything about being a mother, it was because of Sylvie who had loved her fiercely and expected too much of her and, much of the time, too much for Tess sometimes, had let her be.

There were piles of photos, shots of Sylvie's work, snaps of the house and beach, old pictures of Delphine and Max when they were little. In all of them Delphine stood a little behind her brother, her face creased with an anxiousness that Tess found unexpected and touching. Sylvie was in some of them. She looked young and distracted and separate, like she was there by mistake. When Mia was that age, Tess was younger still. Would she have been ready, back then, if Sylvie had forced her to listen? She had felt so alone in those years, out of her depth. What would it have done to her then to discover that Dave was not Dave? Did Sylvie understand that, was that why she had not written again, because she was afraid it might drown her?

Tess sighed, looking at the photos, at Max who never got to grow old, and put them to one side. They were Delphine's memories. She would send them to Delphine. Perhaps she could even deliver them herself. She wasn't the Butterfly Girl any more, she hadn't been that for a lifetime, but she had still let herself be pinned, fixed under the glass of the past, and she never had drunk Orangina beside the Eiffel Tower. Perhaps she could finally persuade Delphine to show her Paris.

She was nearly finished when, at the bottom of a drawer, in an envelope with some dried pressed flowers that crumbled when she touched them, she found a photograph of Dave. It must have been Tess who had taken it because he was standing on the cliff with Sylvie. Sylvie was turning away, her attention caught by something out of frame, but Dave looked straight at the camera, a challenge in his smile as though he was daring it not to see. Tess's impulse was to tear it in half but she thought of her promise to Mia and put it on the table, face down where she didn't have to see it.

Shelagh Healey, she intoned in her head. Shelagh Healey. Shelagh Healey.

She wished there was a way to be sure that what you did would bring more comfort than pain.

Tess would never have noticed the cassette tape if the box's broken corner hadn't scratched her hand. Kate Bush, *The Kick Inside*. The title in Nat's distinctive handwriting and underneath, *For your very own kick inside, Holly Blue, because it's never too early for KB*. In France they had listened to it over and over, Bush's unearthly voice coiling over and around them as they lay naked in Sylvie's bed by the window, watching the bats swooping in the rose-pink sky. It was only back in London that Tess realised she had left it behind. She bought another copy but then he left and she never listened to it again.

The box was cracked along the hinge, she had to take it apart to open it. On the spine of the sleeve Nat had drawn a little butterfly. Tess slotted the tape into Sylvie's Walkman and pressed play. She was half-expecting the batteries to be dead but immediately she was caught up in the soaring, plunging melody of 'Oh To Be In Love'. *I could have been anyone. You could have been anyone's dream.* The smell of heat and pine needles, of wild strawberries and skin.

The music broke off. There was a metallic scrape and then a hiss.

'Fuck, Tessie, this song.'

Tess's breath stopped. His voice, unmistakably, too close to the microphone, smudged and soft with wine.

'I'm spoiling it, I know, I can see you frowning at me, that little notch between your eyebrows, but do you know what I'd do if I could? I'd hide a message like this one inside all the places we've been happiest. So that afterwards you'd never be able to go back to any of them without remembering . . . '

A ragged whimper that might have been him or the machine, another scrape, and then the piano and Kate Bush's child's voice swooping back into the silence.

Her hands shaking, Tess tore off the earphones. She could still hear Kate Bush's voice leaking out, the chords of the chorus over and over like a magic spell. She fumbled with the buttons, stop and then eject, scrabbling the cassette out of the Walkman. Jamming the tip of her little finger into one of the spools at its centre she turned it until there was a curve of tape sticking out from the base and then she pulled it, yanking it out in wild loops until the casing was empty and the tape and everything on it lay in a shining brown tangle in her lap.

She wanted to scream. No, not to scream, to sing out until the earth shook, until the walls around him fell, sending the plates smashing from their shelves, and the ground broke open beneath his feet.

'You want to talk to me about remembering? You have a daughter. Remember her?'

The pure clear note of her rage and contempt exploding him like a glass.

Tess rang Dee Bourke. She told her about the photographs, the one Mia had found, the second one in Sylvie's desk.

'I need to know,' she said. 'I need to be able to stop thinking about it.'

'And what about Mia?'

Tess looked at the desk, its sloughed-off skin of bubble wrap and black plastic. She thought of the two of them, in McDonald's and on the night bus and curled up in Tess's bed, and of Sylvie who might have been punishing her but might just have been waiting until she was ready, until she had the strength to bear it. She thought of Mia in the kitchen, her face pinched and white. *If I don't know who he is, then who am I?*

'She needs to know too.'

26

He said what he had to say. He kept it brief. Mac looked at the ceiling. He tried clearing his throat, once he even coughed, but Mac just went on looking at the ceiling, his thumb absently clicking and unclicking his pen.

The day before he had sat down and tried to commit what he wanted to say to paper. Mia, he wrote at the top of the page, and then, underneath it,

Mia
Mia
Mia
Mia
Mia

The school holidays. When he saw what she had written, the line of question marks like bullet holes in his screen, he wanted to throw up. He couldn't believe he had been so stupid. He scrambled out an excuse but Mia didn't reply, not that night and not all the next day. He knew he should leave it but he went on messaging her, he couldn't stop. He had to turn his phone and his computer off when Vanessa was supposed to be in class because he was afraid of what he might do, the damage he could wreak, and the whole time he was filled with a cold sick fear that he had destroyed the one good thing he had made, that she would never contact him again.

By the time she finally replied, that single perfect letter *K*, any doubt he might have had was gone. It was simple. He buzzed Mac's PA and made an appointment.

He waited. Mac stared at the ceiling, clicking his pen.

'So?' he said eventually. 'Are you going to tell him or am I?'

Mac didn't answer. His clicking pen was a finger in his chest, jabbing at him. He could feel his anger rising. 'Mac?'

Mac dropped his pen and sat up. His smile seemed to pain him. 'I hadn't expected you to be so reasonable.'

'AED is our biggest client. I know we can't afford to lose them. Which isn't to say that what Skinner is asking for doesn't cross a line.'

'No, well. Fortunately for you, that line is no longer your concern.'

'I think I just told you I'd do it.'

'If only it was that simple.'

'What the – you're taking me off the team?'

'No,' Mac said flatly. 'I'm firing you.'

He started to protest, to plead, but Mac sighed wearily and shook his head. 'You're not in the squad now. GenSync is a business. We exist to serve our clients' interests. I'm sorry, this isn't easy to say, but you're a liability. It's over.'

'But what about my team, my other clients? You always said I did a good job.'

'Until you didn't. Look, mate, it's tough, I know, but this is a tough business. The world has moved on since you joined. It's time you did too.'

His anger was so sudden and explosive it almost knocked him off his feet. Staggering forward he punched one-two across the smoked glass desk, one fist finding Mac's giant phone, the other crunching into the screen of his computer.

'Yeah?' he raged. 'And what if I tell you that the moment I walk out of here I'm going straight to the press? That I'm going to give them every last detail right from Day One, Brian Richards and the squad all the way through to you and Skinner and his fucking vigilante army. You think I won't be a liability then?'

Grabbing the edge of Mac's desk with both hands, he forced his thigh under the heavy glass top. The computer slid away from him, falling with a crash to the floor. Then Mac's arm was round his neck and his right wrist wrenched up behind him. He writhed furiously, trying to jerk his head backwards against Mac's face, but Mac only gripped him tighter, his forearm hard against his windpipe, choking off his air.

'You listen to me, mate,' Mac hissed. 'Because I'm going to give you some advice. A final inspirational pep talk before you walk out of this office and never come back. You talk to anyone, ever, about me or about any of our clients, and I'll take you down. Credit history, employer references, criminal record, your social media accounts, the full bells-and-whistles executive package. A beautiful thing when it's done right, don't you think? An entire life fucked at a stroke and not a damn thing to be done about it.'

Abruptly Mac let him go. He stumbled forward, gasping. His arm hung awkwardly from his shoulder. It should hurt, he knew, but it didn't, not yet. His knuckles were bleeding. Cracks swept through the glass of the shattered computer's screen. It looked like a butterfly wing. Mac stepped over it, pressing a button on his phone.

'Angie, if you could come in?'

Mac's assistant Angie opened the door. She was holding an envelope. She looked at the shattered computer screen, the papers scattered on the floor, then at Mac. Mac nodded. She placed the envelope carefully on the desk and backed out, shutting the door behind her.

'Your severance terms are in there,' Mac said. 'I recommend you accept them. I need your pass for the building. Also your phone and your laptop.'

He looked at the envelope. He didn't pick it up. He thought of Mia, of the strings and strings of messages tethering her to him. He could feel pain edging closer, the dark lick of its shadow. 'Sorry. I can't do that.'

'Those items are company property. If you leave this building with them, we will press charges and any settlement will be immediately invalid.'

'And if you take them, there's every chance you'll blow the cover of both of our operatives on the Northford job.'

Mac's expression didn't change. 'I've spoken to Raff. He's confident they have it under control.'

'Right. So the key players from the French activist group that our two agents will claim to belong to, who have been in regular contact with their UK counterparts for more than a year, you're happy that they both vanish without trace two weeks before the protest? You don't think that's fundamentally going to compromise our guys on the ground?'

He saw Mac falter. 'According to Raff . . . '

'They're my dogs and I'm his boss. How would he know?'

They made a deal. Though he would no longer be employed by GenSync, he would continue to run his dogs until the Northford protest was wrapped. In exchange Mac signed off a new severance package, including a six-month notice period on full pay. Neither trusted the other but they both knew the deal would hold. There was too much at stake for it not to.

He had three weeks, four if he was lucky. Then she would be gone.

They gave him back his laptop. Vijay didn't meet his eye as he explained the revised protocols. Under the new system, his communications would no longer be automatically uploaded to the web. They would go through Raff who would authorise them for release.

He felt sick, at himself as much as anything. He should have known Mac wouldn't risk leaving him unmonitored. He thought of his hours-long conversations with Mia, Raff's filthy little fingerprints on every word, and a ripple of fear ran through him.

'Access is also limited,' Vijay said. 'You won't be able to log into the accounts remotely the way you used to, only from your desktop here in the office.'

'But that's bullshit! You know as well as I do that the evenings is when most of these messages go out. So what, I'm supposed to live in the office from now on?'

Vijay stared at his keyboard and said nothing. Perhaps it was the hunch of Vijay's shoulders or the sick pulse of panic in his gut, but he had a sudden jolting memory of Astrid standing in the car park by the van, Kim's bank card in her hand. He swallowed, slowly letting out his breath. Until that moment he hadn't realised he was holding it.

The best UCOs are like the best sportsmen, Andy used to say. The greater the pressure, the better they play.

He put a hand on Vijay's shoulder. 'Look, Vee mate, I'm sorry. I'm not blaming you, I know you're just doing your job. It's fucked up, though, right, Raff suddenly in charge of every word I say?'

He was looking closely or he might have missed the flicker passing over Vijay's face. Mac liked Raff because Raff took care that he did, but Raff never bothered with people like Vijay. Perhaps if Raff had paid attention he would have seen the way

Vijay stiffened when Raff called him ITVee or joked about crappy terrestrial television and what he wouldn't give for a satellite dish, but Raff never looked at Vijay or anyone else on the tech team for that matter. There wasn't anything they had that Raff wanted.

He leaned down, lowering his voice.

'I'm going to ask you something, Vijay. I know I probably shouldn't but I'm going to, because for once in my life I have the chance to do the right thing and I can't walk away from that, not without knowing I've tried.'

He could see Vijay was listening. He leaned closer.

'These new protocols, I don't like it but I get it. My dogs, they're not mine, they belong to the company, and that's fine. Except there's this one. Remember that dog, Vanessa Morales, the one we set up as a test, the experiment into teenager user patterns? I should have closed her out months ago, I know I should, only there was this girl who friended her, the only one who showed any interest in environmental activism, remember her? Anyway, I thought she might give us something interesting so I kept her on. It was clear from the start that she was troubled, but I didn't really think about it and then somehow, I don't know how, it suddenly got seriously intense, like her friendship with the dog was the only thing holding her together so I ran with it. I mean, shit, she was a child, barely thirteen, I thought maybe it would get her through whatever she was – I should never have done it, it was stupid, but Vee, if we end it, if we cut her off dead without any explanation, I think it might crush her. What if she did something stupid? It would be my fault. Christ, Vee, she's just a kid.'

Vijay was silent, his face sombre.

'Morales isn't even on the wall,' he added. 'We've never deployed her for any of our clients. I don't think anyone outside of your tech team knows she exists. I'm not asking for support but if there was a way of taking her off the system, disabling the cookies, if you could just give me time to close her down . . . '

He didn't expect Vijay to answer. He let the silence lengthen, extend its possibilities.

'This work we do, the dogs,' he said quietly. 'Don't you ever wonder how it affects the people out there who think they're real, what it does to someone, believing all those lies?'

Vijay was waiting across the road when he left the office. They walked together towards the canal. Vee was jumpy, glancing over his shoulder. It was done, he said. Vanessa Morales's Facebook account was no longer connected to the GenSync system. As far as Raff and the team were concerned, she had been decommissioned. A dead dog. By the water a group of teenage girls crowded on a bench, drinking Coke and giggling.

'I hope she's OK,' Vijay said, 'that girl.' Then he was gone.

He went to a mobile phone shop and bought a new smartphone. In the balti restaurant next door he set it up and installed the Facebook app. Then he switched the screen off. He drank beer and ate his curry, scooping it up with swabs of bread. Beside him the phone gleamed, like deep water. There was something exquisite about the waiting, stretching it out till the tautness was almost too much, until it sang inside him.

It was getting dark as he walked home, the yellow moon pocked like a bruised apple. He put a hand on his phone in his pocket and it was like the power from the battery was flowing into him, quickening his heart. He was safe, at least for now. She was still his. At home he turned on the phone and touched the app. His thumbnail was stained with turmeric, sickly yellow like the moon.

u awake? he typed and he thought of the years before Vanessa, all the times he had talked to her when she wasn't there. His questions one on top of the other like narrow clouds, reaching up into the stratosphere. Her side blank and blue.

His phone buzzed. **yeah u?**

He closed his eyes, breathing her in.

nah im sleeping, he typed back.

;-)

zzzzzzz

sssssshhhhhhh

zzzzhahazzzzz

laughing or snoring

loring no snaughing no zzzzzzzzz

eva snaughed yourself awake?

It couldn't last. Without the GenSync systems, without the scraped photos and the fake friends, he could never keep it up. It would end, he knew, just as he had known in France, the precise shape of the pain to come pressing like a sheathed blade against the surface of every perfect day, the moment when, running and running, the road was suddenly air beneath his feet and, like a character in a cartoon, he looked down and fell.

He would fall again this time.

oh man just dozed off while typing I HAVE TO SLEEP

She sent a photo of a panda flaked on a tree branch, legs hanging down. He sent back a puppy asleep in its food bowl.

me at lunch after triple maths 2moro%, he typed. **yes holiday girl TRIPLE MATHS**

There was a long pause. He checked but she was still online. He waited. Another message appeared on his screen.

no school on the week-
end tho rite?

the weekends not till
saturday :(

wanna meet irl?

He stared at the message. His mouth was dry. There had to be
a way to stall her, to keep his distance and yet somehow hold her
close. His mind was a blank. His phone pinged.

if u don't want 2 just say

What if she does something stupid, he had said to Vijay. He
should have known this would happen. He should have planned for
it. He didn't know why he had never planned for it. Another ping.

gotta go nite

Her hurt split him in two. He typed hurriedly, clumsily, his
thumbs too slow.

sorry thought i heard my dad

And then,

YEAH I wanna meet u :) when?

27

It is raining when Tess wakes Mia up, the heatwave of the past weeks already like something imagined and impossible. Her window is open and the cool air smells of metal. Mia bites her thumbnail and tries not to think about where she and Vanessa Morales can go if it is still raining this afternoon, if she will even come. She clicks on her phone but the last message is the one she sent last night.

gnite + c u 2moro 🖤

The appointment with Denise Bourke is scheduled for ten thirty. Tess makes pancakes for breakfast, pressing blueberries into them to make smiley faces the way she used to when Mia was little. Mia pours maple syrup on them, watching it pool on the plate. She is wearing the butterfly necklace. When she turns it catches the light.

'He wrote a song about you, you know,' Tess says. 'Before you were born.'

Mia stops pouring. She wants to say she remembers but she doesn't trust herself to speak.

Tess hums a few bars. 'I can't remember the verses but the chorus went like this: *Three hearts now instead of two, me and you and*

301

Holly Blue. That was what he always called you, Holly Blue, after the butterfly.'

Mia looks at her plate. Her pancake grins at her, baring its black teeth.

'He wrote it down, the song,' Tess says. 'I don't know what happened to it. I always wondered if maybe . . . '

'Maybe what?'

'If maybe he took it with him. When he left. A little part of you.'

They are both silent. Mia doesn't know how she feels. It is like there is something pressing down on her heart that keeps it from feeling anything at all.

'Sing it again,' she says and Tess does, and the song mixes with the sound of the rain on the kitchen roof and runs through her, cold and warm at the same time.

They take the train to Croydon. They don't talk much. Mia plays Fruit Ninja on her phone and Tess pretends to read the paper. She wants to tell Mia everything is going to be OK but she can't be certain that it will be, so she presses her arm against Mia's and doesn't say anything.

Mia sweeps her finger over the screen, slicing a pineapple, an orange and a watermelon with a single slash. She hasn't told her mother about Vanessa Morales. It's not like it's that big of a deal anyway. They have arranged to meet at the boating lake at Broomfield Park so it isn't any different from meeting Yaz or anyone else from school. Mia won't even have to take the bus. All week she has wondered if Vanessa will bail. A part of her sort of hopes she will. She worries it won't be the same as it is when they are talking online, so easy and warm like they have known each other all their lives. Everything is different when you are with someone in real life, when you can see their embarrassment or their boredom, when you don't have time to think about the best possible way to say something before you say it. If it all goes wrong, they won't be able to go back to how they were before. No one ever can.

The private detective tells Mia to call her Dee. She takes them into the little conference room. Tess and Mia sit together on the tiny sofa. Dee moves the box of tissues to one side and places printouts of the photographs Tess and Mia emailed to her on the table in front of them, side by side. She holds her laptop in her lap.

'I wanted to see you together because I want us all to be very clear,' she says and she looks at Tess and then at Mia. She doesn't smile. 'It isn't always easy to find someone. I don't mean the process of finding. I mean the finding out. The knowing. It puts certain things to rest, for sure. But it can also start new things. Expectations. Hopes. Stuff you didn't know before which changes the past and the way you remember it. Some people don't want that. They find it makes things harder than they were before.'

Mia looks down at the photos of her dad, her hands in a fist between her thighs.

'Mee?' Tess says softly.

Mia nods.

'We've talked about it a lot,' Tess says to Dee. 'Neither of us knows yet how we'll feel when we know. But we know we have to know.'

'Mia?' Dee prompts and Mia nods again.

'One thing we both wanted to know,' Tess says. 'The investigation, will you tell us what you find out all in one go at the end or as you go along?'

Mia's hand creeps into Tess's lap. Tess takes it in both of hers, holding it tight. In her mind, in a dark place she tries not to see, are all the things that could happen once they start this, once Mia tells Yaz and Yaz tells someone else and suddenly it isn't theirs any more, except it is because he is Mia's father and that will never change. She can feel the skitter inside her, the pebbles starting to fall. If it was up to her they would walk out of this office and she would bear not knowing because not knowing was something private, something contained, but she has promised Mia. All Tess can do is make another silent promise, that she will always be there, that, whatever is to come, they will survive it together. She has to think of Mia.

'Only we thought as you went along might be easier,' Tess says, keeping her voice very steady. 'So we don't worry about what you haven't told us. And also so that if at any point we wanted to stop we could.'

Dee nods slowly. 'Of course. I understand. The difficulty in this case is – let me start at the beginning. As you know, I used to be a police officer. A few days ago I met up with an old colleague from the Met. I wanted to see if she was willing to look at the photos you sent me, maybe even run them through the police database. I thought if I could persuade her, it would us save considerable time and money. When she refused, I gave her copies of the photos anyway, I suppose I hoped she might change her mind, and . . . '

'And?' Tess asks.

Dee clears her throat. 'I think this is the moment you were talking about. When you can choose to ask me to stop.'

Tess glances uncertainly at Mia and squeezes her hand.

'Mee?' she asks, but Mia shakes her head.

'I don't want to stop.'

'OK,' Dee says. 'My colleague didn't change her mind, not about the databases, but when she saw the photos, and especially when I had confirmed the details of your description, the burn on his hand, the whale tattoo . . . '

Tess feels the blood drain from her face. 'She knew him.'

'Yes.'

'Oh God.'

'I can give you his name now,' Dee says. 'If you want it. Or you can wait until I've had time to put together a proper file. It's up to you.'

They are both silent. Tess grips Mia's hand more tightly. She would take it all on, she thinks, the pain both past and still to come, if Mia could live free and in peace. You are only ever as happy as your unhappiest child.

'It's up to you, Mee,' she says. 'Do you want to know now or would you rather wait?'

Mia hunches her shoulders. She looks at the photos laid out on Dee Bourke's table, the one of him with his hand on the bump of her, the other one with Sylvie on the beach.

'I don't know,' she says.

'In that case would you let me give you some advice?' Dee asks. Mia nods.

'A name by itself has no meaning. What gives meaning to a person is their life. The things they have done, the places they have lived. The people they have known. We can find out all of those things about your father. Not today but soon.'

'Is it going to cost more than €3,000?' Mia asks.

'It won't cost anything. It's covered by what your mum's paid me already.'

Tess looks up at Dee who shrugs, like that's the end of the discussion. Tess wants to thank her but her voice doesn't seem to be working.

'Oh,' Mia says. She can't stop looking at the photos. At her dad who is still her dad as much as ever, maybe even more so now that she knows he's really real, but who is also a different man with another name and another story, full of people and places and things that she doesn't know, that have nothing to do with the dad in her head. She thinks of the baby geese she watched on YouTube, born on a sheer cliff in Greenland surrounded by foxes that wanted to eat them. They were too young to fly. All they could do was throw themselves off the cliff with their stubby wings held out and hope they didn't die on the way down.

'Do you think—?' She breaks off.

'Go on,' Dee says.

'Maybe it's stupid but I just thought – I thought maybe if you found out all those things you could keep them here till we're ready.'

Dee looks at Tess. Tess lets the breath run very slowly out of her lungs until there is nothing left but the weight of not breathing. She nods.

'We could do that,' Dee says to Mia. 'If that's what you want.'

'Mum?'

'I – I think that's a good idea.'

'But only if we agree that when one of us decides they're ready, that's OK,' Mia says. 'The other one can't stop them.'

Tess bites the inside of her cheek. This is it, she sees that. Her Dave is gone. Whoever he is, he is Mia's story now, hers to discover or leave alone.

'Deal?' Mia asks and Tess nods again.

'Deal.'

He sits in the car outside his flat. A light drizzle flecks the windscreen. The satnav on his dashboard says the traffic on the M40 is heavy, that the estimated journey time is two hours and thirty-four minutes. In less than four hours he will see her. After thirteen years of waiting he will finally have the chance to explain.

It is crazy. He can't do it. Mia is expecting a girl her own age. She knows what Vanessa looks like, or thinks she does. Vanessa Morales's Facebook page is full of photos of her and her dog, scraped from a Mexican Facebook account. How will Mia react when she discovers that all this time Vanessa was him? Will she give him the chance to explain why he did it, how desperate he has been to know her? Will she even believe him when he says he is her father? Kids these days are warned constantly about stranger danger and the risks of online grooming. There is no way

Mia will assume his motives are good. She'll scream her head off. She'll call the police.

Although maybe that's not true. OK, so she won't be expecting him but he is hardly a stranger. From the moment they began to chat online, there has been a connection between them, an irresistible force drawing them together like all this time they were waiting for the other one to come. It was why she asked to meet him, it had to be, because she felt it too. Like him she knew there was something special between them, something precious and rare. That didn't go away because a person turned out to be different from what you expected.

And anyway, wasn't it possible that she might be glad? She must have wondered why he left, why he never came back. Whatever the truth was, it was always better to know it. Not knowing wore away at you. It ground you into dust. He is her father. She has never talked about him to Vanessa but she can't have forgotten him. She must hold the idea of him inside her, even if he is only an absence, a blank sheet of paper with nothing on it.

Except it won't be blank. Tess will have told her things about him. Some good things, maybe, that they loved each other once, that they both loved Mia, but also how it fell apart, how he fell apart, the terrible day when he left. He closes his eyes, pressing his thumb and forefinger hard against his eyeballs, but he can't stop the images from pushing their way in, Tess standing in the doorway, the blood draining from her face, her arms over her belly, shielding their child. The urgent fear in her voice as she said his name, just his name, over and over like he wasn't even there, like he was standing outside on the landing, like he might be able to save her. He had only meant to push her out of the way, to get out of that flat while he still had the strength in him to do it, but somehow the strap of his stupid fucking squad-issue Casio watch had caught in the chain of her necklace and, when he pulled free, she cried out, her hand flying to her neck, and the way she looked at him then, petrified, yes, but pleading too, desperate for him to explain, to undo what he had done—

If Mia knows all that, she may be afraid of him. The realisation is like a stone falling inside him. She may think he is dangerous, that he means to hurt her. It seems impossible to him that she could ever think that, impossible that after all they have shared over the last weeks she could imagine he means her the slightest shred of harm, but what does he know about what is possible, when what you think is real turns out to be something else instead?

He can't go. He can't risk it. He should message her now and say that Vanessa's mother is insisting that she babysit a cousin or walk the dog or go to the dentist, that she tried to argue but her mother won't listen, there's nothing she can do to change her mind. Surely Mia would understand that. She is a kid, she knows kids don't get to control their lives, however much they want to or think that they should.

And then what? He only has a few weeks left. In a month, maybe less, Vanessa Morales will be deleted. What use is it, to put things off? If he is to stay in Mia's life he has to meet her, to explain it to her, if not today, then soon. All cancelling will do is make Mia trust him a little less. He thinks for the millionth time about his careless message about the maths test, Mia's line of question marks. She already doubts him. She may not know it yet but she does. That's why she asked to meet. She wants to know Vanessa is who she says she is. She wants to know the truth.

Perhaps he should write to her. In a letter he could explain everything, the squad and Dave Taylor and falling in love with her mother and how the violent rage was never his but only borrowed, a scythe so he could cut his way out. He will never tell his story to the newspapers but he could tell it to her, so that she might finally know him for who he truly is. Not Dave Taylor or Vanessa Morales or the self he started with but something in between and always incomplete, because for thirteen years the most important part of himself has been missing. He could write to her now and when he sees her this afternoon he could hand her the letter, ask her to read it while he waits.

And if she refuses to read it, if she tears the letter up? Then he will write to her again. Again and again and again until she realises he is never going to stop. Until she finally gives in. He is her father. Whatever he has done, whatever mistakes he has made, he will always be her father. Nothing can change that.

His phone rings loudly, startling him. For a brief wild moment he is certain it is her. It is only as he looks at the screen that he remembers she doesn't have his number. Orchard Court. He takes a breath. 'Hello?'

'Hi, it's Sonya.' Sonya's voice is quiet and sad. 'It's your grandmother, she's had a stroke. She's alive, the ambulance came very quickly, but so far she's not regained consciousness. I'm so sorry. They were taking her straight in, if you call the hospital they should be able to give you a clearer picture.' She gives him the details. 'I know you'll be wanting to get straight down there, so I wondered if you wanted to let your brother in Australia know yourself or if you'd rather we . . . '

'If you could do it. Please.'

'Of course. Send her our love, won't you? Tell her we are all wishing her well.'

He stares out of the windscreen at the rain. He can hear Sonya breathing.

'This is it, isn't it?' he says at last.

'It might not be. Where there's life there's hope.'

'Right.'

'But if you're asking should you drop everything and go, then yes, I think you should.'

He wants to say something else but he doesn't know what, so he thanks her and hangs up. Vanessa is supposed to be meeting Mia by the lake in Broomfield Park. There is a kiosk there, according to Mia, selling coffees and ice cream. He pictures her there, her hands in the pockets of the grey hoodie he knows from her profile picture, her hair falling over her face. Her blue, blue eyes. The thought of it burns a hole through the centre of him.

He needs to ring the hospital. It is on the way to London, he can call in on his way. Of course if it is as serious as Sonya says, they might not let him see her. She might be undergoing surgery or in the ICU. There might be allocated visiting hours. If she has not yet come round, if she is still unconscious, she won't even know he is there. In which case a few hours won't make a difference. He could meet with Mia in Palmers Green and be back at the hospital by evening. He can't imagine Eileen in a hospital bed. She has always hated hospitals. A severe stroke, Sonya said, but Eileen is a fighter. She will outlive them all.

He doesn't know what to do. Clasping the steering wheel, he presses his forehead against his knuckles and cries.

The train clatters through a tunnel. There is music playing through her earbuds but Mia isn't listening. Dee knows his name. Soon she will know everything about him. His whole self, locked up in the safe in Dee's office until one day Mia is ready to take it out. He is real, she thinks, but his realness is not her responsibility, not yet. It makes her feel strange. Mostly, though, what she feels is relief.

Something electric still goes through her when she looks at his picture, only it's much fainter now, not the feeling so much as its echo. After she and her mum talked, after he stopped being a secret, she set the photo as her screensaver. She liked how it felt, the ordinariness of it. But suddenly, as the train curves back into daylight, she doesn't want him there any more. Opening her photos, she chooses a picture of her and her mum on the beach in France and uploads that instead. In the picture her mum is smiling at her in that way she has, the way that makes Mia roll her eyes, like she could smile at her forever.

She saves the photo of her dad in her folder. She likes to know he is there, one photo jumbled up with all the others, in case she ever needs him. But mostly she wants to leave him in Dee's office, where Dee is the one in charge.

He drives very fast. It calms him a little, the white noise of the engine and the tyres on the road, the steady tick of white lines under his wheels. At the hospital, they direct him to the ICU on the first floor. The room is long and low-ceilinged with beds down both sides. The beds are hedged in with screens and IV poles and machines trailing tangles of cables. Squares of cold light fall from the grids of white bulbs set into the ceiling tiles and the machines bleep softly to themselves.

A nurse shows him to a bed at the far end. Eileen is jacked half-upright, her head tipped back against the pillow. Her eyes are closed. Fat tubes run out of her mouth and nose. Her hospital gown is pulled down off one shoulder and wires are taped to her throat and below her collarbone. She looks small and broken, like a dead bird.

He sits down beside her. Her hand lies on the sheet, a thin clear tube inserted between the bones. He doesn't want to touch it in case he disturbs something. He stares at her swollen knuckles, the dark worms of the veins under the skin. He wonders where her watch is. Stan gave her that watch as a silver wedding present. She never takes it off. Beside him the ventilator wheezes and clicks, wheezes and clicks, over and over, marking time.

'Talk to her,' the nurse says gently. 'Tell her you're here. You may not think she can hear you, but we do know that the brain often continues to process sound in coma patients and that the voice of a loved one can be very reassuring.'

He nods. There are so many things he wants to ask her but he doesn't. He is afraid of what she might say.

'I'll ask the doctor to come and see you,' she says and, as she walks away, the squeak of her shoes merges with the ventilator, the bleeps of the machines. A prayer for the dying.

'Hey, Nan,' he says. 'It's me.'

Mia squats down beside the garden wall and peels the plastic bag off the last of the honeysuckle cuttings. She has done everything just the way they said to on the internet, watered them regularly and kept them in indirect sunlight and checked the condensation level inside the bags so they didn't rot, but the other ones died all the same. Holding the pot in both hands, she turns it slowly. The leaves haven't shrivelled up and dropped off like they did with the other cuttings. There is even a new leaf forming near the top of the stem, a tiny folded flake of green. Carefully Mia eases the plant from its pot, rubbing away a little of the earth with her thumb. The roots are short still, perhaps only a couple of centimetres, but she thinks they look longer than last time. Another week, according to the website, and it will be ready to be planted in the garden. She knows already where she is going to put it, in the corner at the back where it can grow up against the fence. It may still die, of course, but she hopes it won't. She likes the idea that it will be like Bertrand's garden in France, that bees and butterflies will come and on summer evenings their small square of north London will smell only of honeysuckle.

It is raining again. Wiping her hands on her jeans, she checks her phone again. Vanessa hasn't messaged. Perhaps she is already on the bus. It is going to be fine, Mia tells herself. They will walk around the park together and they will talk and laugh and eat ice cream, and Vanessa will tell her things she doesn't know, interesting important things that no one else her age ever talks about. When Mia looks back she will wonder why she ever worried at all.

There is still a small scared part of her that really, really hopes Vanessa doesn't come.

The doctor arrives. Calmly she explains to him that a brain scan has revealed a massive ischaemic stroke. They have administered drugs to minimise the risk of stroke reoccurring and for the pain, they are monitoring her carefully, but there is little else they can do. Damage to the brain is extensive. Eileen is unable to breathe or swallow unaided. While there remains the small possibility that she may regain consciousness, she will never recover.

'At some point we will need to talk to you about options,' the doctor says. 'But not yet, not today. Unless you have anything you want to ask me?'

He shakes his head. When the doctor is gone, he pulls his chair closer to the bed. He slips his hand under Eileen's, palm to palm, stroking her papery skin with his thumb.

'There's something I need to tell you,' he says. 'You have a great-granddaughter. Her name is Mia. She's twelve, she'll be thirteen in a few weeks, and she's funny and clever and brave and her eyes are blue like yours.'

He wonders if perhaps her hand moves slightly in his. He searches her face for signs of responsiveness, a flutter of the eyelids. Beside him the ventilator wheezes, pushing up her chest, letting it fall.

'I'm supposed to be meeting her this afternoon. The first time ever. So I was thinking maybe I could bring her back here with me afterwards so you could meet her too. That would be something worth waking up for, wouldn't it, to meet her?'

In his pocket his phone rings. He ignores it. The nurse hurries over. 'I'm sorry,' she says, gesturing at a sign on the wall. The sign shows a mobile phone with a red line through it. 'You're going to have to switch that off.'

He takes the phone out of his pocket. It's later than he thought. Even if he leaves right now, he won't make it to the park on time. The missed call was from an unknown international number. He thinks of Sonya, her promise to call Paul. He knows already that his brother won't come back, that there will be a hundred reasons why it is absolutely impossible right now for Paul to leave Sydney. As he walks out into the corridor his phone rings again.

'Hey mate, it's me. The care home called. Are you with Nan? Is she OK?'

Straight away Paul's accent gets under his skin. You're not a fucking Australian, he snaps in his head, you come from Middlesex, for Christ's sake, but when he opens his mouth he just feels very tired. He leans against the corridor wall, closing his eyes. He tells Paul what the doctor has told him.

'Shit,' Paul says. 'So they're saying this is it?'

'I think so.'

There is a silence.

'Fuck but I'll miss her,' Paul says at last.

You haven't seen her for twenty fucking years, the voice in his head spits back.

'Yeah,' he says. 'Me too.'

'Look, I'm sorry I can't be there. Take care of her for me, won't you? And listen, mate, just so you know, I called Jayden.'

'You did what?'

'I called my nephew, OK? And before you go off on one, I did it because I knew you wouldn't and because, whatever happened between you and Kim, she's still his Nanna. You won't know this because he didn't want you to, but these last few months he's been going to see her. He and I talked about it a lot when he was over here, about what she'd meant to you and me growing

314

up. He wanted to know her before it was too late. You should be glad. He's a good lad, your son. If he'd waited for you he'd have missed his chance. He asked me for the details of the hospital. He's on his way.'

Paul says goodbye. He thinks he says it back. He puts his phone in his pocket and leans against the wall. The corridor is silent, the shiny vinyl floor striped bright with reflected light. He tries to imagine Jayden pushing open the swing doors from the stairwell and coming towards him, but he can't do it. He can't summon his face or his physique or the way he walks. It has been too long. All he can think of is Jayden as a little kid, the way he hid behind his mother on the days that he came home, like he was a stranger.

I know him, his nan said last time, pointing at the photo of Paul and Michelle and Jayden and Bianca. He comes here. He thought then that she meant Paul, but she hadn't meant Paul. She meant Jayden. His son and his brother, his son and his grand-mother, sticking together despite him, despite everything, the tie of blood unbroken.

Jayden is on his way. He could leave. Or he could stay. They could sit with Eileen together. Eileen would like that. It might be the last thing she remembers, the two of them, sitting by her bed-side. Father and son.

Jayden knows he is here. He is expecting him.

He thinks of Mia, standing by the kiosk, her face as she turns and sees that it is him.

It is nearly half past two. Quickly he opens the Facebook app and begins to type.

Mia looks in the mirror. Clothes are scattered on the bed and on her bedroom floor. She doesn't know why it matters so much sud-denly what she is wearing when she meets Vanessa, but it does. It feels like the most important thing in the world.

Her butterfly wings are propped up against her bedroom wall. Her mum suggested maybe putting them up on the wall but when she showed them to Yaz, Yaz got her to explain the whole story behind them and then said she thought Mia should use them for publicity. She suggested a new Butterfly Girl photograph, only with Mia this time instead of Tess, or maybe even the two of them together. It's like the next generation, she said. The life cycle of a Butterfly Girl. Yaz doesn't worry about climate change, not the way Mia does, not yet anyway, but she has really good ideas. Tess thinks so too. She has promised to take Mia to meet her new/old friend, Nat. Apparently Nat knows a lot about environmental protest, she can help them decide the best thing to do. But we will do something, Mia says firmly. We have to. There isn't much time.

Nat was in the (dis)organisation with Tess so she knew Mia's dad. You can ask her about him, her mum said, if you want to. Perhaps she will remember things I don't. Mia thinks that for now she would rather talk about Yaz's Butterfly Girl idea, but there is still something comforting in knowing that Nat knew him, that he was real to her. Mia doesn't know how to explain it exactly, except that it makes her feel more real herself.

She hasn't told her mum about Vanessa. She hasn't even told Yaz yet. Perhaps tomorrow, if the afternoon goes well, she will say something. She hasn't decided. She takes a breath, swallowing the butterflies in her stomach, and grabs her jeans from the floor. She's still not sure they're what she wants to be wearing but there isn't time to worry about that now. She glances at herself in the mirror one last time. She has to go.

She is sitting on the stairs tying her trainer laces when her phone pings. The message is long, it takes up the whole screen. She curls her legs up as she reads it, her chin on her knees.

i hope this gets 2 u in time but i cant come 2day im so sorry my dad found out about my fb acc + it all came out about us + me coming 2 c u + he lost it hes so strict + he thinks everyone online is evil so now im grounded also hes taken away my phone im sending this from my laptop because i said i needed 2 do homework but theyr blockin that 2 + ive had 2 promise 2 delete my acct so im sorry but i wont b able 2 msg u anymore i shdnt even b sending this if he knew my dad wd freak but i wanted u 2 know i wont eva 4get u im serious i think ur amazin truly the best + ive neva had a friend like u im gonna miss u loads

b happy & fly high ok? cos ill be watchin

ur butterfly friend 4eva Vanessa ♥♥♥

Author's Note

Trespass is a work of fiction, and the events and characters it depicts spring entirely from my imagination. But it was Mark Stone who planted the seed of this novel in my mind.

For seven years after his move to Nottingham in 2003, Mark Stone was a dedicated climate activist with groups such as Earth First! and Climate Camp. The son of an accountant, Stone established a reputation for being the go-to master of protest-camp logistics, while the ready supply of cash from his job as a freelance climber earned him the nickname Flash. From 2003 to 2010 he travelled to eleven countries, including France, Spain, Italy, Poland and the USA, gathering information and playing a frontline part in almost every high-profile anti-capitalist and environmental protest. During this time, according to friends, he slept with at least ten fellow activists. His longest relationship, with Lisa Jones (not her real name), lasted six years. He was close to Lisa's family. He rode with her in the mourners' car at her father's funeral.

But in October 2010 Mark Stone was ambushed by angry colleagues who had begun to doubt his identity. By January 2011 the story was all over the newspapers. Mark Stone was revealed to be

Mark Kennedy, an undercover police officer. Kennedy was part of the National Public Order Intelligence Unit, a shadowy squad with a mission to infiltrate protest groups. He was also married. He and his wife had two children, aged twelve and ten.

For years I thought about Mark Kennedy, the undercover cop with the tattoo on his forearm that showed his skin being peeled back to reveal the mechanical workings of a robot underneath. What did that say, I wondered, about the mental state of a man who had long since ceased to be himself? I thought about his wife who, in the days after the story broke, asked for privacy for herself and her children 'to enable us to deal with the difficult issues that have arisen'.* Mostly, though, I thought about Lisa Jones. About what it would be like to discover that the man you had shared six years of your life with was a complete stranger. That every single thing he had ever told you about himself – his age, his date of birth, his family history, what he did for a living, even his name – was a lie.

Since 2011 the revelations have just kept on coming. It is now clear that, between 1968 and 2010, at least 144 undercover police officers infiltrated more than a thousand protest groups, the vast majority of them left-wing and progressive organisations that presented a perceived challenge to the status quo. Many of those undercover officers pursued sexual relationships under their false identities. At least three are known to have fathered children. All of them, in line with established undercover protocols, faked mental health or family problems at the end of their tours, enabling them to vanish without trace. An undisclosed number left behind partners who struggled to come to terms with their abandonment. The true identities of more than half of these officers remain unknown.

These disclosures have shocked the public. They have also shocked

---

* https://www.independent.ie/regionals/corkman/news/family-upset-by-undercover-cops-admission-of-infidelity-27082341.html

politicians. Incredibly, and despite the fact that, according to Kennedy, each officer cost the taxpayer a cool £250,000 a year, police chiefs had never considered it necessary to consult Parliament about their activities. For more than forty years a small group of senior officers kept the existence of these spies a closely guarded secret.

Perhaps unsurprisingly, those officers have played down the allegations. Since Kennedy was exposed, the Met has insisted that it is 'grossly unprofessional' and 'never acceptable' for undercover officers to have sex with people they are targeting. When eight women involved in sexual relationships with undercover officers brought a legal action against them in 2012, claiming to have suffered intense emotional trauma and pain, the Met issued an unprecedented public apology and settled with seven of the women out of court.

One, however, fought on. In 2016 Kate Wilson, who was involved with Mark Kennedy, sued the Met and the National Police Chiefs Council (NPCC) for 'egregious and serious violations' of her rights to freedom from inhuman and degrading treatment, her right to privacy and her right to freedom of expression. The Met responded by claiming that sexual relationships for undercover officers were banned and that, apart from Kennedy's supervising officer, no other officer had any knowledge of his activities. But in a landmark ruling published in September 2021, the Investigatory Powers Tribunal (IPT) judged that 'either senior officers were quite extraordinarily naive [or] totally unquestioning, or chose to turn a blind eye to conduct which was, certainly in the case of [Kennedy], useful to the operation.'

The tribunal also found that the Met and the NPCC's failure to guard against the risk of undercover officers entering sexual relationships with women amounted to unlawful discrimination against women. Its judgement that 'the undercover operation could not be justified as "necessary in a democratic society"' . . . reveal[s] disturbing and lamentable failings at the most fundamental levels'. As I write this, the Met and the NPCC have been ordered to pay Wilson a total of £229,471 'by way of just satisfaction for breaches of her human rights'. Such awards by the IPT, which hears allegations of abuse by the state, are rare.

What effect this case will have on the future of undercover policing remains unclear. Following a string of allegations about the activities of undercover units, including the disclosure that Scotland Yard had spied on the campaign group fighting for justice for the murdered teenager Stephen Lawrence, Theresa May commissioned a public inquiry into undercover policing in 2014. After years of delay, the Undercover Policing Inquiry (UCPI) has finally begun to hear evidence from at least 250 police witnesses. Chaired by former High Court judge Sir John Mitting, it will investigate the conduct of two units, the Special Demonstration Squad, which ran from 1968 until 2008, and the National Public Order Intelligence Unit, which operated between 1999 and 2010. In addition to the matter of sexual relationships between officers and activists, the UCPI has been charged with examining how undercover officers were permitted to steal the names of dead children to create fake identities without the knowledge or approval of their families. It is also intended to probe claims that undercover officers were authorised by police to give false testimony in court and failed to disclose vital evidence which wrongly convicted fellow activists.

I am not holding my breath. Already the UCPI has pushed publication of its findings to the Home Office to the end of 2023. That date is only too likely to slip further. It transpires that, with the exception of criminal offences, police officers, however senior, can only be held accountable for failures of management while they remain in post. The way this is going, by the time there are any answers, the relevant top brass will be long gone, safely retired onto the golf course. Meanwhile the cost of the inquiry continues to rise. To date the bill stands at a mind-boggling £42 million.

This book is not intended as a political polemic. It is first and foremost a work of imagination, the fictional story of a woman and her daughter who suffer monstrously at the hands of the state and must find their own ways to come to terms with that. It is also, however, the story of many real women who are still fighting to be heard. I hope that in its small way my book might work to amplify their voices and let them know that they are not alone. That we are angry too.

London, January 2022

Acknowledgements

The world of undercover policing is, by definition, a shadowy one. We owe a debt to the courageous activists, campaigners and journalists who have made it their business to unearth its stories and ensure that they are told. I am especially grateful to Rob Evans and Paul Lewis whose tireless reporting for the *Guardian* has done so much to keep this issue in the news. Their book, *Undercover: The True Story of Britain's Secret Police*, proved an invaluable resource in writing this novel, as did *Secret Manoeuvres in the Dark: Corporate and Police Spying on Activists*, a fearless investigation into corporate espionage by academic and civil rights advocate Eveline Lubbers.

Thanks as always to my indefatigable agent, Clare Alexander, and to the brilliant team at Virago: Susan de Soissons, Kate Hibbert, Andy Hine, Nithya Rae, Nico Taylor and most of all Lennie Goodings, whose insight and acuity has so shaped this book.

Finally, a heartfelt thank you to the dedicated band of environmental protesters who went into battle decades ago, long before the rest of us grasped that there was a battle to be fought, and who have never given up. If the world wakes up soon enough to save this extraordinary planet of ours, it will be because of you.

Credits

The epigraph from *The Journals of Sylvia Plath* © Sylvia Plath (London: Faber and Faber, 1982) reproduced with permission of Faber and Faber

'Paparazzi', written by Rob Fusari/Stefani Germanotta; lyrics © Sony/ATV Music Publishing LLC, 2008

'OMG', written by Will Adams; lyrics © BMG Rights Management, 2010

'Umbrella', written by Christopher A. Stewart/Shawn C. Carter/ Terius Youngdell Nash/Thaddis Laphonia Harrell; lyrics © Peermusic Publishing, Sony/ATV Music Publishing LLC, Warner Chappell Music, Inc, 2008

'Oh To Be In Love', © Kate Bush, 1978